Sarah Harvey is in her mid-twenties. She lives in Northampton and has had short stories published in *Just Seventeen* and *Cosmopolitan*'s short story collection *Girls Just Want To Have Fun*. *Misbehaving* is her first novel.

# Misbehaving

## Sarah Harvey

**HEADLINE**

First published in 1999
by HEADLINE BOOK PUBLISHING

10 9 8 7 6 5 4 3 2 1

ISBN 0 7472 6176 8

Typeset by
Letterpart Limited, Reigate, Surrey

Printed and bound in Great Britain by
Mackays of Chatham plc, Chatham, Kent

HEADLINE BOOK PUBLISHING
A division of Hodder Headline PLC
338 Euston Road
London NW1 3BH

To Oi
S'cuse me, where's the party?
Really Really
Always
Les Chunk

# Acknowledgements

My thanks and love to Imogen and Barbie, whose madness keeps me sane, and whose love keeps me going. To Ayshea, my partner in a lot of crimes. To Sam, Rachael and Liz, the other three musketeers (why did I get stuck with the aftershave?); and also to the following friends who've helped, inspired or encouraged me in many different ways: Trevor (a true gentleman and dear friend) and Sue; Gorgeous-Gogo-Dancing Gazza; Sexy Michelle; my lovely Nuala and her lovely Sarah; Anne (whose wild streak is no longer so well hidden); Lovely Lesley and Naughty Maureen; Beautiful Anna; Elizia; Carolyn; Claire; Big Al (Big Kiss!); Small D; Mr A; Tom E; Tina; Kathy; Jules; Chrissy; and special thanks to Fat (now wonderfully thin) Jack for all the proof reading I've forced her to do over the years; and all at NGH.

Love and thanks also to my sister Louise, and to Des, Nomi Bear and Smiles, who always lift me up when I'm down. To my brother James, for his contribution (he knows which bit!). My mum, Diane, for putting up with me at risk to her sanity and carpet; my dad, Brucey Baby, love you; Sil, James and Viv; and to my grandma, Mabs, whose ability to look good in leather trousers well into her seventies will always inspire me.

Finally my grateful thanks to Joanna Briscoe, Luigi Bonomi and Clare Foss, for their faith, encouragement and enthusiasm, and Frances, Jo and Sarah for their lovely legs.

# Chapter One

I watch in horrified fascination the sight of my boyfriend's naked bum heaving into the air then trembling earthward again with all the force of a roller coaster on a downward run. The impact the two bodies make results in a simultaneous groan of pleasure from them and a sort of moaning, almost silent gasp of horror from me. Oblivious to his audience, Max begins the series of thrusts that indicate he's about to come. She sinks long pink-painted fingernails into the tensed flesh of his gluteus maximus. He frantically increases pace, the groaning duet gets louder, then he sighs, she screams, and they sink, hugging and sweating, against each other. Max murmurs something along the lines of that was bloody wonderful, and buries his face between her copious tits. She begins the congratulatory adulation that he always expects after sex, indicating that this is certainly not the first time they've got this closely acquainted.

I always wondered idly what I'd do if I came home and found Max in bed with another woman. You know how when you run the scenario through your mind you suddenly develop a rapier wit, all the little razor sharp one-liners, the punch that would knock out Mike Tyson, the dignified exit? Well, I'm sorry, it doesn't work out like that. Gone are the visions of Mae West reincarnate imparting a wittily crushing rejoinder as she lounges exotically against the door frame. Gone are the Glenn Close-influenced scenes of burning oil over bare bottoms, or the more realistic standby of a bucket of icy cold water. Gone even are the visions of being incredibly free-spirited, and whipping off my clothes with wild abandon to dive butt naked and hopeful under the duvet to join in.

What actually happens is that my bottom lip begins to tremble, my face creases up rather unattractively, like an old and wrinkled boxer dog's, and I burst into a cacophony of rather noisy sobs.

I feel very strange as I stand there, tears and make-up streaming down my face. I also feel like I should be applauding, not crying. Max is an actor. I haven't seen him perform that well for ages, either on stage or in bed.

Alerted by the alien sound of a dementedly wailing woman, they finally unclasp each other's naughty bits and notice me.

Oddly enough their faces now emulate the look of horror that slid on to mine when I first walked bare-footed into the bedroom, to find my boyfriend of over five years in bed with my aerobics instructor.

It had to be her, didn't it? She of the perfect butt, cellulite-defying body and gravity-defying tits.

Despite the fact that I've seen every inch of Max's naked body, from the tiny chicken pox scar under his peculiarly shaped left nipple to the brown patchy birthmark shaped like Italy on his bottom, he grabs the duvet and whips it around them in a fit of belated and spurious modesty.

'Oh my god, Alex . . .' he stutters wildly. 'Look . . . er, it's not what you think.'

It's not what I think? I find them starkers and going for it like two professionals in a blue movie and he tells me it's not what I think? Well, if this isn't sex in its most basic form, then what is it? Some new kind of aerobic workout?

For some inexplicable reason I start to giggle. It's a pretty manic sort of giggle. The sort that instantly recalls visions of straitjackets and padded cells, and patients hoovering lawns in their night clothes.

As I sprint out of the room and out of the house to my car, the giggle gets caught up in the crying until the whole thing turns into a fit of hysterical hiccuping sobs. I fumble with my car keys, vainly attempting to manoeuvre them into the lock through a veil of tears.

Despite the fact that the lock appears to have shrunk from all the water I'm shedding, I finally manage to get in my car just as Max appears, hopping barefoot down the road after me, clutching the duvet to his nether regions like a long, trailing, feather-stuffed fig leaf.

'Alex, wait . . .' he shouts, reaching the car and grabbing hold of the door. I slam it shut, narrowly avoiding amputating two of his fingers, and fire up the engine of my poor little car with the vicious clutch revving of a Formula One driver waiting for the lights to change.

'Alex, please.' Max looks desperate, 'You can't just drive off, I'm caught . . .'

Yeah, the little bastard's been caught all right. I

crunch the car into gear and reverse without looking, narrowly missing a small black cat, a fire hydrant, and Max's Achilles heel.

I feel like someone's just punched me in the gut and then stuck a couple of fingers down my throat.

I think I'm going to be sick.

I think I need the windscreen wipers on my eyes instead of on the car.

I can't see a thing. I rub the back of my hand across my face, leaving a streak of black mascara across my flesh, and pushing the gear stick into first and my foot down on the accelerator, begin to speed away.

It's only as I reach the end of the road that I realise the strange flapping noise I can hear is Max's duvet caught in my car door, trailing along behind me like a madly billowing drag chute. I look in my rear-view mirror just in time to catch the aforementioned bum with the birthmark shaped like Italy, turning a pale blush pink as its naked bastard of an owner sprints frantically back up the road towards home and sanctuary.

As always in a crisis my driving goes on to autopilot and my car heads off towards Emma's house.

Emma is my best friend. A girl needs a few things in life to keep her sane. My top ten of girlie essentials reads as follows, in reverse order:

10) An account card for at least one of the major department stores
9) A sympathetic boss
8) A sympathetic bank manager
7) A good hairdresser

6)  Chocolate and other edibles
5)  A place to call home
4)  A sense of humour
3)  A solid gaggle of good mates
2)  Family
1)  Best Friend

I know my list lacks all the usual sensible things like good health, etc., etc., and a good man doesn't even get a look in (my mother and several of my friends would argue that there is no such thing as a good man), but I'm talking about the essentials that a girl needs to get her through life other than a considerate, faithful, funny, intelligent, sexy lover. In fact it's usually when you find out that your man isn't all of the above that the list of girl's essentials kicks in with a vengeance. In other words, when your man lets you down, your girlfriends usually pick you back up again, dust you off and set you back at a trot on that shit-covered path called life

Fighting my way through the London traffic, I pull into the quiet road in Chelsea where Emma lives in a quaint old mews cottage belonging to her totally loaded but totally lunatic parents.

I manage to park without killing anything and, staggering out of the car, begin to hammer on Ems's front door and persistently ring her bell like an escapee from a mental hospital.

Through the glass I can make out Emma's outline as she trails slowly downstairs. She pulls open the door. It's ten-thirty on a fine spring Saturday morning, and her green eyes are narrowed to two gummy sleep-deprived slits following a Friday night of drunken, end-of-week debauchery. Her long brown bob is a pillow-frizzed mess, and her make-up is smudged around her eyes. Obviously a very heavy night before.

'Hi, Lex.' She peers blearily at me, and manages to motivate her cheek muscles into a dog-tired but pleased-to-see-me grin. 'When did you get back?'

My confused and muddled brain has unfortunately forgotten what manners are. I have sunk to the level where logical thought is a thing of the past and my body is now running on basic instincts.

Without uttering a word, I barge past her and head upstairs, storm into the kitchen at the back of the house, throw the switch on the kettle, and reach for the choccy biccie tin.

'Alex, what's the matter?' Emma, suddenly wide awake, hurries after me. 'Oh my god, look at your eyes! You look like a negative of Chi Chi the Panda with severe hayfever.' Emma's right. My normally pale skin is completely ashen and my sepia-brown eyes are shot through with bloodshot pink. She pulls a peach-coloured tissue out of the pocket of her dressing gown and dabs ineffectually at the smudges of my mascara and eyeliner as I sorrowfully, and still silently, chain eat plain chocolate Hob Nobs.

'Lex,' she snaps in exasperation born of worry, 'stop overdosing on biscuits and talk to me.' She pulls the tin out of my grasp. I had it clutched to my chest like a comforter and suddenly feel very naked and vulnerable without it. I lean back against the kitchen worktop, and blink away a fresh shower of tears.

'I just found Max in bed with another woman,' I mumble through the crumbs.

Ems helps herself to a handful of Hob Nobs, then silently hands me back the biscuit tin.

'Oh, dear.'

Understatement of the decade.

'How do you feel?'

How do I feel? 'Totally gutted' would be the most adequate – and succinct – statement I could come up with. But in the end I don't have to answer.

'Stupid question,' Emma answers herself. 'You feel like shit, of course you do.' She steers me into one of the kitchen chairs with gentle hands on my shaking shoulders, and then turns back to the kettle which appears to have rather obligingly boiled at great speed and is now throwing out an awful lot of steam, and grumbling like a miserable old man with loose and clicking false teeth.

'It helps if you put water in them first,' she sighs, carrying the spitting, protesting object over to the sink and filling it.

She reaches into one of the cupboards, throws tea bags into mugs and pulls out another packet of Hob Nobs which she tears open and tips into the rapidly emptying biscuit tin.

We both wait in silence until the kettle steams to a head.

'Now.' Tea poured, she sits down at a right angle to me at the solid scrubbed yew kitchen table. 'Tell me exactly what happened?'

I sniff heavily and reach for her kitchen roll, blow and begin.

'Well, you know the magazine sent me up to Scotland for three days to review that new health spa?'

'Do I know! Didn't I try and get you to swap places with me? You go into the bank with all the merchant wankers, whilst I swan off up North to do a write up on a pampering palace for posh people. I think that's what I said to you, but did you listen? No, of course you didn't . . .'

'Yeah, well,' I interrupt, 'I wish you *had* gone instead. The place turned out to be an absolute dive. It was a real hose-you-down-with-cold-water-then-slap-you-about-with-wet-towels job, and I'm sure they dug the mud for the facials straight from the vegetable patch every morning, so I thought I'd finish early and drive back and surprise Max. And, boy, was he surprised!'

I sink my nose into my tea and nearly strip the skin off my lips because it's so hot.

'Jeez!' I blow frantically on them and then on my tea. 'Well, anyway, I got home and snuck in really quietly. I knew he'd still be in bed because it's Saturday, so I was going to do something stupid like slip out of my clothes and just slide on in there with him. You know, say hello properly . . .'

'I get the picture.' Ems smiles wryly.

'Anyway, I head up to the bedroom on tiptoe, and there they were, naked, in our bedroom, in our bed, on my new Caroline Charles sheets that I saved for absolutely ages to buy . . . bastard!' I reach for another chocolate and oat panacea.

'Who was it, was it someone you knew?'

'Oh, I knew her all right,' I growl through a mouthful, wiping away more tears with the sleeve of my jacket.

'Well, who was it?' Ems probes impatiently. She

leans forward and composes her face, trying to keep the very fine balance between interested and concerned friend, and detail vulture.

I swallow hard. Despite the tea, my throat's suddenly very dry.

'It was Madeleine Hurst.'

I can tell by Emma's face that she recognises the name, but doesn't quite know where from.

'You know, her from the fitness studios in Knightsbridge? The one who does the abs-and-arse class?'

'Oh,' says Emma flatly.

This single syllable says it all. Madeleine Hurst is blonde and beautiful, and fit in every sense of the word. How many times have I envied her perfectly firm thighs and incredibly small backside, and the boobs that if they weren't trapped within the confines of a firmly stitched sports bra would have knocked her out every time we jogged on the spot? Her make-up never sweats off no matter how gruelling the work out, and her hair always returns to shape afterwards with a leisurely flick of the fingers through its long and shining blonde tresses, whilst I and my cronies, nowhere near as streamlined in our straining Lycra, slope off shining sweatily, and panting unfitly, to the showers.

'It's bad enough finding Max in bed with another woman,' I sigh heavily, 'but with her! It's just adding insult to injury.'

'So you'd have felt happier if you'd found him in bed with some flat-chested ugly old boot, would you? That would have done your ego a power of good, wouldn't it?' Emma replies, anger fuelling her sarcasm.

'No, but she makes me feel so inadequate . . .'

'I thought that was Max's job,' she interrupts crossly. 'I always thought that guy was a complete arsehole!'

'Now you tell me!' I wail.

'Don't give me that "now you tell me" crap.' Emma looks sternly at me. 'I've been telling you that for the last six years.'

'But I've only been *with* him for six years.'

'Exactly,' she tuts huffily, not noticing that the biscuit she's had dunked in her tea for the past two minutes has completely disintegrated. 'Never did like him. Don't tell me you haven't been having your doubts too, 'cause I know you have.'

'Yeah,' I admit reluctantly,' I suppose I have, and after this morning it looks like they were pretty well-founded too, doesn't it! You know, I don't think it was the first time.'

'How could you tell?'

'I just know,' I mumble, shoving another biscuit in my mouth.

'So what are you going to do?'

'Do? There's nothing *to* do. We're through, aren't we? Over. Finished. I find my boyfriend in bed with someone else. I think that sort of signals the end of the relationship, doesn't it?'

'You don't want to talk to him about it?'

'What's there to talk about?' I gingerly test the tea with my tongue. It's cool enough to drink, but suddenly I feel a real need for something stronger. 'Maybe if the relationship were firmer we could get through this, but you know how we've been getting along lately.'

Emma nods.

'About as well as two totally incompatible people can,' she sighs. 'Look, in a way he's done you a favour.' She puts a hand on my arm and squeezes reassuringly. 'It's a bit like putting down an injured animal, you know. Cruel to be kind. Finish it quickly so the pain's less. It was a horrible way for it to end, Lexy, and it may not feel like it now, but I think you'll soon realise that this is a good thing.'

'You're right . . . it doesn't feel like it now,' I wail, blowing crumbs like a whale blows water.

'I'm only trying to get you to look on the bright side.' Ems grins hopefully.

'There's a bright side to this?' I snivel doubtfully, pulling off another sheet of kitchen towel and blowing noisily.

'Sure there is. You've just left Max.'

'I should be happy about that?' I ask her incredulously.

'I'd be bloody delirious.'

'Yeah, but you're not me!'

'Thank goodness! Ugh!' she shudders. 'If I were that means I'd have *slept with him*!'

She says the 'him' like she's talking about something totally disgusting, Beelzebub for instance. Maybe Max is totally disgusting. Maybe that's unfair. We had some good times, he had a nice side, he must have been semi-okay for me to stick it for so long, mustn't he? Either that or I'm totally gullible and stupid.

At the moment I feel totally gullible and stupid.

'What am I going to do?' I wail. 'I feel like life as I know it has just ended. Yesterday I had a boyfriend, I had a home . . . now it's all gone down the plug hole. I'm suddenly single again, and I'm homeless. It's Max's house. I was nothing more than an overpaying lodger, who came in pretty useful for sex and slave labour at the same time as subsidising his bank balance.'

'See, I told you that you're better off without him.' Emma grins weakly at me.

'Better off emotionally maybe, but now I'm homeless. Trying to find a decent flat around here is like trying to find water in the Gobi, especially for what I can afford to pay. I may as well just sod off down to Sainsbury's now, and pick out the largest cardboard box they've got.'

'Well, that's one problem I can solve.' Emma gets to the biscuit grit at the bottom of her mug and grimaces. 'You can move in here.'

'Really?' I ask hopefully, perking up a little.

'Sure. Why not?' Ems says more to herself than me. 'I've got the room. I'd been toying with the idea of getting someone in just to stop Mother moving into the spare bedroom every time she comes up to town, so you'd be doing me a favour.'

'You think you can cope with having me full-time?'

'Why not? I'm sure we won't end up hating each other, or wanting to claw each other's eyes out, or stab each other or anything.'

'I thought you were trying to get me to look on the bright side? Look, when I said I was homeless, I wasn't hinting. If you don't think it would work, I could always go back to Mother's for a while until I find something.'

'God, no!' Emma's eyes widen with horror at the

thought. 'I'm your best friend. Do you really think I'd let you go through that?'

'My mum's not that bad, she has her sane moments. Unlike yours.'

Emma's mother is Joan Crawford reincarnate. In fact she's Joan Crawford and Debbie Reynolds in the same body, with the same joint body mass. 'Paranoid schizophrenic' would be a pretty apt description; a living, breathing, self-obsessed nightmare. It's amazing Ems has turned out as sane as she has, although I must admit she can have her mad moments.

'No, so long as we have a few ground rules, I think we'll be all right. In fact, I think it could be pretty good . . . What do you think?'

'Well, Max always moaned that I spent half my life with you anyway, and I really wouldn't want to commute all the way from Mum and Dad's . . .'

Although the offer is amazingly tempting, I still have my doubts. Everything seems to be moving so quickly. Max gets a hard on and I get an instant life change. Besides you have to look at moving in together in a friendship situation in roughly the same way as you would moving in with your lover. Obviously without the sex part. Ems and I have been mates for what seems like decades, but is in fact about seventeen years. We've grown up together, gone through puberty together, got ready for first dates together, gone job hunting, man hunting, even found and bemoaned our first wrinkles together. In fact we've spent our entire formative years in each other's pockets, but we've never actually lived together. This could be the start of the end of a beautiful relationship.

'It doesn't have to be permanent,' I venture hesitantly.

Emma nods her agreement. 'If we find that we're starting to loathe each other with a passion . . .'

'I'll move out,' I finish for her.

She grins at me. The idea is obviously starting to appeal.

'This could be a lot of fun,' she ventures.

'It could be a nightmare.'

'We get on brilliantly.'

'At the moment.'

'Don't be so pessimistic.'

'What would Theo think?'

Theo Cole, Emma's boyfriend of approximately nineteen months, is often to be found draped across the sofa in her living room, remote in one hand, six pack in the other. He and Emma are total opposites. Emma is a whizz kid, a bright female spark in a male-dominated-sexist-pig-of-a-futures floor at a bank in the City. She's cool, calm, and collected on the outside, but a seething fire brand when roused.

She's also a bit of a nymphomaniac. Well, I don't suppose that's very fair. I'm labelling her, aren't I? Emma enjoys sex. I mean, she *really* enjoys sex. So because she's female and enjoys sex, she's a nympho, isn't she? If she were male and enjoyed sex, then she'd be a stud or something.

She says that she thinks on her feet, and relaxes on her back.

Theo, a musician, is permanently relaxed, be it on his back or otherwise. He's as laid back as a suntanning sloth, roused only by Jimi Hendrix and Guinness. Fortunately their differences seem to complement each other. He is the calm to Emma's storm, the Yin to her Yang. Or as another friend, Serena, once put it in a more unkind moment – a wet blanket on her blazing hot barbecue.

'Theo? Think?' Emma jokes. 'You don't have to worry about that. He probably won't even notice that you're here. It takes him long enough to notice that I'm around. He's so laid back, he's almost horizontal.'

'He's permanently horizontal when you two are together. God, that could be awkward. If I'm expected to go out every time you two have sex, then I may as well go and get that cardboard box . . .'

'Uh-uh.' Emma shakes her head. 'No inhibitions, okay? One of the ground rules will have to be that you can make as much noise during sex as you want to, and the other person either ignores it or vows to compete.'

'Compete? Pah! I don't think I'll be getting much of that for a while.'

'I'll buy you something with batteries for your birthday,' she giggles.

'Yeah, a torch. Then I can see how empty my bed is at night,' I moan half-heartedly. 'It's no hardship. Sex is overrated anyway.'

Emma's face registers shock horror.

'Sex, overrated? Blimey! It's a good job you *have* split up with Max if that's what you think.'

My handbag starts to ring, making us both jump. I haul out my mobile and check out the number on the caller display. It's Max's.

I suddenly feel rather sick. Emma has always had this great knack of taking my mind off my immediate problems. Now suddenly the problem himself comes back into focus by phoning me. I can feel the tears threatening to start again.

I look at the phone and then I look back at Emma, blinking like an owl woken during the day.

'Well,' she demands impatiently, 'are you going to answer it or what?'

I remain dumb and motionless.

'Is it Max?'

I manage a small stilted nod.

'Do you want me to answer it for you?'

I nod again. 'I don't know what to say to him.' My voice is almost a whisper.

Ems reaches across, picks up my phone, and presses the call connect button.

'Fuck off, Max,' she says into the receiver and then switches off the power. 'There,' she grins at me. 'It's as simple as that.'

Despite my mood, I can't stop my mouth from twisting into a small smile. 'I'm going to have to talk to him sooner or later.'

'No, you're not. You don't have to speak to him at all. Why put yourself through the heartache?'

'There are things to sort out,' I utter lamely.

'Like what? We've already established that you and Max were two totally separate people who just happened to be living under the same roof, and sleeping in the same bed. The house is his, you've got separate accounts, separate friends, separate everything. What do you need to talk to him for?'

'Perhaps I just want the chance to call him all the names under the sun, kick him where it hurts and break a few of his favourite things. Maybe that's what I need.'

'Maybe,' says Ems. 'But I still think it would hurt you more than it would hurt him. You know what I think you really need at the moment?'

'A bottle of vodka?' I snivel.

'How about a big hug?'

In the end, after a drunken weekend hiding my misery behind a vodka bottle, and hiding from Max behind the answer machine, leaving my mobile phone switched off, ignoring the backlog of messages on my voicemail that I know will be wiped from memory in twenty-four hours, I chicken out of a confrontation and slope round to the house on Monday afternoon, when I know Max will be camped on his agent's casting couch begging for work where he doesn't have to get dressed up in a furry costume and entertain a horde of shrieking children.

I feel a sort of stomach-sliding, sickening inner lurch as I put my key in the lock and let myself in.

It's only been two days, but already I feel like I don't belong here, like I'm trespassing. The house seems eerily quiet and unwelcoming as I traipse miserably in carrying my empty boxes.

I've been living with Max for nearly two of the six years we've been together, but it's amazing how much of the stuff in the house isn't mine. Once I've packed my clothes, cleared my bits out of the bathroom, and taken a few odds and sods from the kitchen, it's as though I've never actually been here. I never made much of an impression on the house. Obviously didn't make much of an impression on Max either.

Upstairs in the bedroom I clear out my wardrobe

then, turning, look forlornly at the sheets still on the bed. Max hasn't even had the decency to change them. I saved long and hard by forgoing my daily bar of Dairy Milk for a few months, and then fought my way through manically battling women in the January sales to buy them. They were a fêted acquisition, a coveted thing finally gained. Now I don't want them anymore.

The insult added to my injury is the presence of a long thick golden blonde hair on the crisp cream linen of one of the pillowcases. It's just lying there, taunting me. Something inside me snaps. I was just going to come round, get my things, and leave quietly, but now . . .

I may not want the blasted things, but I'm damned if I'm going to leave them for Max to shag on. Scrabbling around in my handbag, I pull out my cherished Mont Blanc, the one my mother gave me to congratulate me for publishing my first short in a magazine. It's sacrilege on both counts, but as I empty dark blue ink all over the sheets I feel a strange sense of euphoria coming over me.

This is good. Wanton vandalism. I can see now where graffiti artists get their kicks, and why rock bands get high on trashing hotel rooms.

I look around for something else to destroy, running my hand along the row of designer outfits in Max's wardrobe. I balk at the thought of slashing the expensive materials with a pair of sharp scissors. It's been done before, it's a bit passé, old hat, verging on criminal, I tell myself. I may feel daring, bold and reckless at the moment but I'm not really, and I know this high will swing to a low the minute I walk out of the door and I'd feel awful for having done it. The thought of Max chasing after me with the same pair of scissors when he's found his precious clothes in tatters really doesn't appeal either, although knowing Max's mentality his revenge would probably be to get his QC daddy to sue me for damages.

I decide that something more subtle is called for. The sheets are my obvious in-your-face revenge. It may seem like cutting off my nose to spite my face as they were actually *my* sheets in the first place, but I know it will hurt Max more than me, because when he gets home he's going to have to do some housework. To Max housework is not just a dirty job, it's a dirty word. Women's work. (Yes, he has actually called it this. No, I don't know why I stayed with him for so long either.)

I decide that if I want to get my own back, then I want something more subtle, not so in-your-face, and definitely not traceable in case of retribution.

Fetching Max's cordless drill from the cupboard under the stairs, I select the finest drill bit in the row and happily hammer a minuscule hole in the bath. I stand back and survey my handiwork. You can hardly see it. In fact, you wouldn't spot it if you weren't looking for it. Your eye would pass over the hole, imagining it to be some speck of dirt that missed the weekly polish with Jiff – and considering I'm the only one in this place that uses the Jiff, it's soon going to have a few real dirt spots to hide amidst.

Just to make sure, I fill the bath with cold water and then go off to pack the rest of my things. When I return to the bathroom an hour later, and remove the side panel with nervous yet excited trepidation, I am rewarded by the sight of a small damp patch beginning to form atop the boards on which the bath rests. Almost perfectly on cue, a drop of water gathers momentum, slides toward the narrow gap between the boards, and slips downwards.

Directly below the bathroom is the newly decorated sitting room. Taking up one corner of this, balanced smugly on the polished wooden floorboards, is Max's pride and joy: his wide-screen TV. He likes nothing better than to settle down on the sofa with a glass of wine in one hand and the remote in the other, and watch the videos he's recorded of every single TV appearance he's ever made.

This love of his egotistical little life is positioned directly below the bath – or should I say directly below the newly *leaking* bath?

This is what I mean. The beauty of subtlety.

Just to make sure, to help it on its way so to speak, I happily trot downstairs, manic grin firmly in place on previously miserable face, and, making certain the TV is unplugged from the mains, rummage once more in Max's tool box. I emerge with a pair of wire cutters, remove the back from the set and happily snip at a few harmless-looking little wires. I then plug it back in, set the switch to on, as Max always leaves it, gather up the last of my things, and go.

I'm halfway down the short front path, when as a final no-going-back gesture, I return to the front door and post my key back through the letterbox. I then dance to my waiting car, throw the last box in the boot, flip the lid shut with the back of my heel and drive off whistling 'Toreador'.

★  ★  ★

Back at the mews, Emma is waiting with tea, sympathy and a freshly cut set of keys, I now have access not only to the front door, but to the garage which she never uses, preferring instead to leave her rusting red MG blocking next door's frontage, much to their constant disgust, plus a key to the back garden, a short narrow wilderness of neglect which Emma says is her contribution to ecology, with a bit of patio thrown in for civilisation.

Emma helps me carry my stuff through to the spare room, where I've spent the last two nights. It's a large room at the back of the house, overlooking the wildly unkempt garden. It's a nice room, light and spacious, but the decor is a bit eau de nothing. Cream carpet, cream walls, cream bed linen, cream muslin at the windows. There's no warmth, no personal touches . . . it's not home.

I feel my nice happy high begin to fade into the not-so-rosy sunset.

'Feel free to decorate if you want.' Emma looks around her disparagingly. 'In fact do what you want to it.'

'Won't your mum and dad mind?'

'Well, Dad never comes here anyway, and Mother wouldn't notice if you painted it puke yellow with violet spots. She'd probably just think it was the blurred-vision after-effects of a lifetime of gin with no tonic, and go back to Harley Street for another pot of little pink pills.

'Is that the last of it?' She indicates the box she's just dumped on the bed.

I nod.

'Okay, do you want a hand unpacking?'

I shake my head.

'I'll leave you on your own for a bit then . . . to settle in.'

She smiles at me, shuts the door and I'm alone.

I sink down on to the double divan and survey the heap of boxes around me that are my life. I haven't got much to show for the past twenty-seven years, just a few boxes full of clothes and junk and unfinished manuscripts.

The euphoria from my earlier happily abandoned vandalism is rapidly wearing off. It feels strange, being here, the material part of my life packed up around me. No matter how evident it was physically that the house in Battersea was Max's, I'd come to look upon it as home.

Now, in the space of just forty-eight hours, my whole life has changed completely. No more home, no more Max, no more usual routine, no more life as I knew it.

The future, before premeditated, now completely unknown.

'I'm not going to cry,' I tell myself determinedly.

'I *am not* going to cry,' I repeat, as the first few salty tears begin to wash down my cheeks.

# Chapter Two

Despite the overwhelming urge to do a Mrs Bennet and retire to my room for a lengthy period of purdah, life ('It's life, Jim, but not as we know it') must go on. I spend a week of annual leave painting Emma's spare room sunshine yellow, under the misapprehension that the bright colour will cheer me up, drinking myself silly every evening, fluctuating between eating too much junk and not eating anything at all, and riding my emotions like a roller coaster.

Max must have had a bit of a shock coming home to a house completely wiped clean of any trace of me.

After initially trying to contact me several times a day, only for his calls to be ignored and unanswered, he has now given up trying to contact me at all. Whereas I used to stare at my mobile phone in horror if it dared to have his number on caller display when it rang, I now stare at it in miserable unfulfilled anticipation as it sits there silently mocking me with its inactivity.

Not only that. Max must know where I am, but he hasn't even come within a hair's breadth of Emma's place. I'm determined that I wouldn't have him back, but it'd be quite nice to have the opportunity to tell him that. In fact, I really think that it's his duty as the cheating party to give me the chance to tell him what a no-good bastard he is.

It's a scenario that helps me through the long lonely nights where I lie in the big double bed in Emma's spare room and stare at the newly painted ceiling, a fledgling insomniac.

In my fantasy, Max is down in the street on his knees, begging and pleading for me to give him another chance, telling me what a fool he is, and how wonderful I am, totally humiliating himself in his desperate desire to win me back. The scene has various different endings, mainly centred around me pouring something disgusting out of the window on to his head, and crushing his hopes with a mindblowingly clever and witty little speech that leaves him kicking himself all the way home for his total and utter stupidity.

I know I didn't want a confrontation before, but I think I may have missed an important part of the healing process by avoiding one.

When I haven't been staring at the phone, willing it to ring, whilst at the same time hoping desperately that it won't, I've been on it, informing close friends and relatives of my current state of affairs, and my new temporary address.

This is the hard bit. I don't know how to tell people, and they don't know how to react. Everybody's so sympathetic and nice, but as soon as I mention Max's name, all I want to do is rant, swear, be abusive, or bawl my eyes out.

They've invented greetings cards for everything

else under the sun. Why couldn't I just pick up a stationery set like they have for birthday party invites? 'This is to announce that Alex Gray and Max Montcrief have split. Please bring a bottle.'

I can't even find enough courage to phone my mother. For some inexplicable reason, whilst I thought the only use Max had for his rectum was to talk out of it, she thought it was a storage place for brilliant sunshine. I couldn't cope with her grief at the moment as well as my own.

On Friday night, I make my first expedition out of the house.

I've been invited round to my brother's flat for dinner. It's an indication of the sad state of affairs I'm in that I actually agree to go. Jem can cook as well as an elephant in flippers can tap dance. I console myself with the fact he's pretty good company and the alcohol is always plenteous, even if the food is usually inedible.

Besides, I figure if I play the pathetic role well enough, he might tell Mother for me. I arrive at the converted warehouse where he has an apartment on the second floor at about eight o'clock, and buzz the intercom. It's my first public outing since last weekend.

'Hello?' my brother's voice crackles through the stainless steel grille.

'It's me.'

'Who's me?'

'Cut the crap and let me in, Jem.'

Since he split up with his long-term girlfriend six months ago, he has been converting his flat into a palace of subtle and sophisticated seduction. It's one of these timber-floored, high-ceilinged places which lends itself to minimalism and lots of candles. I've always loved Jem's flat, but now practically homeless myself, my envy becomes almost palpable.

He does his usual brotherly love routine of suffocating me in a bear hug, and blowing a fat wet raspberry against my cheek. I don't know whether he's pleased to see me or the two bottles of Australian white I'm clutching, one in each hand like alcoholic crutches.

'How you doing, little sis?' He has the same note of concern in his voice I hear in everybody who speaks to me at the moment, like I'm a recuperating invalid or something.

I shrug non-committally. It's only been six days and I feel like a lump of shit that somebody's trodden on with very big feet. I've spent the majority of the time in tears, torn between hating Max with a passion, and loving him with a passion. Somehow the hating parts are easier to bear. There's something very healing about shouting 'Bastard! Bastard! Bastard!' at the top of your lungs constantly, like a mantra. It's much more conducive to solace than staring at old photographs of the two of you supposedly in love, whilst snivelling into your twenty-second loo roll.

There's a strange smell emanating from the kitchen. I don't know what it is, I wouldn't like to guess, and I daren't ask in case it's what I'm expected to eat tonight. I just hope this dinner hasn't coincided with Jem's day to boil-wash his underwear, because that's what it smells like.

Sticking my two bottles in to cool, he pulls a pre-chilled bottle of Sauvignon Blanc and two glasses from the fridge, and takes them through to the table in the corner of his vast sitting room which is already set for dinner.

'So how are you doing then?' he repeats.

'You already asked me that.'

'Yeah, and you didn't answer me.'

There's another buzz on the intercom.

'Saved by the buzzer. Is somebody else coming for dinner?' I try to feign enthusiasm, I'm not really up to scintillating company at the moment.

'No,' Jem grins at me, 'that'll be dinner itself.'

Relief! Dinner's delivered instead of massacred by my brother. My stomach, which has been knotted and uncomfortable since the bedroom scene last Saturday, unknots a little and decides that perhaps after almost a week it's ready to receive a normal quantity of food. I've lost almost half a stone in six days on a diet of constant junk. I'm not complaining. It's always nice to lose a little weight at my age without having to force yourself to give up the usual pleasures of chocolate, alcohol, and my personal favourite iced fresh-cream Belgian buns with lemon curd, of which I managed to eat four in a row on Monday afternoon.

Jem bounds downstairs, and then reappears carrying two large, grease-stained, brown paper bags.

'Grub's up! By the looks of you, you need it. You've lost weight. You look too thin. Gaunt. That's not attractive.'

'Who needs to be attractive?' I mutter morosely.

'You do. Now more so than ever if you want to nab yourself another unsuspecting bloke.' He's trying to joke with me, but I can't make myself laugh.

He waits. My face remains deadpan. He laughs again himself in an encouraging sort of way, but I continue to stare at him like a morose camel.

'Look, I know it hurts, but you have to move on, Lex.' He stops unloading cartons from the bags on to the dining table, and frowns at me, stern but concerned.

'It's only been six days. I think I need a little bit more time to get over it, don't you?'

'Yep, so long as you don't wallow. You and Max aren't going to get back together, are you?' He screws up the empty bags and heads for the kitchen.

'You never know,' I cut in hesitantly, following him.

Jem raises his eyebrows at me, foot poised over the pedal bin.

'No, probably not,' I acquiesce. 'I'd never trust him again.'

'And things weren't exactly brilliant between you, now were they?'

I shake my head.

'Well, in that case, you'd better pick up your bicycle, honey, and get back on it.'

'Like you did when Alison left?'

'S'pose,' he admits, taking warmed plates out of the oven and leading the way out of the kitchen to the dining table.

'How did you manage to recover?' I ask, parking my bum on a wooden seat.

'Life goes on,' my brother states philosophically. 'Besides, I like myself. When a relationship ends, it's really easy to start asking, "What's wrong with me?" I could easily have done that when Ali went. You know, blamed myself . . . but it wasn't really anybody's fault. We're both good people, we just weren't good together.'

My brother farts, picks his nose, belches loudly, eats

cold takeaway for breakfast, wears the same pair of socks for three days running, could ruin a ready meal prepared by Anton Mosimann, admits to watching *Baywatch* for the tits and arse, and *still* manages to like himself. That's confidence for you.

'You don't have to be perfect to be a good person,' says Jem, as though he's reading my mind.

'Are you sure?'

'Well, whose idea of perfect do you feel you have to conform to?' He deftly pulls the cork on the bottle of white and hands me a glass, 'Perfect is only a concept. It varies from person to person. Everybody has different ideals. Find your own set of values, live up to them as best you can, and then you'll be happy with yourself. Whatever you do, don't feel you have to conform to somebody else's ideals because then you can only feel miserable and a failure if you don't manage it. If somebody is worth loving, then they'll love you for what you are whether you eat onion bhajis for breakfast, or fart so hard in bed you wake up embedded in the ceiling plaster.'

He *can* read my mind.

'You have to learn to be comfortable with yourself, then you'll feel comfortable with other people and they'll reciprocate.'

I never knew my brother was such a philosopher.

'I know you probably don't think it at the moment, but you will meet someone else.' He smiles reassuringly at me, and begins to ladle rice from one of the cartons on to our plates. 'There's more than one person for everyone. I don't believe in all this, You'll-only-really-love-once crap. You'll meet someone else and you'll fall in love again. You'll just love in a different way. Doesn't make it any less important than before, just different. You wait, you'll see what I mean. Either that or you'll meet someone who'll make you realise that you were never in love with Max in the first place . . .'

'You think so?'

'I know so.' He refills my wine glass.

'How about you, anything interesting in the romance stakes?' I ask, trying to work the conversation away from me.

'Well, I'm working on a little something.' He smiles enigmatically.

'Oh yes? And who is this little something?'

'Well, it's not exactly a who, more of a collective.'

'You what?' Either Jem's arranging an orgy, or a little more explanation's required here.

He looks a bit shifty and pretends to be very interested in the contents of the Chop Suey. The orgy theory gains ground.

'What are you up to, Jeremy?' I look down my nose at him, trying to fathom what secret lies behind those laughing dark eyes.

'Are you going to eat something or what?' He engineers a rapid subject change, turning his attention to a spare rib which he picks up with his fingers and begins to tear at with strong white teeth.

'You're not going to fob me off that easily.' I put down my wine glass and, crossing my arms, stare at him until he has to return my gaze. 'You're up to something, and I want to know what it is.'

Jem sighs, puts down his spare rib, and licks dark brown sticky barbecue sauce from his fingers.

'Just between you and me?'

'Scout's honour.'

'You were never a scout.'

'Okay, guide's honour then.'

'You weren't . . .'

'I know, I know,' I cut in, 'I wasn't a guide either, but I'm your sister. If you can't trust me, who can you trust?'

He looks at me consideringly for a moment.

'Just between you and me?' he repeats.

I nod.

Jem hesitates, and then grins.

'Okay, I'll show you. But not a word to anyone, okay?'

'Why not? You're not doing something illegal, are you?'

'No, don't be daft, nothing like that. It's just, some people might have a . . . well, they might have a sort of *moral* – if that's the right word – problem with it.'

I was right, he *is* arranging an orgy.

Temporarily abandoning food, he leads me through to his spare bedroom which has been redesignated as an office by the strategic positioning of a computer in one corner.

Jem presses power buttons and the machine whirs into life. He presses a few more buttons, whizzes the mouse around his desk, and a file appears on screen: a long and somewhat complicated list of names and categories.

'What's that then?' I peer closer, my eyes adjusting to the brightness of the screen in the dim light of the room.

'It's my hit list,' he tells me, trying very hard to keep the smirk off his face.

'Hit list?'

'Yep. The fourteen or so lucky women who could win the chance to share my duvet on a cold night . . . or a hot one. Don't mind which really so long as we're both naked and up for it. All listed in alphabetical order and cross-referenced to telephone numbers, local haunts, and with a star rating on how likely it is that they might actually fancy me back.'

'Hit list!' I snort in disgust, scanning the names. 'You should rename it the Tit List! I know most of the girls on here, and nearly all of them could flaunt it on page three without the slightest feelings of inadequacy or embarrassment. Honestly, Jem, you're a slut in the worst possible sense of the word.'

He grins sheepishly.

'That's only one list.'

'You mean, you have more than one?'

'Yeah, that's the B List.'

'B?'

He looks at me sideways and sidles away from me a little.

'B for bonk,' he mutters, only half ashamed.

No wonder he's shifted round to the other side of the desk. If he was standing any closer I'd hit him.

'I do have a list that covers more . . . er . . . well, less . . . er . . . sexual intentions.'

'Oh, so you have a list for permanent meaningful relationships then?'

'Well, sort of.'

'What's that filed under? B for boring? A for Asphyxiating?'

'Well, I haven't quite got round to typing that one up yet. I thought I'd work my way through B first, maybe elevate the status of some of the ones on the bonk list, sort of like a tiered interview system.' He grins happily at me, warming to his subject again, ignoring my glare of disapproval.

'What, like try before you buy?'

My sarcasm flies straight over his head.

'Exactly. See, you've got the idea now. It's quite clever really,' he's saying modestly. 'All the girls are down in order of preference, with room for special comments, and a space for their score at the end.'

'Their score!'

'Yep. It's quite a complicated system actually,' he says proudly. 'Marks out of ten for personality, sense of humour, intelligence, body, sexual inventiveness . . .' He trails off as he finally notices the look of absolute and condemnatory disapproval that's settled on my face.

'Don't be such a downer, Alex. You plan nothing, you get nothing.' He shrugs, 'Besides, it's only a bit of fun.'

'Fun?' I'm totally gobsmacked by the fact that my charming, relatively intelligent brother has drawn up a list of the unsuspecting women he's aiming to get into bed, and actually left room for marks out of ten! 'Would you think it was fun if some girl gave you marks out of ten *after* going to bed with her? You're scouting round her room trying to locate your underpants, and she's holding up score cards . . .'

'Well, it depends on whether I got a ten.' Jem grins. 'Come on, Lexy. It's a bit of fun, a game. And, believe me, it's one most guys play in their heads. I admit, not everybody writes it down . . .'

He hastily closes down his computer and heads

back through to our cooling Chinese where he picks at a glutinous string of noodle.

'*You* may think it's a bit of fun, but would the girls on that list think it was very funny? It just reinforces my theory that all men are lying, cheating, rat-faced bastards who like to play stupid games with women.'

'All men? Come on, Alex, don't you think you're just the teeniest bit biased towards mankind at the moment? We're not all the same as Max. I may have drawn up a stupid list to cheer myself up on a lonely night in, but I certainly don't for a minute think I'm actually going to get to fill the thing in. Well, not the whole thing anyway, I'm not sure if number ten actually likes me, and number thirteen has just started going out with my mate Martin . . .'

I slump back down into my chair, and stare despondently at the congealing, untouched pile of food on my plate. I sink my face into my wine, suddenly overcome by the instantaneous gloom that descends, then disappears, then descends, then disappears – like a lift being constantly called between floors.

'Why did he do it, Jem?'

My brother puts a warm affectionate hand over my own.

''Cause he's a total dick,' he replies gently. 'You know, I never liked to say it before, Alex, but Max wasn't right for you.' He looks at me over the rim of his wine glass and smiles awkwardly.

'Well, why on earth *didn't* you say anything?'

'Would you have listened? Besides, I figured it was better if you worked it out for yourself. And you did, didn't you, so I was right.'

'Yeah!' I reply indignantly. 'But only 'cause I walked in on him in bed with someone else!'

'Oh, come on, Lex, you'd been having major problems before that and you know it. Finding Max in bed with another woman was just the kick up the arse you needed to knock the blinkers off your eyes.'

'Yeah,' I admit reluctantly, finally forking cold King Prawn into my mouth. 'I suppose you're right.'

'Hey.' He grins. 'I'm your big brother, I'm always right.'

I dispute this last only with a sardonic raising of eyebrows.

'But what am I going to do?' I ask, chewing sadly. 'I can't remember what it's like to be on my own. It feels weird. I feel sort of displaced. It's been me and Max for so long, I don't know if I can remember how to be just me.'

'You're going to enjoy being single, that's what,' he replies emphatically. 'Believe me, it may not feel like it at the moment, but it's one hell of a lot of fun! Trust me, I know what I'm talking about. You can do what you want, when you want, with whom you want, and as many times as you want to. And you don't have to ask anyone else's permission first!

'Look, I know it's corny, Lex, but don't think of this as an ending, think of it as a new beginning.' He refills both our glasses and raises his to me in a toast. 'To only being answerable to yourself – and to being able to fart in bed without apologising afterwards. Cheers!'

Having ventured out the night before, I'm ready for a slobby Saturday night in watching some mindless television. Unfortunately, my friends have other ideas.

'It'll do you good to get out.' Emma attempts to coax me off the squishy sofa in the sitting room, where I've got pretty comfortable, thank you. 'You can't sit in the house and vegetate for the rest of your natural.'

'But I went out last night,' I grumble, burrowing my bum further into the comfortable seat of Emma's Ikea special.

'You can hardly call a night in with Jem going out.'

I ignore her, and concentrate on Paul Daniels instead. He's just helped a bespangled Debbie McGee into one of those boxes where all you can see are her head and her feet.

'We're eating out. You like eating out.'

Paul's sawing Debbie in half. I bet she wishes it were the other way around.

'Serena's buying dinner.'

Then again, if he lay down in the box his toupee would probably drop off and I doubt if his feet would reach as far as the holes at the bottom.

'Look, Lex, if it doesn't drive you round the bend staying cooped up in this place all the time, it's going to make *me* go mad, okay? I know it hasn't been very long since you and Max split up, but you can't let it get on top of you.'

I wonder if Debbie lets Paul get on top of her? I wonder if his toupee drops off then? I always think one of the worst things about sex is getting your lover's hair in your mouth . . .

'Alex!' Emma shrieks. 'I'm going out and you're coming with me – whether you like it or not!' She grabs me by both hands and cantilevers me off the sofa. 'Now, go and wash your hair, shave your legs and put some make-up on,' she orders, steering me by the shoulders toward the bathroom. 'I promised Serena we'd meet her at the pub at eight, so get your arse into gear and get a move on!'

'But what about Paul Daniels?' I complain.

'I'm sure his ratings figures will drop by fifty percent without you,' Emma drawls sarcastically. 'Just hurry up and get changed. I'll call you if he draws blood, okay?'

Serena is only twenty-three and devastatingly pretty, with a willowy figure and long shining blonde hair. The sort of girl we lesser mortals look at and mentally spit at from instantaneous jealousy. She is, however, an absolute sweetie-pie and is therefore allowed to be our friend so long as she promises not to look too gorgeous whenever we go out together. Unfortunately, even dressed in a tatty old cardigan and jeans, in which I would look like a bag lady, Serena just manages to look understated and sexy. It's fortunate that we love her too much to hate her, or I'd really hate her.

We meet her at a favourite haunt of ours, a quaint old place by the river where the stone walls are pinned together by huge black metal beams, like a fractured leg, and so many hanging baskets are hung from these walls that their weight is probably making the building sink into its own foundations. Serena's at the bar, being drooled over by a spotty young barman. We elbow our way through the usual Saturday night crowd of revellers to join her.

'Bastard!' is the very first thing she says to me, enveloping me in a hug.

'I assume you're referring to Max and not me?' I ask her dryly.

'Are you okay?' she coos, as though talking to a child that's just fallen and grazed a knee. Any minute now she'll be offering me Smarties to try and make me feel better. I'm wrong, she buys me a double vodka instead.

'God, men are such bastards!' she repeats, as we head outside into the sunshine-filled garden. She says this incredibly loudly, oblivious to the numerous members of the opposite sex lounging on benches quaffing beer and lager around us.

'Aren't they just?' Emma agrees wholeheartedly. Having also accepted a large glass of vodka, Coke, ice and lemon from Serena, she slides in next to me on the rickety picnic bench.

'I can't believe Max would do something like that . . .'

'I can.' Emma disdainfully slurps on an ice cube.

'It must have been awful, just walking in on them like that.'

'Well, it wasn't exactly the best moment of my entire life, no,' I reply dryly, burying my nose in my glass.

'What you need is another man,' she states emphatically. 'I always say the best way to get over one man is to find a new one.'

'I thought you'd just decided that all men are bastards? Besides I don't want another man,' I reply, staring into the murky depths of my drink. 'The last one left a sour taste in my mouth.'

'Mmmm.' Serena rips open a packet of Smoky Bacon crisps, and gazes rather thoughtfully at me.

'You know, I didn't like to say it at the time, but I never thought he was right for you,' she finally says through a mouthful of crumbs.

Not another one! Why do they all tell me this now? Why didn't they warn me before that we were so bloody incompatible? Or is it just some strange phenomenon that as soon as you split up with a man, all of your friends and family decide that he wasn't right for you anyway, like some mass psychic communication?

'You're much better off without him. You need somebody more . . . more . . .' Serena looks at the sky for inspiration, but apparently fluffy clouds don't do for her what they did for Wordsworth. 'More . . .' she repeats again.

'More what?' asks Ems.

'Oh, I don't know.' Serena shrugs and smiles apologetically. 'Just more of everything, I suppose. Max was so egocentric. The only bit of your life that he was interested in was the bit that revolved around him. I mean, how long were you two together? Three years? Four?'

'Over five years,' I mutter miserably.

'Yeah, five years, and I'm one of your best friends, right, and I think I must only have met him about ten or twelve times? Yeah, twelve times at the most . . . and that was twelve times too many,' she adds in an almost inaudible murmur.

Emma and Serena look at each other conspiratorially. There's an exchange going on here that I recognise but can't interpret.

'What?' I demand.

They look at each other again, then back at me.

'What is it?' I repeat, agitatedly. 'There's something you're not telling me, isn't there?'

Serena smiles vaguely, and asks Emma some inane question about work.

'Oi!' I demand loudly. 'What was that look about? Don't deny it didn't happen, I saw it. It was about Max, wasn't it?'

They look at one another again.

'Wasn't it?'

'Well, I didn't want to tell you at the time . . . I mean, he *was* drunk.' Serena refuses to meet my eyes.

'Tell me what?'

'He came on to Serena.' Emma shoots straight from the hip. 'And, yes, he was drunk,' she looks apologetically at our friend, 'but he wasn't *that* drunk.'

It's like I've just been slapped in the face.

'You're winding me up, aren't you?' I ask, my mouth falling open stupidly.

Emma shakes her head. 'I'm sorry.'

'When?'

'At my twenty-first birthday party.' Ren scratches at the splintered surface of the table with a fingernail.

'Over two years ago. Why on earth didn't you say anything?'

'We decided it wasn't worth making a fuss about,' Emma says.

'We're only telling you now, in case you think you've lost something worth having.'

I shake my head.

'How could I have been so bloody stupid?'

'Well . . . love's blind, isn't it?' Emma smiles sympathetically at me.

'If that's what it was.'

'You loved him.'

'Maybe I just *thought* I did.'

'Everyone want the same again?' Emma gets to her feet and rummages in her handbag for some cash. 'I think we could do with another.'

'Sorry, Lex.' As soon as Emma's gone, Serena puts a long-fingered hand over mine, her pearlescent pink nail varnish sparkling in the sunlight.

'What are *you* apologising for?'

'For not saying anything at the time. I wish I had done now.'

'Yeah, so do I.' I push my mass of long brown curls out of my eyes, and rest my face despondently in my hands.

'And Emma's wrong. He was so pissed he didn't know his arse from his elbow,' she adds, hoping this will make me feel better about it.

I don't reply.

'You don't hate me, do you?' Ren asks anxiously.

I look up at her in surprise.

'Why on earth should I hate you? It was him that came on to you, wasn't it? You didn't encourage him, did you . . . did you?'

'Of course not!' Serena states indignantly. 'Come on, Lex, you've known me since I was a kid, do you honestly think I'd do that to you?'

'No . . . I'm sorry, Ren.' I hang my head again. 'I'm just a bit shell shocked, that's all. I don't know what I'm thinking, doing or saying half the time. You know, I realised things weren't all hunky-dory between us, but I never dreamt he was doing a thing like that behind my back.'

'Men can be such bastards,' she sighs a

returns with more drinks. 'Why should they be the only ones allowed to get away with it?'

'Who get away with what?' asks Ems, handing me another large vodka.

'Men. They get to do what the hell they want. You bonk around when you're a man and you're a stud. Bonk around when you're a woman and you're a slut.' Serena, picks lemon pips from the bottom of her glass. 'Or a whore or a tart or a bike or a slapper . . .'

'Yep. Thanks,' Emma interrupts her. 'We get the picture.'

'Yeah, but haven't you noticed that there isn't a female equivalent of stud?'

'Is there a female equivalent of misogynist?' I ask crossly. 'Because I think I'm going to become one.'

'Not all men are like Max.' Emma throws Serena a quit-it-or-die look. 'You'll find somebody else, I promise you.'

I think Emma is about the eighth person to use this old platitude on me. I'm surprised at her.

'I'm not sure that I want to find someone else, I think I'm a bit off men at the moment. I might go for a few years of celibacy.'

'You're a bit off Max. There's a big difference and don't you forget it.' Emma swirls the ice around her glass. 'And as for celibacy – pah! He's ruined your sex life for the past five years, don't let him ruin it for any longer.'

'It's too sad that you've only ever been with one man in your entire life,' Serena muses. 'Because it means you don't know what you're missing out on.'

'I thought monogamy was all the rage at the

moment?' I mutter morosely, quickly knocking back my second drink and contemplating a third. 'In which case I'm the height of fashion for a change.'

'Not so far as I'm aware. You know what you need, don't you? You need to go a bit mad, and have some raging affairs. Sod getting involved emotionally. Just go out, find somebody you fancy, and indulge in a spot of no-strings-attached passion.'

'You mean, sleep with a man just for the sex?'

'Why not? Men do it all the time.'

'But I can't sleep with somebody I don't know and don't love.'

'Men do it all the time.' Serena repeats. 'If they spot a woman who's got enough going for her physically to get their hormones racing, then they just go for it, regardless of anything like love or compatibility.'

'Yeah, but the problem is, women need more mental stimulus. He may be the sexiest-looking man you've ever seen, but if we didn't get on, or he'd got no brain, then I just couldn't get turned on.'

'How do you know? Have you tried it?'

'Well, no, you know I haven't. I was a bit of a late developer in that area . . .'

'Don't knock it till you've tried it then. It's the nineties, Lex. Women have just as much right to a sex drive as men in this day and age.'

'The problem is, I'm not totally sure that I have – got a sex drive, that is.'

'You've just been sleeping with the wrong man.' Emma rummages round in her bag, and pulls out a packet of Marlboro Lights and offers them round 'Believe me, baby, everybody's got it.'

'You just need the right person to make you realise

where it's at.' Serena refuses a cigarette, but nods her agreement.

Emma directs the end of her cigarette on to the flame of her lighter and inhales deeply. 'You know, Ren talks a load of crap half the time.'

'Hey!' Serena rallies, insulted.

'Well, you do,' Emma continues. 'That's a fact. But I think she may just have a point, Alex. You've been with Max for a hell of a long time. You two have never been right together but you've stayed put through I don't know what . . . fear maybe, a need for security. Anyway . . . I think it's about time you started to live a little. Lighten up, have a few affairs like Ren said. Learn to enjoy yourself. Have fun.'

'So I'm just supposed to turn from frigid to free love overnight, am I?' I ask them incredulously.

'You're not frigid. Did Max tell you that? Jeez, Alex, you shouldn't listen to that jerk. You just need to find somebody you're sexually compatible with, that's all.'

'And how do you propose I do that then?'

'It's not that difficult. We do share a planet with a rather large number of the opposite sex, you know. Take a look around you. This place is full of men. This town is full of them. There must be somebody you know that you've looked at and thought, Phwaw! Wouldn't mind a bit of that.'

'Er . . . well, no, nobody immediately springs to mind.'

'Don't you know anybody that you fancy?' Ren looks at me in amazement.

'Tom Cruise?' I offer.

'Dream on, Alex,' Ems laughs. 'Isn't there anybody at work?'

'No way! I work with a bunch of creeps and you know it.'

'Well, what about Lucian, your post boy?' Ren starts to drool into her drink. 'I saw him whisking round the office on those firm Lycra-clad legs of his last time I came to take you out to lunch.'

'Lucian?' I cough, inhaling half a mouthful of vodka into my lungs.

'Don't sound so shocked. You never know what's hidden behind the façade. That gorgeous himbo may not be able to talk about Proust, Faust and the Bauhaus in eight different languages, he may not even be able to tie his own shoelaces, but he might be able to fire up your libido to one hundred degrees in eight seconds flat with his tongue.'

'I don't think I'm Lucian's type.'

'Why on earth not? Don't run yourself down, Alex. You're a really pretty girl . . .'

'That's just the problem.'

'Lucian only likes really pretty boys,' Emma explains.

'Okay,' Ren giggles, shrugging, 'so maybe not Lucian. I was just using him as an example. You never know what passions may lurk beneath the exterior of a man, or what passion somebody you'd normally dismiss as not your type may be able to evoke in you. The best sex I ever had was with someone who'd been chasing me for months, and I really thought I didn't fancy him. Then I stopped running for long enough actually to shag the guy and it was great. I suppose what I'm saying is, you need to just forget all your preconceived ideas about what you think you want in a man, and don't set too much store on first impressions either. You're not looking for a long-term relationship, somebody who can pass on good genes to your children and keep you amused for at least two decades. You're looking for down-to-earth, give-me-a-mind-blowing-orgasm-and-then-bugger-off, healthy, heady sex. And who knows? That unassuming little clerk from accounts you wouldn't let your friends see you out with may be the biggest love god on this planet so far as your own personal libido's concerned. They say Casanova was no oil painting, and a good few inches shorter than Paul Daniels in stack heels, but he managed to do pretty well for himself. Forget emotional compatibility and go for some fun and fornication.'

'You sound just like a man.'

'Ah ha!' she crows ecstatically. 'Exactly my point! You have to reassess your values. When you go out man hunting, you're normally looking for all the qualities that you think you need for a long-term relationship. When you go looking to get laid, you don't worry about whether they've got good job prospects, would make a decent father, and can manage to retain their own teeth and hair for another few years.'

'It's physical, not emotional,' agrees Emma.

'So how can you tell if a man's worth . . . you know . . . going for? Or do you just have to take pot luck?'

'It's in the eyes,' Serena sighs.

'And the attitude,' adds Emma. 'Sometimes you get it wrong, but it's normally pretty easy to tell whether they're going to be good or not.'

'So what about him?' I point towards the interior of the pub.

'Who?'

'The barman who served us when we first came in.'

'Shy and inexperienced,' announces Emma with conviction.

'You think so? He was practically drooling down Ren's cleavage.'

'Exactly, not cool at all. He was looking at her tits instead of her face. Not a good way to impress.'

'So how do you do this? How do you read the signs? Or do you just have to go round bonking indiscriminately in the hope that you might get lucky and hit the compatibility jackpot?'

'It's just something you pick up as you go along.' Serena shrugs.

'You learn to read the signs.' Emma starts on her next bit of lemon. 'The more relationships you have, the more you notice the similarities. Like when men lie, they all get this same sort of trapped expression on their face, the eyes start to dart, they won't look at you, they get all arsey and defensive. Didn't you ever notice that with Max?'

'All of the time, now you mention it. Shame I didn't know what it meant, eh?'

'And when a man's good in bed,' Serena continues, 'he usually has an air of . . . not so much confidence, people can be confident and still be crap in the sack . . . no, it's more an air of self-assurance in a flirty but relaxed sort of way. It's hard to describe, but you know it when you see it.'

'How many men have you actually slept with?'

'Lucky seven,' smiles Serena, pulling one of her own stray blonde hairs out of her Coke.

'I don't need to ask you.' I smile wryly at Emma,

who looks down at the table and grins to herself.

'Maybe you don't, but I do.' Serena's attention is instantly turned away from me and towards Emma. 'Come on, tell all.'

'Sorry.' She shrugs. 'Can't disclose that sort of information on the grounds that I may incriminate myself.'

'But it's not fair, Lex knows.'

'Lex knows a lot of things about me that she shouldn't.'

Serena wobbles her bottom lip in fake distress.

'But I thought I was your friend too? It's not fair to keep things from me.'

Emma grins at her. 'Okay, okay . . . anything to keep you happy. Eighteen.'

'Eighteen!' Serena pretends to faint from shock. 'I think you need to add a few more to your list to redress the balance, Lexy. Say we take the difference between me and Emma – that means that you need about twelve.'

'I don't know twelve men I'd want to sleep with. In fact, at the moment, I think I'd find it difficult to come up with one.'

'There must be a few men you know that you fancy?'

I shrug. 'Like I said, I can't actually think of anyone. Besides, it's not my style. I'd rather just be happy with one person, than slappy with several.'

Serena shakes her head.

'It'd do you good, Alex. You've been stuck in a dead end, dead dull relationship with Max the Moron for god knows how long. You need to get out and get a life, play the field a bit.'

'Well, Emma's happy. You're happy aren't you, Ems?' I turn to her pleadingly. I need someone to restore my faith in monogamous relationships.

To my chagrin she pulls a face, which is hardly an indication of a reassuringly positive affirmation to follow.

'I don't know.' She shrugs. 'I mean, I do love Theo, but sometimes . . .' She shakes her head. 'I don't want to put him down or anything, but I do sometimes feel there must be more to life. He's a great guy, and we have a brilliant time when we're together, but how often do we actually *get* together? I never really feel like I'm very high on his list of priorities. In fact,' her lips purse crossly, 'nowadays I feel like he runs out of paper before he even gets to my name! No, Alex, I think Ren's right. I think you should get out and enjoy yourself. It'd do you good.'

'Well, if you're that keen on the idea, why don't you do it yourself?'

'Alex, come on. I'm twenty-eight and I've slept with eighteen people. I have been "doing it myself" for the past ten years. Albeit rather quietly and enigmatically. It'll be nice to have a new recruit.'

'Make that recruits, in the plural. I'm convinced.' Serena drains the last of her Diet Coke and plonks her glass down firmly on the table. 'I think it's time we all took control of our own lives, turned the tables so to speak. If men can play fast and loose, then why can't we? I think we should all take a leaf out of the open book that is man, and start acting like they do. Love 'em and leave 'em.'

'Hump 'em and dump 'em?' laughs Emma.

'Shag 'em then bag 'em?' Serena snorts.

'You're not being serious, are you?' I ask incredulously.

'Well, I'm single.' Serena shrugs.

'And I'm neglected,' says Ems.

'You've been dumped on,' Serena adds.

'Thank you so much for reminding me,' I mutter dryly.

'What are we waiting for? I mean, we shouldn't dish out advice to you that we wouldn't take ourselves, now should we?'

'Well, I'm up for it.' Emma grins. 'It's got to be better than waiting around for Theo to forget to call me yet again. So what are the rules?' She puts down her glass and, rummaging once again in her voluminous hand bag, pulls out a pen.

'Rules?'

'There are always rules in a competition.'

'This is a competition now?' My gaze swivels between my two friends like a spectator in Wimbledon week.

'Don't you think that would spice things up a bit? How many men can we bonk? How many hearts can we break? Set ourselves a time limit. Let's see . . . who can shag the most guys in say . . . two months? See who hits top targets.' Serena's definitely getting over excited now. My little doubts start growing into slightly fatter, more insistent doubts.

'The winner could get a prize, and we could have incentives, like whoever hits twenty first could get a bottle of champagne or something.'

'I don't know about a prize. If you managed to bonk that many men in two months, I think you'd need a medal and a thorough health check.'

'Perhaps Serena's a little over the top,' Ems agrees, 'but we could have an overall winner . . . how about whoever gets the highest score gets crowned official princess of pull? And the loser has to take the other two out to that gorgeous little Italian restaurant in the High Street and let them gorge on whatever they want. What do you think?'

'I think we should just cut the crap and just go straight to the Italian restaurant,' I reply, frowning in concern.

'Great idea,' they cry enthusiastically, draining the last of their drinks and standing up.

'Pasta's great for building up stamina, and we're going to need as much of *that* as we can get,' interrupts Ems, taking my arm and grinning lasciviously.

Serena takes my other arm. 'We can discuss the plan of action whilst we eat.'

'Plan of action?' I ask worriedly, as they tow me out to the car park.

'Yeah, the guidelines to the game.' Ren grins.

'The rules of rumpy-pumpy,' laughs Emma. 'Why let men have the monopoly on being bastards? Look out, guys, the girls are about to put the "Miss" into misbehaving.'

# Chapter Three

There's a message from Max on Emma's answer machine when we get back.

'Alex, it's me. Pick up the phone, I know you're there . . .'

Well, that's where you were wrong, mate, 'cause I was out stuffing far too much *crespelle* and gallons of Frascati down my neck, and trying to persuade my two best mates they're totally mad. So there! I blow a drunken raspberry at the phone.

'Alex . . . look, this is ridiculous. We need to talk . . . I'll be at home tomorrow. I'll expect you at one o'clock.'

Typical Max. No 'if you can' or 'by your leave', just a summons that I'm expected to obey.

'Are ya . . . are ya gunnago?' slurs Emma, hanging on to the hat stand to stop herself from falling over.

'Dunno. I rillydunno. Gunnagobed now.'

Hello, floor.

I wake up the next morning with a nagging headache, and a nagging feeling that perhaps I should go and see Max.

I want to hear what sort of explanation he's got, if

he has one. Maybe he's just asked me round to blow me up about the sheets, the driller-killered bath and the hopefully exploded TV set. But then again, you never know. I might just get an apology. Maybe. Emma gives me a pep talk before I go, over a hearty condemned woman's breakfast of bacon and eggs.

'No matter how much he grovels, don't give in to him, Alex.'

'Max, grovel? I hardly think so.'

'Well, why do you think he's asked to see you? He wants you back, Alex.'

'You think so?'

'Well, he hasn't asked you round to do the house-work, has he?'

'Knowing Max, that's the precise reason,' I joke weakly.

'Just be careful, babes. You're just at that difficult stage where it seems like it would be so much easier to forgive and forget and go home. You need to give yourself time to get over this part. Don't rush back, Lex, you'll regret it. You're missing your life the way it was, not Max. I know what it's like, I've been through this myself. You get to a point where you feel so bloody disorientated all you want to do is go home, but it's not what you need, trust me.'

'I know,' I reply. 'At the moment, all I really need . . .'

'Yes?' encourages Emma.

'Is an Alka Seltzer. Be an angel . . .'

I spend about twenty minutes sitting in my car, just looking at the front of the house, memories of happier times flooding back to me. I can feel fried egg and undigested bacon rind churning in my stomach, and I've got a lump in my throat the size of a button mushroom. This is no good. I need to be strong when I walk through that door, not choked with emotion, my throat already clogged with the threat of upset, my hands trembling as they rest against the steering wheel.

It hurts, but to give me that strength, I think of Max in bed with Madeleine, naked and bucking like a stud horse with something to prove. The Max I thought I loved was an image that I created. The real Max is the man who lied to me, the man who tried to get one of my best friends into bed. It's like pricking yourself with a needle until you go numb to the pain. I replay every vivid moment of his infidelity until I am immune enough to get out of the car, walk up the short path and ring the doorbell.

Max opens the door. It's the first time I've seen him in over a week. Somehow it feels more like a month. He's dressed in Levis and a creased white T-shirt, and looks tired and slightly rumpled, like he's just got out of bed.

I can feel the hot tears prick at the back of my eyes as soon as I see his familiar face, but I blink them back and concentrate on the fact that this man is an arsehole. He may be cute, but he's an arsehole. Very cute. I'd forgotten about the dimple he gets in his chin when he smiles. Arsehole, Alex. And the way his glossy dark hair flops over one cornflower blue eye. BIG Arsehole, Alex. Forget cute, just think, Arsehole. Okay?

'Alex, I thought you weren't going to come.'

I have to step over a heap of mail addressed to me

to get into the hallway. Max obviously just picked up his, and left mine where it fell.

He moves forward as if to embrace me, then obviously changes his mind, and reverses awkwardly into the sitting room. I follow him silently through. The usually immaculate room is incredibly untidy. Max is one of those people who demands an impeccable home, but expects anybody other than himself to ensure it stays that way.

'Er . . . do you want a coffee or something?' he asks, running a hand through his shiny conker hair.

I've already glanced through to the kitchen and spotted the sink piled high with dirty crockery.

I ignore the offer. I might get poisoned. Even if I didn't, it would probably choke me. Even if it didn't choke me, he'd probably expect me to wash it all up first.

I look awkwardly about the room, not knowing quite what to do with myself. I don't really want to sit down, but I'm not enjoying just standing here like a spare part. Max looks at me and sort of half smiles again. At least he sort of looks at me. His eyes are darting from side to side like the ball in a tennis match. I remember what Ems said about men who won't look you in the eye.

'So how have you been?'

How have I been? I find him in bed with another woman, and he has the gall to ask how I've been like I've just been away on a business trip or something? If I wasn't already lost for words, I'd be completely speechless. I simply stare blankly back at him. I don't know if he finds it unnerving that I haven't spoken a word to him yet. I hope he does. I don't want to be the only one who feels bloody brain-numbingly awkward.

'I may as well come straight to the point.' Max sits down in the wing chair by the fire so I go and perch on the sofa opposite, carefully taking the part of it that's as far away from him as possible.

Despite saying this, he's silent for a few more moments.

A week's worth of newspapers are in an untidy pile next to the sofa, the surface of the top one covered in a fine layer of dust.

He takes a deep breath, like he's just about to deliver a long soliloquy on stage. 'I want you to come home, Alex.'

There, he's said it.

Emma was right. I didn't think she would be, but she was spot on.

I wait for a rush of emotion to hit me. A surge of joy, perhaps. A flood of panic. Nothing happens. The numbness is still there

'I want us to try again,' Max continues. 'We've both made mistakes, but I think our relationship is strong enough to work through them.'

I finally find my voice.

'We've both made mistakes?' I repeat.

'Yes.' Max nods gravely. 'We've both made mistakes, but I think we can get over this, Alex. I'm happy for you to move back in.'

Is that it? No word of apology, no explanation, just, Come home and we'll work it out? Not even that. 'I'm happy for you to move back in', like he's magnanimously forgiving me for walking out on him. I think my mouth drops open a little bit at this point. I find Max in our bed with someone else, going for it like a jack rabbit in mating season, and this is all I get?

'That's very magnanimous of you,' I say quietly.

I think he suddenly realises it needs a bit more than this to make me fall at his feet in adoring subservience.

He flicks the button marked Charm, and moving over to sit next to me, takes one of my hands in both of his and looks up at me from under long sooty eyelashes, his blue eyes suddenly misty with longing.

'I've really missed you, Alex,' he whispers huskily, with just the slightest, sexiest break in his voice.

For a moment my heart lurches on the edge, and then an amazing thing happens. A little voice inside my head begins to laugh.

Oh, Max. If only you could act this well when you're on stage! It'd be move over Ewan McGregor. Fortunately what is designed to have me falling under the old spell, has totally the opposite effect. Jem was right. It's like my blinkers have fallen off or something. I can now see Max for what he really is. Mr Manipulator.

I know Max, and I know what he wants. He wants his old life back. The one where everything was done for him, where the domestic side of things ran without his input in either thought or deed, leaving him free to lead a life of duplicity and debauchery. Where emotional support is a one-sided game of cricket, with me as the box defending Max's goolies from the googlies thrown by life.

After a week he's suddenly realised that trousers left on the floor stay where they are unless someone picks them up, that crockery and cutlery aren't self-washing, that grass grows, dust settles, and you can't live on takeaways every night for the rest of your life. His orderly little life just isn't orderly without his own personal home help to do everything for him. He thinks he wants me back and he's planned all of the things to say which he thinks will help him achieve this aim.

The thing is, I know Max well enough to be able to add my own translation to the whole, obviously pre-rehearsed speech that now follows.

'I miss you,' he repeats, even more softly this time. 'Things aren't the same without you.'

*I can't cook. I've just run out of clean underwear, and the Hoover hasn't ventured out of the closet since you left.*

'I just sit around the house on my own and it seems so empty without you.'

*I can't quite afford the mortgage and a social life without your regular financial contributions.*

'I need to be with you.'

*I'm not getting as much sex as I used to with two women on the go at the same time.*

'I miss your touch.'

*How do you get the cap off the can of Mr Sheen?*

'I miss your smell.'

*I've been wearing the same shirt for the past week, I thought the bathroom was self-cleaning, and there's something strange and stinking growing in the salad shelf of the fridge.*

When he finally finishes, head hanging, my hand still clutched in his, he sighs a little sigh, and then looks up at me again from under said long sooty eyelashes, and attempts a pathetic, brave little smile.

'Come back to me, Alex. I need you.'

It's not working. I rearrange my features into what I hope is a suitably hard expression.

'I love you, Alex.' The voice drops lower, the hand squeezes tighter.

Now I know he's lying. The only person Max loves is himself.

'Who are you trying to kid, Max? If you wanted to be with me you wouldn't have started a relationship with someone else.'

This is the longest sentence I've spoken since I got here. It takes a lot out of me, I can tell you.

Max attempts to look mortally wounded.

'I wasn't having a relationship with her.'

'Oh, yeah? What do you call it then?'

'Having sex does not constitute a relationship. What *we* had was a relationship.'

'Oh, so because I got to do all of the "usual" relationship stuff, like wash your dirty socks, do your ironing, cook all of your meals, and clean your house, I'm supposed to feel privileged, am I? I'm supposed to overlook the fact that you shagged my aerobics instructor! That was purely recreational, was it? A bit of sport, exercise. You didn't fancy jogging or football, so you thought you'd try some extra-curricular shagging instead? Well, you can stuff it where the sun doesn't shine, Max, because I don't want to come back! I don't know if I love you. I don't think I even like you very much anymore.'

He drops my hands and backs off, blinking in what I think is supposed to be his attempt at hurt bewilderment.

'But, Alex, I need you . . .'

'You need someone to stroke your ego and polish your BAFTAs,' I spit back, 'and that ain't gonna be me. Why don't you ask Madeleine? She seems to be pretty obliging so far as your wants and needs are concerned.'

He drops the hurt act, and his eyes narrow like a cobra about to strike.

'You do realise this is all your fault?'

Ah! Now we have the real Max speaking.

'Basically, if you'd done more than lie there like a limp lettuce leaf then I wouldn't have needed to sleep with anyone else,' he hisses in a low malicious voice.

Punch number one. Thrown well below the belt, technically disqualified, but still damaging.

'It's not surprising that I went elsewhere. Sex with you was about as much fun as stuffing giblets back into a dead turkey,' he continues nastily, warming to his theme. 'If you hadn't been so inadequate and so . . . so . . . FRIGID . . . then I wouldn't have to get my kicks with someone else.'

'Frigid?' I manage to say this without my lips moving.

'Colder than a polar bear's backside. I know you were inexperienced when we met,' Max sneers, 'but you'd have thought you'd have learnt something after six years.'

'Well, I'd have thought so too,' I reply, grabbing my bag and standing up. 'Perhaps if I'd been with someone who had any knowledge to impart, I might have done.'

I have the satisfaction of seeing his sneer fall on to the floor and break. When I get to the door, I stop and turn around.

'You know, there was the *one* thing being with you taught me, Max . . .' My imagination draws on a cigarette, and blows a cloud of smoke into his gawping face, Mae West-style.

'How to fake it.'

Despite this last communication with Max the Prat which could easily have turned me into the female equivalent of a monogamous misogynist – monogamous because my manhating would be directed at one man only – and despite the over-the-top enthusiasm of my friends who are still raring to start our own competitive and actual reality version of Jem's virtual reality hit list, I still don't think the ball would actually have started rolling if a little bird – well, a great big fat bird, one of the sort that does a massive dump on your head as it flies past thumbing its beak at you – hadn't forwarded a piece of spectacular news to me in a rather unspectacular way.

Life has moved on exactly one month and two weeks. I'm getting there, but it's been a struggle, you know, like trying to run through knee-deep mud. It no longer seems quite so strange to wake up in Emma's spare room every morning, alone, but I still feel like a shoulder that's come out of joint.

Anyway, the bird, in the shape of my brother, imparts the news, all 'casual like', and in passing, as I'm attempting to cook us dinner in his kitchen. I'm just bashing a piece of steak, slurping Burgundy, and thinking that for somebody who's an appalling chef, my brother's certainly got a wide range of kitchen appliances, when out he comes with it, as though he's just telling me that he's heard the price of coffee at the Co-op has gone up by two pence this week or something.

'Max is doing what!' I shriek at my brother in absolute disbelief.

Jem adopts a please-don't-massacre-the-messenger-with-a-meat-cleaver stance.

'You heard,' he whimpers, nervously eyeing the mallet clutched in my rigid fist, and wishing he'd told me after dinner, when I'd had a few glasses of wine, and wasn't pounding two pieces of meat to death with a steak hammer.

'Yeah, I heard, but I don't think I heard right.'

'Trust me, it's gospel.'

'It's a load of fucking crap, that's what it is,' I yell, re-attacking the steak with increased verve. Swing, wallop. The wooden mallet practically breaks through the meat and impacts with Jem's chopping board.

'I know it's shitty, Alex . . .'

Swing, wallop.

'. . . Max is unbelievable really . . .'

Swing, wallop.

'. . . the cow's already dead, Alex!'

I stop, sigh, and lean my forehead on the end of the mallet so that I get a little red indentation in my skin.

'No, you're right. I shouldn't be taking it out on you or the food.'

Jem also sighs, with relief.

'I should be taking it out on that low-down, dirty, stinking, rat-faced creep of a bastard ex of mine instead!' I hammer home the steak mallet like a butch bloke at a fairground trying to prove his muscles on a test-your-strength machine. A bell doesn't ring, but the steak finally gives up the ghost and splits into two, one piece slithering off the board on to the kitchen floor, and the other bit shooting off and sticking to the newly painted walls.

Jem grabs a wine bottle. I don't know whether he's going to smash it on the counter and use it in self-defence, or pour me a drink.

He does the latter, and hands me a goldfish bowl-sized glass of Cabernet Sauvignon.

'You shouldn't let it get to you, Lex. That's probably exactly what he wants.' He takes the steak mallet out of my other hand and steers me towards a chair. 'You should just rise above it. You don't want him back, do you?'

'No,' I manage pretty positively.

'Then it's not a problem, is it?'

'But . . .'

'No,' Jem states firmly. 'There are no buts. Max is getting married . . .'

There. He's said it again. Max is getting married. My Max! No, strike that. He's not mine anymore, is he? He's definitely not mine anymore, the bastard's getting married, and it was only six weeks ago that he asked me to go back to him!

'And to do something that major this quickly, then he's probably doing it for all the wrong reasons,' Jem continues. 'So think about it. They'll probably just end up making each other miserable. Now doesn't that make you feel better?'

Strangely enough it does. I imagine Max married and miserable, babies spewing rusk on his Ben Shermans, wife nagging constantly in the background. He will hate it with a passion. Max is too selfish to be married. I feel a bit of a bitch taking pleasure from the anticipation of his pain, but only a *bit* of a bitch, a little teeny-weeny insignificant fraction of a bit.

Taking over chef's duties, Jem grinds pepper over the piece of steak that survived my wrath, and slaps it into the top part of his oven. He also peels the other decimated piece of steak from the floor and the wall and chucks that on to the grill as well.

'The floor's clean!' He rolls his eyeballs at me when I look at him in outrage. I frown dubiously.

'I'll eat that bit, okay?' he offers. 'Jeez, Lex, have some more wine and loosen up a bit. You couldn't have picked a better revenge scenario yourself. Can you imagine Max as a married man?'

'Well, I used to be able to, yes, at one point. Married to *me*, to be precise.'

'Well, you had a lucky escape then, didn't you? 'Cause now he's marrying some other poor fool.'

He deftly slices a tomato, realises he's used the same board that I murdered the beef on, and chucks it into his swing bin.

'Just think of all the things about Max that really pissed you off . . .'

'Like sleeping around!' I growl.

'Yeah, like sleeping around, taking you for granted, putting you down . . .'

'Changing channels whilst I was in the middle of watching something without even asking. Complaining if the house was a mess but never lifting a finger himself. Leaving his clothes where they fell and expecting them to miraculously wash and iron themselves, then walk back into his wardrobe.' I take up the theme.

'See, you've got the idea.' Jem grins, washing and breaking a lettuce. 'And just tell yourself that you don't have to do any of that anymore, 'cause some other mug has just signed up for a life sentence of it.'

He tosses the lettuce into a bowl, and then refilling my glass, pours himself a drink, and starts man-handling a cucumber.

'Fancy some garlic bread?'

'Don't mind if I do . . . morning breath doesn't matter to me anymore, does it?'

'Is that the only joy of being single that you can think of?' My brother looks at me pityingly. 'You know, I sometimes wonder if we're really related. There are so many other things that are good about the solo state. Like sex.' He happily sloshes half a bottle of fat-free dressing over his salad then chucks in some wooden server spoons. 'You've got the chance to try something new now, haven't you? See what it's like with somebody other than Max. You know, maybe try a few for size.'

My facial features rearrange themselves into a shocked expression.

'There's no harm in a bit of sexual experimenta-tion,' is his response.

'No, only in catching incurable diseases, getting a reputation, and not liking myself very much.'

'I didn't say you had to metamorphose into a total tart, now did I? Just let your hair down and have some fun. You've been stuck in a relationship for the majority of your youth, Alex, don't waste the rest of it. You'll be thirty in three years, and then you'll be past it.'

He grins broadly. Jem's thirtieth birthday is in a few

weeks' time, so I think he's joking. I bloody well hope he's joking!

'But surely this is the time of life when I should be settling down and having children and a mortgage? Not running round bonking as many men as I can.'

'Do you think giving birth is as painful as paying a mortgage every month?' Jem muses, posting a dripping lettuce leaf into his mouth and chewing thoughtfully.

'I'm being serious, Jeremy!'

'Oooh. She called me Jeremy. Now I know I'm in trouble.'

I shake my head in despair.

'Why's it so hard to have a serious conversation with you sometimes? You're my brother, you're supposed to be a good influence. You're not supposed to be telling your little sister to whip off her knickers at every opportunity.'

'I'm trying to be a good influence, Alex. Watching you with Max has been like watching a favourite plant trying to grow in the shade of a bloody big thorn bush.'

'You mean, I'm stunted?' I ask huffily.

'Only emotionally.'

'That makes it better?'

'Look, Alex, all I'm saying is, you've been tied to Max's nappy tabs for far too long. I think you've already had a stint at being a mother . . . to a twenty-nine-year-old big kid. Get a life! Have some fun, for goodness' sake. Leave the marriage/mortgage/ responsibility bit to someone else for a while, and enjoy life while you can. Now, I hope you're hungry?

Dinner's ready, and I seem to have cooked enough to feed the five thousand.'

Jem entertains me throughout dinner by painting bitchy pictures of the horrors of married life for Max and Madeleine. The problem is, these uplifting thoughts maintain me only for about five minutes after I'm out of his company. By the time I've got back to Ems's house they've had the society wedding of the year, and they're living together in roses-round-the-door bliss, with two point five gorgeous children, a dog that never sheds, shits, or licks its own, and a state of permanent wedded euphoria, the neverending honeymoon of life, idolised by all as the perfect couple, going on *Mr & Mrs* and getting the perfect score, taking over from Richard and Judy . . .

The usual plaintive wail brings my friend running.

'Emmmmmmaaaaa!!!'

'What . . . what?' she stutters, stumbling out of her bedroom in a red fluffy bathrobe, eyes pink and slitty from being woken.

'Max is getting married.' I blink at her pitifully through a wall of tears.

'Oh,' she responds.

'You don't seem very surprised?'

'Well, it's cheaper than getting a housekeeper, and you get sex thrown in on top.' She rubs a huge lump of sleep out of her left eye.

'Emma!'

She shakes her head wearily. 'I'm sorry, Alex, but nothing Max could do would surprise me. The guy's a total jerk.'

'But why is he doing it? Jeez, Ems, we've only been split up for just over a month.'

'Maybe he loves her?' she offers. 'Whoever?'

'Madeleine,' I mutter grumpily. 'That's not what I wanted to hear, Emma.'

'I'm your friend, and friends don't lie to each other.' She reaches out and squeezes my shoulder affectionately. 'Look, do you want a cup of tea or something?'

'No.'

'How about something a bit stronger? I think there's a bottle of something in the fridge. It's only a really cheap white that Theo brought round last week and hasn't bothered to come back and actually drink with me, but it's cold. It's either that or Meths.'

'Meths sounds good. Do I get it in a brown paper bag?'

Emma raises her eyes heavenward and goes to the kitchen to fetch two glasses.

'We only split just over a month ago,' I repeat to her when she comes back into the sitting room bearing alcohol. I sound like Marvin the Paranoid Android, all flat, morose and feeling totally sorry for myself.

'Nearly two,' Emma corrects me. 'And sorry to be the one to remind you, but he has been seeing her for a bit longer than that, hasn't he? Besides, you know what Max is like. He can't be on his own for more than five minutes. He went straight from his parents' to that house, and then he asked you to move in with him three weeks later.'

'Well, like you say, it was cheaper than getting a cleaner.' I laugh weakly. 'Oh, Ems, I know he's been a bastard, but I can't help missing him. We did have some good times together.'

'The Max you miss isn't the real Max.'

'So you're saying everything I thought we had was fake?'

'No . . . of course it wasn't, but it's really easy to forget the bad bits and paint a rosy picture of something that wasn't that wonderful. Ultimately he showed his true colours. Don't forget that you left him, and definitely don't forget the reasons why.'

'He's just doing it to get back at me, to take the piss. Poor little Alex, who can't even get another date, let alone get married.'

'Can't or won't?'

'Can't or won't what?'

'Get another date, stupid. You could be out every night if you really wanted.'

'Yeah, with dorks, plebs and social rejects.'

'So, what does it matter if you date the odd dork? At least you'd only be *dating* a moron. Madeleine Hurst is marrying one!'

A small snigger escapes me.

'That's better.' Ems sloshes more wine into my glass. 'You never know, your smile might find its way home soon.'

'Would an apologetic one do as a starter? I've been a pain recently, haven't I?'

'Only recently?' Emma rolls her eyeballs and dives nose first into her wine glass.

'You know, I just wish there was some way I could get back at him.' I swallow Theo's cheap white, topping up my already high alcohol level.

'That's childish.'

'I know, but it would make me feel better.'

'What, like attempting to blow up his TV set or

drilling a few holes in his bath tub?' Emma says slyly.

I go crimson.

'*Moi*! Deliberately vandalise somebody else's property?' I feign outraged innocence. 'I wouldn't do anything like that.'

'You know, bitterness normally only hurts the person who's feeling it,' Ems waxes philosophical. 'If Max is doing it just to piss you off, then he's a bloody idiot, because ultimately the only people he'll be hurting are himself and Madeleine.'

'Hmm, that's pretty much what Jem said.'

'But anyway,' she continues, 'if he *is* doing it to piss you off, then the best thing you can do is show him that it's not working.'

'And how do you propose I do that then?'

Emma lifts a magazine, and thumbing through to the problem page, pulls out a piece of paper slotted there.

'Filed under the Agony Aunt page for safe keeping. 'She grins and hands it to me. It's a paper napkin from a certain Italian restaurant we're known to frequent. Scrawled on it, in a mixture of Emma's and Serena's handwriting, is a list entitled, 'The Hit Back List'.

'Start playing him at his own game, Lex.'

I haven't had one of these girlie get-together-to-go-out sessions for ages. The music's blaring, alcohol is in abundance, the slightly singed smell of heating curling tongs and a heady mix of three different perfumes hangs on the air, the room is strewn with clothes, and Serena is parading round in her eighth outfit.

'This reminds me of when I was sixteen.' I pout

into my hand mirror, sucking in my cheeks as I apply blusher to the apples, frowning as I spot a pair of fine lines under my eyes that I hadn't really noticed before.

'When you were sixteen, I was only twelve.' Serena admires her slim figure in the full-length mirror.

'Piss off, Ren!' Attempting to ignore my lines, I try to concentrate on my better features.

'When I was sixteen, I was thin,' Emma moans, pinching her thighs. 'And I thought cellulite was a form of low-fat spread!'

Full lips, quite good cheekbones, large brown eyes that I was once told by a drunken admirer were beautiful. Not bad for an old bird, in a dark room and standing as far away from the gorgeous Ren as possible!

'Does this look okay?' Serena slips into one of Emma's few designer outfits, a little black dress with emphasis on the little.

'You look gorgeous,' Ems sighs jealously. 'How come it's my dress and I don't look that good in it?'

'Doesn't it make my bum look big?' Ren peers anxiously over her shoulder into the mirror, at her tiny muscular rear. The whole thing is about the size of just one of my bum cheeks.

I look over my shoulder. 'You've got a bum? When did you get that then?'

'I always wanted a cleavage,' Emma sighs, 'and I got a bum instead. When I was younger I said to God, "You know this puberty thing? Well, please make me look like Sam Fox." '

'So what happened?'

'I ended up looking like Sam Fox all right, only I

look like Sam Fox back to front and doing a hand stand.' She slaps her arse cheeks in disgust.

I end up back in the first outfit I tried on over an hour ago, a pair of deep purple velvet hipsters and a matching halter top. It looks good, but I'll have to remember to breathe in all evening as my stomach's on display.

A loud honking from outside heralds the arrival of the taxi.

'Ready?'

'Ready as I'll ever be.' I breathe in. Not only does my stomach flatten, but my boobs lift too. I should breathe in more often.

'Let the games commence.' Emma holds out her hand, Serena puts hers on top in a gesture of solidarity, and they both indicate for me to do the same.

'I feel like a Ninja Turtle,' I mutter, embarrassed.

'No, we're the Three Musketeers.'

'I'll be Athos.'

'I'll be Porthos.'

'I'm not being a bloody aftershave!'

'You can be D'Artagnan then.'

'Well, technically speaking he wasn't actually a musketeer.'

'Well, technically speaking, neither are we.'

'Look, just shut up and psych up, okay!'

'Evenin', ladies.' The surprisingly petite bouncer waves us through into the night club, with a lift of his black silk bomber-jacketed sleeve, and a flirtatious wink. It's nearly midnight. We've hit a succession of bars and a succession of bottles, but as usual when you really need the courage of a drunkard, you stay stone cold sober, no matter how much alcohol you pour into your body.

We walk through into the huge air-conditioned, laser-lit, smoke-filled hangar that is the main club area. The place itself is a bit like an octopus with incredibly short stumpy legs. You've got the main room, which is a huge domed area and houses a split-level dance floor already heaving with bodies, and all around, off the main room, are little separate areas housing bars or chill out places. Some stairs to the other side of the dance floor lead to a balcony area which sweeps the whole circumference of the upper level of the central dome. People go up there to see and be seen: hanging over the railings, chilling out, chatting, laughing, drinking bottled water, watching the dancers and hawking for talent. Or to find a dark uninterrupted hideaway in which to grope a recently achieved conquest. This is apparently our ultimate aim. Tonight is the opening night of the games.

I head straight for the nearest bar, and rooting around in my 'bag', wave a twenty in the direction of several pint pullers who are running around on the wet floor behind it.

Serena informed me that you simply don't take handbags to night clubs anymore. My joke that I'd have nothing to dance round was greeted with a look of absolute horror, as though I was being serious.

I don't think even in my younger clubbing days that I ever quite got sad enough or drunk enough to dance round my handbag, but what I don't have, however, is my portable face repair kit. The 'bag' Serena has furnished me with is yet another Rick

Moranis sequel. 'Honey, I shrunk the handbag'. It's designed to fit snugly into the palm of my hand whilst I get on down and boogie. Basically it's just a purse in disguise. There's enough room for some cash, a lip liner, an eyeliner, and – also supplied by an over-hopeful Serena – a condom, but no room for my usual cosmetic arsenal of hairspray, lipstick, blusher, emergency foundation, hairbrush, perfume, etc. I even have to detach my front door key from the huge bunch of keys I normally lug round with me every-where I go like a security blanket. *And* I have to leave my mobile phone at home. Help, Mummy.

Ren and Emma are standing at the edge of the dance floor, as I stagger back through the throng clutching three bottles of Bud.

The beat of the music is intoxicating. It's a call to my feet and my hips and my knees and my arse to start swaying like a cocktail being gently stirred by a swizzle stick.

'Put one foot on the dance floor with that bottle and the bouncers will bodily remove you,' warns Serena.

'Well, that's one way of getting the instant atten-tion of a man.'

'No way. Bouncers are strictly off limits. You'd just be another notch on their bulkhead, and it's you that's adding up the conquests tonight, not the other way around.'

I quickly finish what is for me about my seventh bottle of the evening, and then follow my friends on to the crowded dance floor, where bodies gyrate to the heady beat and sweat glistens under the glitter balls. Lasers lick across our faces, strobing funkily in time to the music, which is more than can be said for me.

It's been so long since I went to a nightclub, I've forgotten how to dance. I'm too busy concentrating on my feet to scout the room for 'talent', as Serena puts it. I manage to get back into the beat fairly quickly. The only bit that throws me is when an up tempo record suddenly gets an unexpected slow bit bang in the middle. The hordes of frenetically wiggling dancers – including me – don't know what to do with themselves. Musicians must have a really cruel sense of humour. A stop-dancing-and-look-like-a-prat bit seems to be added to all of the better tracks.

I'm starting to think that our mission is really Mission Impossible. All of the bars that we've been to have been packed to the brim with people out for a good time, opposite sexes eyeing each other like bargains at a Sunday market, people pairing up like animals in the mating season. The thing is, I've talent scouted every room and hit a big fat zero in the find-myself-a-fanciable-male stakes. I've been off the market for so long I think I've forgotten how to trade. It's really weird going out with the express purpose of picking up a man. I think it must be like going shopping. When you're broke, you find so many gorgeous things you'd die to buy. When you've got money, the shops are empty.

Serena, however, a hormone-seeking missile, a testosterone targeter, is doing pretty well for herself. She's already been chatted up twice, and we've only been in the club long enough to visit the ladies once, and despite the fact it's pretty difficult to see through the fug of a thousand cigarettes, and the cold smoky haze of an enthusiastic dry ice machine, she's already homing in on some guy she fancies the pants off.

'Oooh, look. I think that's Nicky Taylor over there. You see the one in the blue Ralph Lauren shirt?' She points to a blond guy with chiselled cheek bones and a Crispian from Kula Shaker haircut. 'Isn't he gorgeous? Number one, here I come! Don't wait up, girlies . . .' And she's off like a bloodhound, weaving through the crowd to sniff him out, her lithe body still writhing to the rhythm of the music as she moves, like a snake, dancing to a charmer's tune.

'Is that really fair, picking someone you know? Surely that gives her a head start?' I complain, as I watch her move in for the kill.

'Well, we didn't specify in the rules that it couldn't be someone you know.' Emma shrugs.

'The rules were pretty open, weren't they?'

'Like Serena's legs.' Ems points to where Serena, target located, contact made, is already getting up close and personal with the delectable Nicky,

'Not seen anything *you* fancy yet then?'

'God, you make it sound like we're in a cake shop or something.'

'We are,' Emma grins.'

'Well, so far I've seen some pretty manky-looking cakes, like the last drying out Danish that nobody wants.'

'Hell, Lex, you're not looking for someone to start a permanent relationship with. You haven't got to wake up with them every morning, wash their socks, or take them home to meet your parents.'

'No,' I admit reluctantly, 'I suppose not.'

'Well then . . .'

'Well then nothing. Why should I lower my standards?'

'Because by your standards even Johnny Depp wouldn't get a look-in.'

'Oh, I think he might pass . . . just.'

'Don't know about you, but I need something with ice in it.' She fans herself with her hand, then leads the way off the dance floor.

We fight our way through the bar again.

'Yo, Ems.'

A hand reaches through the crowd and grabs her by the shoulder. The hand is followed by what I think is a man. I say 'I think', because it's very hard to tell. The whatever it is and Emma embrace like old friends.

'Ain't seen you for like ages, man,' it drawls in a croaking voice. 'How ya' doin'?'

'Great. Life's a breeze . . .'

Emma introduces me.

'Alex, this is Skidmark.'

The thing holds out his hand to me, and I take it tentatively. He must be a Mason or something, because he doesn't actually shake my hand, just does some weird pressure things with his thumb in my palm, whilst his little finger dances foxtrot across the back of my knuckles.

'Pleased to meet you . . . er . . .'

'Just call me Skid, man,' he drawls, finally releasing my hand.

'Skid's a friend of Theo's,' says Emma.

I might have guessed. Theo doesn't know any normal people. Skid reminds me of a Muppet. He has shoulder-length wavy hair streaked blue, blond, and bright vermilion, through which two piercing ice blue, but totally stoned eyes peer, like a wild animal lurking in a lair. He appears to be wearing an outfit made out of squashed recycled egg boxes, you know, the pale blue synthetic kind that squeak if you try to bend them. I'm shocked when he turns to the bar and I notice the obscure but expensive designer label stitched to the back of the matching shirt. I'm even more surprised when he pulls a roll of notes the size of a loo roll out of his pocket and pays for our drinks.

'Is he a drug dealer or something?' I ask, watching open-mouthed as he peels a twenty from the bunch.

'Lex! Don't be so judgmental. Just because he looks a bit weird doesn't mean he's a coke head. As a matter of fact, he's got his own business.'

'Doing what? Organised raves? Organised crime?'

'He makes furniture, very beautiful furniture, reproduction pieces mainly. He's got a waiting list of two years for some of his pieces.'

Skid catches the end of our conversation.

'I like to work with my hands, man.' The pale blue eyes focus in on me, and then swim straight out of focus again. 'I know everybody thinks wood is like . . . dead and hard . . . but it ain't. It's soft . . . like velvet. If you love it, you can mould it, and if you're quiet enough you can hear it breathing.'

'Mmmm . . . profound,' I reply, finding myself grinning at him like someone who's just been approached by a cigarette-cadging mental case in the middle of a crowded shopping centre, and doesn't quite know how to handle it.

The DJ cuts the funk, and slaps on Village People.

'Whoah . . . cool song. D'ya wanna dance or some-fin'?' He turns to Emma.

Skid doesn't look like the kind of guy who would dance to YMCA. Then again, as I'm learning pretty fast, you shouldn't judge a skidmark by its tyre tread.

'Sure.' Emma puts her bottle down.

''R'ya comin, Al?' The eyes and hair swivel back to me.

I bite back Emma's usual retort of, 'No, it's just the way I'm standing,' and shake my head. 'I think I might just sit this one out, thanks.'

Skid holds out a hand to Emma.

'You know, I think he might possibly be number one on my list,' she whispers as he tows her past me.

'Are you sure? I mean, I know you like them weird, just look at Theo, but this guy's in a league of his own. And it's a bit close to home, isn't it?'

'Theo and I don't see each other anymore, do we? I'm a free agent, I can do what I want.'

'And that means sleeping with a guy who looks permanently like he's on his way to a fancy dress party?'

'Told you before, Lex, it's not all about looks. Skid's a great laugh, and humour can be incredibly sexy.'

Emma and he disappear into the crowd already arm-gesturing on the dance floor.

'And then there was one,' I murmur to myself, wrapping my lips around the neck of my Bud bottle and taking a big swig.

After about thirty seconds, I decide that I should have gone with them. I don't like being in a club on my own. I feel vulnerable. I suppose I should be scouring the crowd for potential men; this is supposed to be a competition after all, and the other two are racing ahead of me.

I move over to the edge of the dance floor.

'Young man!' everybody shouts in unison flinging their arms in the air.

I decide it's time for another trip to the loos.

When I return, re-lip-linered and little else thanks to Ren's cruel limitation of my MAC supplies, the music has thankfully moved back to the usual mix of dance/garage/funk that I'm familiar with. I buy myself another drink, and then move back to the dance floor trying to spot Emma or Ren.

A strange guy dances up and, grabbing my arm, tries to get me to boogie with him.

'Piss off!' I snap.

So he does.

Shit! I chide myself. I'm supposed to be out on a pulling mission. That was a potential one-nighter and I just blew him straight out the window without even thinking. He was quite cute too.

It's no good, my automatic reflex isn't to go out and grab myself a man, it's to fight them all off with a big stick like some vestal virgin.

I may as well go home. Emma's nowhere to be seen, and although I've finally spotted Serena, she's lip-locked to Nicky Taylor. Like Siamese twins, they've been joined at the mouth for the past half an hour. How they can dance with their lips plugged into each other I don't know, but they're managing, and pretty well. Then again, Serena really can dance. She's one of those lucky people who seem to slide into the rhythm with the ease of a well-oiled willy into something hot, wet and warm. I think she's definitely hit her number one. The way their bodies are moving against each other, if they weren't still fully clothed I'd think she was actually going for a tick on her list on the dance floor.

I look at my watch. It's gone one o'clock in the morning. I'm damned if I'm going to stay here until three. I'm knackered, and for some reason I now feel more than a little bit pissed. I think tiredness has let the alcohol take effect. My whole body is crying out for sleep, apart from my stomach which is sort of hinting that a greasy Salmonella burger from one of the vans outside would be rather delicious, which means I've definitely had *far, far* too much to drink.

I decide to go outside and hail a taxi, and wobble off towards the cloakroom to pick up my coat.

'Hi, Sexy Lexy,' says a familiar voice, as I stagger past the penultimate bar of the club. 'Not leaving, are you?'

I turn to find myself face to face with Laurence Chambers, or should I say Leery Larry as we in the office call him. Larry is a hot shot libel lawyer who does work for the newspaper for whose Sunday magazine I write. He is a slime ball chat-up merchant extraordinaire. Now he's lounging against the bar, looking cool and expensive in a Romeo Gigli suit. I must have my beer goggles well and truly in place, because from being somebody I wouldn't normally touch with someone else's barge pole, he suddenly looks kind of attractive.

'I was actually, yes,' I reply to his question, teetering dangerously on my borrowed heels as I halt in mid-flight.

'That's a shame,' he tuts. 'I've only just got here,

and the most attractive woman in the place is leaving. Story of my life. Don't go, Alex. Come and have a drink with me. I'm on a boys' night out and there's too much testosterone in our corner. We need some female company.'

I hesitate for a moment.

'Come on, Alex . . . come and have a drink,' he coaxes.

I look back at the dance floor, and suddenly see Emma. She's still dancing with Theo's friend, who's side sliding like a seventies reject to something that really calls for some funky hip thrusting. She spots me, smiles, waves and points to her watch, mouthing, 'Twenty minutes, okay?'

She's obviously changed her mind about road testing Skidmark's sexual prowess.

'Just a little drink, how about it?' Larry encourages.

He waves a couple of bottles of champagne at me.

'Okay.' I shrug. Hell, what have I got to lose? I've got to wait for Emma anyway now. I may as well be drinking somebody else's champagne whilst I do it, even if that somebody else is Leery Larry.

He indicates for me to pick up another two bottles from the counter, and then leads me across the club to a darkened corner. Through the fug of dry ice and cigar smoke I can make out a group of men in suits lounging on squashy blue velvet sofas, drinking profusely and holding a free-for-all conversation interspersed with laughter and profanities that rages almost unintelligibly above the music.

'Works night out,' explains Larry briefly. 'Come and swim with the sharks.' Relinquishing half his champagne booty to another suit, he takes my arm and leads me through the throng to a sofa set against the rear wall, parking me between two guys in almost identical dark grey Hugo Boss.

'Reinforcements, thank god. I haven't had a drink for at least . . . ooh, let me see now . . . forty seconds.' The blond guy to my left howls with laughter at his own lack of wit, and commandeering one of the bottles, proceeds to open it with much show and unnecessary froth, the cork shooting off into the crowd on the dance floor, smacking some poor unsuspecting dancer on the back of his head.

Larry slides into a seat opposite me and traps my knees with his long legs.

'Marcus,' he says, squeezing proprietorially, 'this is Alex Gray. She's a writer down at the rag. Alex, this is Marcus Wentworth.' He indicates the blond prat, who winks heavily at me and hands me a glass of champagne, with a rather slurred, 'Hello, Gorgeous.'

'And, believe it or not, this is another Alex – Alexander Pinter,' continues Larry. The guy on my right leans across and offers me his hand. He appears to be slightly more sober than the rest of the group.

'Hi, Alex. A writer, are you?'

'For my sins, yes.'

'Nah,' he drawls. 'Can't be. You're too good-looking to be a hack.'

I'm drunk enough to be pleased by such obvious flattery. Besides, Alex Pinter is rather gorgeous. Either that or my beer goggles are now taking on a rosy pink champagne tint.

'You know, I think it must be an omen that we're both called Alex . . .' He slides in closer to me, and tops up my hardly touched glass.

'Yeah, omen as in Damien,' cuts in a voice. 'Hi, I'm Tony.' The owner of the voice slides out of the shadows and holds out an elegantly manicured hand. 'Larry didn't bother to introduce us, he always keeps the best-looking women to himself.'

'Sod off, Tony.' Alex puts a hand on my knee, and grins at the olive-skinned Italian.

'Larry didn't introduce him for a reason,' he pretends to whisper conspiratorially to me, ensuring that his colleague can overhear. 'He's a total tart, a wolf in wolf's clothing. He's the kind of guy your mother warned you about.'

'Oh, yeah.' Tony grins to reveal amazingly straight white teeth.' And *he*'s the kind of guy that'd hit on your mother the minute you left the room! Stay away from him, Alex.' He squeezes on to the sofa between me and Marcus Wentworth, who's just passed out face down on the arm and is drooling out of the side of his mouth on to the blue velvet upholstery.

'You just stick with me.' He puts his hand on my other knee, tops up what little space is left in my glass, then hands it back to me. 'I'll look after you.'

I knock back my champagne, looking from left to right in overindulged glee. Sexy man to the left of me, sexy man to the right of me. Oh, happy day. Perhaps this pulling lark isn't going to be so difficult after all?

'Er . . . excuse me . . . but Alex is here to have a drink with me, aren't you, darling?'

Larry leans over and refills the section of my glass that I've just emptied. 'You two just remember that, okay?'

'Are you pulling rank now, Laurence?' The male

Alex leans forward and locks gazes with Leery. 'You only have seniority in the office, you know. You can't get all the perks out of office time too.'

Wow! I'm being fought over. This is a novel experience. I know they're only acting up to each other, but it's pretty nice all the same. It's rather good to be surrounded by attractive men, all vying for my attention and flirting like they're on a mission. I suddenly remember my own mission. Perhaps it won't be so difficult after all. I mean, Alex is gorgeous and Tony is . . . well . . . gorgeous. What a dilemma. I've gone from no chance to double my luck in an instant.

Within half an hour I've danced twice with Larry, four times with Alex, and three times with Tony, who gets ten out of ten for tenacity, and nought out of ten for hand control – they keep sliding under my skirt, like they're magnetised and my fanny's made of metal. I've been reluctantly introduced to more men in suits who keep appearing like identical rabbits out of hats, I've got more phone numbers than the local directory, I've gone through nearly one of the bottles of champagne on my own, and Emma is a forgotten face amidst a large dancing crowd.

I finally get away from Tony, the wild hand rover, and slump back down next to Larry on the Cilla sofa.

'There you are,' he breathes huskily. 'I was beginning to think Tony had whisked you away from me. Have another glass of champagne, darling.'

Smiling seductively at me, Larry tops up my glass yet again. I take a large slurp, and giggle as the bubbles hit the back of my throat. I didn't notice when the manoeuvre occurred but Larry now has one hand attached to the back of my neck, a thumb rubbing slowly up and down against the delicate flesh, and his thigh pressed firmly against mine.

'You know,' I let the bubbles run over my tongue once again, then smile through a warm alcoholic haze at Leery Larry, 'this stuff must be bloody good . . . I've always thought you were about as attractive as day-old dog doo, but now . . .' I salute him with my glass '. . . I say now, Leery Larry, my old lovey, you actually look kind of sexy.'

I'm dead. I'm in pain. My head's been run over by a steam roller. Somebody's spot welded my tongue to the roof of my mouth. It must be cold because my body's shaking like a frightened whippet, so why do I feel so hot and horrible? I try to open my eyes, but overnight my eyelashes have turned into zips – broken zips whose little metal teeth are firmly meshed together. I know what's going to happen. As soon as I've managed to force open my eyes, I'll see a nice nurse with a big smile, in a crisp blue uniform, leaning over me, ready to mop my fevered brow. I must be in hospital. You can't feel this bad and not be in hospital.

I open my eyes. No nurse, no Lucozade, no nothing.

I close my eyes again. A little memory escapes from the dense fog-encrusted woodland that is my brain and skips merrily across a sun-filled clearing, shouting, 'Nightclub, nightclub, nightclub,' in a childish sing-song voice.

Ah, yes. That's where I was. So where am I now? I try opening my eyes again. I think I must have passed out *in* the nightclub. A bass beat is still booming in my head, and two glitterballs are rotating where my eyeballs used to be. My eyes continue to spin and defract light, but I finally focus enough to realise that I'm not in the nightclub anymore. I am in fact in a large bed, in a totally unfamiliar bedroom. My eyes swivel around the room, whilst my body stiffens and remains perfectly still, taking in first the mirrored ceiling, then the acres of cream shag pile, then the creased linen sheets twisted around my naked body.

Naked body. Ooops! I am totally devoid of clothes.

I'm stark naked, I'm in a strange bed, and suddenly have a horrible realisation that, even worse, there is something in the bed with me.

The 'something' is lying beside me, heavily asleep, snoring slightly, mouth open, the sunlight streaming through the blinds at the window and picking out all the lines in his late-forty-something face.

I am in bed with Larry.

I just about suppress the scream that attempts to burst out of my throat like a lemming on a suicide mission.

Oh, my god! What have I done?

Despite the fact that I've forgotten how to move my own body, it's a gut reaction to get the hell out of that bed. I've never moved so fast in my life.

My clothes are in a trail leading away from the bed and out of the room. I stumble out of bed and follow them through to a huge drawing room, doing a reverse strip as I go. By the time I get to a large beige suede couch, I'm only missing one stocking and my shoes. I find them tucked under a glass Art Deco coffee table upon which sits my mini bag, two glasses, a barely touched bottle of Poilly Fuisse, and a half-eaten hamburger. The stocking is draped over a statue of Aphrodite on a table in one corner of the room, as though removed and flung with total abandonment.

Fully clothed once more, my sole driving aim becomes to get the hell out of here before Sleeping Ugly wakes up.

I'd call a taxi, but I don't even know where the hell I am. The whole of one wall of the drawing room is made of tinted glass, through which I can see the Thames snaking green and solid below. I must be somewhere in Docklands.

A grunting sort of snorting kind of snore from the master bedroom sends me diving for the exit.

Slipping the latch on the front door, I make my way into a pot plant-infested lobby, with carpet thicker than my mother's pet dog, and call for the lift, expecting Larry to wake up and demand breakfast in bed at any moment.

Downstairs in a glass jungle of an atrium, I luck out. The kindly doorman takes pity on me, calls a cab from his cupboard-sized rest room, and invites me to join him for a cup of tea while I wait for it to arrive.

'Good night was it?' he asks, taking in my shaking hands, pallid features, and the black bags under my eyes large enough to hold the weekly shop.

'You know, I really wish I knew,' I sigh, blowing weakly on the strong sweet brew to cool it. 'But my brain's a blank from two o'clock on.'

Emma is waiting for me, standing at the top of the staircase, hands on hips, scowl on face.

'Where the hell did you get to last night, my girl?'

she growls, then bursts into fits of laughter at the sight of my mortified face.

'Ren, you can quit calling the police, Cinderella's just got home from the ball.'

'I'm going to have a shower, then I'm going to bed.' With a great effort, I haul myself up the stairs and try to push past her towards my room.

'Oh, no, you're not, madam. You're supposed to turn into a pumpkin at midnight, not midday.' Emma looks at her watch. 'We want to hear all about last night. Where the hell have you been, Alex? We've been worried sick.'

'Don't ask.' I shake my head, then stop because it aches too much.

Serena comes out of the kitchen, blonde hair tied on the top of her head, casual in jeans and a sweat-shirt, and looking far too fresh for someone who was out clubbing and boozing until three in the morning.

'Where have you been?' She throws herself upon me in a hug born of worry that rattles my already shrunken brain so that it cowers inside my skull like a chastised puppy.

'I don't know where I've been,' I mumble. 'But I know where I'm going, and that will have to do for now. I'm going to the bathroom.'

In Emma's bathroom, which is the height of luxury but bloody untidy, with bottles of everything your body could ever need or wish for overflowing on shelves, along the side of the bath and on the window ledge, I take off my clothes once again and throw them in the wicker basket we use for dirty laundry.

I then struggle into the shower, close my eyes, and stand stock still under a blast of hot water for ten minutes. I finally get up enough energy to soap myself, and wash my sticky smoke-filled hair.

As the hot jets of water needle into my flesh like a violent Shiatsu massager with sharp pointy finger-nails, I also finally face the thing I've been attempting to block out of my mind all morning.

I have had my first one-night stand – and I can't remember a single thing about it, which is a pretty mixed blessing considering it was with Leery Larry.

I should feel different, I just feel hungover.

I get out of the shower and, swathing my body in a big fluffy towel, go through to my bedroom, where I stand in front of the full-length mirror next to the wardrobe. I let the towel drop so that I'm standing naked. I don't feel any different, and I don't look any different either. There are no tell-tale finger-sized bruises, no passion scratch marks. Maybe nothing happened? I think hopefully. Yeah, right. I was naked and in bed with Leery Larry Chambers and he didn't do anything about it? That's like saying the Honey Monster would pass over a bowl of Sugar Puffs. I don't think so. Pulling on my jeans and a sweatshirt, I spend as long as possible drying my hair, before plucking up the courage to go out and face my friends.

Serena's cooking Sunday lunch, standing at the oven, stirring cheese sauce for the large cauliflower which is currently bubbling in a pan. Emma's seated at the kitchen table, shelling peas into a bowl, drink-ing a glass of Swartland, and reading the Sunday paper.

The windows are steamed and the room is hot from cooking.

She looks up as I enter the room, and smiles.

'How are you feeling, babe?'

'Dead,' I reply, grabbing a glass from the side and pouring myself some red wine. I get the glass halfway to my face before breathing in the heavy smell of fermented grape, and almost gagging.

'Want a coffee?' asks Serena, watching me in sympathetic amusement.

They give me a few moments to compose myself before moving gently in for the kill.

'So . . . got anything you want to tell us then?' Emma pops a whole pea pod into her mouth and chews.

'Nope,' I mutter, pretending to read the cartoon supplement of Ems's paper.

They're silent again for a few more moments.

Suddenly uncomfortable, I get up and poke the chicken that's roasting merrily in the oven, going a glorious golden suntan brown, just for something to do, to feel like I've escaped their friendly questioning gazes.

Serena hands me a mug of coffee.

'Well, *I've* got a confession to make, even if you haven't.' She smiles and wiggles her eyebrows at me playfully.

'You didn't?' Emma's mouth pops open like one of her pea pods. 'But you came home with me last night, and I know you slept alone . . .'

'There are other places apart from a bedroom.' Serena grins and, turning back to the oven, prods her potatoes.

'Such as?' Emma prompts.

'The end cubicle in the ladies' loos on the chill out

floor.' She pushes her long hair out of her face and laughs uproariously. 'Don't look so shocked,' she remarks to Ems, turning back to her sauce. 'I saw a certain long-haired lover from Hampstead Heath sneaking out at about seven this morning, shoes in hand.'

Emma says nothing, merely grins into her wine glass and then looks back expectantly at me.

'Now you know our escapades, are you going to tell us what you got up to last night? Or should it be who you got down with?'

I shake my head and sink back down on to my seat at the kitchen table, clutching my warm coffee mug like a comforter.

'You know, I really wish I could,' I sigh, 'but unfortunately everything's a total blank. Last thing I remember is drinking champagne in the club with Larry Chambers and a few of his cronies . . .'

'Leery Larry the litigator?' cuts in Emma, pulling a face.

'The one and only,' I sigh again, a heavy exhalation of air. 'As far as I recall I was having a pretty good time. He may be an arsehole, but he works with some pretty tasty guys. Anyway, I vaguely recall a group of us going outside to look for a taxi, and then that's it. Well, that's it until I woke up this morning any-way . . .' I trail off

'And?' they chorus in unison.

'And I was totally stark bollock naked, and Larry the Letch was lying next to me snoring. Okay?' I shout back at them, shame making me aggressive.

The gits both start to laugh.

'It could have been worse. You could have woken

up with Larry and all the others in bed with you,' Serena snorts, then puts her hand over her mouth in self chastisement for taking the piss out of such a sorry object as me.

'How could you go to bed with Leery, Alex?' Emma shakes her head in despair.

'How can you go to bed with someone called Skidmark?' I mean, just the name's a turn off for starters,' I counter.

'He's incredibly good-looking.'

'I'm surprised you can tell. All I could see was lots of psychedelic hair.'

'Oh, and we're especially proud of our own conquest last night, are we?' Emma asks sarcastically. 'At least mine was young enough to *have* a full head of hair.'

'There's nothing wrong with older men,' I defend myself, pushing to the back of my mind all the things that are actually very wrong about Leery Larry.

'No, only certain older men,' says Emma as if she can read my thoughts.

Laughing loudly, Serena swings open one of the kitchen cupboard doors. Attached to the inside is a child's blackboard and a piece of chalk on a string. On the left hand side of the board Serena has neatly written in our names: Ems, Ren, Lex.

'Look what we got.' She smiles. 'Thought we could use it to keep tabs.'

'Can we have the score on the kitchen door, please, Miss Simmons?' says Emma in her best Brucie Forsyth voice. 'Alex, this is far more of an occasion for you, my darling, despite the choice of partner, so I think you should go first.'

'I don't know if it counts,' I say sheepishly. 'Firstly I really can't remember a thing, thank goodness, and secondly the rules state quite clearly that we're supposed to be the one doing the pulling, and I get the awful feeling it was me that was led down the garden path like a lamb to the slaughter.'

'Well, you shouldn't mix your drinks, like you shouldn't mix your metaphors,' Serena giggles. 'What do you think, Ems? Shall we let her have it or not?'

'I don't see why not,' Emma agrees magnanimously. 'We all make mistakes, don't we?'

Serena runs a chalk mark next to my name, one next to hers, and another beside Emma's. 'One all,' she announces. 'Even Stevens. A dead heat so far, girls. So now it's onwards and ever upwards.'

'Shouldn't that be onwards and ever upright?' Emma smirks.

My hangover lasts until Sunday night, but the feelings of mortification stay with me a lot longer. I go back to work on Monday morning, and slope around the *Sunday Best* offices like an illegal immigrant waiting to get caught, and if I dare to venture into the outer limits of the rest of the building where the real newspaper hacks live, I start acting like Tom Cruise in *Mission Impossible*, diving in and out of doorways and dark corners. Fortunately Larry doesn't come into the building that often. By the end of the week, the nightmare is starting to recede a little, and I'm starting to relax a bit. Come mid-morning coffee break, I decide I need some self-indulgence to go with my coffee and head off to the staff canteen to stock up on cholesterol.

I'm just contemplating the rows of calorie-and fat-laden cakes, tongs in hand, trying to capture a particularly skittish doughnut, when a voice speaks behind me.

'Hiya, Sexy Lexy.'

I nearly jump out of my skin. Larry is so close behind me I can feel the warmth of his breath on the back of my neck as he speaks.

'You shouldn't be having one of those. It'll ruin your figure, and you wouldn't want to do anything to destroy something so lovely, now would you?' He runs a caressing hand over my arse, making me jump again. The doughnut I had just managed to trap between the plastic tongs shoots out of their grasp and lands on the floor. The jam spilling out of its broken sides makes it look like a suicide jumper.

'Oh, dear,' purrs Larry. 'Look at the mess we just made. Never mind, somebody will clean it up. What time shall I pick you up tonight?'

'I beg your pardon?'

'I thought we could do something. Dinner at the Estuary maybe, then back to my place for . . . dessert.'

'Er . . . I can't, I'm washing my hair tonight.'

'Now that's a poor excuse if ever I heard one.'

I haven't the time or the ingenuity to think of a polite response to this, so I just go for brutal truth.

'Yeah, you're right, Larry. It is an excuse. I don't want to go out with you, tonight or ever. I was totally out of my tree on Saturday night. If I'd been sober I wouldn't have come within fifty feet of you, okay?'

To my surprise Larry carries on smiling.

'But I thought we had something together?' He purses his lips in amusement, as though chiding a naughty but well-loved child. 'We did have something, didn't we?'

'Yeah, sex,' I reply bluntly. 'Having sex does not constitute a relationship.'

Oh my god! I'm quoting Max. I'm turning into a man. No, worse, I'm turning into a bastard! I should hang my head in shame, but there's this strange sort of feeling creeping over me, a feeling of – well, almost power. If this were a film, you'd get the lightning flash and the manic laughter at this moment in time, as the Alex I know myself to be turns from the mild-mannered Jekyll into Horrible Hyde, the destroyer of men's hearts.

Larry is still smiling, though. It's bloody disconcerting.

'Well, actually, no. We didn't.' He grins.

'We didn't what?'

'Have sex.'

'But . . .'

'You passed out.'

'I did?'

'The most fun I got was taking off your clothes to put you to bed. Love the red silk undies by the way.' He leers at me. 'Oh, that and watching your reaction when you thought we'd . . . er . . . you know, shagged each other's brains out.' He grins at me lewdly, 'Don't worry Alex, we didn't. But I can wait.'

He saunters off, hands in pockets, to join a group of suits in the other corner of the room.

He's been winding me up. The powerful feeling deflates like a pricked balloon to be replaced with a groaning, sinking, I've been had, I'm a moron and he knows it, kind of feeling. It's not nice.

I always thought the guy was a jerk. I was totally and utterly wrong. He's not a jerk, he's an arsehole of the highest degree. He is a flea on the dog's bottom of humanity. God, men are such devious bastards!

I can see him now, in a little giggling group of cronies in the corner. It doesn't take a mastermind to work out what they're talking about, especially as the muted whispering and guffaws of laughter are accompanied by scornful glances in my direction at pertinent intervals. And men think women are cliquey bitches!

Could my day get any worse?

I phone Emma.

'Meet me for lunch,' I rasp desperately.

We meet up in a wine bar that's pretty much equidistant between us, and is therefore a regular lunchtime haunt. It's one of those places with wooden everything, lots of greenery, acid jazz playing softly in the background, and huge blackboards instead of menus.

I get there a few minutes earlier than her, and manage to gulp my way through nearly a whole large glass of Frascati before she shows up. As the alcohol creeps warmingly through my stomach lining and into my blood stream, I begin to relax just a little. After being goosed by Larry in the canteen, I tried to escape back to the *Sunday Best* section of the building. Unfortunately Larry decided to follow me, and the whole morning after that has been a constant stream of comments and innuendoes. What makes it worse is that, despite everything, Larry is still hitting on me.

Incredible or what? He makes me look like an idiot

in front of everybody, but still he thinks I'm game for a quickie in the photocopy room.

At half-past eleven a courier arrives with a huge bouquet of roses. There's a card. *'Lunch at La Scala at one o'clock. In anticipation, L.'*

This was the point where I decided the only safe course of action was to leave the building and escape to my best friend and a bottle of wine – or should that be my best friend, a bottle of wine?

'Well, it could have been worse.' Emma always has to try and find a bright side. 'At least you now know you didn't shag a wrinkly, and he can't be a complete jerk off otherwise he might just have taken advantage of you given the state you were obviously in.'

'I don't think even Larry's into necrophilia, but he had the chance to have a bloody good look, and now he's seen the goods he definitely wants to sample.'

'Well, you could be flattered by that, I suppose.'

'I could be, but I'm bloody not,' I snort, downing my second glass of white in one go. 'Why do men think that a good way to get into a woman's knickers is to totally humiliate her?'

'Would you like some food to go with your liquid lunch?' Emma asks, her voice heavy with concern and sarcasm.

I shake my head. 'I feel decidedly nauseous,' I reply.

'I'm not surprised, considering the amount of alcohol you've consumed over the past few days. Man cannot live by wine alone . . .'

I attempt to disprove this theory by asking the waiter for another bottle.

'You'll be late back.' Emma purses her lips.

'Who gives a toss?' I reply snappily. 'In fact, I'm not going to go back,' I state emphatically. 'Ever,' I add as a dramatic afterthought.

'Ever? That's a bit drastic isn't it?'

'Well, maybe not ever, but I'm not going back this afternoon. I'm going to get some therapy. I'm going shopping. Want to come?'

'Unfortunately some of us are committed to our careers, and can't just swan off to Harvey Nicks every time we feel a touch grumpy,' Emma drawls sarcastically. She stands up and takes her jacket off the back of her chair.

'I've got to get back to work. Don't spend too much—'

'I'll spend as much as I want to,' I huff. 'It's my money.'

She sighs and shakes her head.

'I was going to say, don't spend too much time feeling bad about Larry. You can't change the past. It's better to regret doing something than to regret not having done something. Besides, he enjoys winding people up. He's probably loving every minute of your discomfort. Don't give him the satisfaction. 'Bye, babe.' She hugs me and plants an affectionate kiss on my cheek. 'See you tonight. And keep smiling, okay?'

An afternoon of shopping therapy turns out to be an afternoon of shopping aversion therapy.

The streets are packed with rampaging school children on half-term holiday, some of them going it alone, some of them accompanied by harassed, teeth-grinding parents. It rains. I get soaked. The sun comes out again with a vengeance, and it's suddenly far too hot. I go into a chemist to buy a few bits that come to about a fiver, and end up leaving my eighty-quid sunglasses in there, never to be seen again. I get into a fight with some granny over the last of a particular blouse on a rail, win, buy the blasted thing, then suddenly realise that if some blue-rinse granny wanted it that badly then why the hell am I even contemplating wearing it? I find the most gorgeous, wonderful pair of trousers I've ever seen in my life, made of the softest burgundy moleskin, cut by an artist and within my price range, only to find that they've just sold the last pair in my size and won't be getting any more in, ever.

I end the afternoon by trying to hail a taxi at six o'clock in the evening in Kensington High Street, mad hopeful fool that I am. I finally arrive back at the mews, late, dishevelled, hot, cross, and even more pissed off than I was earlier.

'Never go shopping in a bad mood,' I grumble to Emma, whom I find in the kitchen poised over steaming saucepans, covered in flour, with open cook books ranged about her. 'I've just bought a dress I'd be embarrassed to drop off at Oxfam, let alone wear in public.'

'So your therapy didn't work then?' she asks, tossing oregano into a bubbling pan.

'Nope. It just made the day seem worse. This has without doubt been one of the shittiest ever, so I stopped by the offy on my way home and got some takeaway happiness.' I hold up my two carrier bags full of cheap wine.

'Oooh, lovely.' Emma looks at my carriers with far more enthusiasm than she looked at my sour face when I walked through the door. 'I've made pasta. Let's eat, drink, and try and get you a bit merry.'

The phone begins to ring. Emma stops rummaging in one of the kitchen drawers for the corkscrew and flips the receiver off the wall while I slump down at the table, scowl firmly in place, and pick strings off a lump of half grated mozzarella.

'Hello,' she chirps cheerily, tucking the phone under her chin, then her tone changes to totally flat and unwelcoming,

'Oh, right. Hold on, I'll ask.'

She covers the receiver with her hand.

'It's Max the Prat,' she whispers crossly. 'He wants to know where the household insurance documents are? Apparently he's had a bit of a problem with his TV. Do you want to talk to him or shall I tell him to go search up his own arse . . .' She trails off as the set, miserable scowl on my face finally takes a hike and I collapse face first on to the table in fits of hysterical laughter.

Max's phone call was the boot up the bum I needed, the burst of amusement necessary to get me off the bottom of my emotional roller coaster and rocketing back up towards the top again. I go into work the next day, decidedly more cheerful and determined to ignore anything Larry Chambers has to throw at me. I've decided that if he carries on spreading rumours, I'm going to counter attack and start saying that nothing happened because he couldn't get it up. That'll take the wind out of his blustering sails, the poke out of his pecker so to speak.

This thought makes me giggle, as does a vision of

Max watching his much-loved TV explode in a pool of bath water. I get on the tube with a mad smile on my face, and despite the fact that I spend the fifteen-minute journey swinging from a sweaty leather strap with somebody's equally sweaty armpit positioned directly above my nostrils, I get off the tube with the smile still firmly in place, and take it to work with me.

Unfortunately, as is sadly usual with my smiles at the moment, its life span is extremely short.

Mary Piccolo, cookery features and work best mate, is at my desk before I've even had a chance to switch on my PC.

'What's this I hear about you and Laurence Chambers?' she asks me, wide-eyed with interest.

'Er . . . what exactly is it you've heard?' I ask her nervously, the smile fading into oblivion.

'Well, news is that you're a bit of an item. I didn't think he was your type, Lex?'

'You're right, he's not.'

'So it's all wrong then, you didn't spend the night with him?'

'Well . . . er, technically speaking . . . no, not in the way that you mean spend the night, anyway.'

'What do you mean by, "Well . . . er, technically speaking . . . no"?' she mocks me. 'That doesn't mean, "Well . . . er, technically speaking . . . yes" by any chance, does it?'

Typical! I'm already getting a reputation and I haven't even done anything yet. I think carefully before I reply. I could make matters worse with my counter attack plan, make people think I would be a willing participant in a game of hide the sausage with Larry Chambers. I could just go for out and out denial. Then again, what the hell? People believe what they want to believe anyway. I may as well make Larry squirm as much as I have been.

'Well,' I grimace sweetly at Mary, 'let's just say the opportunity arose, but Larry's . . . er . . . vital bits, didn't.'

# Chapter Four

Quote (unknown source):
**Definition of 'easy'** – A woman who has the sexual morals of a man.

Rules of Play:
1) Women in charge/control at all times.
2) Love 'em and leave 'em. A one-night stand is a one-night stand. No going back for second helpings. (This rule will be waived if desperate for a shag, and it's offered on a plate.)
3) Never give them your phone number.
4) Take their phone number, promise to call, but never do.
5) Never tell them you love them, unless very drunk and therefore able to deny it when sober.
6) Fall asleep immediately after orgasm regardless of whether they've come yet.
7) Talk about them with your friends afterwards.
8) Flirt outrageously with their mates, then swear you were just being friendly for their sake.
9) Run a mile at the mention of the words

'commitment' or 'relationship'. (The use of the phrase 'When will I see you again?' is strictly prohibited.)

10) Never apologise.

11) Safe sex, or no sex.

Duration two-month game-play period.

Winner:    Whoever shags and bags the most men within game-play period.

Outcome:  Loser buys outrageously extravagant dinner at favourite Italian restaurant.

Mason is big, blond, blue-eyed and bolshie. He emanates arrogance, and I don't find him at all attractive. What is Emma playing at?

'You'll really like him,' she assured me, having announced her intention of setting me up with one of her work mates. She's my best friend, I trust her, so I thought 'what the hell?' and went for it.

I'm not doing very well for myself. Emma and Serena have got into the game with the ease of natural players. The hunted becoming the hunter. Men falling at their feet like toppling dominoes. Boadicea would have snapped them up as new recruits with a click of her sinewy fingers, calloused from flinging spears at stray males. I find it a lot harder. I like to sit back and let men do all the running – which is strictly against the rules, as apparently it denotes a relinquishing of control. Besides, the men aren't actually running in my direction at the moment anyway, so the girls have decided in their wisdom that a blind date is called for. This is apparently allowed because we are in charge of all the arrangements, and therefore no control is relinquished to the man. I wish I'd listened to my gut, which has been complaining bitterly all day, and stayed at home with a six pack and a family-sized packet of dry-roasted peanuts, but I didn't. So now here I am, stuck in a wine bar with Mason, Mr Egotistical Bore of the century.

I've only been here for half an hour and I've already heard his entire life story, including details of his amazingly successful career, his parents' huge house in Hampshire, his time as a rugby international, what he does and doesn't find attractive in women, what women find attractive in him, and the fact that Kenneth Branagh is his second cousin twice removed or something.

I think he knows that my name is Alex and I drink medium white wine.

'Would you like another Martini, Alice?'

Wrong.

I nod. I think that's all I've managed to do since I got here, that and yawn surreptitiously.

'Well, would you get me a Caffrey's while you're at the bar. I just need to pop to the loo.'

Seeing as I already bought the first round, I add 'tight' to his list of many faults, and debate whether to make my escape before he returns from the Gents.

Too late. He must piss as fast as he talks. I'm just groping around under the table for my handbag when I see him heading back towards me.

'Sorry, forgot to give you this.' He thrusts a twenty at me, and smiles apologetically.

'Back in a mo.'

Well, okay, so he's not that tight, but he's still an

arsehole, and I'm stuck now, aren't I? I can hardly disappear clutching his money. Mentally cursing my so-called best friend, I fight my way through the noisy crowd to the bar, and make myself feel better by asking the nervous young barman for 'A large one, darling' in a very obvious male letching kind of fashion.

Mason improves very slightly as the evening progresses.

Unfortunately, I think he's just improving by degrees as my alcohol level increases. I just sit back, listen, and drink a hell of a lot. The more I drink, the less I hear, but by half-past nine I've still managed to find out that his favourite colour is blue, his mother's maiden name is Lang, he only wears Armani, he drives a Saab at the moment but is going to buy a Mercedes when the new plates come out, he's an only child, he speaks three languages, he earns eighty thou' a year, has a flat in Chelsea, he's allergic to cheese, his mother's, best friend's, sister's, husband's uncle is Lord Snowdon, he hates politics, his ideal woman is a fifteen-year-old French model I've never heard of, he's slept with thirty-two women in the past twelve years, and he still thinks my name's Alice.

The next time I head for the bar, I cut the crap, sod the glass and buy myself a bottle of Jacob's Creek, which I steadily drink down to the sediment in the space of the next hour.

Cocooned in my alcohol-induced ear muffs, Mason becomes nothing but a moving mouth with no voice.

Yak, yak, yak, yak. His lips are constantly moving as

though motorised, but I'm not listening to him any-more. It's like being back at school, where the only skill I was truly excellent at was looking like I was paying attention when really I was off on another planet completely. His mouth is happy to motor on, whilst I do an impression of a deaf nodding dog with an alcohol problem.

To wile away the time, I indulge in one of my favourite pastimes: rewriting the history of the people around me judged on appearance alone, which is entirely unfair but a bloody good laugh.

By half-past ten I've decided that the girl in the flowery leggings and broderie anglaise blouse, with golden-brown hair to her waist, a leather biker jacket and DMs, is obviously the love child of Sandy Shaw and Meatloaf, an up-and-coming singer like her parents, who have disowned her due to her love of grunge and the fact that she thinks the best way to get ahead is to give her manager blow jobs in the back of his stretch limousine, hence the huge pink lips like a full-blown fuchsia – from so much sucking.

The crop-haired guy in the Moss Bros suit leads a double life. Strait-laced accountant by day, after mid-night he abandons his sock garters, slips into some-thing Lycra and spangly and sets off down to Soho to disco the night away in one of those cage things you see suspended at prominent points throughout the dance floor in seedy boogie bars.

The little balding Chinese man at the table in the corner, drinking espresso and reading the *Telegraph*, is an Elvis impersonator, who likes nothing better than to don a quiffed wig and a high-collared white stud-ded suit, and strut around to 'Jail House Rock' with shaking legs and thrusting pelvic movements.

The Chanel-suited lady at the bar, with the chignon and the conference name badge, isn't really a solicitor but a sex toy sales rep, whose huge embossed briefcase actually contains an assorted array of rubber perversions she sells to bored housewives on Clapham Common.

When I get bored with this, I call on an old favourite of a fantasy and end up mentally working my way through the *Kama Sutra* with Tom Cruise as my willing partner. When Tom is a worn out, panting, satiated heap in the corner of my bedroom, and I can entertain myself no more, I check my watch, realise that it is an acceptable time to cut and run, stop Mason in full flow about his last time out to dinner with 'Ken and Em' before they split, push back my chair and announce my intention of leaving.

Surprisingly enough, Mason offers me a lift home.

Surprisingly enough, I accept. It might have something to do with the fact that when I stood up the room began to gyrate faster than the spangly Lycra-wearing accountant disco dancer. I think even the effort of hailing a taxi would have been enough to unbalance me. How much have I had to drink in the past few hours? I know that I eat too much if I'm bored, but I didn't realise this habit extended to alcohol consumption as well. Thank goodness Mason's car is only just round the corner.

I hang from his arm like an old granny needing assistance to cross the road. I think Mason thinks his luck is in; he's had me looking rapt and sexual – the Tom fantasy – for the past hour, and now I'm clutching his arm like I never want to let go. He doesn't realise that the only reason I'm doing it is because I have a sneaking suspicion that if I do, I might just fall over.

For the first time in the entire evening, he is quiet. We drive back to Chelsea in complete silence, broken only by the occasional 'Left here', 'Next right', 'Straight over the mini roundabout' from me – the most I've said all evening. As we get closer to home, I suddenly decide I don't really want Mason to know where I live, and direct him into the road just beyond ours instead.

He pulls the large leather-upholstered car to a halt, and pounces as I'm struggling through an alcohol-induced fug to release my seat belt.

So much for role reversal, I think, as he lunges forward to attach himself bodily and lippily to me. Mason has just behaved how I'm supposed to.

It's a bit like removing a sucking leech from an open wound, but I manage to extricate myself from the clinch.

Rather than taking the hint from me struggling away like a cat that really doesn't want to be petted, Mason just grins at me happily, like an over eager Saint Bernard who's just indulged a favourite in a vigorous tongue wash, aware only of the compliment on his side that he actually wants to kiss me, rather than the thought that I might not want my tonsils to be tickled by his particular tongue.

Mason is obviously hot to trot.

Unfortunately, I'm not.

Opportunity knocks, and I won't answer the door.

Larry was struck from the scores on the door after it transpired that I didn't actually – phew and double phew – sleep with him. Strike one.

If it's up to me, Mason won't even get an innings.

Strike two.

Why? He's not ugly. He's got a fit bod. He's single, solvent. Thirty-two other women have found him acceptable enough to sleep with, what makes me so fussy?

Oh, what the hell? This one's for the girls and my dismal score rating.

I take a deep breath, push an open-mouthed Mason back against his seat, and kiss him as though my life depends on it.

He's so surprised by this full-on tactic that at first he doesn't respond. He simply lies there like a dead fish, mouth gaping slightly open, eyes staring bulbously.

I'm sorry, but I just can't get turned on kissing a halibut in rigor mortis. Perhaps this wasn't such a good idea.

I close my eyes, determined to battle on, and am rewarded with a faint movement from below, a little lip response, weak at first but then warming up quite fast until he's kissing me as hard as I was kissing him.

He's actually quite a good kisser. To my surprise I can feel a small flicker of arousal begin to lick at the pit of my stomach. At last!

I open my eyes.

Mason's are sort of half closed. You know how a dog's face goes when you scratch just the right spot on its belly?

The flicker fades and dies.

I close my eyes again and just concentrate on the kissing, instead of the who, and that nice warm glow begins to burn again. But when I open my eyes for a second time the feeling fades just as fast.

And then I realise what the problem is. He may be turning me on physically, but my head is steadfastly refusing to join in the fun and games.

He has very practised hands, which are currently running lightly over the base of my spine, and my body is responding to them like an engine being fine-tuned by a skilled mechanic. But just because he can tune up your valves, it doesn't mean he knows how to get behind the wheel and drive you to the best advantage.

I try the eyes thing again. Yep, definitely. Close my eyes, get horny feelings. Open my eyes, horny feelings fade rather rapidly.

Damn. This isn't supposed to happen. How do men do it? Do they have a shut-off valve or something? Whatever I do, I can't just let my libido take over. This may feel rather nice, but it certainly doesn't feel right. I don't find this man attractive. Hell, I don't even like the guy, so what on earth am I doing this for?

There's only one thing left to do. I make like I'm a real journalist, make my excuses, and leave.


Serena and Ems are on the sofa sharing a duvet, eating popcorn and watching tapes of old *Friends* episodes. They freeze-frame Ross and Rachel in emotional combat, and look up expectantly.

'Well?' they ask in tandem as I stagger through the door and flop down next to them.

I shake my head. My grimace says it all really.

'Okay,' they reply in tandem, offer me some popcorn, make a space under the duvet, and set the video back to play.

★ ★ ★

'Yes, Mother, I'm fine.'

'No, Mother, I'm not a snivelling, sodden, unhappy, unkempt heap. Life's great.'

'Yes, of course there's life after Max. I couldn't be happier.'

'Of course I'm happy. Would I lie to you?'

'Yes, of course I know Jem split with Alison last year.'

'No, of course I wasn't copying him!'

'Yes, you did tell me Mrs Kempson's daughter's just had another baby. Four times actually.'

'Well, you'll just have to adopt some, won't you!'

'No . . . no . . . I'm sorry, I'm not uptight. I'm fine, okay?'

'Yes, well, thank you, that would be lovely. Of course I'll visit when I can, but life here is so hectic, work's endless, and it's just one long round of parties and invitations at the moment. You know the sort of thing.'

'I know you worry, but I'm not overdoing things, honestly.'

'Yes, you too.'

'I will, I promise.'

'Okay. Speak to you soon. 'Bye.'

'Yes, of course. 'Bye.'

'Mother, please don't cry.'

'Yes, of course. 'Bye.'

'Okay, Mother.'

'Fine.'

'You too.'

''Bye.'

'Yes, I promise.'

''BYE!'

I slam the handset back in the cradle so hard a bell somewhere inside the telephone's plastic casing rings in alarm.

Why are parents such hard work?

My mother's finding my break up with Max harder to cope with than I am. Thank goodness she lives far enough away not to be able to pop round every five minutes, I don't think I could cope with her grief first hand as well as my own. Grief. Yes, I admit that's the word I used, because despite the bravado for Mother's sake, I am still miserable over Max.

I'm at a point where, despite still hating the bastard for everything he did, I'm missing him dreadfully. Well, I don't know if it's so much him that I miss, as familiarity, my own home, the things we used to do together. It's hard to explain, but it's pretty miserable and kind of lonely.

Still, I suppose it's good for my writing.

They say great suffering produces great art.

Whilst working for *Sunday Best*, I am also attempting to write the novel of the decade. I should be at my PC 'channelling my emotions', bashing out forty chapters of something heartrendingly meaningful and wonderful.

Personally, I think great suffering sells chocolate and alcohol.

All I feel like doing at the moment is slobbing out in front of something mindless on the TV with the hugest box of Black Magic I can find, a large bottle of blue label vodka, and a box of man size.

I, however, have to go to work. It's ten a.m. on a Friday morning. I normally manage to wangle my week so I don't have to go in on a Friday. I'm quite proud of myself for having invented the three-day weekend.

Today, however, is the day that our editor, Rodney Slater, is finally giving up the helm and leaving the rats to sail the ship alone. He hits bus-pass time at approximately five-thirty-five this morning and is abandoning us for the dubious joy of spending his twilight years playing golf, and planting petunias in his handkerchief-sized garden in Putney.

We are therefore throwing him a retirement party, and given a choice between staying at home and getting pissed and maudlin on my own, or going to work and getting pissed and maudlin in company, the latter wins.

Once a Fleet Street legend, Rodney is now nick-named Slaphappy Slater, not only because of his laid back attitude to getting the magazine out, but because he has a pretty bad habit of pinching, patting and squeezing backsides every time a female dares to get too near to his side of the desk.

An ageing Lothario who looks like Friar Tuck after a partially successful diet, he has the sort of lank greasy hair that you grow from one side of your head for the express purpose of sweeping it over to the other side to cover a balding pate, and wears sepia-tinted glasses that are so large they dwarf his head, but have the sort of lenses that make eyes look twice their usual size.

Rodney has been loosening the reins as he slides happily towards retirement so much that if he wasn't leaving today, he would have tripped over them any minute, and fallen flat on his face in front of the management.

The lax atmosphere means I normally manage to type up my piece in a morning, slide it under Rodney's eyes for the obligatory ten seconds, like feeding a piece of paper through a photocopier, then spend the rest of the week adding another few thousand words to hopefully the new epic of the decade, my attempt at a millennium *Gone With the Wind*, jokingly working titled by Ems *One Fart and You're Outta Here*. Unfortunately, the play-away days may soon be over.

I don't know what it's going to be like with Rodney gone.

Currently, working at *Sunday Best* is a bit like working in an unruly, undisciplined kindergarten.

Despite the fact that we're supposed to be living in days of sexual equality, the open-plan office is dominated by a little clique of males we call the 'Bully Boys'. The in-crowd, with whom nobody particularly wants to be in.

The 'Boys' in question consist of Damien Lawrence, our deputy editor, a frustrated investigative journalist, Harvey Manson, features, who's far too good for us, and doesn't he know it; Big Eric Tearny, the photographer in residence, who looks like a growth-induced Will Carling; and the baby of the bunch, Nigel May Davies, a young wannabe with more ambition in his little finger than the worst kind of on-your-back, legs-in-the-air starlet.

Rodney is the indulgent mentor to this little gang, a chain-smoking Fagin to a bunch of Artless Dodgers.

I arrive at work at my usual clocking in time of ten-thirty to find that the 'Boys' have been down to Soho and bought an inflatable sheep, which, filled with helium, is now tied to Rodney's desk, floating next to the 'Happy' part of his 'Happy Retirement' banner.

Of course, being the children that they are, the boys couldn't resist playing with the helium in other ways, and we now have an office full of temporarily squeaky voices. Damien is currently stampeding through the adjoining glass-fronted office, which houses the secretarial pool – well, with only three secretaries, it's more of a paddling pool – canister in hand, attempting to harass the girls.

This could be considered as either very brave or very stupid.

Sandra, Rodney's PA and sort of unofficial office manager, is six foot and muscled, and doesn't suffer fools gladly.

As the secretaries decrease in rank, they decrease in size and attitude.

Glenda, the next in line, is five foot five and fourteen stone, fierce if she doesn't like you but putty in your hands if she does. Then there's young Jenny, the secretarial junior, who is pretty, plump, and just about five foot two, and hasn't been with us for long enough to have developed the 'If you're messing me about, fuck off or die painfully' mentality that years of working with newsmen has engendered in the other two. Damien, who thinks he can get away with anything because he looks a little bit like Clive Owen, swallows a mouthful of helium into his lungs and, taking his life into his hands, prances up behind Sandra, grabs her almost non-existent waist and warbles, ''Ello, darlin', fancy a shag?' in her ear.

'Crikey, I sound more feminine than you now, Sand,' he squeaks, sliding behind her as she lugs

Tupperware boxes out of the secretaries' glass fish bowl and into the main office.

Sandra herself has a voice like Rod Stewart – gravelly and low, like a man's. In fact it has been a source of constant speculation throughout the building that Sandra is a man who's undergone a not particularly successful sex change. She has a permanent five o'clock shadow, a receding hair line, the sort of pot belly normally cultivated by years of evenings spent nose down in a pint glass, and no boobs. As if to compensate, God has possessed her of a rapier wit, much envied by myself.

'Your voice doesn't sound any different, Damien. Isn't it about time your balls dropped? Most men reach puberty in their teens, you know.'

He slinks off with his tail between his legs, and Sandra returns to folding napkins into the shape of water lilies for the finger buffet, and fighting to keep a drooling Rupert Murdoch, the fat furry spoilt office moggy, away from a plate of tuna and cucumber sandwiches that are beginning to curl at the edges in the heat of the office lights.

The finger buffet is a sorry-looking affair.

We were all asked to bring something along – or contribute, as Sandra put it. Pride of place is a huge chocolate and cream cake especially baked by Rodney's long-suffering wife Margaret. It, unfortunately, is the only thing that looks vaguely edible. Gathered around it, like humble servants worshipping a higher rank, are sausage rolls with cement pastry made by Jenny; delicate little fairy cakes decorated with whipped cream and angelica made by the fair hand of lovely Lucian the post boy, who whisks around the building delivering post and advice in Lycra cycling shorts by day, and then becomes a raging dancing queen by night; and some very dubious-looking crab cakes produced by a fiercely proud Glenda. Lionel, the office vegetarian health freak, who writes the fitness page and is a particularly active union rep, has provided a Tofu something. Don't ask me what it is. It looks nasty, rather like something you discover in a covered dish at the back of the fridge on an annual clear out, or me the morning after a particularly heavy night out, all pale, shadowed and sweating.

I cheated and went for ready made, grabbing a quiche from the food section at M & S on my way in.

It would appear most other people in the office had the same idea.

There are now twelve quiches sitting on the desks which have been shoved together for the buffet. For some strange reason, they are all cheese and tomato.

Everybody looks at them despondently.

Only Mary is over the moon.

'That's my next week's feature sorted.' She beams at me. 'The Quiche Niche. *Sunday Best* taste tests the top ten quiches.'

Rodney arrives around about midday, to a straggling greetings line of clapping, cheering colleagues.

He is then thrust quite forcefully backwards into a wheely chair decorated with blown up luminous condoms, and whizzed around the office at high speed to a chorus of 'For He's a Jolly Good Fellow', whose lack of tunefulness is made up for by volume and boundless enthusiasm.

When he's finally brought back to a standstill,

Rodney gets somewhat shakily to his feet, takes off his glasses and wipes his perspiring brow with the spotty hanky that was sitting jauntily in the top pocket of his suit jacket. He also uses the same hanky to wipe his eyes, and blow his red nose very loudly, then shoves it back in his breast pocket.

'Speech! Speech! Speech!'

'Aren't we supposed to have the presentation first?' objects Sandra, hurrying in with the gift-wrapped electric rotivator and obligatory carriage clock we all chipped in to buy, carried one under each muscular arm.

The boys are persuaded to postpone the festivities until the big wigs come down from the top floor, the 'penthouse suite' we call it, housing those who must be obeyed: the Editor-in-Chief, whom everyone privately calls the Idiot-in-Chief, his minions and the money men.

They arrive bang on five o'clock, a collection of sombre suits. You almost expect men in police sunglasses and ear pieces to come in and secure the building before they arrive.

My heart sinks to my sale-bought Chanel boots when I see Larry lurking at the back of the group. I avoid him, whilst trying not to be too ostentatious about it, lurking amidst the sausage rolls, hiding behind the chocolate cake which is the size of the *Queen Mary* in dry dock.

Fortunately, as anticipated, Mary the office foghorn has passed the news of Larry's apparent lack of upward mobility around the building quicker than a bush fire spreads through the dry and dusty outback. He's as keen to avoid me as I am to avoid him, and we dance a very distant synchronised tango about the room in our efforts always to be somewhere where the other is not.

Sandra does her presentation and Rodney is yet again enticed to give a speech, which is mercifully short as he's already drunk, although this fortunately comes across as him being choked with emotion rather than chock full of cheap white wine.

The Editor-in-Chief gets to hand over the usual obligatory gold watch and cheque, eyes the finger buffet with distaste and leaves as quickly as possible, his people towed behind him like a straggling trail of baby ducks following mother, Larry bringing up the rear, much to our mutual relief.

When the big wigs leave, the serious drinking starts. Those who had, for appearance's sake, been sipping with pursed disdainful lips on little white plastic cups of mineral water, head for the row of wine boxes set up on the side and get stuck in with a vengeance.

This is why I didn't mind coming in to work today, because today work is not work, work is a party.

I contemplate the buffet table, trying to decide between the lesser of evils.

'Who's taking over when Rodders has gone then?' Mary wanders over and offers me more cheap warm rank wine, which I'm starting to think might actually be wine vinegar.

'Haven't got a clue.' I select a relatively innocuous-looking fairy cake and start to pick off the angelica. 'Are they replacing him? Rodney hasn't said anything, I thought they might go for a bit of natural wastage.'

'The natural wastage has just retired,' Mary dubiously selects a curling sandwich. 'That's what they've got to replace.'

'Why? He doesn't really do anything, does he?'

Damien, the fountain of all company knowledge because he makes it his business to know everybody else's business, wanders over chewing valiantly on one of Jenny's concrete sausage rolls.

'Apparently they're moving in some whizz kid from Hong Kong,' he says, gingerly pressing his front teeth to make sure they're not wobbling.

'A Chinese, eh? The ethnic minorities could do with a little more representation in this place.' Lionel sidles over to join us, shovelling Tofu into his mouth. He also has Tofu trembling on his thin lips, and in his straggly John the Baptist beard.

'Did somebody mention Chinese?' Nigel, who was also looking at the buffet as though it might eat him, rather than the other way round, looks up hopefully.

'I could kill for King Prawns in Oyster Sauce.'

'Sounds like a good idea to me . . . who's on for a Chinese?' somebody else takes up the chorus.

'It's more like Chinese whispers,' I comment to Mary who nods her agreement.

'But it's a bloody good idea.'

We decide to head off en masse for Mr Woo's, a restaurant in Soho, leaving Rupert Murdoch thoughtfully licking cheese from Mary's first place-winning quiche.

Mr Woo's aren't particularly pleased to see us, a rowdy party of about twenty people in varying states of sobriety who haven't booked, spilling in and taking over, demanding instant seating, instant food and instant alcohol.

The maitre d', or the Chinese restaurant equivalent, launches into a furious flood of Cantonese, which roughly translates as 'no bookie, no eatie', and only agrees to seat us after a hefty bribe from Damien and Nigel, and a promise of a mention in Mary's next restaurant feature.

Two doubtful waiters push a couple of the largest tables together, seat us, give us menus, then head off to the bar for forty bottles of Chinese lager. Two each, just to get us going.

It's like the feeding of the five thousand. Dish after dish makes its way through the Western-style swing doors leading from the kitchen into the restaurant, to be deposited on the little candle-fired burners in the middle of our table.

I am pulled from the lingering food torpor of the past couple of months by the sight and smell of the Special Chow Mein alone.

The food here is wonderful. I used to eat here quite a lot . . . with Max.

My appetite levels dip again at the thought of him. Still, at least it's good for my waistband. I was starting to get housewifely content and slightly porky living with him. Now I'm back down to my fighting weight of dead on nine stone.

I sit back and slug some beer from my bottle, while everybody else makes up for my lack of appetite, falling on the blue china dishes like a ravenous wolf pack on a fresh catch, growling at each other and fighting over the crispy duck.

Even Lionel, complaining bitterly about the levels

of monosodium glutamate he is being forced to consume, still manages to wolf two platefuls piled with spring rolls, Chow Mein, Sweet and Sour, and – despite declaring himself a strict vegan – five Spare Ribs in barbecue sauce, before sidling off home just in time to avoid paying his share of the bill, which when it comes is astronomical.

A totally piddled Rodney insists on putting it on his now defunct expense account.

'Whadda they gonna do about it?' he slurs, signing the cheque with a flourish, 'Sack me?'

Damien struggles to his feet and raises a bottle of Chinese lager in the air.

'A toast. To Rodders – may he have a long and happy retirement.'

'Yeah, whadda you gonna do with all your spare time, Rodney?' Big Eric leans back in his chair and picks at his teeth with one of Jenny's hair grips, pinched straight from her gleaming blonde tresses.

Rodney also gets to his feet.

'I,' he announces happily, waving his glass in the air, 'am going to bloody enjoy meself. No more bleedin' early mornings or late nights for me . . .'

'When did he do those then?' Mary asks.

'Dunno,' I reply. 'Must have missed it.'

'Oh, no, I've worked 'ard all me life, and now it's time for me to sit back and relax . . .'

'A continuation of the past twenty years then,' I say to Mary.

'Rest on me laurels . . .'

'Instead of his arse,' she whispers.

'And enjoy the fruits of my labours.'

'A large pension, a deposit account in the Caymans

full of back handers and hush money, and an ageing mistress in a council penthouse in Peckham,' I whisper back to Mary.

'Cheers, everybody! Good 'ealth!' and Rodney knocks back his eighth drink in one go.

'Cheers,' we all echo in varying states of enthusiasm.

'And to start it all off,' he continues, eyeing his now empty glass almost sorrowfully, 'I'm going to go nightclubbin' and strut my funky stuff!'

He rolls drunkenly sideways. I'm almost on my feet to catch him before he falls, but then realise, as he emulates the same roll but to the other side, that he's actually dancing.

'How abart it? Who's with me then?'

Rodney, disco king apparent.

We work our way through various bars, before moving on to a nightclub. The only abstainers are Mary, whose babysitter has to be home by eleven, and Glenda, who like Mrs Slocombe has her pussy to attend to.

The bouncers at the Oasis are a forbidding wall of solid muscle. You'd swear one of them was Mike Tyson's younger brother, and the other looks like Popeye's arch enemy Bluto, only bigger.

'What's the age limit?' hisses Damien, running a hand through his almost black mop of hair.

'Over twenty-fives,' I reply, looking at Jenny, who's not quite twenty-one.

'I meant, the other way.' He indicates Rodney, who's started to boogie again.

'Do you think they let pensioners in?'

'Don't be sarky.'

'I'm not, I'm being serious. Some places have

126

strange door codes. Look at Peter Stringfellow.'

'Well, I don't think any of us would get in there. We're all either too fat, too old, or just plain ugly.'

'Speak for yourself.' Damien preens in one of the smoked black glass side doors. 'I've been to Stringfellow's loads of time without any hassle.'

'You may have gone there, but did you actually get in?' jokes Nigel, who is also assessing his own reflection with obvious satisfaction.

Big Eric's not wearing a tie. Harvey's in jeans. Rodney is drunk and ancient. But by sticking closely together as a group, doubtfuls on the inside, vaguely normal on the outside, we all manage to get in.

Rodney, who married very young, confessed to me in the last bar that he's never been to a nightclub before in his entire life. He staggers into the huge, smoke-filled, air-conditioned room, eyeballs popping out of his head at the sight of the crowds of scantily dressed women boogieing to the booming beat of the music, bumping and grinding under the lasers over head.

He grabs an abandoned free ticket from a nearby shelf and fans himself with it, muttering and grinning.

'Bloody 'el!' he gasps. 'They're in their bleedin' undies.'

Whilst Rodney heads for the dance floor, leaving a trail of drool as he goes, and everybody else heads for the bar, I go to the loos to freshen up.

It's a bit *déjà vu* being here again so soon, but I suppose as I am I may as well try and get to number one on my hit list. My score on the kitchen door remains sadly at zero, while the other two are chalking up a storm. But you can bet your boots on one thing: there's no way I'm getting pissed and going home with an arsehole again. I don't want a repeat of the 'Larry Experience'. Then again, the only men I seem to meet are 'Larrys'. I wish I could summon up some enthusiasm for my task. I'm beginning to wonder why we ever decided to do this stupid challenge in the first place. Serena's going for it great guns, and Emma rolls home all the time with bandy legs and a big grin. I'm the only useless one, still too inhibited by my hang ups.

I think of Larry.

I think of Emma's friend Mason.

Strike one and Strike two.

It's all very well vowing to play men at their own game in the heat of the moment, but when it comes to the crunch – the alternative heat of the moment – I just can't do it. I just can't go through with it.

Sometimes I forget what made me want to go through with it all in the first place. Max, that's what. Max and his morals, or rather lack of them. Max, the lying, cheating bastard. Max the user. Max who asked me to go back, and then asked someone else to marry him only weeks later.

'Screw Max,' I say too loudly to my reflection in the mirror.

The girl beside me, repainting her pouting lips pillar box red in the cold hard clinical light, looks at me and smiles wryly.

'Screw them all, that's what I say. Bastards!' she says, wrinkling her nose.

Screw them all. That's what I'm supposed to be doing, isn't it?

Screwing the lot of them. Revenge of the oppressed sex.

Hump 'em and dump 'em.

I can hear Emma's voice now.

'Go out and get 'em girl.' That's what she'd be telling me. 'Stop skulking in the lav like a wimp. Act like a man!'

Determinedly I slap on another layer of lippy, undo another two buttons on my top, so that my black lace bra slips into view whenever I move, and head back out on a mission.

The others are in full party mode.

Rodney is dancing to Sash with Sandra, looking about him with a big grin, like an old stud horse put out to grass in a field full of young frisky fillies.

Sandra, feet planted firmly to the same spot on the floor, sways her large bottom in time to the music, a centrifugal force to Rodney's frenetic ping-pong ball.

Rodney can't dance. Not in this era anyway. He'd probably have got away with it in the seventies. The sort of side shuffle, slide back, side shuffle, slide back, movement he's doing would fit quite well to a little bit of 'Night Fever', if he threw a few hand signals and finger twirls as well.

His swept over grey hair is going dark with perspiration, his forehead shining wetly under the laser lights which twirl and spin above him.

For the first time in his life he has abandoned the obligatory suit jacket. His tie is hanging at half mast and his armpits are great dark circular stains of sweat, but he doesn't care, he's going for it big time.

'*On cor oon fwar.*' Rodney howls along to Sash, joyously eyeing the jigging bosoms of the frantically dancing young lovelies around him, like a chocoholic let loose in Cadbury World for the first time.

Lucian, still in cycling shorts, dayglo orange ones today, DMs and a skinny rib Paul Smith T-shirt, is strutting his stuff like something out of Hot Gossip nearby, watched at times by an admiring Sandra who refuses to believe that such a 'nice-looking boy' could be gay.

Nigel the junior, Damien, and Big Eric the photographer are attempting their own version of a tequila slammer contest at one of the many bars.

Salt on hand, lick, lemon suck, tequila swallow.

All in unison, like a synchronised swimming team diving into alcohol.

I'm not sure if they've got the sequence of events quite right, but they don't seem to care.

Young Nigel, looking decidedly green, is gamely struggling to keep up with his older, more experienced companions. He's doing okay until some kind soul points out the worm at the bottom of the bottle, then he turns the most amazing shade of pistachio, clamps a hand over his mouth, and sprints for the door marked Gents faster than a bargain hunter on the first day of the Harvey Nicks Christmas sale.

Harvey, who has fancied Jenny since she first started working for us, has summoned up the courage to ask her for a dance, and is now contemplating bribing the DJ to throw on a few slow numbers. He is saved the effort as Rodney, bouncing past after a slim blonde in a silver spangly bikini, Lycra tights, stacked Westwood sandals and nothing else, bumps into Jenny and sends her flying straight into Harvey's waiting arms, where they then continue to sway together despite the tempo, with closed eyes and mutually blissful expressions.

I attempt to lounge nonchalantly against the bar, scanning the room for likely candidates.

Life, I decide, after an eyeball turn about the room, would be so much easier if I wasn't so bloody fussy.

I know I'm not exactly Miss World, I have asked myself what right I have to be so choosy, but I am.

The mental script in my head goes something like this.

He's not bad, nice hair, nice arms, but his eyes are a bit too close together and they're brown. I don't think I like brown eyes.

Mmm, that one's quite nice. But then again, he's got a funny mouth. He's okay until he smiles, and then he looks like Freddie Mercury, and I never fancied Freddie Mercury. Blue Chinos over in the corner . . . promising, nice arse, can really dance which is rare for a lot of men. Nice face, too, but he looks a bit skinny. Chest isn't broad enough. No, definitely not hunky enough for me, I like my men with a bit of meat on them.

Now *he* looks hunky, definitely. Nice arms, broad chest, good legs . . . or is he just fat? And that face. Yuk! No, thank you.

Man in the short-sleeved Ralph Lauren. No, nice face but saggy arse. Nothing worse than a man with a saggy arse.

Guy in the Red or Dead T-shirt? Bloody gorgeous, but dances like a tone-deaf elephant on roller skates whilst imagining he's Wayne Sleep.

And on it goes.

The thing is, am I supposed to fancy whoever it is that I pull – if I pull?

And how do you go about doing it man-style?

Women have their own subtle signals to send out if they see a man they fancy. It's a game of flirtation, catch his eye once too often, maybe smile a little, then leave the rest to him. Thinking about it, we have it easy.

How do men do it? I need some clarification on this one. Emma, Serena and I have made up our own rules, but we're all women. Maybe I need to hear it from the horse's mouth.

The horse being a man, of course.

To act like a man in this situation, I need to know how a man would act in this situation. I think that's the problem. I'm trying to be how I think a man would be, but I don't really know how a man would be. Do you follow me?

I need to be a good journalist and do some research.

I sidle over to Damien and Eric, who have abandoned the drinking game following the defection of Nigel to hug porcelain, and are now deep in conversation, contemplating the 'hot totty' on the dance floor.

Damien: 'What about her?' (*sucks the head off his pint of lager*)

Eric: 'Which one?'

Damien: 'Blondie over there, the one falling out the front of her dress.'

Eric: 'Nice tits ... shame about everything else. Nah.'

Damien: 'Now *she's* a bit of all right.'

132

Eric: 'Which one?' (*scans the room like a shortsighted mole*)

Damien: 'The brunette over there, the one with the legs and the tits.'

Eric: 'Cor, yeah, wouldn't mind giving her a large portion.' (*eyes popping out of his head*)

Damien: 'Go on then, mate.' (*nudges him in the ribs with a well-placed encouraging elbow*)

Eric: 'Nah!'

Damien: 'She's begging for you.' (*looking leery*)

Eric: 'You think so?' (*looking hopeful*)

Damien: 'Look at it. Go on, you're in there, I'm telling you. Go on . . .'

Urged by Damien, Eric struts on to the dance floor. I watch closely, fascinated.

Eric's technique is to slide up behind the chosen woman and begin to dance, getting closer and closer until he's almost grinding against her. She pretends not to notice him. He moves in a little closer. A light deliberate brush of his hands over her hips and she turns to face him, feigning indignation.

'All right, darling? Fancy a dance?'

'I already am dancing,' she replies.

'I meant naked and horizontally.' Eric grins broadly. I wait for her to slap his face, but instead she starts laughing. The next thing I know they're heading off the dance floor together and he's buying her a drink at the bar, giving a sly thumbs up behind his back to Damien.

So that's how they do it.

Am I ready to go for it on just one lesson?

What the hell! I knock back a double vodka.

Right, first of all find somebody I fancy, because

from the conversation you do actually have to fancy them. Well, I've tried that one. I run through my list of possibles again, and finally settle for the guy in the blue Chinos as being the one with the least demerit points against him.

He's still on the dance floor, strutting his funky stuff, so I have a few more drinks for Dutch courage, wait until a record I like comes on, then just go for it. I feel like a Kamikaze pilot zooming to certain death. If I could close my eyes I would, but I'd probably fall over.

I can't quite go for the whole Eric hands-on-hips direct approach, so I just boogie as close as I can get until he finally notices me hovering behind him like an annoying bluebottle, and turns round to look at me.

I smile weakly, then take a deep breath and just plunge in.

'All right? Fancy a dance?' It sounds bloody strange coming out of my mouth.

He looks me up and down like I'm something he's just trodden in.

'Get a life.'

He turns back to his mates, who all guffaw with laughter.

Ground open wide and swallow me whole!

Stung by humiliation, I scuttle away and disappear into the Ladies with a face redder than a baboon's backside.

It's nearly two in the morning. I finally pluck up the courage to emerge from the toilets, where I've spent the last hour, face still blazing like a barbecue. I slink back out into the club, tail between my legs. Thankfully, people have started to leave, including he of the blue Chinos, Mr Humiliator.

My party is coming to the end of a long day's drinking.

Rodney, feet trailing, is propped up by his face, which is wedged into the cleavage of an extremely drunk bleached blonde who looks like a young Diana Dors.

Harvey and Jenny are still locked around each other like the two sides of a twisting interwoven pretzel.

Big Eric's offering to photograph a stunning brunette and launch her on Page Three.

Handsome young Nigel's shoved his stomach back down his throat, and is now the centre of attention in a group of drunken giggling girls who are convinced he's Peter André.

Even Sandra is being chatted up by the bouncer who looks like Bluto.

Everybody's doing it.

Everybody except me.

'All on your own then?' says a voice at my elbow.

It's Damien.

'Certainly looks that way,' I sigh, contemplating my own failure.

'Well, I'd offer you another drink, but I think it's chucking out time.'

'Doesn't matter. I think I've had about three times as much as I should anyway.'

We lapse into an almost companionable silence for a few moments. Damien and I tolerate each other. I think he's a bit of a jerk, and Damien knows this, but we get on okay, so long as we don't talk to each other.

'Won't be the same without old Rodders steering the helm.' He jerks his head towards Rodney.

'Well, he hardly did much steering, did he?' I retort. 'It's a bit like taking the figurehead off the front of the ship. You can still sail perfectly well without it, and after a while people will forget it was ever there.'

A bit like Max really. The good ship Alex won't sink without that deserting rat. I grab Damien's bottle of Bud, and neck it.

I end up sharing a taxi home with him, Harvey and Jenny.

The lovebirds spend the entire journey locked on to each other's lips, like two fighting sink plungers, slurping at each other's wet slippery tongues like kids eating melting ice cream cones.

I stare in embarrassment out of the side window, whilst Damien, ever on the lookout for a story, chats to the cab driver about any famous clients he's ferried in the hope of some dirt being dished.

Harvey and Jenny get out at the same place, even though I know she lives nowhere near Harvey's. After all the office avoidance, skirting round each other, taking it in turns to gaze longingly when the other wasn't, all the basic farting about for four months, they're certainly moving fast now.

Why are relationships so bloody complicated? Why do Jenny and Harvey now make it look so simple?

'Isn't that sweet?' says Damien watching them walk hand in hand up to Harvey's front door, then stop to kiss in the shadows.

'Love . . . pah!' I spit. 'Who needs it?'

'My, we do sound disillusioned. Has that boyfriend of yours been upsetting you again?'

This is not a concerned question, this is a tease.

'I'm not with Max anymore,' I reply grumpily.

Damien, whose attention had been focussed out of the window, turns back to me and pulls a wry, surprised kind of face.

'Well, you certainly kept that one quiet.'

'Well, I'm hardly likely to discuss my private life with you, am I?' I spit at him. 'Not unless I want the whole world to know about it.'

'Is that what you really think of me? Honestly, Alex, I'm not all bad.'

'You're not?'

'Of course I'm not.' He gives me a hurt puppy dog look.

I give him a look which clearly states that I'm not convinced.

'Why do you hate me so much?' he asks me sorrowfully.

I try to determine whether the hurt attitude is genuine or not.

'I don't hate you, I'm completely indifferent.'

'Well, that's a challenge to a man if ever there was one,' he laughs, eyeing me up unashamedly, arrogant as ever.

Now I know why I dislike Damien. It's because he reminds me of Max. Confidently cocky, good-looking, a click-your-fingers-and-they-come-running kind of guy. Just the sort of man my friends and I started our scheme to wreak revenge upon.

That would be a bit of a coup. Hump and dump

Damien. Put him in his place. The problem is with him I get the feeling it would be a race to see who could dump who first, and he's far more practised than I am. Who'd end up humiliating whom? I ask myself. And is it worth shagging such an arse, just to prove a point?

Damien has a place not far from Emma's in Chelsea, a ground-floor apartment in a converted Victorian house, a little bit like the place Max and I used to share.

I wait for him to shoot out of the cab and leave me with the fare, but instead he pays the driver, then turns to me and smiles in a pretty nice, friendly sort of fashion. 'Fancy coming in for a coffee?'

What implications does a question like that hold coming from a man like Damien? I don't know whether it's the six glasses of warm white wine followed by several Buds and a large quantity of blue label vodka dancing merrily in my stomach, or the thought of my dismal score rate that dims my senses, but when I open my mouth to say 'No Way, Jose', I actually hear myself saying, 'Okay.' It sounds like my own voice, but it's somehow dislocated from the rest of my body, sort of disembodied, like a head that's been chopped off. It's certainly dislocated from my brain, which immediately starts to bleat silently with horror at the thought of being alone in Damien's apartment – with Damien. Nonetheless, only minutes later that's where I find myself.

It's a surprisingly nice place for someone like him. I don't know what I expected. I mean, I've never really had cause to imagine how he lived, but I suppose I would have placed him in a house share in Islington with patterned carpet, brown nylon duvet covers, and Arsenal posters instead of wallpaper.

Damien's flat has stripped floor boards, a pale oak kitchen, a state of the art sound system, eau de nil walls, and Liberty print blinds at the windows.

The biggest surprise of all, though, is that on his own Damien is actually pretty good company.

I like most of his CD collection, and the way he's decorated his apartment; he offers me real coffee instead of instant, and chocolate Hob Nobs which earns him several brownie points instantaneously.

He's flirty but not dirty, witty without being crude, very well read, and surprisingly easy to talk to.

This is a side of Damien I've never been introduced to before.

Perhaps the wise cracks and juvenile behaviour are a part of his character reserved for use only with his cronies at the office.

I even manage to flirt back a little bit. Not a lot, just a little. Enough for the coffee to move on to brandy, Radiohead to move on to Portishead, and Damien to move from the pale lilac leather armchair he was perched in, to the sofa where I am currently reclining far too comfortably.

He starts off at the other end of the long three-seater, but gradually squeaks his way along the soft leather until his thigh is pressing against mine.

He yawns and stretches and his arm slides along the back of my neck.

I'm just about to slap him down for being so bloody sixteen-year-old-in-the-cinema childish, when I feel his fingers begin to knead at the knotted muscles of my shoulders. Despite myself, it feels incredibly good.

Strike that, it feels bloody wonderful. There are so many knots in my shoulder muscles you'd think they'd been home to a whole jamboree of rope-fiddling sea scouts for the past few weeks.

Damien rubs away until I'm leaning forward and he's almost bodily behind me, both hands kneading at my muscles like a chef pounding bread dough, pushing with his thumbs, pressing away, popping the lactic acid, until I'm as floppy and pliable as a rag doll.

God, he's good at this. What with the alcohol and the mind-blowing back rub, I'm floating off to another dimension.

In fact I'm so disconnected, I don't even object when his hands slide around from the back to the front and transfer their attention to my boobs, slipping under the cotton of my shirt, his thumbs connecting with my nipples, rubbing them to a peak with slow, soft, casually calculated movements.

The next thing I know we're kissing.

'I am kissing Damien,' a little voice announces in my head. The little voice sounds very surprised and slightly indignant, and adds a rider to the first comment. 'I really think you should stop kissing Damien,' it says.

My body throws a V and carries on.

'Stop kissing Damien this minute!' the little voice commands, in a definite stop now. 'He's seducing you. It's not supposed to happen like this!'

Unfortunately the rest of me doesn't respond. You see, kissing Damien is a not altogether unpleasant experience. I'm very surprised at this. Then again, I still feel rather disembodied, as though I'm watching myself from a corner of the room or something.

The little voice, seeing beyond this evening to tomorrow morning and the rest of my life, and sensing severe mortification and mortal danger to my pride, rolls up its sleeves and prepares to do battle with my mind which, drunken and stupid, is failing to see sense. My mind, you see, is concentrating far too much on what's happening to my body, and it's decided that it's rather enjoying the sensations, and doesn't give a toss really about who's inducing them. It's a bit like those old Warner Brothers cartoons. I've got a good conscience and a bad conscience having a running battle in my head. They're currently having a nose to nose argument that goes something along these lines:

'It's being offered on a plate.'

'You don't fancy Damien.'

'But I'm getting turned on.'

'But you're a good girl really, you don't have sex for the sake of sensation alone.'

'If I was a man I would.'

'If you were a man, would you shag a female version of Damien?'

'Good-looking. Fit. Bit of a bimbo. Yep, definitely.'

'But you're not a man.'

'Think male mentality. Remember – rules are rules. Sad girl with no score.'

'Why are we playing this stupid game in the first place?'

Good finally grabs bad by the throat and slaps it round the face a few times to try and dispel the drunken torpor. It works. With a mental shriek of horror, I finally realise just what it is that I'm doing.

I decide that I want to pull away, but there's nowhere for me to go. I'm pinned to the end of the sofa by the weight of Damien's body. I'd fall off the edge, but for the fact that I think he'd follow me, and we'd end up in a rather compromising position on the floor.

Finally, when the good conscience has pinned the bad conscience to the floor in a Big Daddy-style bellyflop, and is growling at it to submit, Damien stops the fight by himself pulling away. He grins at me with his mouth and his eyebrows, and whispers for me to 'stay there', 'cause he'll be 'back in a moment'.

I stay, but only because I'm struggling to regain breath and some leg control. What do I do now? I've wimped out of the last two encounters, and now the black coffee is loosening the grip of the alcohol, like a spatula releasing the sides of an omelette from a non-stick pan whose non-stick is gone, I desperately want to wimp out of this one too.

When Damien dims the lights on the way back from the bathroom, panic sets in. It's not the fact that he's trying to set the mood, it's the fact that while in the bathroom, he completely abandoned his clothes.

He struts back into the room, wearing nothing but a big grin, a pair of Mickey Mouse socks, and a raging hard-on already sporting a luminous condom which glows eerily green in the dim light.

My mouth drops open.

Trust me, this is not an invitation for oral sex.

'Damien's in the nude, Damien's in the nude!' keeps running through my head like some childish playground taunt.

I gaze in amazement at the confident, swaggering figure in front of me. He has slightly knock knees, and rather a lot of dark curly chest hair which tapers to a fine line just above his sternum that travels southward to meet a certain appendage which is determinedly pointing northward.

'Ready?' he rasps.

There's only one thing I can do.

I start to laugh. Quietly at first, and then the giggles just run away with me until I'm guffawing like an asthmatic donkey, with tears streaming down my cheeks. Damien's willy deflates faster than a bouncy castle that's just been spiked by an illegal stiletto heel. Imagine the Leaning Tower of Pizza standing tall, slightly angular, and very proud of itself, suddenly toppling earthward like the last domino in a shunted row. It sort of retreats between his balls like a disgruntled tortoise trying to hide, and Damien suddenly discovers some modesty, covering his shrunken hard on with his hands and looking at me in wide-eyed, totally mortified outrage.

Grabbing my handbag, I stagger away from him, backwards, my face contorted into a clown's mask of mirth as I attempt to halt the hysterics. I manage to just about control myself until I step out of his apartment into the night and, collapsing against the wrought-iron railings, begin to absolutely howl with laughter.

A scowling red face appears briefly at Damien's living-room window.

'Strike three!' I yell at it, before it scuttles back into the shadows, and I head off down the middle of the road swinging my handbag.

★ ★ ★

'Did you pull?'

This is now Emma's standard greeting. She no longer says hello when she first sees me.

I am seated at the kitchen table feeling sorry for myself. We don't possess an ice bag, we don't even possess a handy bag of frozen vegetables. I have had to resort – oh, what a shame and a waste – to filling an old bath cap with Cookies and Cream ice cream, tying it up with a piece of string, and plonking that on my throbbing head instead.

'I did,' I mutter through a mouthful of morning-after tongue fur, 'but then I'm afraid I wimped out again. I'm sorry.' I hang my head in my untouched muesli in shame. 'I tried, I really did. I just get to the crunch and I can't go through with it. I think I should give up. I'm obviously not cut out to be a male chauvinist pig.'

'Nonsense!' Emma laughs. 'You'll get there eventually, don't let the failures put you off.'

Failures? Thank you, best friend, that's just the word I needed to hear. Failure.

'You can't give up yet. It's like falling off a horse,' she continues. 'Pick yourself up, dust yourself down, then get straight back on and ride for your life.'

I think of Damien in the nude with his Disney socks and luminous willy. I think of riding for my life atop that luminous willy with my hands gripping his ankle motifs. I already feel slightly sick from my hangover. Now I just want to go and stick my head down the toilet and barf my guts up.

'Would you ride for your life on Damien Lawrence?' I ask her.

'Damien!' she repeats in horror. 'Damien! Is that who you were with last night? Jeez, Lex, what were you doing going out with that creep?'

'I was being indiscriminate.'

'You can say that again!' Ems's eyes are wide with horror. 'I know the rules say go for anything that has the proper appendages, but there's nothing about having to sleep with pond scum!'

'But isn't that what I'm supposed to do? Aren't men indiscriminate?'

'Only when drunk or desperate. Were you drunk?'

'Well, I'd had quite a few. But I must admit. I'm actually getting pretty desperate. I must have been to agree to go in for coffee with him in the first place. Fortunately I wasn't drunk or desperate enough actually to get naked with the idiot.'

'Thank goodness for that!'

'But surely he comes under the "If it's offered on a plate, take it" rule?'

'Damien doesn't come on a plate, he's scraped off the heel of your shoe. Come on, Lex, I know we've got rules, but you've got to keep this thing in perspective. There's no point in ruining your future bonkability or endangering your health just to prove a point.'

'Yeah, but I don't seem to be doing very well so far. It's been four weeks, and I haven't even had one one-night-stand. Serena's already on to number three.'

'Yeah, she has taken to playing the game with frightening skill, hasn't she?'

'And you're going great guns . . .'

'Mmmmm.' Ems glosses over this one, presumably to avoid hurting my feelings further by comparing her

145

rampant success with my own sad failure.

'Ahhhh!' I shriek, and bang my head against the wooden surface of the table. 'How am I going to face him at the office? I'm already scuttling round like a cockroach avoiding Larry and he only comes into the building a couple of times a week. Damien's in the same bloody office!'

'Well, it would have been ten times worse if you'd actually slept with the guy.'

'I know. Thank god I'm away for the next couple of weeks.'

'Not another trip into the unknown?'

'Yep, I'm supposed to be going to the Cotswolds,' I sigh,' then on to one of those awful holiday camp things down in Devon. You know, *Hi-De-Hi* mixed with *Colditz*. My life is just so, so exciting.'

'It's a damn' sight better than being stuck in a room with forty hormonally rampant men yelling into telephones all day.'

'You think? I'd swap you any day. I'd be bound to find a few targets in a place with so many men.'

'Sounds good to me. I'll swap you my power suit for your overnight bag.'

'I wish. Tell me, what's it really like being the only woman in a room full of men?'

'Oh, hell,' Emma sighs dramatically, picking up my spoon and dipping into the melting bag of ice cream perched on my head. 'Simply hell!'

# *Chapter Five*

Monday morning. I load my usual kit – dicta-phone, laptop, enough luggage for a month – into the boot of my Fiesta.

Despite the constant travelling I still haven't turned into one of those people who can just throw a couple of separates and some accessories into a case and have outfits for any occasion. I always pack enough clothes to last me for twice as long as I'm going and to cover any contingency. If I was going husky trekking in the Arctic I'd pack a bikini; tropical beach-hogging in the Seychelles and I'd stick in a woolly jumper and hot water bottle just in case.

The weather in the Cotswolds isn't exactly tropical, unless you think of tropical rain forests instead of tropical beaches. A fine drizzle dogs me all the way up the M40, and it's only as dusk gently begins to fall that the gentle April sun fights her way through the clouds to illuminate the honeyed countryside around me, her rays soaking up the droplets of glistening water scattered everywhere, like kitchen towel on spilt champagne.

Despite my grumbling reluctance to go on this trip,

my mood lifts higher the further I travel into the heart of Warwickshire.

I'd forgotten how gorgeous it is in this part of the world.

In fact, I'm so inspired by the glorious countryside around me that I change from Radio One to Classic FM and add a little Vivaldi to the whole scenario.

By the time I reach the hotel, I'm ready for a little stately splendour. You know the sort of thing: long driveway Darcy could gallop his sweating mount down; beautiful gardens in which to take a turn with Mr Rochester; ivy climbing up to the bedroom windows, ready to be scaled by a desperately love-sick Gregg Wise.

I'm not disappointed.

When I reach the main gated entrance to The Priory, the place I'm reviewing, I'm greeted by a long and winding drive, dark-leaved trees standing sentinel to either side. Darcy doesn't cross my path on his thoroughbred as I drive down admiring the estate around me, but the place is pretty romantic all the same.

The drive leads to a huge old house built of Cotswold stone, the many-paned windows spilling golden light into the dusk of early evening.

A porter in a green and gold waistcoat hurries from the house to help me with my bags, waits patiently while I check in, then leads me up the left fork of the ornately carved double staircase to a Renaissance-style painted room with a four-poster bed and a view of a walled flower garden complete with fountain, atop which, standing on tip-toe, his arrow pointed directly at me, is Cupid taking a prolonged pee.

If I were a location scout I'd go into raptures over the place. As I'm a writer I go into absolute over-the-top raptures instead, overtip the porter, and whip out my laptop.

I can't believe the paper has finally sent me somewhere worth going to. I think Rodney must have had a final passionate fling with his budget.

When my computer thesaurus has run out of synonyms for gorgeous, I take a shower, change into the obligatory little black dress, and go down to the oak-panelled dining room for dinner.

I've dined on my own in so many places as part of my job, it's something that usually doesn't bother me in the slightest. I think other people find it more disconcerting than I do. A single woman eating alone seems to have about the same effect on a restaurant as a young mother whipping out her boobs to breast feed in public. I can feel the respective looks of curiosity, sympathy and disapproval radiating from different areas of the room.

After an amazing meal, I take pity on the poor uncomfortable people around me, think of my thighs, sod dessert, and head for the bar. At least here I have a reason, in others' eyes, to be on my own – I am obviously on the pull. At least when they know – or think they know – why I am on my own, they can accept my solitary status. I used to go for the old lone drinker's standbys of a newspaper, good paperback, or even, when pushed, my portable PC. Now I don't feel the need for such props. If a man can go into a bar and drink alone, then in my newfound role of gender stereotyping reversal, so can I.

Despite this new assertiveness, I still feel a little

self-conscious as I park my bum on a bar stool and order a glass of white. Restaurants are fine. I have a knife and fork and food to play with, a menu to study with a professional eye. Bars I find a little trickier, I'm not really in the bar to review it, you see. I'm in the bar to get pissed.

I'm lucky. The barman, the sweetest type of gay, is bored and welcomes company. He compliments me on my dress whilst he serves me my first glass of wine, and within five minutes I've found out that his name is Aidan, he's twenty-five, originally from Edinburgh, he split up with his long-term boyfriend just over a year ago and came down here to get away from it all, is a graphic – but frustrated fashion – designer by day, and has been working in the hotel bar in the evenings for the past few months to meet new people and his new mortgage.

'So what do you do then, sweetie?' He finally asks me the dreaded question.

'I'm a sales rep,' I lie. I never tell anybody what I do when I'm out 'casing a joint'. Tell them I'm doing a write up for an almost national newspaper and I get unusually good service. I need to see what's the norm.

'That surprises me.' He puts down a gleaming pint glass, and picks up another. 'You don't look the type. What do you sell?'

'Industrial laundry products.' Another lie, but I suppose newspapers are always washing other people's dirty linen in public.

'Really? You ought to have a word with the house-keeper here. We're having big shake ups at the moment. I think we're looking for new suppliers for lots of different things.'

Oops! Don't know a thing about what I'm supposed to be selling. I try to think of cleaning products, but all I can come up with is Jiff, Blue Loo, and Mr Sheen. I'm going to have to think of something easier to bluff or I'll end up getting caught out.

'Mmmmm. Thanks . . .' I murmur non-committally, brain buzzing frantically as I try to think of another subject to switch to. 'So what's the weather been like here then?' I ask banally.

I'm fortunately saved by the appearance of a young girl in her late-teens with long white-blonde hair down her back and a face like a petulant ferret, who arrives to assist Aidan for the latter part of the evening. Apparently the hotel bar is frequented by locals as well as guests, and is gradually filling as we speak. She of the ferret face, appears also to have a ferret brain, and has to be shown how to work the Electronic till about eight times. By the time Aidan comes back to me he's as wound up as an oversprung clockwork toy and wants to grumble, so fortunately no further mention is made of my so-called employment.

'What a waste of space,' he moans in his beautiful Scottish burr, 'she's so empty-headed we could use her for storage. Everything I say to her goes in one ear and floats straight out the other on a stream of warm air. Don't know why they took her on, she's more of a hindrance than a help.'

'Quite attractive, though. I suppose she's good for business.'

'Attractive? You think? You ever heard that song? Nice legs . . .'

'. . . shame about the face?' I finish for him, trying

to suppress a giggle. 'Aidan, it's cruel to bitch.'

'Yeah, and it's cruel to make me work with that bubble head.'

'The customers seem to like her.' I watch as a group of males, who were all slowly drinking pints, suddenly switch to speedily guzzling the bottled beer that's kept on the lowest shelf. Every time she bends to get another bottle, the drooling mob are greeted by a show of slim thigh, and a flash of white lace knickers underneath a skirt that is little more than a slightly wide belt. Oh, to have thin enough thighs to wear it myself, I think, slightly envious of all the attention she's eliciting.

'Mmmmm, well, you know what most men are like, sweetie. Brain down the front of their underpants.' He purses his lips in jealous disapproval. 'You know, I used to see this guy – before John, the bastard that dumped me, that is. Now, he was *such* a tart. Swung both ways purely so he could have a wider choice of who to bonk. I swear he used to think, eat and breathe through his libido. Well . . .'

The grumbling stops dead. A man has just entered the room and sat down on a bar stool a few feet away from me. Aidan's ready smile is instantly renewed.

'Now here's what I call a real man,' he leans in and whispers conspiratorially, unconsciously licking his lips. 'Such a waste, though. He's so straight it's untrue. I'd try to convert him but I'd only be torturing myself with dreams of what can never be.'

He winks at me.

'Well, I'd better serve him in the only way I can, before *she* shows us up. Back in a mo.'

The blonde ferret and he then fight it out over who

is going to serve the new arrival, while I take a look at the object of such rivalry.

He is in his early-to mid-thirties, casually comfortable in moleskin trousers and a pale green Ralph Lauren shirt. He has short brown hair, cut close around the sides and slightly longer on top, a few grey hairs peppering their way through, a slightly crooked nose, and a nice mouth. It's an attractive face, but not instantly striking.

I watch, curious as to why Aidan and Ferret Face are making such a fuss of the guy. Perhaps he has a bucket of that '*je ne sais quoi*' that Emma and Serena swear by. I must admit, he seems fun. He has an infectiously dirty laugh that makes me want to giggle along with him, even though I can't quite catch what's being said.

The thing that strikes me the most is that he looks so happy. He's relaxed, obviously follows the Jem theory of being comfortable with oneself, and said dirty laugh is ever ready as he chats to Aidan, who won the cat fight to serve him.

Yep, I decide, he's definitely attractive, there's something about him. I peer a bit closer. He has blue eyes, or at least I think they're blue, it's hard to see from here. I edge a little closer still. Yep, they're blue all right. Well, a sort of bluey-green with a few flecks of hazel thrown in for effect; a cornucopia of colour, sparkling and changing like the patterns in a kaleidoscope.

I suddenly realise that those bluey-greeny-hazel-flecked eyes are focussed on mine. He's caught me staring. He smiles. Normally I'd do the usual female thing of looking away with a disgusted sort of expression on my face as if I thought he was about as attractive as an old dish cloth used to clean the cat's bowl. Or if I fancied him, looking away coyly and slightly more slowly under my eyelashes, then perhaps looking back again a few moments later with a sort of I'm-demure-but-come-and-get-me-big-boy smile. Or then again, I'd probably go for the old standby of looking dead embarrassed and hiding my face in my drink.

I don't, though. The eyes are so merry and so friendly, I actually manage to smile back quite easily and normally.

Ferret catches the smile and starts to look daggers at me. Any minute now, she'll whip off her stilettos and start stabbing me with them. Fortunately for me she is soon distracted by a new arrival to the rowdy group of leering businessmen further down the bar.

A toupee has walked into the room wearing a managing director. I say it this way round because the hair piece has far more presence than the pale and greying specimen of dubious maledom beneath it. It, however, has to be the saddest toupee in the history of hair pieces, which says an awful lot about the man, doesn't it? It looks like he's scraped up an old grey Scania-squashed rodent from the road, and unceremoniously slapped it on to his head, without washing out the road grit or back combing its flattened fur.

On to my fourth glass of wine, including half a carafe of a bloody good house white consumed with dinner, I feel bubbles of laughter begin to well in my throat, and have to swallow the rest of my drink to quench them.

Aidan shimmies over with a bottle and tops me up.

'One of the richest men in the country, him.' He follows my gaze. 'Sells poultry.'

'Is that a demonstration model he's wearing on his head?' The giggles begin to start again. 'He looks a right turkey in it, doesn't he?'

Aidan touches my arm, and stifles guilty laughter.

'It is awful, isn't it? He's here for a conference, you know. Booked out half the hotel, he has.'

'A dead chicken convention. How exciting!'

'Apparently he's single.'

'I'm not surprised.' I cough as my wine goes down the wrong way. 'I wonder what he's got for pubic hair? A petrified gerbil clinging to his groin?'

Aidan thrusts his knuckles into his mouth to stifle the giggles.

'I'd be petrified if I found myself down his underpants,' he snorts. 'He's one of the richest men in the country, though,' he repeats, as though this makes him instantly desirable.

'You think he'd be able to buy a decent wig then, wouldn't you?'

'Mmm.' Aidan nods his agreement. 'Or scrap the cover-up look completely. Somebody should tell him it's trendy to be bald.' He picks up a cloth and begins to polish some pint glasses, steaming and fresh from the hot wash machine. 'I mean, look at the Mitchell bruvvers. They've got bonces like billiard balls with five o'clock shadow, and they seem to do all right for themselves. My last feller . . . well, the one before the one before John the Bastard that dumped me . . . he had a number one all over, and talk about sexy! He used to feel like a little mole . . .

'Oooh, excuse me, the gorgeous Jake's got a half-empty glass and if I don't head over there this minute, *she*'ll beat me to it, and we don't want to let *her* loose on the pumps, now do we? The last time she tried to pour somebody a pint they got a two-inch head. You know, not everybody likes a girl who gives generous head, do they?'

Aidan shoots back to serve 'the gorgeous Jake' with the sexy laugh, leaving Ferret Face to get caught by Wiggy who, following the advice of his half-cut cronies, orders a bottle of bottom-shelf best.

Sighing tetchily, looking daggers at Aidan now, instead of me, Ferret Face bends down to get Wiggy a bottle of Budweiser, whereupon he falls in complete and utter lust at first sight with her scanty white panties, and proceeds to burst every blood vessel in his pudding grey face to chat her up.

'What's a nice girl like you doing in a place like this then?' is his first pathetic attempt.

'I work here, don't I?' she replies in a flat sarcastic monotone. 'Look.' She pulls out the name tag attached to her top, and runs a finger over the engraved letters like a blind man reading braille. 'It says Baaar Staaaff.' She enunciates the words like a primary school teacher talking down to a difficult toddler. 'Bit like bastard but instead of the D at the end there's an F. You know, as in F off.'

I wonder what charm school she went to? Wiggy isn't listening, though.

'Helen,' he says, dragging his eyes away from the cleavage she just shoved in his face, and reading the name above the title. 'That's a lovely name for a lovely girl. Did you know, you're a helluva girl,

Helen. Fair *belle Hélène*, I'd like to eat you for dessert.'

I begin to giggle into my wine glass. I can't help it, I've never heard such crass lines in my life.

Wiggy tries to lean his elbow on the bar in cool dude fashion, misses, and jerks his head up quickly as he realises his chin has nothing to rest on, shooting the road accident rodent into a skid across his bald bonce until it's resting at a forty-five degree angle to the top of his head.

Completely oblivious to his wonky wig, he gazes goofily at the Ferret and begins to croon rather tunelessly a song about beautiful girls.

By this point I'm almost drowning in white wine, snorkelling alcohol up my nose as I snort with barely suppressed laughter.

'The gorgeous Jake' is also collapsing into his Caffrey's, shoulders shaking with mirth. We catch eyes, brimful of laughter.

This time I look away. Don't ask me why but I suddenly feel a bit gauche.

' "Tell her I luuuuurve her, tell her I neeeeed her body . . ." ' Wiggy continues to wail, making it up as he goes along.

I look across again, Jake looks back, we raise eyeballs to heaven in mutual derision. He shakes his head, mouth curling.

'If I promise you that it's not a chat up line, can I buy you a drink?' I almost look around me to make sure that it's actually me he's talking to, but Blondie has cut dead Wiggy's wooing, cut the daggers, and is now mowing me down with an imaginary sub-machine gun.

'If I told you that I was disappointed that it wasn't,

would you still want to buy me one?' I reply jokily, with a sudden boldness I almost instantly regret. Fortunately it makes him laugh again.

'Now *that* was a line if ever I heard one.' He grins as I blush the same colour as the heart of the log fire burning merrily in the grate at the other end of the room. He beckons to Ferret Face. who, once panting to serve him, is now as reluctant as an unthirsty horse being led to a mill pond. I'm sure if no one was looking she'd spit in my glass.

Aidan's in the cellar changing a beer barrel. When Ferret Face has finally managed to grasp the rudiments of serving drinks that you don't just flip a top off, my neighbour at the bar comes over.

'Jake.' He puts down the two full glasses, and holds out a hand.

'I know,' I reply, taking it.

'And you . . .?'

'Oh, sorry. Alex.'

'You know, this is going to sound like another line, but you look kind of familiar.'

'You're right.' I laugh, liking the way his handshake is firm and warm. 'That does sound like another line.'

'Well, it wasn't, but it was my turn anyway. You started it.' He slides on to a stool next to me. 'No, seriously, joking apart, I know your face from somewhere.'

I sometimes have people say this to me. It might have something to do with the fact that there's an outrageously flattering piccie of me next to my byline in every edition of *Sunday Best*. Because it's such an amazing picture – expert make-up artist, right lighting, computerised spot removal – it looks like me, yet it doesn't. In comparison to the photo of Alex, the *Sunday Best* travel writer, the real Alex, i.e. me, is sort of like a George Michael or Liz Hurley look alike: similar enough to make people do a double take, but disappointing up close. Still, because it *is* similar – I mean, under all the doctoring it is me after all – and because our circulation is pretty wide, I do get the occasional 'Don't I know you from somewhere?' comment. Don't get me wrong. I don't get mobbed in the streets or autograph-hunted in Sainsbury's, unlike Max who had quite a fan club at one time after he played a particularly dashing officer in a Sunday evening period drama. Big head that he is, he adored every single minute of his brief spell of fame, and kept his side burns for at least eight months after the last episode was screened. I just get the occasional flicker of near recognition.

'Well, everybody tells me I'm the spitting image of Elle Macpherson,' I joke.

Aidan comes back from the cellar grumbling that he's wrecked a cherished fingernail whilst changing a barrel.

'So you two have met then?' He holds out his hand for me to inspect said nail, and I tut sympathetically. 'Good, I was going to tell you to keep Alex company, Jake. She's on her own, and we don't want that sad pathetic lot giving her a hard time too, now do we?' He indicates the rowdy businessmen with a jerk of his head, and winks surreptitiously at me.

I think I'm being set up. Aidan, who realises that any love or lust sent from his direction will, by this particular male, go unrequited, is obviously prepared to be magnanimous.

'Don't you worry, Alex hen, Jake'll look after you. Get him to give you a guided tour, why don't you? The gardens are absoloootly beautiful this time of night.' He winks at me again, Mr Obvious. 'Wildly romantic – moonlight, scent of roses, that sort of thing.'

Jake, who's laughing almost as much at Aidan's hard sell Cilla Black tactics as he was at Wiggy's wooing of Ferret Face, attempts to pull a straight face and asks me what I think of the hotel.

'It's gorgeous,' I enthuse. 'This is the sort of house I used to dream of living in when I was a child. You know, when you go through that phase of being adamant that you're adopted, and your real parents are wealthy, royal, and have room for a pony?'

He laughs. 'Glad you like the place.'

'Oh? You sound like you have a vested interest?'

He nods. 'It's a family business.'

'Oh, right.' That explains the toadying from the bar staff. 'You work here?'

He shakes his head.

'No, I've been working abroad. My parents own the hotel, but my father's been ill, and things have started to slide a little. They need some help pulling the place around. They've let it go a bit, been too preoccupied with other things.'

'So you've come back to run it for them?'

He shakes his head.

I'm just helping out for a while. It's not really my line.'

'So what is?'

He smiles wryly. 'Let's just say I'm a sort of trouble shooter. Something needs sorting out, putting back on track, then I get called in to do it.' He seems as coy as I am to disclose his own line of business, and rapidly changes the emphasis to me.

'Aidan says that you're some sort of rep?'

'Mmmmm. 'I do the non-committal murmur again.

So that's what he and Aidan were talking about earlier . . . me. Don't ask me why but I feel absurdly pleased that I have evidence of some interest on his part. I move the conversation back on to safer ground.

'You seem to be "pulling this place round" pretty well. So far it's one of the best hotels I've been to this year.'

'Thanks, we're doing our best. You travel a lot then?'

'It's part of my job. I've stayed in some hell holes in my time, I can tell you.'

'Mmm,' he agrees. 'My only qualification for help-ing my folks sort this place out is that I must have stayed in some of the worst hotels on the planet. I don't know an awful lot about the trade, but I do know a hell of a lot about what to avoid.'

'Yeah,' I laugh. 'I stopped in a place once where it was so damp even the woodlice wore waders. You didn't need to book an en suite, you could just stand under the trickle of damp in the corner of the room.'

He laughs his agreement.

'I know the feeling. I think my worst one was this place in Torquay. I'd gone down for a conference and the main hotel was overbooked. In fact, I think the whole town was pretty much booked out. The company I worked for then was a pretty important client, so in desperation they shipped me and some colleagues out to what they called an annexe, but which was actually another hotel just down the road. I think I went from five-star to no-star in one hundred yards. You've never seen anything like it in your life. I thought I'd died and gone back to my boyhood. I mean, talk about scout hut – I'm surprised we didn't have to sleep in iron-framed bunk beds.

'It was two to a room, not counting the cockroaches, and about one bathroom between six people, in at ten or you got locked out, breakfast at eight on the dot or you lucked out – although you could always eat the mushrooms growing on the ceiling if you got too hungry. Oh, well,' he sighs, 'the conference was all about team-building; three nights in that hotel taught us more than any of the lectures.'

'Tell me about it,' I agree. 'In some of these places it's survival of the fittest, and the bed bugs are usually more acclimatised than you are . . .'

'And better fed,' he jokes. 'At least they're always guaranteed to get room service.'

I've never found it so easy to talk to somebody that I don't know. Come to think of it, it's easier to have a conversation with Jake than it is with some people I *do* know pretty well.

He's bright and witty, and the time that I spend talking to him flows as freely as the alcohol Aidan keeps pouring into my glass. Every time it hits the bar empty, my new friend swoops in like a Saint Bernard on a rescue mission and tops me up.

By the time last orders is a distant memory, and the pumps are fast asleep under their beer mat blankets,

it's just me, Jake, a rather good bottle of Pouilly
Fumé, and an open fire.

The lights have been turned off and we sit side by
side in the warm flickering golden light of the fire,
nursing our glasses and chatting like old friends.

Up close, there are lines around his eyes, lines that
crease when he smiles. In the past few hours I've
discovered that Jake smiles a lot. I've also discovered
that we both love to travel, share the same tastes in
music and a mutual appreciation of good food and
wine. We've briefly touched on politics, argued about
sexual equality, told several bad jokes, and now we're
both pretty drunk in a warm, happy relaxed kind of
way.

Jake picks up the bottle which is placed between us
on the floor. It's empty.

'Fancy another?'

'If I have any more to drink you'll have to get a
doctor out!' I giggle.

'Why, does it make you ill?'

'No, but you'll get a bad back lugging me up two
flights of stairs to my room after I pass out.'

'Well, how about that guided tour then?' He looks
sideways at me, the soft light from the flames flickering over his face like a caress, and raises his eyebrows
questioningly.

I look at the grandfather clock ticking quietly away
in one corner of the room. It's gone midnight.

'Do you really think we should at this time of
night? What about the other residents?'

'Passed out by now, I should think, judging by the
quantity of alcohol that was consumed in this bar
tonight.

'How about it?' he asks, standing up and holding out a hand. 'I can show you the folly where Lady Elizabeth Beauchamp was caught in a secret tryst with a local monk, and murdered by her jealous husband . . . and the avenue where a ghost is said to walk each night, carrying his head under his arm, after being butchered by his own brother.'

'Well, with incentives like that, how can I refuse?'

Outside the night sky is a throw of black velvet, with stars strewn across its surface like glitter flung by an unseen hand. It's warm, a soft breeze ruffling the leaves on the trees so that they whisper in the darkness.

Jake leads me around to the back of the house, every sound, no matter how small, eerily magnified in the quiet of the night.

'These are the formal gardens,' he stage whispers.

'Never?' I reply sarcastically.

'Look, I'm the guide, okay? I'm supposed to be giving you a tour, and you're supposed to be rapt with attention at everything I say.'

'Okay. Sorry.' I stifle a smile and attempt to regain a straight face. 'Is this okay?'

'What?'

'Do I look rapt enough for you?'

He promptly puts me in a head lock, and frog-marches me out on to the lawn.

'I'm the Priory ghost,' I giggle, breathing in the lemony tang of his aftershave.

'These are the formal gardens,' he repeats, silencing any further interruptions from me with a mock glare. 'Said to have been designed by Calamity Jones . . .'

I start to sing 'Whip Crackaway'.

He lets go of my head and sits down in the middle of the lawn.

'Okay, shan't guided tour you then,' he slurs, pretending to be highly offended.

'Oh, please, please, please, please, pleeeeease. I promise I won't interrupt. Why don't you show me the spot where Lady Elizabeth had her bunk up with the sex maniac monk?'

'Who said it was the monk that was a sex maniac?' he mutters, pretending to sulk. 'It could have been Lady Liz who did all the chatting up.'

'Oh, come on, it's usually the man who makes the first move.'

'Untrue!' he states categorically. 'Complete crap.'

'Trust me, it was the monk.' I slump down next to him. 'He led her into bad habits . . . "Would you like to take a little communion in my cassock your lady-ship?", "Boy, have I got an interesting holy relic down my underpants, your ladyship", "This isn't the only shaved and shiny head I've got – wanna see the other one?", "Honestly, your ladyship, naked flagellation is good for the soul", "But, your lordship, I thought you said to treat her ladyship to a religiously good serv-ice?" '

Jake's sulky face finally cracks and splits into a huge grin.

'Now are you going to show me where Lady Liz lost it or what?' I cajole.

He gets to his feet, takes both my hands, and hauls me up.

'Walk this way,' he mouths, and begins to stagger across the lawn, still clutching on to one of my hands.

I stagger after him, bum slightly damp from the night dew on the grass. He tows me around the side of the east wing, through a kitchen garden that smells of a wonderful confusion of tarragon and thyme, parsley, mint, basil, and other herbs I can't spell.

'Don't tell me,' I giggle, doing a Vincent Price impression, 'this is the kitchen garden where walks at midnight the ghost of some mad French chef, meat cleaver in one hand, garlic bulb in the other, looking for some poor unsuspecting victim to try out his new recipes on . . .'

I stop short as we cut through a box hedge, and realise that we are by the swimming pool.

'Lady Liz bonked the monk in the pool?' I blink up at him in confusion. 'Don't tell me, she was disgraced after having a water baby nine months later?'

'I don't think the pool was here in the late-seventeenth century.'

'Of course it wasn't, how silly of me.' I hiccup softly. 'They hadn't invented swimming costumes then, had they?'

'Nope,' he replies. 'They'd have had to have gone skinny dipping.'

We look at each other, then at the pool lying inky black and dappled silver by the moonlight, its surface gently undulating like silk blown in a soft breeze. Look at each other again, grin inanely, and in unspoken agreement start to run towards it, whooping and hollering like children.

We get to the edge of the pool and I balk. I'm still fully clothed, and the black water looks suddenly icy. I make a sort of mad dash to the very last Cotswold stone paving slab then stop dead just before I fall, teetering on the edge like a spinning top about to topple over.

Not Jake. Slowing only enough to grin at me as he flies past, he launches himself forward and straight into the water, the splashback as he hits the surface soaking my feet and lower legs.

He resurfaces, blowing water like a whale, merry eyes dancing with laughter. 'Coward! Get your arse in here now!' he calls, hands rotating like a sea lion's flippers as he floats on his back fifteen feet away from me.

I frown dubiously.

'I'm very drunk,' I call back, 'but although the alcohol might be insulating my brain, it's not going to insulate my body, is it?'

'It's heated.'

Still I hesitate.

'Come on in, the water's lovely.'

'Haven't I heard that line before?' I reply dubiously. 'Alex!'

I kick off one shoe, and dip in a stockinged toe.

'Doesn't feel very heated to me,' I mutter, as lukewarm water soaks the silk.

'It's hotter than it looks.' He grins, rolling on to his stomach and swimming over to me, arms cutting strongly through the water.

Still hesitating on the edge, I shriek as his hand curls around my ankle. One swift jerk and I'm off balance and falling.

He catches me just before I go under, and rights me. I'm gasping at the sudden shock, hair streaming wetly into my eyes. He gently pushes damp locks out of my face, and for a moment I think he's going to kiss me, but he simply grins wickedly at me and swims away, Patrick Duffy in *The Man from Atlantis*, body wriggling like an eel as he surface dives and disappears into the cut glass blackness of the water.

I tread water, enjoying the feel of it, soft, warm and caressing against my skin.

'It's gorgeous,' I call after he surfaces at the other end of the pool.

'Told you. Do you think I'd have been so cruel as to tip you in here if it wasn't?'

He disappears underwater again and resurfaces just in front of me, dripping like a seal, holding my lost shoes.

'There's only one problem,' I continue as he lobs my dead Pied à Terre pair on to the side of the pool.

'Oh, yeah? What's that then?'

'I think I'm sinking.' My water-logged clothes suddenly feel like they weigh more than I do. I manage a brave wave as I disappear below the surface weighted down by one hundredweight of sopping cashmere.

Jake hauls me upright once again.

'*Baywatch* eat your heart out,' I giggle as he tows me to the side.

'I was thinking more along the lines of Greenpeace,' he mutters through gritted teeth. 'You know, save the whale?'

'Well, I know I'm no Pamela Anderson . . .' I mutter huffily.

'If you were Pamela Anderson, you'd bloody well float on your own,' he grumbles.

Leaving me clutching gratefully to the side of the pool, he gets out first, then taking my hand, hauls me out of the water.

I stand there in my sopping wet black cashmere looking like a drowned mole. He has drops of water on the ends of his eyelashes. His eyes don't look bluey-green in this light, they look a sort of sludgey brown, but they're still laughing.

Still holding on to my hand, he lifts his other hand and rubs a line of black mascara from under my eye with his thumb. The thumb dips, traces the contour of my cheek bone, then runs softly, caressingly, over my lips.

With my shoes off he is a little over two inches taller than me – a good height, I find, for our bodies to slot together comfortably as we draw close in an embrace.

We kiss. How can I describe the way it feels as our lips meet and move together, as our tongues slide against each other, warm and wet and caressing? Perhaps it's like the feel of the very first rays of a summer sun gently stroking your naked flesh, or the juice of ripe strawberries flowing into your mouth with the first bite of succulent fruit. Pretty poetic for me, but hell, this is a sensation I haven't experienced before. His mouth is more tempting and more delicious than anything Cadbury's could ever create. It's like delving into a bag of chocolate raisins. You just can't stop eating them, compelled to indulge until you've totally overindulged.

Instant sexual chemistry.

The thing is, according to the ground rules I'm supposed to be the one who does the picking up, so will this count?

Sod the ground rules! flashes through my mind as his kiss moves lower. It was a pretty mutual picking up anyway. Isn't that what equality is all about? A mutual effort in something.

'I've got a pretty good bottle of brandy in my room.' His lips and breath brush against my neck as he speaks.

I smile my agreement, and he takes my hand.

We tiptoe, dripping, up the stairs, shoes in hand, giggling like teenagers.

The brandy is forgotten the minute we step inside the door.

He pulls me to him and we begin to kiss again, my arms automatically twining about him, my hands caressing his neck, gently stroking the soft close-cropped hair at the back of his head, pulling him closer to me.

I wait for the usual warning bells, the automatic body shut down, but I'm waiting in vain. The longer we kiss, the more turned on I become. Even when I open my eyes the feeling remains, increases even, as his own eyes, which were closed too, open lazily, and smile down at me.

This shouldn't feel so comfortable and relaxed. I don't know this man. I met him three hours ago, and now I'm standing here in his bedroom buzzing with desire as he pulls my cashmere dress over my head and lets it fall to the floor.

It's like I've stepped out of reality. Is it really my hands that are undoing the buttons of his soaking wet Ralph Lauren shirt, and my mouth that is tracing the curve of his neck? My tongue that is running lightly yet greedily over his nipples as I push his shirt away from his broad shoulders?

Gradually we undress each other, breath intermingling, fingers slipping under material to meet flesh.

He has a broad chest, strong arms, good legs, and a cute bum. But what is immediately striking to me is the difference between him and Max. Max was slim and lithe and pretty and – well, I see it now, Max was a boy.

Jake is, in every sense of the word, a man.

'You're beautiful,' he murmurs, hands gently squeezing the full flesh of my breasts, the tips of his fingers running teasingly across my nipples as they stiffen ecstatically at his touch.

So are you, I reply mentally, loving the strong muscular feel of his body, revelling in the contrast with the softness of his skin under my fingertips.

We fall back upon the bed together, sheets twisting, lips and limbs brushing, hands, mouths and minds exploring, savouring. Roughly gentle, languidly urgent.

How can something so hard, feel so soft? Skin, velvet and hot to the touch. I have an uncontrollable longing to take him in my mouth and taste him, to run my tongue along every curve and line and bump and ridge, as his own tongue wanders lazily across the most sensitive parts of my body.

I used to get bored before it even started with Max. Now I just want this to go on forever and never to stop. The feel of his skin, the smell and the taste of him, are dizzyingly erotic. I place a finger under his chin and pull him to me, tasting myself on his lips and tongue.

I wake, feel him lying alongside me, his body against mine, his soft breath warm against the back of my neck, his arm encircling my waist.

It's still dark, but birds are singing somewhere outside.

Now what do I do? What does it say in the rules about afterwards? Do I just lie here and enjoy the feel of his skin against mine, bask in the wonderful warm afterglow that is still tingling through my body like the after effects of a violent electric shock? I'm amazed at how comfortable it feels to be lying in the arms of a practical stranger, how good his skin feels against mine.

My eyelids flutter shut, the regular rise and fall of his chest lulling me back towards sleep.

My eyes snap open.

I haven't done this before. I can't stay here and sleep. I can't wake up in the morning and face him. Gently, I pull away.

He murmurs in his sleep and rolls over on to his front, face suddenly illuminated by the dawn light streaming in through the gap in the gauzy curtains, long golden-brown eyelashes curled against the soft down of his cheek.

How could I have thought his face was just *nice*? He has a beautiful face. Strong, well defined, and beautiful.

Play by the rules, Lex, I remind myself. Love 'em and leave 'em.

Besides, I'm probably just another notch on his bedpost, which judging by the pure artistry with which he makes love is a scored mass of marked wood.

God, just thinking about last night sends my stomach shooting into my diaphragm with desire.

I tentatively reach out and run a soft caress across

the smooth firm skin of his back, then snatch my hand back, like I've done something wrong.

Oh, boy, am I confused.

I just want to get dressed and get out of here.

I want to leave him my phone number.

No, I want to sod going back to work and stay in this warm and welcoming haven with my newly discovered love god forever.

He stirs, mouth moving silently in sleep.

I long to kiss him again, to feel his mouth against mine . . .

I can't wake him up. How can I face him again after . . . after . . . I feel my insides begin to melt. It's a strange sensation, your mind telling you to run, and your body begging you to stay and do it again, and to hell with the consequences, to hell with having to face an almost total stranger who's explored more of you than . . . Time to go. I mean, I'll always know where to find him, won't I?

Chanting 'Love 'em and leave 'em, love 'em and leave 'em' like a mantra, I pull on my still-sodden dress, hurry back to my room, and pack at lightning speed.

Downstairs, I wake the dozing night receptionist, pay my bill and slip out to the car park.

Outside it's at the point where night is just morphing into day, where the moon is momentarily brighter than the sun before fading into a shadow, palely insignificant beside her brilliance.

I've had about two hours sleep, so why do I feel like I'm walking a few inches off the ground, like I'm treading a bouncy castle with delicate footsteps?

Sod the book, I've just discovered the real joy of sex.

My next stop is the holiday camp from hell. I'm going to be half a day early for a place I never wanted to go to in the first place, but I'm singing all the way down the M5.

## Chapter Six

I lug suitcase, overnight bag, laptop, myself, up the stairs of the mews, and collapse wearily, but happily, on the top step.

'Heeelllllooooo.' Emma bounds out of the kitchen waving a potato-encrusted metal masher, and hugs me affectionately, smearing spud into my hair with her enthusiasm.

'God, it seems like ages since you went away,' she cries, squeezing the last ounce of strength out of my knackered body. 'You know, I *really* missed you.'

I don't know whether to be flattered by the fact that she missed me, or insulted by the fact that she seems so surprised about it.

She lets go of me, and thoughtfully licks potato from her fingers.

'I must have got used to having your miserable face around the place . . .'

Okay, I take the insulted option. I attempt to look offended, but it doesn't work. This stupid smirk is sitting on my face, and flatly refusing to get off. It's been there for eight days now, miraculously surviving the Howkins Holiday experience, apparently undaunted by the compulsory clock golf, the

Hawaiian evening with grass skirts made from astro turf and Pina Coladas that were all Pina and nothing else, the early-morning twenty decibel surround sound speaker wake-up call, the stand-up comedian bluer than a bottle of Azure Bay and about as funny as a painfully heavy period.

Oh, and singing for your supper. Two rounds of 'Oh, I Do Like to Be Beside the Seaside', before being granted the dubious pleasure of shepherd's pie made with reconstituted potato, and peas that stayed as bullet-hard cooked as they were frozen. Yet still I look like Jim Carrey on speed.

Emma stares at me curiously.

'Now that's something else I haven't seen for a while.' She inspects my smile like an expert on the Antiques Road Show. 'Alex Gray's smile, very rare piece, last seen in about 1992, one-off original, totally priceless.'

Emma tilts her head to one side as she observes me, then begins prowling round me like a big cat moving in for the kill.

'You did it, didn't you?' she says eventually, peering into my face as though inspecting it for blemishes.

Is it that obvious? I mean, I was tempted to get a T-shirt printed, but there's obviously no need, it's emblazoned all over me.

'You've only bloody well gone and shagged someone, haven't you?' Emma states bluntly.

I simply continue to smile.

Eat your heart out Mona Lisa.

'What was it like . . . what was he like . . . was it good . . . did you enjoy it . . . who was he . . .' She shoots a volley of questions at me, giving me no time to answer any of them, in fact not really needing answers, just waiting to see if the stupid grin slips from my face at all.

It doesn't. Not even the smallest fraction of a slip occurs. The grin, cheesier than extra mature Cheddar, remains as firmly fixed as a broken mug handle set with Araldite. In fact, the grin stays put for some time. Even when Emma instantly phones all of our friends to spread the good news, inviting Serena round for a chalking ceremony celebrated with sausage, mash, Diet Coke, and a million and one questions.

It only begins to slip a little when I wake up four days later on Monday morning and realise that I've got to go in to work today. You know, work, where Dayglo Damien lurks.

I slide into the office like James Bond on a mission to stay incognito. The temperature has become positively balmy, the sort of fresh pretty weather as portrayed in clothes softener adverts where you bung some nice fragrant liquid in your washing machine, and suddenly get transported into the opening scene of *The Sound of Music*.

Well, anyway, despite the gentle heat fanning London's dusty Monday morning commuters, I'm togged up in full secret agent outfit, from my dark glasses to my ankle-length raincoat, with Emma's Portobello Road rat hat (big and made of some sort of unidentified synthetic fur) pulled down over my ears.

I don't know why I'm dressed like this. The plan is to slide past Damien unnoticed, but due to the fact that everyone else around me is floating about in summer gear, I stand out like a polar bear in a cage full of plucked parrots.

I return the hat to the wild in the small park I pass through, between the tube station and the office, where a grey squirrel promptly falls in love with it. Immediately I get into work, I realise the place is different somehow. I know Rodney's gone, but that's not it.

I take off my dark glasses which are making everything from little Jenny to the computers look jaundiced.

That's not it.

*I* feel different. *Boy*, do I feel different. Despite the fact that I'm overly conscious of my absolute desire to avoid Damien for as long as possible, I'm still on a pretty good après-amazing-sex high. But it's not that either.

Somehow, there appears to have been a total change in atmosphere in the office. The old laid back ambience has gone.

Then I realise what it is. It's ten o'clock on a Monday morning. I'm normally one of the first ones in, but today everybody's already here, and instead of the usual groups ranged about the room, chatting about their weekends, drinking coffee, laughing and joking, they're all working. I mean, actually at their workstations, computer keys tapping, telephones ringing, photocopier zapping, working!

Then I remember. Two weeks ago – Rodney retires. Last week – New Boss starts. It's all becoming clearer.

I seek out Mary for enlightenment.

She's at her desk.

I can tell this because her desk is almost spotless.

Usually, you have to hunt for Mary behind piles of cookery books, free samples, wilting pot plants, and files spewing out sheaths of paper covered in ideas and recipes.

'Mare! What on earth's going on in this place?'

'Hi, Lexy!' Mary looks up, her golden-brown curls bobbing, and grins. 'Welcome back to the Hive of Industry.'

'I take it this is all the doing of the new boss?' I indicate the said industry with a sweep of my hand.

She nods.

'Sure is.'

'Wow, the new broom must really be sweeping clean?'

'He's not a new broom,' Mary giggles. 'He's one of those supersonic Hoovers with attachments. Brrrrm!' she revs jokingly.

'What's he like?'

'Wonderful.' She indicates the wall behind her head, where the assorted debris from her desk is now stacked neatly on ranks of carved beech. 'Look, he got me my shelves. I asked . . . nay, I pleaded and *begged* Rodney to get me some shelves for the whole two years I've been here . . . and within one week of Jack Daniels starting I have them. Doesn't that tell you something?'

'Jack Daniels? You're joking, aren't you?'

She laughs, but shakes her head.

'But that's a drink.'

'Yeah, I know, and he's a real tonic, I can tell you!'

'Where's Damien?'

'Away on an assignment, back next week. Why?'

Good. A minor reprieve.

'Oh, nothing. Just wondered.' I perch on the edge of Mary's desk, wondering whether to fish, or just to wait and see if he's said anything, because if he has, I dare say I'll find out sooner rather than later. Never one to want to wait for anything, I decide to fish.

'Maaary . . .' I use my best I'm-not-really-interested-but-tell-me-anyway voice. 'Has Damien said anything to anybody about – well about Rodney's leaving do?'

'Nothing other than complaining that Glenda's crab cakes gave him food poisoning. He didn't come in for a few days afterwards. Why?'

'Oh, nothing.' I slide off the desk and begin to head towards my own. 'Nothing at all. See you later.'

Somebody's been at my desk with the Mr Sheen. My computer, which normally looks like Stig of the Dump sitting amidst its own electrically generated dust cloud, is gleaming brightly. It's cream. I've never realised that but always thought it was a browny sort of beige. The African violet which has been sitting in deathly, crisp-leaved, rigor mortis on my desk for the past six months, has been removed and replaced by a large, glossy-leaved, very green and very alive something or other that looks a little bit like a cross between cannabis and a money plant. This could be good for staff morale. Grow your own dope or dosh.

I even have a desk tidy, a little red cylindrical thing into which some kind soul has shovelled my stolen biros and paper clip necklace.

It's a very weird sensation to go away for a week and come back to total change. It's a little bit disconcerting. I feel like I've walked into a remake of *The Stepford Wives*. The Stepney Hacks.

The new boss is obviously a fast worker. It was rumoured that he was some hot shot being sent in to shake us all up a bit. It would appear that for once the rumours are true. I hardly recognise my fellow workmates as they scuttle round the office, looking busy. I mean, I know looking busy is something they've managed to perfect over the years without actually *being* busy, but trust me, this is the real thing.

They have some strange motivational practices in those Asian countries. Perhaps he's got everybody doing communal exercise and chanting before they start work every morning. Perhaps we'll all end up in little matching high-collared blue suit numbers, bowing to his effigy as we walk in the door. Or is that Japanese rather than Hong Kongese?

The most radical change, however, is in our Sand. Our Sand is our Sand no more. She has metamorphosed from a big hairy caterpillar into . . . well, a big hairy caterpillar in a posh frock.

She is wearing what is obviously an eighteen-hour girdle with built-in Wonderbra forcing her almost non-existent bust into cleavage-inducing life. Forget Wonderbra. This one must be a MiracleBra. Where can I get one?

She's shaved off her moustache and has had her hair styled into lots of tiny kiss curls which feather forward flatteringly over her face to hide a multitude of sins, including the receding hairline, laughter lines and several broken veins. She has also slid her constrained body into a chiffon floral offering so feminine, floaty and diaphanous, she should be wearing a matching hat and wafting around the gardens of Buck Palace with a Spode bone china cup of Earl Gray in one hand and a piece of strawberry shortcake in the other. Far, far different from her usual slacks and baggy cardi, I can tell you.

The new boss is obviously an improvement on Rampant Rodney to have had this amazing transformational effect on our Sandra.

Even her voice when she says 'Hello' as I walk into the office has lost some of its gravel-in-a-coffee-grinder quality. She now sounds deep, low and husky, as opposed to butch.

I decide to do some digging in her direction.

'So what's he like then, our new boss?'

'Oh, Mr Daniels is a lovely, lovely man!' She beams.

Sandra doesn't talk like this. She doesn't call people *Mr* So and So, she'd never describe anybody as lovely, lovely, and she quite simply *does not* beam at people. I decide that the real Sandra has been abducted by aliens, and is probably even as we speak having strange experiments carried out on her recumbent body whilst this replicant floats around our office like Princess Margaret interbred with Fatima Whitbread. Could I sell the story to the *Sport*, I wonder?

Sandra's inter-office line rings.

'Yes, this is Sandie. Of course, Mr Daniels. Right away, Mr Daniels.'

Sandie (?!?) leaves me standing open-mouthed as she practically skips into the inner sanctum. It's like watching a grouchy old nag suddenly transformed into a skittish young mare by the arrival of a sleek young stallion. Our new boss must be something pretty special to have had this radical an effect on Sandra's hormones. This could be interesting. Then again, just because Sandra is obviously already infatuated with him doesn't mean that he's gorgeous. She has pretty suspect taste when it comes to men. I mean, she's carried a picture of Barry Manilow in her wallet for the past eighteen years.

I try to get a peek into the inner sanctum, but Sandra skips in like a frisky lamb and pulls the door sharply to behind her. All the blinds are down, shrouding Rodney's old office in privacy and some mystery. I can't see in, but I have a vision of Sandra – sorry, Sandie – heaving her bum on to the edge of the desk, crossing her thunderous thighs in their new seamed stockings, and offering to take dictation or do a short hand job.

I'm getting worried.

I sidle over to Mary's desk again, where she is sorting through several colour photographs taken by Big Eric of assorted Pavlovas.

'Is he really nice, or are you just letting me down gently?'

'Who?' Mary looks up from a huge blob of meringue, raspberries and cream.

'The new boss, of course.'

'You haven't seen him yet?'

'I haven't been here, have I?'

'I know, away on another jaunt,' she sighs enviously. 'What wouldn't I do to swap the delights of readers' recipes and taste testing for your job.'

'Well, if you're doing chocolate fudge cake, I'll swap you for my two days in Aviemore next month.'

She wrinkles her nose endearingly at me.

'I'm doing perfect picnics as the weather's picked

up. Perhaps you could combine the two and save me the effort. Aviemore Alfresco?'

'I don't know about that. Every time I go to Scotland it rains. How about Picnic in a Puddle?'

'Hello, children!' a melodious voice calls across the office. It's Astral Astrid, our resident astrologist, dropping off her horoscopes for the week.

Despite the fact that her publicity shot has her done up like Mystic Meg on a gypsy kick, Astral Astrid is in fact perfectly normal Nuala from Neasden, a charmingly pretty middle-aged ex-Dublin housewife, in sweatshirt, blue jeans and canvas pumps. She looks about as mystical as a town centre supermarket.

As usual everybody wants to know their horoscope for the coming week. I grab mine.

*Aries: With Neptune in your solar system you could be in for some difficult times ahead.* Tell me something I don't know. *But rise above the storm and you will weather it.* Very punny, Nuala. *Expect a week of big surprises, with passion being found in unexpected places.*

'I don't know what you're reading those for,' she drawls in her beautiful Irish brogue, 'they're a load of focking crap. I should know, I write the bloddy things. Now, who's going to make me a cup of tea? I've been stuck on the focking tube for hours and I'm as parched as a dried up oasis.'

Passion in unusual places, eh? Perhaps I should start hanging out somewhere different. I know the accepted pick-up joints are pubs, clubs, all-night laundrettes, and Sainsbury's, but if I want to increase the score on my bedroom door, perhaps I should be heading off for llama riding in the West Country, orienteering in Milton Keynes, or bungee jumping off Tower Bridge.

And what about the difficult times? Could this be a reference to the mysterious Jack Daniels? Will I actually have to start working to keep my job?

'Oi, Nuala,' I yell at her, 'what's the week got in store for Arians work wise?'

'Oh, absolutely terrible . . .' she calls back, diving gratefully on Sandra who's just reappeared with a tea trolley.

'Really?' My heart sinks.

'How the hell should I bloody know?' She laughs. 'But if you don't get back to your desk and do some bloody work before Mr Daniels comes out of his lair, you won't need a mystic to predict you'll be in big trouble.'

Sandra wheels across the room, tea trolley clattering over the pale blue carpet. Perched temptingly on a plate are a heap of glistening brown chocolate digestives, an unheard of treat in this place where the tea totes idea of exotic is a packet of Nice.

'Ooh, choccy biccies.' I reach out.

Sandra practically slaps my hand.

'They're for Mr Daniels,' she snorts.

'Daniels doesn't sound very Chinese.' I sulkily go for a far more inferior plain biccy and get away with this theft unreprimanded.

Sandra still looks at me in outrage, however, but it's not over the stolen biscuit.

'He's not.'

I look confused.

'I should have thought a travel writer would know that you don't have to be Chinese to live and work in

Hong Kong,' she says archly, and flounces off amidst a swirl of chiffon frills, jealously protecting her precious choccy biscuits from marauding hands.

I attempt not to go red with embarrassment.

'Of course I know that,' I mutter. 'It would help if I was a travel writer who occasionally got sent somewhere more exotic than Clacton-on-Sea, though.'

'Perhaps you should work on Mr Daniels . . . ask for a few locations where you have to get to your destination by aeroplane instead of car,' suggests Mary, convinced of our new boss's bounteous nature by virtue of the acquisition of her new shelves.

'Yeah, sure. "Excuse me, new boss, but you know I'm due to go to Scotland next month for two days? How about shipping me out to the Seychelles for two weeks instead? It would make much better copy . . ." As if!'

'Well, I got my shelves,' Mary points out happily.

'I think two planks of wood and a few brackets are rather more within the budget than white sandy beaches, palm trees and cocktails.' I sigh heavily. 'Though, god knows I could do with a proper holiday after the past few weeks.'

Mary puts a sympathetic hand over mine.

'Still hung up on Max?'

'Max who?' I jest.

'I take it that's a no, then?'

'Well, let's just say I feel a lot better about myself in certain directions.' I consider telling Mary about my night of mind-blowing passion, but don't. I'm not the only one she gossips with, bless her. Besides I still have very mixed emotions on that front myself. I've picked up the phone to dial The Priory and apologise for my disappearing act about thirty times in the past couple of days, and wimped out each time.

'I'm just tired, Mare, I could do with a break.'

She looks at me curiously.

'What aren't you telling me, Alex? Come on, out with it. You know I can't abide secrets I'm not in on.'

I think of my night at The Priory, and fight the grin that's threatening to spread across my face.

'Look, I'll tell you all about it later over a coffee, okay?' I lie, removing my bum from the edge of her desk. 'This new air of activity is pretty catching. I feel kind of awkward being the only one not doing anything constructive.'

I go back to my desk and begin to transfer my notes on the last couple of weeks from my portable to my PC.

Predictably my report on The Priory is pretty glowing.

I give the place my highest star rating. I'm not being biased. I had a good time there, didn't I?

Perhaps Jake will read the write up and then he'll realise that I looked familiar to him because of the photograph next to my byline. Maybe, just maybe, he'll get in touch and ask for a return game. Are two-night stands allowed in the game rules? I doubt it, it doesn't go with the hit and run policy, but oh, for a full action replay!

Despite my determination to be industrious, I allow myself a little fantasy. Indulge myself by replaying the events of that night in my head like a favourite movie, to be screened over and over.

I imagine Jake's face . . . and then I move on to other interesting parts. It's amazing how every detail of that man is etched so deeply into my mind. The way he looks, the way he feels, the way he smells, the touch of his skin against mine.

I can see him now, it's almost as though he's standing there in front of me, fully clothed of course, because we're in the office, but . . .

'Morning, Mr Daniels.' Lucian sweeps past with his post trolley. Hang on a second, how did he get into my dream? I'm at work . . . shit! I jerk upright. The new boss is in the office, and I have to doze off on my desk!

Okay, if I'm awake how come I can still see Jake? Admittedly he's now fully clothed, but he's walking past Mary's desk as large as life.

'Morning, Mr Daniels,' she simpers.

He smiles broadly. I'd know that smile anywhere.

Mr Daniels. Jack Daniels. Jake?

Oh my god, I'm going to die.

If I'm not going to die, I wish I was.

Somebody tell me I'm asleep and dreaming? I am, I'm still asleep. That's what it is, I'm asleep and having a nightmare.

Time to wake up. I pinch myself. Hard.

'Ow!'

'Alex, what are you doing?' Mary looks over as I shriek with pain.

'Just checking to see if I'm awake,' I reply, rubbing my bruised arm.

'Well,' you'd better be,' she hisses. 'Because that's the new boss over there, and I don't think you'd make a very good first impression if he found you fast asleep on your computer.'

'What sort of first impression do you think I'd make if I abandoned my clothes, abandoned my inhibitions and leapt into bed with him?' I blather stupidly.

'You what?' Mary's eyebrows hit the ceiling. 'What are you on this morning, Alex?'

'I don't know,' I reply, 'but Prozac would be nice.'

I watch as Jake walks across the room, smiling good morning to everybody. Boy, do I remember that smile. It was one of the first things I noticed about him. The casual clothes have gone. He's wearing a grey Armani suit, the hair's a little shorter too, but there's no doubt that the man I see before me is the man I saw below me, and above me, and from various other different angles, one wonderful night less than two weeks ago.

I realise that Mary's talking to me.

'. . . apparently his father used to call him Jack as a joke because he was a publican or something along those lines.'

'Hotelier,' I reply dazedly watching Jake go back into his office.

'Yeah, that's right, a hotelier,' she continues. 'Hey, how do you know . . .'

Without answering, I shoot up from my desk and, leaving a bemused Mary behind me, scuttle out of the office with my head down, and make for the ladies' loos.

Fortunately, they're empty.

I try a spot of deep breathing to calm myself down. It doesn't work. What is it they do in those American soap things? Breathe into a paper bag! That's it, I'll breathe into a paper bag. On second thoughts, I won't. The only paper bags to hand are the sanitary towel disposal ones, and I don't really fancy shoving one of those over my gob.

I splash water on my hot red face, and then lean my forehead against the cool hard mirror above the basin, suppressing an urge to bang my head hard, several times, against the wall.

Why, why, why? This could only happen to me. First Larry, then Damien, and now this. Why do I have such a capacity to dump on my own doorstep? Then again, I didn't know I *was* dumping on my own doorstep. How the hell was I supposed to predict that the first man I decide to add to my list was going to end up as my boss? Even Nuala couldn't have foreseen that one.

I suddenly have a horrible thought. Is this why I got sent to review The Priory in the first place? Did he know who I was all along? Did he sleep with me to get a good review? Now I am getting ridiculous. I give myself a mental slap around the chops. 'Pull yourself together, Alex,' I tell my panic-stricken reflection. I take a few deep breaths and feel a little better.

Now what the hell do I do? I spent a night of wild and totally abandoned passion with the most attractive man I've ever met. I follow the rules. I walk out. Only to find the next week, that I'm bloody working for him! How am I supposed to face him? If I couldn't face him the following morning, how the hell am I supposed to do it now?

What on earth must he think of me?

I've got the urge to walk out the door and keep on walking.

My mother used to say, 'What goes around, comes around.'

I've got a new version. 'If you come and then go, it comes back to haunt you.'

As it is I crawl back to my desk with my face hidden behind one hand and reposition the new plant and my computer so that you'd need X-ray specs to see who was sitting behind them.

I know I can't hide from him forever. This man's my boss. I could quit, but I'd still have to face him to do that. I have visions of marching into his office wearing a paper bag over my head, telling him that I've developed an overwhelming case of agoraphobia and I need to work from home from now on. The problem is a travel writer can't be an agoraphobic, 'cause agoraphobics travel about as well as a month-old cling-film-wrapped cheese sandwich on the London to Glasgow overnighter.

'Alex . . . helloooo . . . earth calling Alex.'

I peer over the top of my plant to see Nigel standing in front of my desk, notebook in one hand, pen in the other.

'Come on.' He jerks with his head towards the inner sanctum, the Editor's office.

'What's going on?'

'Editorial meeting,' he replies. 'Have one every morning now.'

'You're kidding?'

Editorial meetings? We used to kick a few ideas around over morning coffee. Either that or just pick an idea, then go out and get on with it.

Taking a firm mental grip, and holding a huge red folder in front of my even redder face, I follow Nigel, scurry into Jake's office and head for the darkest corner. I know these guys, nobody's going to bother to introduce me, so I figure I can just slide in unnoticed and sit down, stay behind the folder for the entire meeting, and then go back to hiding behind a pot plant for the rest of my working life.

Unfortunately, as I pass his desk, I realise he's looking at me expectantly, waiting for me to introduce myself.

'Er . . . hello.' I peer above the folder, my top set of eyelashes blinking against its plastic edge. 'I'm Alex . . . er . . . Alexandra Gray.' I hold out a very tentative hand, the one that isn't keeping the red folder firmly over my face.

'Ah, yes. Travel. Pleased to meet you, Alexandra.' He stands up and shakes my hand without even a flicker of recognition. 'Take a seat.'

My heart slowly slides back down my throat and settles behind my rib cage where it resumes beating, still not at its normal rate but at least I know I'm not going to die just yet.

He's acting like he doesn't know who I am.

I don't know whether to be relieved or insulted.

I know it's been a week or so, but I doubt I look so different he doesn't recognise me. I mean, he's seen more of me than my gynaecologist, then again I doubt if he was particularly looking at my face. Maybe if I walked in naked and sat on *his* face he'd find me vaguely familiar? Hey, haven't I seen that twat somewhere before? Maybe he bonked so many women last week we've all rolled into one faceless blur of bodies and marks from one to twenty.

Maybe I'm the latest addition to his own personal list. Or just *maybe* he feels used and abused, and wants to forget it ever happened. I mean how would I have felt if roles had been reversed? If Jake had walked out on me in the middle of the night? He probably hates me. But rules are rules, and I can hardly explain that to him. 'Sorry, Jake, I'd have stayed, but Rule Two clearly states . . .'

I perch on a new leather-upholstered upright, next to a new triffid of a plant, and attempt to disappear amidst the foliage for the duration of the meeting.

As he talks, Jake leans back in his chair, with one leg crossed over the other, so that his left ankle rests against his right knee, totally relaxed but so obviously in charge, in control . . . like he was the other night, relaxed but totally in control. Jeez. I know they say that to combat meeting someone who makes you nervous you should imagine them naked, but this is ridiculous! I shake my head, trying to lose an image of Jake and me, hot, naked and laughing, and replace it with the one that's in front of me now. Jake Daniels. My boss. The man who could have me out of the door with a click of his fingers. This thought sobers me up.

He's also had a pretty sobering effect on my colleagues. I don't think I've ever seen them looking so well . . . sort of perky and enthusiastic, all sitting up straight, wide awake, instead of the usual half asleep or hung over; all ready to chip in with ideas, instead of looking around vaguely at each other in the hope that somebody else will have a flash of inspiration and save them the bother.

Jake just exudes cool calm confidence.

Even Harvey is attempting to impress, and Harvey usually thinks he's too good to have to try to do that.

Jake's looking directly at me now. I think he just asked me a question. I wish I knew what the hell it was.

I tentatively come out from behind my folder, my face finally completely revealed. He doesn't miss a beat.

'As you missed the preliminaries last week Alex, perhaps you'd like to tell me a bit about yourself, and how you perceive your role within *Sunday Best*?'

He's looking me directly in the eyes, that clear gaze holding mine. Thoughts of my job are as far removed from my head as Clacton from the Taj Mahal.

'Er . . .' I reply eloquently.

Great, Alex. A writer who's totally lost for words.

I wait all day for him to pick a quiet moment and say something, to call me into his office, to sack me, to give me a pep talk on the proper etiquette for working relationships – hell, even to offer to chase me round the desk a few times before getting down to some serious sex in his swing chair.

Nothing.

We pass each other in an empty corridor, but he simply looks at me and smiles that devastating smile of his.

It seems to be the new work ethic to leave after the boss. I don't have a problem with this, I've been glued behind my desk most of the day, working my socks off, keeping my head low, only daring to dash to the lav or get a cup of tea when he's out of the office. I have no intention of drawing attention to myself by going home before he does. He finally leaves the office at twenty past eight. There's a collective sigh of relief, and a mass exodus immediately afterwards.

By the time I get back to the mews, it's nearly dark.

'Emma!' I shriek, running into the house, banging doors. 'Emma!'

'I'm in here,' she calls from the kitchen.

She's seated at the table reading a financial report from work that's nearly as thick as the local telephone directory.

Catching sight of me, red-faced and agitated, Ems puts it to one side, pulls out the chair at right angles to her and pats the seat invitingly.

'Calm down and sit down, babe. What's up?'

I sit down at the table next to her, as strung out as a cat's guts in a racket factory, clutching on to the solid edge of the table to steady myself.

'The new boss . . . you're not going to believe this . . .'

'He's gorgeous, he's rich, he's asked you to marry him, and you're going to settle down in the country with a great sex life and two point five kids?' Ems laughs.

'Don't joke about it!'

'You mean, he really is gorgeous and rich and he's asked you to marry him . . .'

'Emma! Cut the crap, this is serious!'

She looks at my panic-stricken face.

'Yes, it is, isn't it? Sorry.' Standing up, she flicks on the kettle, reaches into the cupboard, then sits down again and hands me the biscuit tin.

'Okay, go ahead, I'm listening.'

'The new boss . . .' I pant.

'Yes, we'd already got that far.'

I shoot her a venomous look and she lapses into semi-apologetic silence.

'He's the guy that I . . . well . . . you know . . . not

last week, but the week before . . . the guy that I . . .'

'Had mad passionate wonderful sex with?' She's joking again, little realising that she's hit the nail on the head with one well-aimed wallop.

'Well, yes,' I reply weakly.

'Seriously?' Her mouth moves into gawp mode.

I nod, gnawing at my bottom lip in agitation.

'But how?'

'I don't know!' I shriek. 'Sod's Law, Murphy's Law, some bastard down there who hates my guts! I don't know how, he just is!'

'Come back, Rodney, all is forgiven.' Emma exhales incredulously, then called by the steam from the boiled kettle, throws bags into mugs and slops on hot water.

'What am I going to do?' I attempt to shovel three biscuits into my mouth at the same time.

She thinks for a moment.

'Do you need to do anything?'

'Of course I do,' I mumble through my mouthful, chewing frantically, 'I can't work in the same office as him. I'll have to quit!'

'Don't be so melodramatic.'

'I slept with my boss, Emma,' I say slowly and loudly as though spelling it out to a two year old. 'Admittedly, I had no idea that's who he was at the time, but I've still bonked the new Editor. What's going to happen to me now?'

'Maybe you'll get a promotion?' Ems quips. 'Oh, come on, Lex,' she cajoles, as I do my Dying Swan act, face first on to the table. 'It's not that bad . . . lots of people have slept with their boss. At least it wasn't Rodney.'

She sits back down and hands me a cup of tea.

I peel my face off the table and start to ladle about eight sugars into it out of the earthenware bowl.

Emma looks at me and the sugar spoon, and shakes her head in despair.

'It's good for shock,' I mutter grumpily. 'Why me? Why does this have to happen to me?'

'Of all the newspapers in all the world he has to walk into my office.' Ems does a very bad Bogey impression in a doomed attempt to make me laugh. 'If it's any consolation, it was probably just as awkward for him. What did he say when he saw you?'

'He didn't say anything. He just acted like he didn't actually remember me, like we never actually spent over two hours bringing each other to the peak of sexual excitement. Then again, maybe the sex wasn't as memorable for him as it was for me.' I sniff.

'Ah. Now we're getting to it,' says Ems, looking knowledgeable.

'You what?'

'The real problem. Now we're getting to the root.'

'What are you on about?'

'You're not upset because you've ended up with this guy as your boss. You're upset because he's chosen to pretend that what was, for you, probably the most memorable night of your entire sex life never actually happened.'

'That's not it at all,' I growl, suddenly realising that it is. Well, at least some of it.

'Oh, Ems, what am I going to do?'

'You could ask for an action replay.' She grins.

'Don't be so facetious!'

'Why don't you just play him at his own game then?'

'And what's that? Ludo, Scrabble, Tiddlywinks?'

'Now who's being facetious? What I meant was, if he's pretending it didn't happen, then perhaps you should follow his lead and do the same thing. It might be the best way really. Wipe it from your memory and start with a clean slate.'

'Mmmm.' I consider her words. 'Perhaps you're right.'

The only problem is I can't wipe it from my memory, it's seared across my brain in full mind-blowing Technicolour.

'Just forget it ever happened, it's probably the best way.'

I can't forget it because I don't want to wipe it from my memory. I've only ever had amazing sex once in my life and now I'm supposed just to forget it? Oh, why is life so cruel? I need to have amazing sex again. The sooner the better. Sitting in that hot office earlier, I could smell him. Not just the tangy citrus smell of his aftershave, but the fresh smell of his warm skin. Last time that scent was in my nostrils, the taste of it was also on my tongue . . .

I take my mental equivalent of a cold shower, and think of Damien, naked except for his Mickey Mouse socks and dayglo condom. This has about the same effect on my libido as a high-powered hose of cold water on a small flame.

It's sad, really.

I always thought sex was so over-rated. Emma would rave about a hot night with some hunk or other, and I'd wonder what all the fuss was about.

Now I've finally discovered that I do have a sex drive, and it's not the battle-scarred, rusting, round the clock, 900cc Lada I always thought it to be. It's a fast-paced, full throttle, engine revving, fuel-thirsting Ferrari. I know, I know, Ferraris have sleeker bodies than mine. My eternal regret will be that I didn't discover that I enjoy getting naked with members of the opposite sex until after my best body years. I wasted the cellulite-free, smooth-hipped, tight-bottomed years of my teens being a professional virgin, proud of myself for turning down all offers of casual sex and waiting for Mr Right. Perhaps if I'd taken up some of those offers, I'd have realised how wrong Mr Far-From-Right Max really was far, far sooner. It depresses me to think I could have been experiencing what I did with Jake for the last ten years or more.

What depresses me even more, however, is the thought that I may have to wait another ten years to experience it again. That's if I'm lucky. If I'm unlucky I might never experience mind-blowing sex again *at all*.

The door bell heralds the arrival of Serena. I have to go through the whole scenario again, only this time in more detail because she's one of those people who like to hear about every single moment so that she can visualise as we speak.

She, like Emma, finds the whole thing highly amusing.

I wish I found it as funny as they do.

This is going to be so awkward. Every time I look at the guy, all I can think about is that night in his hotel room, where my clothes and my inhibitions were abandoned with alarming alacrity.

Jake Daniels. The first of the hits on my hit list.

Jake Daniels. My new boss.

Perhaps that's how I should look at it. Two different people. One a memory, the other a reality. The problem is separating them in my head when I'm at work. Every time I looked at Jake today I saw him and me and . . . well, you know what happened.

The week at work passes by pretty uneventfully.

Despite the Chinese whispers about a major shake up, cuts, redundancies, nobody has as yet been shown the door.

Having coasted for two years under the misdirection of rampant Rodney, I'm suddenly hit by a rather gripping desire to hang on to my job.

I work my multi-coloured socks off, the continuous tapping of my computer keys sounding like the rattle of gun fire.

I just hope I'm not for the bullet. My job has never really justified a full-time position, I usually spend about three days out of the week working for the paper and the rest of it writing my novel; this week I've been writing epics for my articles instead of for some as yet unknown publisher.

Fortunately, I don't see that much of Jake, he seems to spend the majority of his time in endless meetings with the men upstairs, but I'm still constantly living on my nerves, ready to dash behind a filing cabinet or deliver something for paste up if he comes too close to my desk.

Come the weekend, I'm determined to relax. I've never worked so hard in my entire life as I have in the past week, and I'm totally knackered. I'm going to sleep late, eat healthily, cut the old alcohol intake, give myself a facial, a manicure and a pedicure, and basically wrap myself up in cotton wool for forty-eight hours.

Unfortunately the arrival of the post late on Saturday morning puts paid to any hopes of a stress-free weekend.

First off I'm rather excited by the delivery of a large cream envelope.

'Party invite!' I grin hopefully at Emma, waving it under her nose as she sits at the kitchen table in her dressing gown, troughing through a huge bowl of homemade fruit salad. She's got a towel wrapped round her hair, which is currently being treated to a hot oil pack, and is attempting to open her mouth without cracking the vile-looking pistachio green beauty mask she's got spread all over her face. Why are they called beauty masks when they make you look so bloody ugly while you're wearing them?

I slit open the thick paper with my unused toast knife and, pulling out the card inside, read the embossed gilt lettering.

'He's got to be joking!' I splutter.

'Who?' Ems chases a lone grape around the bowl with her spoon.

'Max.'

'What's he want this time?'

'He's only sent me a bloody invitation to his bloody wedding hasn't he!'

'You're joking?' Emma abandons the fruit salad and gives me her full attention. The face pack finally gives up and cracks as the frown that normally appears whenever Max's name is mentioned settles over her features.

'I wish I was . . . what am I going to do?' I stare at the gold-embossed invite, holding it at arm's length like it's contaminated or something.

'What do you mean, what are you going to do?' Emma takes it from me and reads it disdainfully. 'The bin's in the corner . . . unless, of course, you fancy a ceremonial burning, in which case my lighter's in my handbag.'

'I can't bin it!'

'Why not? Don't tell me you're actually thinking about going?'

'Well, if I don't go he'll think I'm upset about it.'

'But you are upset about it.'

'Yeah, but not in the way he'll think I'm upset about it. If I don't go he'll think I'm slumped in a dark corner somewhere, sobbing my heart out that it's not me floating down the aisle like a fresh cream Pavlova on legs. What I need to do is buy the biggest hat in the universe, go, get in all the photographs looking abso-bloody-lutely deliriously happy for them both, drinks lots of champagne, eat cake with a smile on my face, and generally have the time of my life.'

'Well, I suppose you could always do a number on the "Has anybody got just cause or impediment" part.'

'Unfortunately there's nothing illegal about marrying an arsehole, is there?'

'Are you sure it's a good idea to go?' Emma scratches her cheek and a green flake floats down into her breakfast. 'I mean, I follow the theory, but if you overdo the "oh so happy to be here" bit, then everybody will think it's just a show, and that you *are* devastated you're not the one in meringue with a net curtain draped over your head.'

'That's a thought . . . Will you come with me? You can tell me if I go too OTT.'

'No way.' Emma firmly shakes her head.

'Pleeassse, it says me and guest.'

'I can't come with you. If you're set on going, you've got to take a man.'

'Really? I suppose I could ask Jem.'

'That's not the kind of man I meant.'

'I didn't realise there was more than one sort.'

'I meant a draped-on-your arm, look-how-much-better-than-you-I-can-do kind of man. A bloody drop dead gorgeous one, who's going to drool all over you all evening like you're the best thing since virtually fat-free cake.'

This sounds like a pretty good idea to me, but there are the practicalities to consider, like who, and how.

'Where am I going to get one of those then?' I ask her.

'You could ask Mason.'

'You really think he fits the criteria?' I snort.

'Damien then?' she says slyly, with just the slightest smile.

'Don't even think about it . . . and if you suggest Larry next, I'll wait till you're asleep and stick wax strips under your armpits.'

'Oooh!' Emma shudders at the thought. 'Well, we'd better go out and find you a man then, hadn't we?'

She scrapes back her chair and stands up.

'Get your cement mixer fired up, my girl, and your face on. We're going out.'

★  ★  ★

An hour later, we're heading down the M25 to a drinks party at Emma's parents' house. 'The things I do for you,' she mutters, hunched over the steering wheel like a demon, foot flat on the accelerator, twenty-eight-year-old engine groaning in protest.

'Do for me? They're *your* parents.'

'Exactly, they're my *parents*,' she replies dryly. 'And I'm actually going to socialise with them from choice!'

'So this party you're dragging me off to, you don't actually want to go there?'

'God, no . . . of course I don't want to. But I've had an idea. You're going to borrow Guy.'

'Borrow who?'

'Guy. He's a friend of my father's. We're going to get him to take you to the wedding.'

'A friend of your father's . . . great!' I moan, pulling at the hem of the indecently short velvet cocktail number Emma poured me into, kicking and screaming. 'I turn up at Max's do with some geriatric cigar-smoking pervert, and everybody's supposed to marvel at how well I've done for myself . . .'

'Alex, not all my dad's friends are just like him, you know. Guy's young, he's rich, he's seriously good-looking, he's single . . .'

'Okay, Ems, what's the catch?'

She grins at me. It's a false smile, a falsely reassuring smile, which worries me far more than the fact she's not looking at the road at the moment.

'Why on earth should there be a catch?' she says far too brightly.

'He's young, rich, devastating to look at, and *still* single?' I tilt my head to one side, 'Come on, Ems.'

'Perhaps he just hasn't met the right woman yet . . .

moron!' she screeches as a Scania lorry moves over from the left lane and cuts her up. Moving into the fast lane, she accelerates past him, the car rattling like an old spin dryer at the end of its cycle, and sticks two fingers up to him in her rear-view mirror.

'Emma! What's the catch?' I stop cowering under the dashboard in abject fear, and heave my bum back into the cracked leather of the broken-springed bucket seat.

'Why should there be a catch? Some men are confirmed bachelors . . .'

'EMMA!'

'Okay, okay.' She shrugs, 'So he's got about as much personality as Orville the duck without a ventriloquist's hand up his bum, but he looks the part. Get him in a tux and he's Timothy Dalton's better-looking brother.'

'Oh, great, so all I have to do is just drag him along and hope he keeps his mouth shut all night.'

'He doesn't need to talk, he just has to look good. And, boy, does he look good.'

'I don't think it's a sensible idea, Emma . . .'

'He's gorgeous. In fact, you could say he's the personification of physical perfection.'

'Not if you were pissed, you couldn't,' I reply grouchily.

'He's loaded.'

'So what? I want a decoy not a meal ticket.'

'He drives your favouritest car of all time,' she says in a sing-song temptress kind of voice.

This one catches my interest. Despite the fact that I only drive a 1.6 Fiesta, I've always had an overwhelming passion for sporty cars – cars you can really drive. Especially the only true Italian Stallion.

'He doesn't?' I breathe excitedly.

She nods slowly, biting her bottom lip, then slides her eyes sideways to look at me.

'He sure does. Hot, red, and shares it's name with Fred Flintstone's favourite pet . . .'

'Did you say he was definitely free on the twenty-seventh?'

Emma's parents live in a really affluent bit of Berkshire. My parents also live in Berkshire, in a not quite as affluent but still quite nice part. Going from my end to Emma's is a bit like following an upwardly mobile nature trail.

You can tell you're moving up in the world because the name plates change as you go on. You start off at my parents' end with names like White Gates and Five Acres seared into wood, or intricately crafted in black metal from the local garden centre, then you move on to the posher parts and you get the brass plates stating that you've just arrived at The Grange or Highfield House. By the time you get to Emma's end, you don't get any name plates, just the odd board announcing opening times.

We turn off the main road, and pass between – get this! – the gate houses. (All right, I think they've got about two rooms each that wouldn't house an under-sized pygmy, but it's still pretty impressive, I mean, my first flat in London was even smaller!) We drive down a tree-lined avenue, the lower branches of the old spreading oaks nibbled away by grazing cattle, for about a mile before we get to the house.

Emma's parents' house is one of those big old

Georgian places. You know, the sort that look like wildly overgrown dolls' houses. The drive swings around to the front of the house, now bordered by a high stone wall instead of trees, and loops back on itself around a carriage circle in front of the main doors. Emma parks her little rusting red heap amidst the assorted sleek and sporty BMWs, four wheel drives, Porsches and TVRs already parked haphazardly across the lawn and the drive like an upmarket Knightsbridge dealer's show room.

I get out of the car. It's four o'clock in the afternoon, the sun is shining high in a pale blue sky, moorhens are calling to each other from the lake at the back of the house, horses are galloping high-tailed across the horizon, and the Chemical Brothers are blasting from the house so loud that the Georgian-paned windows are rattling in their frames.

'I see my little brother's at home,' Emma says dryly. Angus is seven years younger than her, and they're always about as pleased to see each other as an English lorry driver finding a French farmer parking his tractor sideways across a main autoroute.

'So what's the reason for this do then?' I ask as the front door bursts open and several already drunk revellers spill out clutching glasses and each other, and stagger off in the direction of the paddock to re-enact a scene from a John Wayne movie.

'You think my parents need a reason to get drunk?' Emma shuts the car door and several flakes of rust fall off the sill on my side. 'I suppose they could cite living with each other for the past thirty years . . .'

As if in response to her last comment, a woman rushes out of the house, sobbing loudly and hauling battered leather luggage in each hand. I'm not surprised she's crying. She's wearing a cocktail dress that looks like a huge blue velvet tent that could house a whole troop of boy scouts. It's a good job it's a nice day. Too strong an easterly, and she'd set sail. I'd cry if I was wearing a dress like that. It's bad enough being manhandled by Emma into this little itchy black velvet job that just needs an alice band and a bigger nose to look down to complete the job, but the midnight blue enormous nun number is something else.

It's then that I realise that the walking theatre curtain is Emma's mother Juliana, or Jules for short, which is pretty apt due to the amount of gold and diamonds she has hanging about her head and hands. She's a walking Cartier advertisement. Each chipolata sausage finger is adorned with one or sometimes two rings, a glittering array, a priceless permanent knuckle duster. They do say that a woman who wears a lot of rings displays a need to be owned or dominated by her man.

Jules attempts to disprove my theory.

'I'm leaving your father,' she barks to Emma as we attempt to walk in at the door just as she barges out of it.

Oblivious to the fact that there is a pretty raucous party in full swing in her house, she starts to load the suitcases into the open back of a dirty green Range-Rover, stops, throws them violently to the ground, turns to her daughter, collapses into her arms like an old ham who's just been stage stabbed, and begins to wail loudly.

Emma, clearly wondering what the hell possessed

her even to think about coming here in the first place, manages to pacify Jules enough to get her back in the house. The place is heaving with an eclectic mix of people, drinking and honking to each other above the music like a raggle-taggle assortment of game birds. The only thing they appear to have in common is a propensity to get pissed in the afternoon. The dress code ranges from ball room to boiler suits; several people are standing around braying loudly to each other still in mud spattered hunting pink. I almost convince myself that it's a fancy dress party when I see a fully vested vicar wandering round, glass of Chablis in each hand, until somebody actually addresses him as 'Reverend'.

Jules allows Emma to lead her through the throng, slumps down on a chair in the kitchen, legs akimbo, copious cleavage heaving as though exhausted, and demands a large gin and tonic. Emma ignores this demand but Jules doesn't seem to notice, accepting the proffered glass of water and downing it in one go, complaining merely at the lack of ice and lemon.

'He's got another woman, a bit on the side,' she announces without any preamble, her face emerging from the water like a dripping Labrador climbing from a lake.

'You're joking, aren't you?' I ask, open-mouthed. Emma's father's about as fanciable as a two-week-old natural yoghurt that hasn't been kept in the fridge.

'Would I joke about something like that? What am I going to do?' she wails. 'I feel so hopeless, so frustrated!'

I consider telling her about my spot of revenge, but decide that she's already unstable enough as it is without any advice from me about cordless drills and prized possessions.

'That really doesn't sound like Dad at all.' Emma hugs Juliana, grimacing at me over her mother's broad shoulder. 'Don't get so upset, I'm sure there must be a rational explanation for everything.'

'Oh, you're such a sensible girl, you're a source of constant comfort to me, darling. What would I do without you?' Jules begins to sob into her shoulder again. Emma and I again exchange glances behind her back, and simultaneously roll our eyes heavenward.

I decide to leave them to it and slope off to get myself a drink. I find a quiet corner in the huge orangery at the back of the house for me and a bottle of purloined Château Neuf du Pape. Original man-hunting mission temporarily shelved, I settle down to get drunk and watch the debauchery going on around me.

Emma's little brother was a spoilt brat of a child. He's now twenty-one, in his last year at Oxford reading Politics, and is, so far as I can make out, still a spoilt brat of a child. He and his friends are cavorting about the house like out of control kids at a birthday party, extremely drunk and some of them, I'm sure, totally doped out, spraying each other with vintage champagne like Silverstone winners, treading garlic prawns into the Turkish carpets, and playing hop-scotch on the black and white chequered floor of the hall.

One of Angus's friends side slides along the terracotta floor tiles of the orangery on the slippery leather soles of his new shoes, catches a shin on a heavy ornamental urn housing a mini palm tree, trips, and cracks his head on a small statue of a naked Persephone.

I think it was safer in the kitchen with Jules and her histrionics.

Perhaps I should go back in there and get on my soap box about the merits of forgive and forget. I know I'm not the best advocate of this right at this moment in time – look at Max and me, or rather the fact that there is no longer a Max and me due to his own similar indiscretion – but surely it's different at Juliana's age? She and Roger have been married for centuries, and unlike Max and me who could argue for the Olympics, normally get on pretty well, each being as mad as the other. This makes a difference, doesn't it?

Emma reappears after fifteen minutes and slumps down next to me, sighing heavily.

'Where's your mother?' I ask her.

'Oh, she's gone upstairs to redo her make up,' replies Emma, grabbing my bottle and drinking straight from it.

'But I thought she was leaving?'

'Oh, that. She's always leaving. It never lasts long. I think the longest she's ever stayed away was three days. Really sweated it out, she did. Practically hanging off the banisters not to phone home, and then when she finally gave in and went back Dad hadn't even noticed. Thought she'd gone to stay with Granny in Sussex for the weekend or something.'

'But what about Roger's other woman?'

'There is no other woman. Apparently she found a credit card bill for some jewellery that she certainly hadn't seen hide nor hair of, and it totally freaked her out. You know what she's like, total drama queen.'

'Well, that sounds pretty dodgy to me.'

'It's Mother's birthday next week. I think it'll all be resolved then.'

'Oh I see . . . surprise present.'

'Which isn't going to stay a surprise if my mother has her way.'

Juliana comes back into the room, eyelids freshly repainted with a streak of blue, cheeks pink and rouged like an old Aunt Sally doll, dyed platinum blonde hair piled back on top of her head like a plate of sculpted mash potato.

To my complete open-mouthed surprise, she comes over to us and hauls me into a gin-sodden embrace.

'Take my advice and don't let them walk all over you, darling,' she breathes in my face. You could get drunk on the fumes alone. 'Give Max a taste of his own medicine before you're too old to enjoy administering the dose.'

Arranging her bosoms in the front of her dress like two overgrown melons in a fruit basket, she totters over to a group where her husband is spouting forth about the merits of dried dog food and vitamin pills for Springer Spaniels, and gooses their bank manager.

I look at Emma.

She shrugs and smiles feebly at me.

'I think I was adopted.'

Suddenly, all female eyes are drawn towards the door.

I'm not given to jaw dropping over the opposite sex, but a complete vision of masculinity has just walked in. Conversations stop as people turn to stare in the instant attention-giving way that only the truly beautiful can command. The object of all this admiration seems remarkably unaware of the effect he's just had on the room, me included. He scratches his chin as he looks kind of nervously about at the heavy drinking, gawping, squawking crowd, then selects a glass of champagne from one of the trays being waved under his nose by the gaggle of young waitresses who rushed to his side like iron filings to a magnet.

'Wow!' I state, taking in the perfectly formed bod, the tousled dark hair, and almost luminous jade green eyes. I search for something more descriptive, but simply, and not very eloquently, repeat the last word that popped involuntarily from my mouth.

'Wow!' This one comes on a stream of hot breath.

'Exactly,' Emma states with a certain pride. 'Now do you see what I mean?'

'That's him?' I ask, open-mouthed.

She nods.

'That . . .' she says, grinning at my reaction '. . . is Guy.'

I don't know whether to be impressed or disappointed. There's no way someone like that is going to want to go out with me, pretence or not.

Gorgeous Guy is immediately accosted by Emma's mother and several of her friends, who viciously bat the waitresses out of the way with their Gucci bags, then stick closely to him as he moves across the room like a pack of ankle-hugging, tail-wagging, tongue-lolling poodles.

'He is gorgeous,' I admit. 'I'm sold.'

Emma smiles, and pushing my hair out of my face, inspects how much of the make up she so carefully applied earlier, is actually still in place.

'Thought you would be. Now let's just see what sort of sales job we can do on him.'

It takes us a while to prise the gorgeous Guy away from his drooling posse of middle-aged admirers. In fact, it's not until evening is settling in, the sun slowly sinking over the bowling green lawns at the back of the house, the sky turning first streaky pink and orange above us, then black as the sun sinks behind the trees, that the vultures finally and reluctantly swap drooling over Guy for drooling over the replenished buffet table, and start to stuff stuffed mushrooms down their gullets in the hope of soaking up some of the vast quantities of alcohol they've consumed throughout the afternoon.

We manage to corner him alone in the orangery.

Close to, he's even more stunning, sort of softened El Greco, with a long lean rangy body, chiselled cheek bones, the most kissable mouth I've ever seen on a man, and sloping eyes like a spoilt Siamese's, framed by the longest thickest lashes ever.

He's the sort of guy you'd see wandering through St Mark's Square at dawn in a tux, hands in pockets, tie loose about his neck, hair tousled and glossy, glorious Italian women throwing roses at him from balcony windows. You know, like in an advert for very expensive champagne or hormonally charged aftershave or something.

When he looks at you, you just want to melt into a pool of drool.

To put it bluntly, he's totally horny.

He should have a score of honey-bodied babes at

his beck and call, a little black book bigger than the A–Z, full of mobile phone numbers. He probably has. Women have been slipping their numbers into his breast and back trouser pocket today. I've seen them do it. The question is whether he's got the acumen to work out how actually to *use* a telephone . . . Honestly, you'd find more intelligence in the remedial class at an infants' school.

Then again, if he had more than one brain cell, he'd probably be an absolute bastard. You see, as it is, he's totally thick . . . very sweet, very nice, a complete Adonis physically, but absolutely, totally, plank-sized thick.

We have to repeat the plot to him about eight times, but he finally gets the message and responds with surprising enthusiasm.

'So you'll do it?' Emma asks, having explained in words of one syllable this time.

A bunch of horrible drunk Hooray Henrys run screaming past the window dressed in clothes stolen from Juliana's abandoned and forgotten suitcases. Amongst them is Angus who, having consumed seven pints of champagne and Guinness, trips over the hem of a red satin off-the-shoulder number that looks remarkably like a circus tent, and falls flat on his face into the ornamental pond.

'Right, so you want me to go to this wedding with Alexandra, yah? But, like, I'm not really going on a date with her.' Guy runs a hand through his tousled hair in an effort to wake up his brain. 'I've just got to pretend, yah?'

He is oblivious to the riot in the garden.

'Yah . . . er, I mean, yes. You know, play act.'

He frowns for a moment while this sinks in, then breaks into a gorgeous, gorgeous smile to reveal the most perfect set of white teeth I've ever seen in my life.

'Okay, yah, great. What fun!' he finally catches on, and begins to laugh like a donkey being castrated without anaesthetic.

'So you'll do it?' Emma and I both sigh in relief, not so much that he's agreed to go to the wedding with me, as for the fact that now we don't have to try and explain the whole thing to him yet again.

'Yah, sure, great. Sounds like a bit of a jape, and I've always fancied trying my hand at a bit of thespianism.'

'Well, I'm sorry,' Emma replies archly, putting an affected hand on my arm,' but we're just good friends and that's as far as it goes!'

The braying laugh stops and he looks at us in confusion.

'Sorry, what?'

Emma and I roll eyeballs at each other.

# Chapter Seven

I'm sitting at my desk on Monday morning devouring a cheese, ham and pickle roll that I brought in for lunch, hiding my face behind last weekend's magazine and working out how to make sure that Guy doesn't speak to an entire soul throughout the whole of the nuptials, when I hear the usual cacophony of good mornings that heralds the arrival of a fellow member of staff. I don't need to look up to recognise the voice that responds.

After a few heart-quivering moments, where I contemplate the best course of action, I decide to go for the direct approach.

Steeling myself, I lower the magazine, look him straight in the eye and speak as steadily as my nerves will allow.

'Morning, Damien.'

The eyes that I'm trying to look straight into swivel from side to side in a desperate attempt to focus on something else, I get a mumbled 'mmnnnn' in response and then he shoots off to do a me and hide behind the assorted equipment on his desk. It suddenly dawns on me that Damien's embarrassed. I mean, it's obvious if I think about it. I'm embarrassed about the whole thing, and I'm not the one who stripped off naked and offered my luminous rubber self for sexual pleasure, only to be howled at with laughter.

I realise with relief that he's certainly not going to say anything about events after Rodney's leaving do, which although only three weeks ago now seem like a decade away. He's got far more to lose by its becoming public knowledge than I have. What would Damien's reputation be worth if the story got out? A sensuous sexy stud muffin – which is how he likes to be thought of – doesn't prance around in nothing but a pair of Mickey Mouse socks and a dayglo condom and get rejected.

I catch him surreptitiously throwing a nervous glance in my direction, and to my horror start to giggle. I chide myself. How could I be so cruel? I'm subjecting him to what Larry put me through, and it's not nice.

Perhaps I'm finally achieving equality in the sex stakes, but if equality's all about being free to ridicule a fellow human being then I'm not sure I want it. I try to smile at Damien instead, then worried that he'll think it's a come on, change it into a sort of curt businesslike nod of acknowledgement.

Think I'll just go back to hiding behind my desk again.

My relief is short-lived.

I'm just settling down behind my rapidly mounting wall of pot plants – the dosh/dope plant has now been joined by several others (the army knew what they were doing when they chose green as camouflage) – when Sandra calls over to me.

'Alex, are you free? Mr Daniels would like to see you in his office.'

Oh, dear.

This must be it. Confession time.

This is the moment I've been dreading, and yes, my stomach does drop to my knees, as I suspected it would, and suddenly I find that no matter how hard I try to get up, my bum is firmly glued to my seat.

I mime having my throat cut to Mary, who grins sympathetically.

I sneak a peek at Jake's horoscope. I know when his birthday is, because Sandra has written it extra large on her wall chart in indelible red pen with two exclamation marks at the end, and then circled in luminous green.

*Libra: Someone will need kicking into touch this week. It's time to take off the gloves and go in fighting. The wool has been pulled over your eyes for too long, and you'll no longer accept underhand behaviour and deception.*

Great.

It takes me ten minutes to walk the thirty feet from my desk to Jake's office door, by which time Sandra is going positively puce with impatience. She puts a hand in the small of my back and pushes me through before I have a chance to think of an excuse not to go in at all.

Jake is at his desk. He has his back to me, and is working on what looks like a totally mind-boggling spreadsheet on his computer, row upon row of figures whizzing before his eyes faster than Damon Hill side-sliding round Silverstone.

'Hi,' he says without looking round. 'Sit down. I won't be a minute.'

219

Well, he sounds friendly enough. Then again, you don't have to behave like a bastard when you fire someone. He's going to kill me with kindness, terminate me with tenderness, sack me with saccharine.

He presses Control S on his computer keyboard, with a satisfying click of keys, scrolls out, and then swings round in his chair to face me.

He's smiling again.

This is far more disconcerting than if he looked grave.

You see, as he swung round that beam of a smile hit me like the arc of light from a lighthouse, flashed over my face at high wattage, and sent a pulse straight through my entire body which made me shiver.

It's a pretty new sensation in my life. In fact, so new it takes me a few minutes to recognise what it is I'm actually feeling.

Lust. Straightforward, gut-twisting, stomach-burning lust.

Oh, goody, something else to make my life more problematic.

I still fancy the guy.

I'm scared to death and as horny as hell. It's a very strange combination, a bit like smoking your first illicit joint, petrified of the consequences but floating off on an erotic high after the first few puffs.

'Alex.'

I manage a response which sounds a bit like, 'Nnn?'

Fortunately Sandra bustles in bearing coffee which gives me a little bit of a chance to recover my composure. He waits until she's left the room before speaking again. 'Sorry we haven't really had a chance to get together before now . . .'

We haven't had a chance to get together! I nearly choke on my coffee. What about The Priory? Don't tell me; it was the worst sex he's ever had and now he's scared to mention it in case I request a repeat performance.

Jake is speaking to me. I struggle to refocus my attention on his words rather than my own thoughts.

'. . . the work you've been doing on travel is great. I like your style. You write very well,' he's saying. 'The places we've been reviewing could be a little more exciting though.'

More exciting! He's having a laugh, isn't he? My heart sinks. He's making fun of me.

'It's good that we promote our own country, but there is more to the world than Britain . . .'

Now he sounds perfectly normal, perfectly serious, am I imagining the innuendo? Perhaps he's toying with me as a way of getting his own back.

I take my courage in both hands, look up, look across, and look him right in the eye, searching for something, I'm not sure what, just something behind that cool façade that will show me the truth. A glimmer, just a flicker maybe of shared intelligence. Our eyes meet.

He's totally unreadable.

He'd be great at poker.

Although I've been holding it back, I'm really tempted to walk in and file my copy on The Priory. Just to see if I get a reaction.

He's still speaking.

'I also don't think we can justify having it as a weekly piece . . . Do you enjoy your job, Alex?'

This one pulls me away from thoughts of heat-filled hotel nights, and back into the current conversation.

I nod slowly.

'Well, personally, I think you're wasting your talents.'

Oh, dear, as I thought, he hates me and this is a preliminary to getting rid of me.

'You're a bloody good writer, Alex.'

I wait miserably for the 'but'.

'But . . .'

Here we go.

'I think you're wasting your time.'

Dole queue here I come. I look at my feet.

'I'd like to move you on to something more challenging.'

Whoopee, I'm not getting the sack, I'm being moved to knitting patterns of the month or the weekend weather check.

Outlook stormy. Floods imminent.

I bite my bottom lip to stop it wobbling.

'Harvey's leaving us.'

'I know,' I mumble.

'He's moving on to better things. Seduced by the lure of the big boys on Fleet Street. Greater journalism,' says Jake with a sardonic raising of his eyebrow, obviously quoting the man himself. He pauses here as though expecting a reply.

'He always said he would,' is all I manage in response.

'It means I need a new feature writer, but I don't have the budget to replace him. Theoretically we already have too many staff writers, and I'm afraid what you're doing doesn't really justify a full-time job.'

Jake leans back in his chair and presses his fingers together under his chin.

I've been sussed! He's going to ask me to go freelance. No more monthly pay cheque. I'll be a starving journo, living in a cold unfurnished garret, writing on the corners of the old newspapers that I have to sleep under . . .

'. . . so I'd like you to combine the two and start writing features for me as well.'

'You would?' A glimmer of hope dares to lighten my heart. I manage to drag my eyes away from the polished tocs of my boots and glance up at him.

He's looking at me with that disconcertingly direct gaze of his. The one that makes you want to start fidgeting like a naughty school girl waiting outside the headmistress's office.

'You really think I'm suitable for this?' I suddenly feel vastly inadequate. The only escape from travel I ever had with old Rodders in charge was to do the odd fill in. Top Ten lists, trivia quizzes, stuff like that. I mean, I used to dream of being given the chance actually to write something more challenging, and then I just settled into a routine and poured my literary frustrations and half my working hours into my unfinished novel.

'You're a good writer, Alex. I don't see that travel keeps you fully occupied, and I think you've been under-utilised. I'm not saying that's your fault, but I think we need to broaden your horizons a little.'

'Get your money's worth,' I blurt without thinking.

'Well, I wouldn't have put it quite like that.' He raises his eyebrows at me, but the smile stays firmly in place. 'I think you're probably aware that my predecessor let things slide somewhat.'

Well, that's the understatement of the decade, but I'm not going to say anything.

'My remit is to turn this magazine around. Make it something people want to read again. I think the importance of our role within the paper has been forgotten by an awful lot of people, most disturbingly by those who actually put *Sunday Best* together. We should be producing a magazine of a much higher standard, with more modern ideas. We need to make *Sunday Best* something people would go to a news stand and actually buy if they weren't getting it for free with their newspaper . . .'

It's like I haven't breathed out for the past ten minutes. I'm not losing my job. In fact, this is more like a promotion. I exhale and relax a little.

'You know how it works. We'll pool ideas, you'll come up with a few of your own, and if they're suitable we'll let you run with them. The usual deadlines will apply in future, but as Harvey's not going for another few weeks, it gives you a bit more time to get your teeth into your first assignment. I'll give you the outline now, and if you could let me see a draft copy in . . . say, three weeks' time?'

I nod. I even manage to throw in some enthusiasm and a small smile.

Jake hands me a blue folder.

'Have a read through this. It contains a précis of what I want this piece to be. A few ideas I'd like you to run with: background, quotes, stuff like that.'

I open the file and glance at the topmost paper.

'The Unfairer Sex.' I read out the heading at the top of the first page.

'Mmm.' Jake nods. 'I see it as woman taking on man's role for a change. Turning around the whole concept of man the eternal predator. What's the changing role of women in the sexual milieu in the run up towards the new millennium? Do they just want equality or are they after total domination? That sort of thing.'

He's taking the piss, isn't he? He has a sort of quirk at the corner of his mouth as he speaks.

'Are women becoming more sexually aggressive? Are they taking control of their own sex lives, or just playing men at their own game? And if that's the case, I want to know who's winning. Make it upbeat, keep it humorous if you can. I'd like to work very closely with you on this one . . . seeing as it's your first piece. But I expect great things from you, Alex. I think you'll perform really well.'

Why does everything he say have a double entendre? Now I know he must be making fun of me. He probably thinks I'm some heartless tart who took what I wanted then walked. Well, that *is* what I'm supposed to be, isn't it? So why am I so upset that this is what Jake thinks?

I bite my bottom lip, hard to stop it wobbling as stupid tears begin to threaten, and feel it go numb.

I've got to say something now. But what?

And then he smiles at me. It's an open, honest, direct, even kind smile. There's no trace of irony, no sarcasm, no malice.

Now I'm totally thrown.

It makes it even worse when he gets up from his chair, comes round to my side of his desk and holds out his hand to me.

'Of course, there'll be a little bit more money. I'm not in a position to offer you much at the moment, I'm afraid . . . an extra two thousand okay for you?'

I nod dumbly.

'Great. I'll get you a new contract drawn up.' He takes my hand. He doesn't shake it like I expected, just holds it briefly. Mine is shaking. His hand is warm and strong and very still.

Then he lets go.

Everything he's just said to me, my common sense, my sense of equilibrium, all of it's wiped out by that brief touch. The feel of his skin against mine again, triggering memories, horny memories of the best bonk I've ever had in my life . . . a memory which kept me smiling for at least a week, and which I now, disturbingly, find highly embarrassing as well as highly erotic.

I stumble out of his office in a sort of stupefied fashion and slump down in my chair. I've just been given a chance that I've always wanted, actually to get to do some proper writing for the magazine, but now I'm not even sure I want to be working here anymore.

I'm a seething mass of mixed emotions. The most memorable sex of my life, and the guy who participated is acting like he doesn't recall a moment of it. Is that what it's about, being a man? Having the most amazing, excellent sex with someone, and then just moving on? Is this where women go wrong? We, who can recount a detailed list of every man we've had – or not had in some cases – an orgasm with. Perhaps that's why I'm finding this whole hit list thing so difficult.

Perhaps I need to be more focussed, more tunnel-visioned. Perhaps, please forgive my crudity, I should adopt the male view of us as a hole between two legs, and just see a man as a dangly thing between two legs. Focus in on the equipment, the tool, so to speak, and not the hydraulics that work this piece of machinery.

My immediate problem, however, is Jake. How can I work with him after what happened between us? He may choose not to remember, but every time I look at him, I get a full colour action replay running through my mind.

Wearily, I lean my forehead against my computer screen and close my eyes.

Nigel turns to Harvey.

'I think Alex is trying a mind transfer to save having to type up her copy. Hey, Alex,' he calls to me, grinning broadly, 'you have to use the keyboard, darling. They haven't fitted your computer with a telekinesis chip yet.'

Thank god for that, because what's going through my mind at the moment is far too X-rated for a family newspaper.

We spend Friday night slobbing at Serena's flat, eating pizza, drinking wine and watching television.

It's an unspoken agreement that we have to be deathly quiet, apart from the odd giggle from the other two, through *Friends* and *Frasier*, but every time the adverts come on I take the opportunity to complain about my situation at work, and the girls once again roll their eyeballs at each other and roll out the old adages of 'never feel you have to say sorry', and 'don't bother regretting it in the morning, because by the morning it's too late to change anything anyway'.

Not that I really regret what happened, or who it happened with, the only bit I regret is that the 'who' turned out to be my new boss.

'Only I could do it,' I sigh heavily, my depression lifted only slightly by the handful of toffee-coated popcorn I shove in my mouth and chew on like a morose camel.

'Rubbish! It happens all the time,' Serena replies through a mouthful of mushroom, spicy sausage and mozzarella. 'People bonking bosses, bosses bonking employees. You're not the only one, you know.'

'Yes, but I bet I'm the only one who didn't know it was my boss at the time.'

'Wanna bet?' Emma's sitting on the floor in between Serena and me, curled up on the sofa, and painting her toenails individual colours with Serena's vast nail varnish collection. 'You've never been to one of our Christmas parties. I've seen secretaries there so drunk they wouldn't know if it was the MD they shagged over the photocopier or Santa Claus.'

'Ooh!' Serena's eyes light up at the thought. 'Perhaps I should come along to one of your shindigs. I could add a few more chalk marks to the score board on the kitchen door.'

'You don't need to add any more.' Emma raises her eyebrows. 'You're already streets ahead of the rest of us.'

'Maybe I should quit, get another job?' I muse, giving up on the popcorn and pilfering the last piece of pizza, strings of cheese refusing stubbornly to unglue themselves from the box, trailing around

Serena's bare toes as I lean back into my seat. 'Prefer-ably one where I haven't had a one-night stand with the guy in charge.'

'What on earth for?' Emma asks incredulously. 'He's not giving you any hassle, is he? Jake either really doesn't remember or he hasn't got a problem with it. If he had he'd have said something. He certainly wouldn't have promoted you. See,' she sniggers, paint-ing the little toenail of her left foot candy pink, 'didn't I say sleeping with the boss might get you a pay rise? And you haven't even had to do it again.'

'Bugger off, Emma!' I reply grumpily.

'You're lucky you didn't lose your job com-pletely . . . you couldn't have been that bad in the sack after all.'

I throw a cushion at Serena, who just delivered this one. She ducks, and the cushion lands softly on her huge, furry, spoilt moggy child substitute, aptly called 'Fat Cat', instead. Fat Cat growls, fluffs out his immense tortoiseshell tail like a feather duster, and stalks majestically from the room.

'Great.' Serena fondly watches him depart towards the minuscule kitchen, to peruse his empty food bowl sulkily. 'Now he's in a mood.'

'Serena!' Emma rolls her eyes heavenward. 'It's a cat.'

'I know that, and you know that, but do you think he does? Besides, he's a very intelligent cat. He's quite capable of moods, you know.'

'Yeah, like Alex.' Emma pulls a face at me to try and make me laugh. 'Oh, for goodness sake,' she sighs when I continue to sport an expression like a sulky baby. 'You were happy . . . for the first time since you left Max, you were actually walking round with a huge grin on your face. I liked you like that, Alex. It made *me* happy. Pleeease can we have the happy Alex back?' She rests her head against my leg, and looks up at me with puppy dog eyes. 'Purleee-ase . . . You've had great sex, you've got a better deal at work – can't you just enjoy these facts without worrying over the trivial details?'

'Well, I'm glad someone thinks it's trivial that the promotion and the great sex both came from the same source,' I reply sniffily.

'Aaaaahhh!' Ems screams, grabs the cushion that so offended Fat Cat, and wallops me with it. 'Alex Gray,' she puffs, pushing her fringe out of her eyes, 'you're my best friend and I love you to death, but for god's sake, snap out of it, will you! It's like living with Marvin the Paranoid Android. You know, recently I think you're only happy if you've got something to be unhappy about.'

I try a fail safe and burst into tears. It's not really put on. I feel so confused and wound up at the moment I don't know which way to turn and crying seems the easy option.

Emma is immediately mortified and conciliatory.

She abandons her nail varnish and the attitude, and scrambles up on to the sofa to give me a hug, her tacky toes sticking to the faded Dralon of Serena's knackered sofa.

'Don't get upset, babe.' Serena wades in with a box of tissues, and refills my wine glass. 'I know things have been a bit fraught, but it's not worth getting your knickers in a twist over something that might not happen.'

'Ren's right. Life's good, Lexy.' Emma pouts glumly at me, mirroring my own expression. 'If only you could see it, you've got great friends who love you, you've got rid of Mad Max – and I don't care what you say, that's a bloody good thing – you've found out that sex actually can be better than a box of Black Magic and a good movie, and you've just been promoted at work. You've always wanted to write more for the magazine, haven't you?'

I press my face into a soft white tissue, sniffle a bit more, then nod.

'Why don't you tell me what you've got to do for your first story?' Serena coos, putting a hand on my shoulder.

'If you really want to know?' I whisper in my best martyred voice.

'Of course we do.' Serena smiles at Emma. 'Don't we, Ems?'

Emma looks kind of unsure about this one. She's already heard the entire script of my meeting with Jake, and taken an hour to persuade me that his subject choice was probably just a complete and rather unfortunate coincidence. The problem is it's hard to persuade somebody of something when you're not sure that you believe it yourself. I don't give Emma a chance to object or tactfully change the subject this time, though.

Actually, I've been dying to interview the girls for my piece. It's a bloody good excuse to pick up some hints from them. I think I'm going seriously wrong somewhere along the line. Before the Jake incident, my game failure rate was a thoroughly half-hearted one hundred per cent. Since Jake I haven't even bothered trying. The times that we've gone out, the others pull out their score cards, pull no punches, and pull the men, whilst I slink off into a corner, drink myself silly, and wonder what I bothered getting all dressed up for. The only reason we're having a girlies' night in tonight, instead of a night out, is because I grumbled my way out of it, unable to face another evening of stalking potentially sexy men.

Basically, there's no getting away from it. I am not a predatory female.

I explain the outline of my brief to Serena, who listens intently until I finish.

'Oooh, you're having a laugh, aren't you?' She does an impression of Kenneth Williams. 'If he set you an assignment like that he must . . .'

Emma elbows her somewhere in the region of the top of her tibia.

'. . . think you've got talent,' she finishes. 'It sounds like it could be quite hard to write. You know, to get a balanced view,' she tails off, grabs her glass of wine, takes a deep slug and smiles inanely at me.

From the kitchen we can hear the sound of plastic scraping across the floor, as Fat Cat noses morosely at his empty supper dish.

'Well, I was kind of hoping you'd let me interview you?' I throw my no longer needed soggy tissue at the bin and miss.

'You ought to ask Sukey.' Serena picks it up from the floor in distaste, and drops it into the rubbish. 'She's been out with a different man every night this week.'

Sukey, Serena's nineteen-year-old sister, has been on an unscheduled visit that was supposed to last a week, but started five weeks ago and still hasn't drawn to a conclusion. Whereas Serena is a gorgeous young thing, Sukey is an even more gorgeous, even younger, young thing with a figure to die for, superbly slim and fit but with curves in all the right places, and a face that could grace the cover of *Vogue* without the slightest embarrassment. You know the sort of thing: the huge eyes, high cheek bones, bee-stung lips look. Hate, hate, hate. She has so many men attempting to get into her knickers, you'd think she was a lingerie service catering for transvestites.

'Where is she?' I ask hopefully

Serena laughs, sucking froth from the fizzing neck of a newly opened bottle of Bud.

'Where do you think? Out . . . with yet another conquest. You know, she only has to look at a man and he's whipping off his trousers in anticipation.'

'Huh!' I grumble. 'If I look at a man the only thing he's "whipping off" is "in the other direction".'

'It's all about sending out the right signals.' Emma nicks Serena's Bud and takes a huge swig, wiping her mouth on the back of her hand.

'Well, I must be sending out a "Don't bother, I'm a boring bastard whose knickers are superglued to her fanny" signal then,' I complain, 'because I never get chatted up.'

'I think it's more of a "Get lost, I'm miserable, I don't want to talk to you, and you just don't stand a chance" kind of signal,' says Ems, not unkindly, reluctantly giving the beer bottle back to Ren.

'Yeah. I'm not being horrible, but you're not exactly approachable when we go out, Lex,' adds Ren. 'You put up this practically impenetrable barrier, and men are pretty scared of rejection, you know.'

'I do?' I ask, suddenly imagining myself with a sort of Ready Brek glow of a force field that instantly zaps any man to dust if he dares come within two feet of me.

I quite like this image.

Emma nods her agreement.

'You don't get chatted up because men are too scared to approach you.'

Maybe they're right? I mean, it's better than my theory that nobody chats me up because I'm about as fanciable as a week-old dead halibut.

'But I thought it was supposed to be us doing the chatting up, not waiting for the man to come to us?' I ask, slightly confused.

'Well, that's the beauty of subtlety and signals.' Emma, picks up a pot of Smartie blue Hard Candy, and starts to paint alternate fingernails on her left hand. 'If you give out the right signals, the man comes to you, but it's you that got him there in the first place by giving out the right signals, so basically the ball's in your court.'

'Yeah,' agrees Serena. 'You see something you want and you've got to go for it.'

She illustrates this philosophy by telling me about her last two conquests. Serena spots a guy in a busy bistro – you know the scenario – and decides that he looks like a bit of all right. She watches him for a while, admiring the way his arse fits his Levis, his tortoiseshell brown hair flops over his blue eyes, and liking the way his mouth and his eyes crinkle when he smiles, and the frequency with which this actually happens. She doesn't rush in. She bides her time until he goes to the bar, then surreptitiously manoeuvres herself so that she's standing next to him. It's crowded, they're continually jostled against each other. Eye contact is made. The next time she's pushed by the crowd, she makes sure she barges into him a little harder. Polite apologies ensue. She smiles and makes a comment about the length of time you have to wait for service, throws in a line about him looking familiar – she admits this is pretty corny, but apparently corny tends to work – and a conversation is started. When she eventually gets served first, she offers to buy him a drink and hey, presto it goes on from there.

I like it. I like the subtlety. I also like the safety. According to Serena, this way if you decide that they're a total jerk when you actually get to talk to them, then you can just get served and sod off.

Another guy was apparently obtained along with the groceries in the local supermarket. He was standing next to a sign that said 'Buy one, get one free'. I think Ren made him a better offer. It's not fair. The only thing I ever pick up in a supermarket is a large bill.

I've scribbled all of this down in the little mental note book I have in my head, for my piece and for future personal reference. I might have to try some of the Serena techniques the next time I go out. If I feel up to it . . . or should that be up *for* it? Not for the first time I'm beginning to wonder why I agreed to the game in the first place. I haven't exactly been going out of my way to play hard, more like hard to get.

Emma's surprisingly reticent about her pulling

techniques. You think a man magnet such as she would have a lot of stories to tell, but you try getting any of them out of her. It's like trying to pull healthy teeth.

'Don't want to be giving any hints to the opposition.' She grins slyly at me. 'I'm hanging on to second place by my bitten fingernails. If I tell you how to pick up men, I might just end up the poor unfortunate at the bottom of the score board who has to foot the bill at the winner's dinner.'

At the moment, *I* am that poor unfortunate, and time is rapidly running out. Serena has an amazing seven chalk marks against her name, Emma has a pretty respectable four, and I have my solitary, but seriously sexy, one.

It's strange. It was so easy just to fall into bed with Jake, easier than falling into the pool with him even, but I'm finding it so hard to get the motivation to do it again with someone else.

Looks like I've been sussed now, though.

Emma and Serena have both clammed up on me.

Since no further answers on how to tune in your libido to the right pulling frequency are forthcoming, I shall have to move on to fresh information fodder.

My big sister Erica's coming over from the States next week, maybe she can give an international slant to my story. How to pick up more than a double Swiss on rye in a deli on Madison. Would you really meet the Tom Hanks of your sleepless dreams if you waited for long enough at the top of the Statue of Liberty? Do all New York males look like Robert de Niro, Al Pacino or Michael Douglas?

'I'll have to grill Erica on how women pull in New York . . .'

'Do you think it varies according to continent?' Emma wanders into the kitchen to raid Serena's fridge for more beer, blowing on her tacky fingernails to dry them. 'I thought the language of love was supposed to be universal?' she calls back to us, dislodging several fridge magnets as, three Bud bottles and a tub of dip balanced between two hands, she attempts to shut the fridge door with her backside.

'When's Erica arriving?' Serena relieves Emma of the dip, and hungrily pulling off the plastic lid, begins to scoop her tortillas into the creamy gunk.

Erica was originally supposed to be stopping with Max and me, but now there is no longer a Max and me, Serena has stepped in and saved the day by offering her spare room.

'Thursday afternoon. Is it still okay for her to stop here?'

'Sure, Sukes is heading back to Edinburgh this weekend. She's finally decided that perhaps she ought to go back to Uni and catch a few lectures before her exams, so the spare room'll be empty again.'

Smiling, Serena relinquishes the crisps and dip to Emma and gathers up Fat Cat instead, who has decided he's too hungry to sulk and is weaving round her ankles, spell-binding for food.

'She's not allergic to cats, is she?' Serena strokes his long furry tail with both hands, and he starts to growl again. His face clearly registers a 'cut the crap and just give us some food' look.

'No, but she's allergic to penicillin so you'd better

wash your coffee mugs before she comes,' I joke, indicating the sink which is housing a washing-up mountain big enough to be seen from the living room.

'That's Sukes, she's such a slut! She says she's just being a typical student. Like it's obligatory never to do any housework, drink cheap beer all day, blow your entire grant in the first week of term on Nicole Fahri, and party until dawn every day.'

'Sounds pretty good to me.' I attempt to steal the bottle of Bud that Emma's just opened, only to get my hand slapped. 'Do you think I could be a mature student?'

'Hardly,' Emma cracks open another bottle and hands it to me. 'You can't even be a mature adult!'

I love airports. There is always such an air of anticipation and excitement to them. Happy people sodding off to foreign climes for a fortnight's break from the drudgery of routine; others, brown and weary but replete, heading home in clothes that are far too skimpy for the British weather, but show off their tan.

Erica's flight's delayed but I don't care. I wander round the shops, buy myself an overpriced sandwich, some fresh juice and a magazine, and sit back in a regulation airport seat with a happy sigh. I eat, and I read, and I people watch, until the monitors finally announce that Erica's flight is now in the baggage hall.

Typically, she is one of the first to sweep through into the arrivals lounge, a porter pushing a trolley laden with Louis Vuitton obsequiously behind her, eyes firmly fixed on her pert bottom and long slim legs.

My sister looks like the me I'd like to be. Slimmer, taller, far more beautiful. Hair darker, shorter and glossier; eyes bigger, browner, with longer lashes. Do you get the idea? Sort of how I think I look on a good day until I catch sight of the reality in the mirror. Erica's elegant, successful, confident. Is she really my sister?

I have this theory that I was adopted, but so far my parents refuse to verify it.

'Alex, my god you've grown!' is the first thing she says to me as she sweeps me into a far from elegant hug, and plants pillar-box red lips on both my cheeks. She's been living and working in New York for nearly three years now, and her typically English public school accent is now softened with the lightest of American burrs. She smells expensive, of perfume that costs three hundred dollars an ounce, and designer wool that probably costs one hundred dollars per square inch or something.

'Erica! I'm nearly twenty-eight. I stopped growing about ten years ago,' I protest, wriggling free from her sisterly embrace in embarrassment.

'Well, in that case, heels must be higher here. You never used to reach above the tip of my nose.'

'It's the weight that came off my mind when I left Max,' I mutter grumpily, straightening my jacket. 'It used to make me stoop.'

'Ah, yes. Max.'

At the mention of the M word, she hugs me again, then holds me at arm's length by my shoulders, her perfectly painted face suddenly awash with sympathy as she inspects me.

'How *are* you?'

'I'm fine.'

'Are you sure?' The normally flawless brow creases.

'Of course I'm sure. Are these all your cases?'

'Sure they are.'

'Ren's only got one spare room, you know. You need an extra room just for this lot.'

'Well, it was very sweet of her to offer, but I'm quite happy to stay in a hotel, you know.'

'No way! I want you on hand while you're here, not stuck in some designer hotel that I'd be too lowly to visit you in.'

Erica laughs, linking her arm through mine.

'Yes, how thoughtless of me, of course you want me nearby . . . don't worry, darling, big sis is back now. I'll look after you – and I'll start by sorting out that son of a bitch Max for you!'

She sweeps me across the airport lounge towards the automatic exit doors, the porter scurrying unbidden behind as though attached to her knicker elastic by his own longing.

'Well, thanks for the offer, but I don't think that son of a bitch Max needs sorting out. In fact, he's pretty much sorted already.' I take a deep breath and then tell her what I'd been putting off in our last few telephone conversations. 'He's getting married.'

Erica watches as the porter loads her luggage into the back of a taxi, hands him a twenty-pound note with a gracious smile, then turns back to me, still smiling.

'You know, I could have sworn you just said that Max is getting married,' she says smoothly, folding her endless legs into the back seat of the taxi, the

panting porter having hung around after his tip for
the sheer pleasure of holding the door open for her.

'That's probably because I just did,' I reply, clamber-
ing far less graciously in after her. Why do I sound
like *I'm* apologising?

'You're joking, aren't you?' The smile hasn't slipped
but it's set a little harder.

'Yeah, sure,' I reply dryly. 'I made it up for my own
amusement.'

'Don't be so facetious, Alex!'

Ignoring Erica, I lean forward to give the driver
directions.

'But to whom?' she asks, tugging at my shoulder.

'*Whom* do you think?' I reply crossly, slumping back
into the seat, and staring out of the window.

'To her?' Erica replies incredulously.

'Just let it go. I really don't care.'

'But I was under the impression that this was all a
bit of a misunderstanding . . . that you two were
sorting things out?'

'I told you on the phone, we're through. There's no
going back.'

'But Mother seemed to think it was just a bit of a
glitch, a lovers' tiff, and that you'd sort things out.'

'Well, you know what she's like. Lives in her own
little happy fantasy world half the time.'

'So you don't want him back? I'm not here to
referee a rematch?'

'No,' I wail. 'For the last time, I'm glad I'm shot of
him. Yes, it hurt. Yes, it was a bitch how it happened.
But no way, not ever, do I want him back.'

'Well, thank goodness for that.' Erica's face breaks
into a huge relieved smile as she rummages in her bag

and, pulling out an atomiser, surreptitiously mists the less than fragrant taxi driver. 'I never thought he was right for you.'

We lug all of Erica's suitcases and the four portions of haddock and chips she insisted on stopping for like she'd just rediscovered *Brigadoon* or something, up the three flights of stairs to Serena's top-floor flat.

Erica eats all of her fish and chips and most of mine. I don't know how she manages to stay so slim and toned. She puts away enough food for a trainee Sumo wrestler. After we've eaten, we install her in Serena's spare room.

Now I know why my sister always has such wonderful clothes. It means that she gets to sit on the bed, holding court and not lifting a perfectly painted fingernail, while I and my friends unpack for her, for the sheer pleasure of seeing what's coming out of the suitcase next. All three of us are mentally noting which things we simply have to borrow – or should that be annexe – before she goes back to the States.

'We're not staying cooped up in here all night, are we?' Erica complains as we fart about, slipping in and out of different outfits. 'Let's hit the town, have some fun. Find some men.' Her voice lowers to a lascivious growl.

'Men?' I query.

'Definitely. I haven't had sex for over five months – I've got an Out of Order sign on my fanny,' she sighs. 'The only diaphragm of mine that's had any use recently is the one that inflates my lungs when I scream with frustration!'

Emma chokes with laughter, white wine hitting the

back of her throat and heading out through her nostrils.

My eyes widen with incredulity.

'Don't look so shocked, Alex. I'm not the last of the vestal virgins, you know. Although I certainly feel like it at the moment! It's been so long since the last time, I've probably grown a new hymen.'

Is this my Erica? Perhaps she was body snatched at the same time as Sandra turned into Sandie.

'What's the matter, Alex? You're looking at me like I've suddenly sprouted a pair of horns or something.'

'I don't know. It's just since you've been in America, you've just got more . . . more . . .' I search for a suitable word that isn't insulting.

'Forward?' Erica suggests herself. 'God, girl,' she laughs, 'there are so few single, attractive, solvent, heterosexual men over there that you just have to get down and get dirty and hang on in there. It's like fighting for the last size twelve Donna Karan in the Harvey Nicks sale.'

'I thought New York was full of Andy Garcia and Al Pacino look a likes? You know, all dark-haired, brooding and macho?'

'Don't believe everything you see in the movies.' She grins. 'The only decent men are either gay or already married.'

'I thought the divorce rate was high over there?'

'Sure, but you have to put your name down at birth to be on the waiting list for a divorcee. Why do you think I've come back to Britain?'

'To visit me?' I reply hopefully.

'Yeah, but I want to do a bit of bargain hunting whilst I'm here. You know, take home a souvenir in the shape of something six foot and masculine.'

Well, I said I wanted to get some tips from my big sister. Erica always knows what she wants, and she always knows how to get it. Whereas I know if I ever decided what I wanted, I wouldn't have a bloody clue how to start achieving it.

The other two don't take too much persuading to borrow an outfit each from Erica and head out to one of our usual haunts, the wine bar I went to with Mason. We find a table and order a couple of bottles of semi-decent Chablis.

It's amazing how many men Erica describes as 'absolutely gorgeous' or 'totally divine'. I suppose three years in a man desert and your standards drop somewhat. What I would class as a little drip is an oasis to my sister.

Perhaps I should try some self-prescribed exile, then maybe I won't have so much trouble spotting even one guy I find vaguely attractive.

'Ooh, he's nice,' purrs Erica, spotting yet another favoured man and pointing him out to me.

I gasp with horror.

It's Mason.

I attempt to slide under the table but it's too late, we've been spotted, and Emma, the disloyal cowbag, is even waving him over.

I make my escape to the bar for more drinks, hoping Mason and his friends will just say hi and then sod off, but when I go back to the table my vacated seat has been filled by his pert backside and he's in full swing on the Ken and Em dialogue.

Erica actually looks interested. Either that or she's also perfected the technique of looking rapt while being mentally a million miles away. I peer closer at her eyes but they don't appear to have that giveaway glaze.

'What's the matter with her?' I whisper to Emma.

'Mason's chatting her up.'

'I know that. What concerns me is that she actually appears to be enjoying herself.'

'Is that so implausible? If you listen, he's actually quite amusing.'

'You can describe somebody talking about themselves without pausing to draw breath for over three hours as *amusing*?'

'If you're referring to your date of disaster, he told me you were really quiet all evening. I think he felt he had to compensate.'

'Well, he certainly did that all right.'

'Maybe you just got off on the wrong foot.'

'Maybe I just didn't like him very much.'

'Well, we can't all be compatible with everybody, can we? Erica seems to like him well enough.'

She's right, Erica's smiling and laughing like she's having a really good time. I feel it my sisterly duty to save her from making a huge mistake, and at the earliest opportunity catch her eye and indicate for her to meet me in the Ladies. I'm in there for five minutes, pretending to do and redo my hair, before she finally follows me in.

'What's up, Alex?'

'Do you know who you're talking to?'

'Yeeess . . .' she replies slowly. 'His name's Mason. Emma introduced us, remember?'

'And it doesn't bother you?'

'Alex, honey, have I missed something here?'

'Look, I know what it's like to be desperate to hook a man . . .' Even if it's just for appearance's sake, I add to myself, thinking of the game in play, and my failure to get on the leader board.

Erica bursts out laughing.

'Honey, you're just a baby! How can you have had a chance to feel desperation?'

'I'm twenty-seven. I *feel* ancient.'

'Well, I'm *thirty-three*. How do you think that makes me feel?'

'Ah, so you are just talking to him 'cause you're desperate.'

'Well, I don't really like to classify myself as desperate, Alex, it kind of smacks of no-hope loser and I trust that's not me. But I am getting to the point where I'd like to get into a serious relationship and actually stay there.'

'You are? But all you ever wanted was a good career.'

'And I got it, Lex. I got the penthouse suite, the company limo, the key to the executive wash room, the lot. And do you know how empty my life feels without someone special to share it with?'

'But you love your job?'

'Sure I love my job, but it's not enough. Now I want the husband and kids bit to go with it. I'm thirty-three and my biological clock's ticking so loud anybody would think I was the crocodile from *Peter Pan*.'

'You'd contemplate having a *baby* with Mason?' I look at her, horrified.

'Well, how about I have sex with him first and see how I feel then?'

'You'd contemplate having *sex* with Mason?' I ask in the same incredulous voice.

'He's single, solvent, heterosexual, fit, has his own teeth and hair, and from what I can make out all his limbs are intact. I'd say he was a pretty good bet.'

'He has the personality of Narcissus.'

'You mean, you want personality on top of all the other attributes?' She's only semi-joking. 'God, Alex, you English are so picky.'

'In case you'd forgotten, you're English too,' I tell her sulkily.

'Ex-pat, darling. Makes a big difference.'

'Yeah, like you lose a tenth of your brain for every year you stay in the States. Erica, Mason is an egotistical, egocentric, self-obsessed, ladder-climbing show off.'

'Yep. Just how we New Yorkers like 'em. You know, I might take him back to America with me.' She pauses to run a slash of red lipstick across her pouting mouth. 'If I get browned off with him, I can always sell him to my girlfriends for a couple of thousand dollars . . . Don't look so concerned, Alex, I think he's really nice.'

'You do?'

'Sure. He's witty, and attentive, and he's pretty bright . . .'

'Excuse me, but are we talking about the same person here?'

'Alex, he thought you were the outwardly shy and quiet, but inwardly repressed nymphomaniac, type.'

'He said that?' I reply in horror.

'Sure. Now see how easy it is to get the wrong impression about somebody?' She links an arm through mine. 'Now come and have another drink, and relax. I promise I'll think before I bonk, okay?'

Maybe Mason wasn't so wrong. Sure, I'm not outwardly shy and quiet, but maybe I am a repressed nymphomaniac.

All I can think about at the moment is sex.

Well, sex with Jake to be more precise.

While I join in the general conversation, still keeping a sisterly eye on Erica and the Ego Man, peruse the room for talent, concede that the guy in the Calvin Klein jeans is kind of sexy, even make the odd bit of eye contact, all the time little pictures keep popping into my head like a slide show, a trailer of the highlights for an amazingly blue movie starring me and my boss.

It's like I've been brainwashed.

I try to concentrate on finding myself another likely candidate for a score on the chalk board.

After three-quarters of an hour, when I've rejected every man in the room for varying reasons, Erica yawns widely, stretching her slender arms above her head, so that her loose-fitting top slides up to reveal her midriff.

'Jeez, I'm pooped. Must be jet lag.'

Ah, ha. Thought so. Mason's finally bored her to tears and this is a hint for little sis to leap to the rescue and get her the hell out of here.

'I'll get our coats and we can go, if you like?'

'Mason's getting mine.' She smiles at me somewhat sheepishly. 'He's gonna give me a lift home. You don't mind, do you?'

I try not to hesitate too long. 'No, just don't wear your seat belt, okay. It hinders your escape.'

She smiles in mystified fashion at me, before having her coat draped around her shoulders by a very attentive Mason distracts her.

'Gee, how chivalrous of you.' She beams a big come-on smile at him.

Uck! I can't stand here and watch my sister actually flirting with Mr Bombastic. I give her a last hug, as though sending her off to the gallows, then head back towards the bar and the others.

'I need another drink.' I slump down beside Ems, and gaze sourly into my empty glass.

'Why? Because Erica scored where you couldn't?'

'Don't be ridiculous!' I snort indignantly. 'Couldn't? I could have had him if I'd wanted to. Like that.' I click my fingers. 'Easy. I just didn't want to.'

Emma grins broadly at me.

'Well done!'

'What?'

'You sounded just like a bloke then. You know, I think you might actually be starting to get somewhere. Now you see that cute guy over there? Well, while you're in the macho mood, why don't you pop over and see if he fancies a quickie in the car park?'

I rest my forehead on the bar in despair.

# Chapter Eight

Mason's following my sister around like a puppy. I think he's in love. I give him ten out of ten for tenacity. It's actually quite nice to see a man so desperately keen, but I finally think of a way to make Erica consider her options more carefully.

I simply point out to her that if she spends all of her time in London seeing Mason, then she may be missing out on the other male delights that our wonderful capital has to offer. I mean, she wouldn't go into just one clothes shop and buy the first dress she saw, would she?

Erica sees the logic of my argument and manages to ditch Mason for a night on the town with the girls, which includes myself, Emma, Serena, and an old mate of mine and Ems's from school, Jude, who's visiting from Oop North for the weekend.

We're all wearing something of Erica's apart from Erica herself who, for some inexplicable reason, swapped dresses with Jude the minute she arrived at the mews. I've nicked the disgustingly gorgeous Moschino dress I've had my beady eye on since Erica first arrived with her bulging suitcases. It's amazing, black and not just figure-hugging but figure-moulding. Like a full-body equivalent of a Wonderbra. I had to fight Serena and Emma for it, but since Erica's my big sister I successfully pulled rank before the real cat fight broke out.

Serena settled for a slinky sequined Gaultier that she looks totally fab in anyway, and Emma's nicked the Galliano that was my second choice if my claws didn't prove to be sharp enough. The international cosmetics company Erica's a creative director for has supplied us with make up for the evening, and to be quite honest, we give a new meaning to the word 'glam'. At least we think we do anyway, and how you feel you look, rather than how you actually look, is really rather a big percentage of the game.

The Oasis is definitely not on the agenda for this evening. We're trying a fresh hunting ground, a new club up West that's supposedly experiencing the same sort of attention from London clubbers as a new baby gets from enraptured relatives. According to one of the girls from accounts, it is the in place of the moment, filled to the brim with delicious men, bursting with testosterone, a plethora of perfect pecs, an abundance of muscled abs and arses . . .

I'm actually quite excited.

I'm surprised what an effect the thought of muscular male bodies has on me nowadays.

Planet Sex lives up to its outrageous name. It's out of this world. An alien spaceship landed on earth, an extra-terrestrial building pulsating with music and throbbing with strangely attired bodies, shuddering and grinding to the beat in an outlandish mating ritual.

I don't need to drink much, you could get high on the atmosphere alone. Swept by the crowd on to the dance floor, I'm delighted to find that I've remembered how to dance. I have rhythm!

With a whoop of joyous abandon, I throw myself into the beat with the enthusiasm of an Olympic diver hurling themself waterwards. The best thing is, Kate from accounts was right. The place is man heaven, filled to the brim with gorgeous morsels who could have come straight off a Jean Paul Gaultier catwalk.

Erica's metaphorically in a vat of chocolate mousse with a large spoon and a big appetite. Mason is a dim and distant memory – emphasis on the dim – as she boogies on to the dance floor and starts to gravitate in the direction of a pair of twins who are beautiful enough to be causing something of a sensation to our left as they do a synchronised shimmy in matching silver body paint and little else.

Jude, her honeyed body poured into a spider's web of a dress by Issey Miyake, slides up behind me and, putting her hands on my shoulders, joins in the rhythm. She tosses her head to the right and her long dark hair, woven into hundreds of plaits, tumbles down her back like frayed rope.

'Don't look now, but there's a *gorgeous* guy over there, and he hasn't taken his eyes off you for the past ten minutes.'

'I said, don't look!' she shrieks as I instantly turn to see.

I snap my head back and face my friend, who surreptitiously peers over my shoulder while pretending that we're deep in conversation.

'He's still looking,' she reports.

'What's he like?'

'I told you . . . gorgeous.'

'Yeah, but gorgeous blond, gorgeous dark, what?'

'Oh, yeah, sorry. Short hair, medium to dark brown, hard to see in this light, medium height, nice face . . . lovely face. Looks a little bit like George Clooney . . .'

'Really?' I ask, incredulous that somebody who looks even just a little bit like George Clooney would be looking at me.

'Really,' Jude confirms, her voice rising in mild panic. 'And he's coming over . . .'

'He's coming over?!?'

Jude nods frantically.

'Alex?' The George Clooney lookalike, who's not really George-ish but still gorgeous on closer inspection, appears in front of me.

He looks familiar.

'It is Alex, isn't it?

I nod.

'It's Alex. 'He holds out his hand. 'I mean, I'm another Alex – Alex Pinter. We met at the Oasis. I work with Laurence Chambers.'

Now that's a night I've tried to wipe from my mind with a good deal of success, I'm pleased to say. I do, however, remember Alex Pinter, and I also remember thinking he was rather sexy.

He smiles at me. It's a nice smile, sort of like Jake's: friendly, sexy, with a hint of laughter and eyes that crinkle at the same time.

I was wrong. He's not rather sexy, he's VERY sexy.

'I'm surprised you remember me,' I tell him somewhat coyly.

Emma's looking at him in open-mouthed admiration. Even Erica, still gyrating in spangly silver-twin heaven, starts to inch back in our direction.

'How could I forget you?' His eyes sweep over me with gratifying admiration. 'You look sensational. Can I buy you and your friends a drink?'

'Well, we . . .'

'That'd be lovely.' Serena elbows me in the ribs. 'Wouldn't it, Lex? Thank you.'

'Great. We're all over there.' He indicates a darkened corner. 'Come and join us.'

'Well . . .' I hesitate.

'Love to.' Serena butts in. 'We'll be over in a minute. Just going to visit the little girls' room.'

'I'll be waiting.' He grins.

'Two minutes.' She smiles seductively. 'We'll be there.'

'What did you do that for?' I gasp as soon as he's gone, suddenly overcome by stupid shyness. 'Maybe I don't want to have a drink with him.'

'Alex, he's stunning, and he likes you, and the three-month deadline is nearly up, and you're last on the board, and it's your birthday soon – and what the hell? He's a man, you're a woman. Just get over it, girl, and go for it. Besides, he said "we" and "all". That means there's more of them, and if they're all like him, then I'll love you forever.'

'You're one of my best friends, you're supposed to do that anyway,' I mutter darkly. Serena decides that I'm the most marvellous friend on earth as we head into Alex Pinter's darkened corner and find eight bottles of Moët and a group of tasty men eagerly awaiting our arrival.

The problem is, it's so *déjà vu*. It could be an exact re-enactment of the last time I met up with this motley crew in a night club. I almost expect a continuity girl to nip out with her Polaroids, stop-watch and tape measure. Amongst the group are Marcus Wentworth, the blond bomb site, who is once again fast asleep, this time on a silver Space Age sofa, mouth wide open, eating upholstery; and Tony, the Wolf in Armani, is already eagerly rubbing those wandering hands and moving in on Serena and Jude simultaneously.

I realise with a sinking heart that if the usual besuited crew are here then it's quite possible that . . . I quickly scout the group, fingers crossed, but sure enough, there he is, the lounge lizard himself, Leery Larry, propped against the bar, attempting to chat up an uninterested barmaid.

Worse is yet to come. I recognise another familiar face slumped on a sofa, glass in one hand, giggling blonde in the other; and despite the fact that my mind is begging my eyes to admit they're being thoroughly deceitful, there's no getting away from the fact that it's Damien.

Oh, hell! They've probably been out getting pissed together and comparing notes about me. You know, 'Well, we would have, but she passed out' and, 'Well, we would have too, but she ran off. What a wash out!'

I find Alex Pinter at my elbow again.

'Lexy, great, you came. Do you want a drink or would you like to dance?' he asks, grey eyes glittering in the strobe lights.

Neither, I want to get the hell out of here. Man

heaven has turned into my own personal man hell.

'Alex? Earth calling Alex . . . drink or dance, what's your pleasure?'

Sod it, I can't spend the rest of my life hiding from them in red-faced embarrassment. I'm supposed to be here to enjoy myself, so I'm bloody well going to. At least if I head back for the dance floor I can get away from . . . from . . . is there a collective term for wankers?

I grab the full glass of champagne Alex is holding out to me and knock it back in one go. 'How about both?' I grin at him.

We dance and laugh our way through the next half an hour, shouting our conversation above the music until the slowies hit. I'm not normally one to stagger round the dance floor clutching another hot sweaty body to tunes I'd normally switch off if they came on the radio, but Alex dances really well, and I don't object as he pulls me against him and begins to sway sensuously to Dina Carroll.

'I've heard some interesting things about you,' he murmurs in my ear.

He has? From what source? I wonder.

'I think we'd be good together.' His hands slide down my back, tenderly caressing the gentle curve where my waist tapers to my hips then slowly inching their way over my arse which he begins to stroke, not unlike someone repeatedly fondling the silken head of a spaniel.

It's quite a pleasant sensation. In fact, I suddenly realise that this man is turning me on and feel this rather silly sense of relief flood through me.

Hur-bloomin'-ray! At last I have proof I'm not a

frigid freak, a hopeless, hormone-deficient, sans-sex sad git.

I'm just settling against him with a happy horny sigh when I spot Erica signalling from the other side of the vast dance floor.

Reluctantly I head back to the corner of the club where my friends and Alex's cronies are having a wild party of their own. Empty Moët bottles litter the tables, one sofa is a heaving mass of male and female body parts – legs everywhere, no hands to be seen. I recognise Serena's patent Bally waving amidst the fray. Damien is still in the same chair but with a different girl, this time a giggling brunette whose tongue is probing so deeply into his left ear that it appears to be seeking a route through to the other side. This time he spots me, but fortunately is obviously in no mood to reminisce either, and apart from a semi-polite nod of recognition, makes no move to speak. Alex heads off to find us more alcohol with an affectionate pat on my bottom that would piss me off if someone else tried it, but merely gets me wondering what it would be like if the affectionate tap turned into a slightly harder affectionate slap on my bare flesh . . .

I give myself a mental slap round the face. Snap out of it, Lex. It's as though somebody has suddenly unlocked my hormones after a few weeks in solitary and now they're running totally wild to make up for missed time. Just because the guy's a pretty good laugh, and has a smile that reminds you of a certain someone who shall remain nameless, doesn't mean you have to take him home and attempt to recreate your sexual awakening.

Erica staggers over to me, waving a champagne cocktail, and clutches my arm. 'There you are, Lexy Wexy. I've been looking for you forever. Do you know . . . do you know . . .' she repeats '. . . you were right, my darling little sis. There's more to life than just one dress.'

'What *is* she on about? More to the point, what is she on? I mean, I've had more than my fair share to drink, but she's rolling around like the *Titanic* in a force-ten gale.

'I think I'm in love,' she gurgles.

Ah, the dress analogy. Light dawns. So does relief. Hurrah, Mason's out of the window.

'That's nice. Who with?' I ask her, detaching her claw-like fingernails from my flesh and steering her towards a silver stool.

'Him over there, the sexy one. He's really lovely. Lovely, lovely, lovely.' She waves drunkenly from side to side on the stool, like a slender poplar being blown in the wind. 'He thinks I'm Liz Hurley.' She hiccups gently. 'Keeps asking for my autograph. I like him. Did I tell you he thinks I'm Liz Hurley?'

'Which one?'

'The one that looks like a thinner Michael Douglas.'

'Larry?' I reply incredulously.

'Yeah, that's the one. Lovely Larry.' She grins.

Well, I've never heard him called that before. Leery, lascivious, Lothario, ludicrous, lecherous, loathsome . . . but never lovely.

'You know, I could really fancy him,' she slurs, eyes narrowing, lips pouting.

My sister fancies Larry. The *Titanic* has found its iceberg and is heading straight for it, full steam ahead! This is a major bummer. Let's just hope it's a side effect of the fact that she's rolling drunk.

'Don't you think he looks like Michael Douglas?' she repeats. 'I really like Michael Douglas.'

'What?' I never realised she had such suspect taste. I mean, Mason should have been an indication, but this . . . I shake my head in disbelief.

'Okay, Rics, maybe you do. I mean, different people find different things beautiful. After all Debbie married Paul, didn't she? But Larry . . .' I shake my head and sigh heavily. 'Imagine Michael Douglas as Gordon Gecko, Lizard Man, the wanton, wilful wanker of Wall Street?'

She nods.

'Then make him ten times slimier, and twenty times more ruthless, and that's Larry.'

'Really?' Unfortunately, rather than being put off, she seems kind of impressed by this information.

'He's a bad man, Erica.' I grab her by the shoulders and force her to look me in the eyes. 'Trust me, you don't want to know, okay? The word "fuckwit" was invented just for Larry, do you understand?'

She nods slowly. Her eyes are still glazed, but I think I'm getting through to her.

'Hey, Riccy baby, come and dance with me.' Eddie Maynard, whom I kind of like as he's one of the less moronic types from Larry's office, bounds up and drags my sister to her feet. 'You don't mind if I steal your gorgeous sister, do you, Lexy?'

'Be my guest. Just look after her, okay?'

'*Avec plaisir.*' He blows me a kiss and drags Erica off to the dance floor. It's hard to tell if she's dancing or just swaying drunkenly against him, but I don't think Eddie really cares.

Alex returns bearing more alcohol, a bottle of Becks in each hand, and a packet of dry roasted peanuts clamped between his teeth.

'Der yer wanna sert dern?'

I pull the peanuts from his mouth.

'Do you want to sit down?' he repeats, indicating an unoccupied chair with a nod of his head.

We both squeeze into the chair, thrown into proximity by design and dynamics, thighs pressed firmly together, hip bones colliding so hard we could add some kindling and spark a fire into life.

'You first.' I lift up so that Alex is sitting slightly below me, my right leg draped over his left, so that I'm sort of sitting on his lap really, pressed into his chest. I can feel his heart beating softly against the curve of my right boob.

Our heads are resting together. He turns to face me, so close that the tip of his nose is almost touching mine.

I sort of half close my eyes expecting him to kiss me, but he doesn't.

'I think I should take you home,' he says after a moment's silence.

'You do?'

'You look absolutely shattered.'

As if to prove his point, a huge yawn which refuses to be stifled escapes my throat and distorts my mouth to Jaws proportions.

'See, I was right. Do you want to go?' he persists.

'What about my sister? I can't just leave her.'

'She's an adult, isn't she? Besides, it's not as if you're leaving her on her own.'

'I know, but she's absolutely rolling . . .'

'Well, if you're worried, why don't you ask one of

the others to keep an eye on her?'

'I don't know . . .'

'She'll be fine. Look, she's over there with your friend Samantha.'

He points to the sofa which was previously hosting a mini orgy. Serena is perched upon Tony's lap, his hands ferreting happily under the hem of her dress while she chats animatedly with Erica, who's swiftly abandoned the dance floor and now thankfully looks slightly more together despite the fact that Eddie is currently fast asleep with his head nestled happily in her plunging cleavage.

'Rics,' I call to her, 'I'm going home now. Do you want to come?'

She turns, smiles, and shakes her head.

'Are you sure?'

She nods and mouths, 'Absolutely.'

'Will you be okay?'

She grins broadly, does a thumbs up, points to the sleeping head in her neckline, and crosses her eyes in amusement.

Alex and I get as far as the taxi door where he pulls me to him and kisses me until all the breath has been squeezed from my body. He kisses me with practised, yet relaxed expertise. He's good. It feels good. The warning bells haven't started ringing yet either.

We kiss in the back of the taxi, all the way to the mews, necking without pause for breath, like teenagers.

'Well, this is me.' I finally and reluctantly drag myself away from him as the black cab pulls up outside the red front door.

Alex smiles slowly.

Again, there's something in those light grey eyes of his that reminds me of Jake. A certain confidence, a hint of laughter. I don't know, but I can see what the others mean now. I just know that Alex is good in bed.

It's the direct gaze, like he's got nothing to hide and a hell of a lot to show me. 'Aren't you going to ask me in for a coffee then?'

Now that's the $64,000 question.

Am I going to ask him in? He's probably got a damn' sight more in mind than just coffee, and I'm still not sure it's what I want too. But what the hell? It's all in the name of research after all.

'Do you want to come in for a coffee, Alex?' I laugh.

'Coffee?' He grins. 'That's a nice idea Sure, thanks.'

'Just a coffee, mind,' I say sternly.

'Sure. Whatever you say.'


He slides in behind me as I fill the kettle at the sink, one arm twining around my waist, the other pushing my hair away from my neck to give access to his lips, which slowly and deliberately begin to kiss their way across the nape and up behind my left ear.

I feel a soft blush of sensation slide up from the pit of my stomach. Coffee momentarily forgotten, I turn to him, sliding my arms around his neck and joining in the kiss with warm abandon.

Alex puts his hands on my waist and, swinging me round, lifts me on to the kitchen table. Coffee mugs, biscuits, debris from earlier, topple to the floor as I fall back across the surface and Alex falls on top of me, both of us laughing as the kiss continues, pretty much uninterrupted by the change in location, as electrically charged and potentially explosive as an exposed live wire.

'Wow!' he murmurs, his warm champagne-sodden tongue searching out my fillings. 'Larry was certainly right about you.'

'You what?' I practically spit the tongue back out again.

Undeterred, he begins to trace a line of kisses down my throat.

'Do it for me, Alex.'

'You what?' I repeat, going as rigid and responsive as a recently deceased hamster.

'Do it for me . . . do for me what you did for Larry.'

He wants me to pass out?

'Do the poodle thing, you outrageous little animal!' he growls. 'Sit up and beg for me, baby. Woof! Grrrrrrr . . . woof!'

Are all men jerks? Or is it just the ones that I meet? Do I have a sign that says, 'Naive, Take Advantage' pinned to my back or something? Sorry, no. According to Larry, the sign reads, 'Easy Lay, Join the Queue for Kinky Sex'.

Alex duly ejected.

Me duly dejected.

Emma and Jude arrive back an hour later.

I'm sitting at the kitchen table, alone and unbonked, having dispatched a bewildered Alex into the night and now trying to drown my sorrows in fat – bacon sandwich, full-fat milk shake, large slab of coffee and walnut cake, a half-full box of pralines, a tub of melting ice cream, and half a pork pie arranged in a semi-circle around me on the table.

They're as high as kites. Jude's smoking something that looks like a dog end and smells suspiciously sweet. Her black eyes are glittering like dew-covered sloes, and she's laughing like an hysterical hyena as she and Ems discuss the antics of some guy desperate to get her out of her Gossard Glossies.

Serena is apparently enjoying yet another conquest back at her little pied-à-terre in St Giles. My sister is nowhere to be seen.

'Where's Erica?'

'Dunno,' shrugs Ems, heading for the fridge and pulling out a bottle of Evian. 'Thought she was with you.'

'Well, she's not,' I snap, in agitation born of worry.

'Ask Jude.' Ems tries and fails to break the plastic seal on the bottle. 'I think she was with her last.'

Jude staggers back from the bathroom, still giggling like a maniac, picks up my half-eaten coffee cake, and begins to fork the remains into her mouth like she hasn't been fed for a week.

'Jude, have you seen Rics?'

'Don't you know?' she replies, crunching into a walnut. 'She went home with that guy you work with.'

'What?'

'That guy you work with . . . you know?' She rolls her eyes in the effort of getting her dope-muddled brain to remember details.

'Damien?' I ask incredulously.

'Damien?' she frowns, shrugging. 'Is he the one

that was about forty with grey hair . . .'

Dear God, please, no!

'. . . an Armani suit, and a face like a thin Michael Douglas?'

Insomnia. I can't sleep. All I can think about is my poor sister in the clutches of Larry the Letch.

All night I pace the floor like an expectant father, then infuriate the usually easygoing Serena by phoning every half an hour from seven o'clock onward to see if Erica's got home yet.

Finally Serena can take no more.

'Look, Lex, I love you,' she mumbles, 'but I've got the hangover of the century, and I've only had about two hours' uninterrupted sleep. I'll get Erica to call you when she gets in, okay? And if you call me one more time this morning then I'm going to come over to your house, wrap the telephone wire round your neck, and slowly throttle you with it! Understood?'

Finally I get a call.

'You stayed the night at Larry's then?' I try to sound casual.

'Sure.'

'What did you do, lie back and think of England?'

'No, I lay back and thought of Alex, and it really put me off. It was like you were sitting on my shoulder, a loud little conscience, going, "Don't do it, Erica, don't do it!" '

'See, I'm good for you,' I tell her, without knowing myself why I'm so relieved.

'You're about as good for my love life as a dose, little sis. Anyway, don't get too excited. I may have backed off and slept in his spare room last night, but he's taking me to dinner tonight. And, hey, who knows? I might just have an evening free from little voices telling me what I can and can't do.'

'You're going out with him again tonight?' I ask jealously. 'I thought you came over here to see your family?'

'Hey,' she teases, 'Larry could *be* family if he asks me nicely. Do you think I should save myself for the wedding night?'

'Wedding night!' I shriek. 'Wedding . . . Hell, if you really have to do it, just bonk him now and get it over with!'

Erica laughs. 'You know, I was hoping you'd say that. See you at lunch.'

Come back, Mason, your sins are forgiven.


I meet Erica at a favourite Italian restaurant in Knightsbridge.

Jem, who's been away on business for the past two weeks, is supposed to be joining us but as usual he's late. He walks in, just as I'm trying to dissuade Erica from furthering her acquaintance with Larry the Letch.

'Crikey! You've only been back in the country two minutes, and you two are already arguing.' My brother's voice interrupts a pretty heated discussion.

'Jeremy!'

Sisterly animosity momentarily forgotten, Erica rears to her feet to greet the brother she hasn't seen in almost a year.

'How are you, darling? America must be good for you, you look fantastic.'

'Wow! So do you. You're so fit. Have you been working out?'

They hug in far too emotional and ebullient a fashion for the other diners around us, then Jem pulls out a chair and sits down between us to referee.

'Come on then, dish the dirt. Why are you two rowing already?'

'We're not arguing, we're having a discussion.' I pour my brother a glass of chilled white wine and pass him a menu.

'Actually,' Erica smiles archly at me, 'I think we're having an argument. Alex thinks she's entitled to run my love life.'

'I feel I have to when my sister is intending to sleep with a total jerk,' I snap.

'So what?' Jem replies, unfolding his napkin. 'You slept with one for five years. I think that entitles Erica to the odd night, don't you?'

He grins at us both, amused at his own wit.

I glare at him.

'I just don't want to see her making the same mistakes I did, okay?'

'Excuse me,' Erica cuts in, 'but I'm the big sister here, I'm supposed to do the guide and advise part, all right? Besides, one person's mistake, is somebody else's big thing.'

'Well, Larry's certainly big in the head department.'

Erica shakes her napkin, and her head.

'I don't know why you're so down on him, Alex.'

'I think our Alex is just down on men in general at the moment,' says Jem, squeezing my hand under the table. 'I'm sure this Larry guy shouldn't take it personally.'

'I think you might be wrong there, Jeremy.' Erica raises her perfectly plucked eyebrows at me. 'Lex isn't down on men at all, unless you count going down . . . in fact she isn't averse to the odd fling herself.' She looks at me knowingly. 'Emma told me about Jake, Alex.'

I stop gnawing on a breadstick, and scowl at my sister.

'Emma's got a big mouth.'

'Oh, yeah?' Jem grins at us both, thoroughly enjoying the altercation. 'Who's Jake then?'

'Nobody,' I mutter.

'Jake Daniels,' says Erica. 'He's Lex's new boss, and she already knows him far more intimately than she should – so god knows why she's lecturing me about the possibility of having a little fun with Larry.'

'Possibility? Possibility! I'd say it was distinctly more than a possibility, wouldn't you?'

'And why should that be a problem for you?'

'Jake Daniels?' interrupts Jem.

'Because Larry's a complete and utter arsewipe, that's why.'

'Jake Daniels?' Jem repeats.

'Yeah,' I finally answer my brother, while trying to out glare Erica.

'I thought he was working in Hong Kong?'

'Just come back . . . you know him?'

'Yeah, I know him. I've known him for years. We were at City together. Well, sort of. He was doing his last year when I started my first. He used to room with Michael Flanagan. You know, Lewis's elder brother? And Harry Lorde – you remember Harry, don't you, Erica? We all used to go out drinking together. We'd start one end of the Kings Road, drink our way to the bottom, then work our way back up again. Really nice guy. Good laugh. Did bloody well, think he got a first. Economics, politics and journalism, so far as I remember. Used to work for Channel Four and then he got head hunted by the publishing group that owns Lexy's place. He's a sort of troubleshooter, doing pretty well for himself so far as I can gather. You could do a lot worse than settle down with someone like Jake Daniels, Alex, I can tell you.'

'Settle down!' I reply in confusion. 'But Jem! I thought you told me I should go out and enjoy myself? Have a bit of fun, you said. Try some promiscuity.'

'Now hang on a minute,' Erica interrupts. 'If you're allowed to be doing the promiscuity thing, then why can't I?'

'I didn't say that!' he protests.

'It's not the promiscuity I object to, Rics.' I turn back to my sister. 'In fact, I'm really happy about the promiscuity. Ask Jem, he thinks a little promiscuity is good for everybody, don't you, Jem? No, what I really object to is Larry himself. He's a total fuckwit.'

'Well, the Larry I know certainly isn't. He's been nothing but a gentleman.'

'Don't you mean nothing like a gentleman? Besides, you don't know Larry, you only met him last night . . .'

'Whoah, hold on!' Jem flags us down with his hands.' Lexy, Erica's old enough to make up her own mind about this guy, okay? If he's a jerk like you say, then don't you think she's got enough sense to realise that for herself?'

'Suppose.' I shrug in reluctant submission.

'What I'm worried about is you,' he finishes.

'You what?'

'This promiscuity being good for you thing, for starters.'

'That's what you told me.'

'You didn't!' Erica says incredulously, eyes wide with outrage. 'Jem, how could you?'

'That's not what I said at all.' He holds up his hands in a defensive gesture. 'I said that Lex should let her hair down a bit. Not rip off all her inhibitions like a stripper on fast forward and run around shagging anything that breathes.'

'Well, you obviously gave her the wrong impression,' Erica says disapprovingly.

'I don't know why you're coming across all Virgin Mary all of a sudden,' I say. 'You told me yourself you only came back to Britain to get laid.'

'You didn't?' Jem asks, goggle-eyed.

An old spinster at the next table quits chewing on a piece of lamb's lettuce and turns up her hearing aid.

'Well, I've been single for such a long time . . .' Erica trails off, twisting her pink linen napkin awkwardly.

'Well, I'm single for the first time in ages.' I turn to Jem. 'I'm supposed to be following your advice and having fun, going out, getting laid, breaking hearts and not giving a damn, aren't I?'

'Are you asking me or telling me?'

'You told me to,' I say like a petulant child.

'You don't usually listen to a word I tell you, Alex, why have you this time?'

'This is all Max's fault!' snaps Erica, suddenly looking and sounding remarkably like our mother. 'It's all very well playing the field but it can be a dangerous game, Alex. Jem probably meant that you should get out and have some fun, not go on a mission.'

'Well, if I'm on a mission, as you put it, then it's mission bloody impossible! I'm not cut out to be promiscuous, Erica.'

'You say that like it's a bad thing.'

'Well, it is when you're in a competition to see who can have the most one-night stands,' I reply without thinking.

The waiter who was homing in to take our order, starts sliding backwards again, muttering something insulting under his breath in Italian about the loose morals of English women.

'Is that what you're up to!' Jem gasps, his big brown eyes almost popping out of his head.

'Well, you kind of started it with your bloody stupid hit list thing,' I retort, my face creasing into a sulk.

'Oh, no!' he cries in a lisping mock-German accent, slapping a hand to his forehead. 'I zink I ave created a monzter!'

'Alex, how could you be so irresponsible?' Erica asks, horrified.

'I'm not irresponsible.' I wave my fork at her. 'We have rules, you know. Safe sex or no sex. Though usually, in my case, it's safe 'cause there's *no* sex.'

'Safe sex isn't just about using a condom,' Erica looks aghast. 'It's about using your head, guarding your emotions as well as your health.'

'Well, there's no need to freak out. Apart from with Jake, I'm a total failure.'

'You're not a failure, Lex. This is my fault, I should have realised how emotionally vulnerable you were.' My brother shakes his head. 'Me and my big mouth.'

'I suppose I didn't help either.' Erica stops twisting the napkin, and twists her mouth into a wry smile instead. 'I suppose I haven't set a very good example.'

'Does that mean you're not going to see Larry again then?' I ask hopefully.

'In your dreams.' She laughs dryly.

'Well, what sort of example do you call that then?' I reply huffily.

'It's called, deciding what you want and going for it.' Erica beckons the waiter, who's been hovering nearby, ears on elastic. 'Which is as good an example as you're going to get, little sis.'

After lunch, she drags me up to Knightsbridge and Harrods on a shopping spree. I called a reluctant truce regarding Larry over lunch – I think very magnanimously on my part – and she now thinks it's okay to include me in her excitement about their dinner date tonight, and drag me round the acres of couture looking for a dress that's suitable for the opera, with dinner at La Scala afterwards. As if she didn't bring enough with her from New York!

After two hours trawling round all the top names, Erica flashing her gold card like it's got a sell by date of today, I'm finally following her through the home department looking for a guilt-gift for Mother whom she hasn't yet visited, laden with her shopping like a Himalayan baggage yak, when I spot them.

Max and Madeleine.

Or should that be, Harold and Hilda?

There they are large as life, wearing his and her Tommy Hilfiger jackets, Levis and Timberland boots, togged out like twins with a twee mother.

It's *the* weirdest sensation, seeing them together. I mean, seeing Max on his own would be bad enough, but Max and Madeleine, hand in hand, right there in front of me . . . Jeez! Don't get me wrong, it's not like a shot of jealousy or anything, it's more like the feeling you get just before a big interview where you really want the job. You know the typical scenario: butterflies buzzing in your stomach, a sudden awareness of your face so that every expression you wear feels contrived and completely wrong.

I tug on Erica's sleeve with my teeth, both hands being fully occupied, and indicate Max with a nod of my head and an expletive muffled by a mouthful of pure wool jacket.

She spots him straight away, then homes in on Madeleine with a critical eye. 'Is that her?' she breathes incredulously.

'Mmm. Sickening, isn't it?' I reply, spitting fibres.

'She looks like Barbie,' Erica sneers disparagingly.

'Is that such a bad thing?'

Erica's rolling up her Ralph Lauren sleeves and moving in for the kill.

'Well, seeing as we've bumped into them, I may as well take the opportunity to tell Max "I'm-so-Wonderful' Montcrief exactly what I think of him and the way he treated you . . .'

Dropping some Dolce & Gabbana, I grab her by the chain shoulder strap of her Chanel bag, and yank her back.

'Look,' I hiss, 'we're just going to slip quietly past them, okay? I don't want to see him, speak to him, or breathe the same air. Understand?'

But it's too late. Even as I speak it becomes painfully obvious that we've been counter-spotted.

'Alex! Hey! Over here.'

I attempt to hide behind a display of Lalique, but to no avail. Max has locked on and is moving in for full collision.

'Oh my god, if it isn't Erica!' He zooms in for an air kiss to each cheek while my sister goes bright red with barely controlled anger. 'Haven't seen you for ages. You're looking absolutely wonderful. You haven't met Madeleine yet, have you?

'Mads, this is Alex's big sister.'

He acts like 'Mads' and I should like one another. The fact that the last time we met she was naked with her legs in the air and Max positioned somewhat incriminatingly between them has obviously slipped his mind.

To her credit, and my slight pleasure, she looks bloody uncomfortable. Max just looks bloody pleased with himself, but that's his usual facial expression anyway. He puts an arm around her shoulders in proprietorial fashion and smiles pleasantly at my sister, who appears the epitome of calm and poise but whose nostrils are flaring in dangerously tell-tale fashion.

'We're just sorting out the wedding list,' he announces smugly. 'You will be coming to the wedding, won't you?' He smirks, turning to me. 'Did you get your invitation?'

God, he's enjoying this one. Max, drama king, has

always loved scenes, especially when he gets to play the key role.

'Of course,' I gush, determined not to let him think for one moment that I'm upset he's getting married. 'Hottest date in my diary for this year. Wouldn't miss it for the world.'

'You know, I'm amazed you managed to get everything organised so quickly,' Erica says pointedly.

Max ignores this, and merely smiles at my sister in frighteningly beatific fashion. 'I've had a marvellous idea! Why don't *you* come to the wedding too? Alex'll need somebody to keep her company.'

'Well, actually, I already have a date . . .' I reply, hoping desperately that Guy's still booked.

'Oh, how nice.' He smiles patronisingly. 'Well, must get on. As you say, there's so much to organise and so little time to do it all in. *Ciao*!'

'Sorting out the bloody wedding list!' snorts Erica, as soon as they're out of earshot. 'Smug bastard!'

'I wonder if they're having intertwined Ms engraved on their crystal?' I muse.

'I think you overdid the enthusiasm about the invite a little bit.'

'Well, I don't want him to think I'm cut up about it – smug bastard!'

'Does Madam wish to order something for the Montcrief/Hurst wedding?' A sales assistant who'd been hovering star-struck in the background closes in for the kill.

'Certainly,' I reply.

Erica looks at me in surprise.

'Actually, I do.'

Ignoring the crystal, the dinner services, and the

beautiful linen, I sod off to the book section and placate myself by buying them a do-it-yourself TV repair guide, and a manual entitled *How To Have Sex With the Same Person for the Rest of Your Life.*

Another night. Another nightclub.

I'm in my usual position, hiding alone in a dark corner, with my drinks lined up in front of me, and my invisible, man-repellent barrier glowing on full beam.

The game for me has turned into purely a spectator sport. I feel like one of those grannies who sits at the back of a court with her knitting, purely for the entertainment value, watching while my friends fish in the sea of people on the dance floor. While I am back tracking as fast as possible, Serena and Emma appear to be on full throttle. With only two weeks to go, it's a race to the last minute to see who comes out on top.

I know I'm the loser. Unless I go out and pull an entire rugby team in one go, then I'm footing the bill at Luigi's. But frankly, my dear, I don't give a damn anyway. I'm worried about Emma. Her ticks on the blackboard are fast on the tail of Serena's row of white marks.

I'm worried about Erica, who tonight has been taken to the River Café by Leery. He, pardon the pun, is really pushing out the boat in his efforts to woo her.

I'm worried about this bloody wedding. I don't want to go but I've got to, which really pisses me off. I'm being forced into doing something I don't want to do by the fear of what other people will think of me. I wish I had the guts to say, Stuff the lot of them! and just do what I want to do, which is stay at home and pretend it's not happening. But I haven't.

I'm still worried about working with Jake. I thought it would have worn off by now, but every time I see him I still get mental pictures of me and him butt naked and bonking.

I'm worried that I don't really know what I want out of life any more . . . hell, the only thing I'm sure about at the moment is that I don't want to be here.

I finish my last vodka and Coke and slope off home early.

Emma staggers back at eight o'clock the next morning, still drunk from the night before, slightly damp as though she's just had a quick shower, her see-through top on inside out, and her knickers stuffed in the pocket of her suede jeans.

I'm sitting at the kitchen table, nursing a cup of coffee, a bowl of soggy cornflakes, and a complex.

She grins blearily at me, eyes almost crossing in their effort to stay open, opens the kitchen cupboard, pulls out a packet of crisps as an impromptu breakfast, slashes a chalk tick against her name on our leader board, then totters off to her bedroom to sleep for the rest of the day.

She re-emerges in time to go out again.

I decide to stop in. My first Saturday night in on my own for ages. A time to relax and recuperate.

The highlight of my evening is switching on *Casualty* and finding that Max is in it. You might wonder why I'm so pleased to see my nemesis in full TV tone

Technicolour, when just the thought of him usually has me reaching for the vodka bottle, but it means I have the pleasure of watching him being rushed into hospital bleeding and comatose, on the verge of death following a pretty ugly accident. I watch with avid interest.

'Yes!' I shriek, thumping the air in triumph as he's attached to a monitor and promptly flatlines.

Unfortunately Charlie attacks his chest with a defibrillator, a burst of electricity to the pulmonary, and the line bleeps back into life.

'Booooo!' I hiss, throwing my chocolate wrapper at the screen.

Ten minutes and a couple of different emergencies later, we're back with Max. He's in an intensive care bed, attached to lots of things that beep and flash lights.

'It's no good,' the totally gorgeous Scottish doctor is saying, tears pricking his beautiful sympathetic eyes. 'It may look like he's alive and well, but he's clinically brain dead.'

'Yeah, tell me something I don't know!' I jeer at the screen. This is the best performance I've ever seen Max give, it's so true to life!

'But we can't just switch him off, he's a human being not a machine!' wails a ham actor into his handkerchief.

Shows how much you know him then, doesn't it, mate? Somebody point me to the switch, I'll 'Off' the bastard.

A nurse tentatively raises the subject of organ donation.

'Just don't try reusing his brain, his heart, or his

dick,' I spit, breaking into my third bar of Bourneville. 'None of them works properly!'

This afternoon I had to meet Jake in his office to discuss how my piece was shaping up. I showed him the notes I'd made about Serena's pick-up techniques, and a little bit I'd written on predatorily desperate career girls who hit their early-thirties and look on anything in designer trousers as a potential sperm donor. (Really hope Erica goes back to NY before it's published!) He seemed pleased with what I'd done. Told me I've great potential as a writer. Waterstone's make a space on your 'G' shelf! Actually managed to look at his face instead of my feet or his arse this time!

I don't feel quite so uncomfortable around him anymore. I'm pretty much convinced he's letting sleeping dogs lie. He's encouraging, which is nice. He was really interested in all my ideas, totally unlike Rodney! He asked me if there was anything else I wanted to discuss with him, but I think I'm on track with what I'm doing now. I'm feeling rather proud of myself for getting through a whole half hour with Jake without imagining him naked every five minutes – only every eight minutes according to my watch, which is a huge improvement. It's pretty difficult keeping a wayward brain off the subject of sex when the topic of conversation is legitimately about that same torrid subject.

The weekend of the wedding arrives faster than I could ever have anticipated. Erica abandons me very unwillingly to my fate as she is finally dragged off to visit Mother in Berkshire, kicking, screaming and pleading for mercy and an early release date.

The only high spot, in what will undoubtedly be one of the lowest memories of my life when I'm an incontinent granny in a bath chair, is the reappearance of the gorgeous Guy who comes round the night before for a wedding rehearsal.

It's a bit like being loaned a Michelangelo for the weekend. You know, look but on no account touch.

'I thought it was only the happy couple that did this sort of thing,' I grumble, tipping peanuts alternately into a dish and my mouth.

'You need a rehearsal more than they do. They've got a script, you've got to ad lib.' Emma comes out of the kitchen carrying an industrial-sized bottle of ice cold Frascati, and four glasses balanced by their stems between her fingers. 'We don't want you telling Max that you met Guy kangaroo trekking in the outback, and him saying you got it together over cold game pie and a bottle of Bolly at an outdoor Pavarotti concert, now do we?'

'We need to keep the story simple,' I say, taking the glasses before she drops them, 'Otherwise things could get very difficult.'

'Well, if you just stick to the easy stuff, like where you met, how long you've been together, that sort of thing . . .'

'I'm still not sure this is such a good idea.'

I haven't seen Guy since the party. Emma's spoken to him a few times just to make sure he's still okay to go ahead with this mad scheme of hers. Apparently he's dead keen to join in the charade, which is all very well but my overwhelming memory was that trying to get facts to stick in his head was like trying to wrap a parcel of live whitebait using wet Sellotape.

'Perhaps we should ring and tell him not to bother coming. I can save face by developing a vicious bout of twenty-four-hour leprosy or something so I don't have to go to the blasted thing.'

'Too late.' Emma grins as the distinctive throaty growl of a fabulous Ferrari dies away outside the cottage, followed by the sound of the front door bell.

'Aren't you going to let him in then?' She grins at me, amused by my discomfiture.

'Let me have a look first. Don't want you going to Max's wedding with just anybody, now do we?' Serena, whose curiosity is level nine on the curiosity Richter scale, pushes me out of the way and peers out of the window.

'Wow!' Her breath steams up the inside of the window. 'Nice car. Nice face. Nice arse. Where did you get him from 'cause I want one! He'll *more* than do. Go get 'em, girl. Oh, and I think you may need these.' She presses a packet of Extra Safe in my pocket.

'What!' I exclaim in horror as though she's just pushed a particularly slimy slug into my pocket instead of a packet of three. 'I'm going to a wedding, not an orgy.'

'So?'

'Well, I didn't know I was supposed to . . . well, you know, *go for it* with Guy? I thought it was all make believe?'

'We're thinking male mentality, remember. If the opportunity, or should that be Guy, arises, then you're prepared, aren't you?'

'I'm not sure that I want to be.'

'Excuse me.' Serena flicks back the blind again and stares down at gorgeous Guy, who's sitting on the bonnet of the Dino, long legs crossed, lighting a Marlboro, waiting for someone to come down and let him in.

'You're telling me that you don't want to *shag that*? That you have no inclination whatsoever to rip off his clothes and see if the body is as good underneath as the bulges imply?'

'Well, no, I don't want to, actually.'

Serena shakes her head in bewilderment and disbelief.

'You'd better start saving your pennies, Alex. If you're really this fussy, then the pasta is definitely going to be on you.'

I'm feeling a little more reassured when Guy comes into the room.

I'd forgotten how stunning he is. I really don't think it would matter if he opened his mouth and started talking like Weed out of *Bill and Ben*, you're so busy gazing into those beautiful green eyes that you don't really take in anything else. Even Serena, who's never backward in coming forward, is rendered speechless by the close-up view.

Emma introduces them.

Serena takes his proffered hand like she's holding something very fragile and extremely expensive.

'Nnnnnnn,' she replies in response to his polite hello, her eyes bulging like a mare in season just introduced to her stud stallion for the day.

Guy seems slightly more lucid.

He bounds over on long legs and greets me like an

old friend rather than somebody he's only met once.

'Alison! Great to see you again! You know, I can't tell you how much I'm looking forward to tomorrow, yah? What fun, eh?'

'Er, yeah, great. But it's Alex, okay?'

'Yah, Alex. Cool. Sorry, come to think, you don't look like an Alison.' He beams broadly at me.

What does an Alison look like? Not me, obviously. I decide that despite the lack of brain power, Guy's really nice. His simple happiness is infectious. He reminds me of a pedigree Labrador that spends its life sleeping, shagging and showing off, all grinning, glossy, gorgeous and waggy-tailed. Life's a breeze and then you die on the job with a big doggy grin on your face and your tongue and your todger hanging out. I like him even more when he hands me a green and gold Harrods carrier, with four bottles of Taittinger in it.

'What's this for?' I exclaim, peering inside. 'You're doing me a huge favour. I should be giving you gifts, not the other way round.'

'Well, I thought as we missed out on the stag and hen nights, we could have our own, yah? What do you think? Good idea? Bit of Dutch courage before the production tomorrow . . . build up towards the performance. Fun, eh?' He runs a hand through his already tousled dark hair and grins at me.

That's the longest sentence I've ever heard Guy string together. I feel like applauding but crack open a bottle of pre-chilled bubbly instead.

Three bottles later, and we haven't done much rehearsing.

The TV is flickering away in the corner of the room

with the sound turned down. Guy and Serena are tangoing shoeless and cheek to cheek around the room, taking it in turns to swig from the third bottle.

Emma and I are slumped side by side on the sofa, finishing the last of the Frascati and debating whether to open the last bottle of champagne.

Guy is crooning rather tunelessly into Serena's small right ear, and she joins in the impromptu duet, her eyes crossing drunkenly.

Emma's thumbing through the copy of *How To Make Love To the Same Person for the Rest of Your Life* that I bought as a wedding present for the M & M couple.

' "Variety is the spice of life," ' she reads, adopting a very bad impression of Miss Jean Brodie that sounds more Pakistani than Scots. ' "If you want your husband to come home to the same woman every night, then let him come home to a different woman every night. Act out his fantasies. Greet him at the door dressed as a schoolgirl one night, an exotic dancer the next. Serve his dinner as a fluffy, flirty bunny girl one night, and a buxom serving wench the next. Keep your marriage alive by using your imagination . . ." Crikey, this bloody book's so male-oriented! What about hubby greeting me at the door after a hard day's work in nothing but a posing pouch and a label attached to his dick saying, "Sod dinner, eat this instead"?'

Guy and Ren stagger past us, clutching on to each other like the last couple left in a marathon dance-a-thon.

'One, two, cha-cha-chaahh. One, two, cha-cha-chaahh!' slurs Guy, as the music changes to something with a distinct Latin beat.

'Do you think he can count past one and two?' I ask Emma.

'Shhhhhhh.' She presses a finger to her lips. 'Don't want to upset him before the bloody wedding, do we?'

'Talking of bloody weddings, aren't we supposed to be sorting out where me and my beloved met? You know, first kiss, first shag, first argument?'

'How about this then. You were skiing in St Moritz . . .'

'I can't ski.'

'Minor technicality. Anyway, where was I? Oh, yes, you were skiing in Klosters and fell down a crevasse in a glacier. Now Guy, who just happens to be second cousin to HRH Prince Charles . . .'

'. . . whizzes past in his helicopter, clad only in a black balaclava and army issue underpants, and chucks a box of chocolates on my head which instantaneously knock me out, leaving me to freeze to death,' I drawl sarcastically. 'Come on, Ems, take a reality pill. Why don't I just say that I met him at a party?'

'Well, that's not very glam and romantic, is it?'

'No, but it's true, and both of us might be able to remember the same story. Besides, I've got a few other details to learn that are pretty important, without having to concoct some elaborate work of fiction about our first encounter.'

'Such as?'

'Well, you know, I think it might be a big help if I knew what his name was as well?

'You know what his name is, silly.' Emma raises her eyeballs to heaven. 'It's Guy.'

'What, *just* Guy, like Madonna's just Madonna?' I

slur, attempting to peel the foil off the last bottle of bubbly. 'Hello, Max's friends and family, this is Guy, just Guy. You know, like Lulu's just Lulu.'

'Oh, I see what you mean.' She scratches her left ear thoughtfully. 'But I'll be blowed if I can remember . . . Guy, what's your surname?'

He stops tangoing for a moment, and scratches his left ear thoughtfully.

'Do you know,' he giggles, confiscating the bottle of bubbly I've just opened and taking a long swig, 'I'll be blowed if I can remember.'

## Chapter Nine

The day of Max and Madeleine's wedding dawns bright and beautiful. Not so me. I wake up still on the sofa, head glued to a cushion by the sheer weight of my hangover.

Emma has crashed out on the rug on the floor, head resting on an oversized bag of ready salted crisps, mouth open, snoring slightly, arms and legs flung everywhere as though she's landed after falling from a great height.

I grab an unsealed bottle of sparkling mineral water from the table, and not caring that it's flat and completely rank, take a long desperate swig.

I don't know why, but for me champagne hangovers are always the worst. Not that I get to drink champagne unless someone else is buying it, but whenever I do I always wake up the next morning feeling like I've been run over by a Panzer tank on night manoeuvres. I wonder how many brain cells the alcohol killed off last night? I wonder if Guy still has enough brain cells left to pass as a human being instead of a very pleasant vegetable?

Dragging myself off the sofa, I chuck a woollen throw over Emma, who's showing no signs of emerging from her coma, and stagger on jelly legs into the bathroom. I take a slow and careful shower, each individual jet of water feeling like knitting needles being jabbed into my head by an irate granny who's just dropped a whole row of pearl stitch.

Wrapped in a robe and feeling slightly more human, I debate whether to start clearing away the debris of the night before. Empty bottles, empty cigarette packets and full ashtrays, screwed up crisp packets, and a couple of dead cheese-encrusted boxes from pizza that I don't remember ordering or eating, litter the drawing room. My stomach starts to bleat pitifully for something solid to soak up some of the acid that's churning away inside me. I decide to sod clearing up and head for the kitchen.

Serena appears from Emma's bedroom, wearing Emma's tatty old robe, looking bandy-legged and knackered but bloody smug. She leans in the doorway, watching me.

'What are you looking so pleased with yourself for?' I ask her, loading bread into the toaster.

The bathroom door opens and Guy wanders past, wearing nothing but a small mascara-covered towel draped about his hips. His hair is wet from the shower, and his muscular body gleams with water where he hasn't dried himself properly. The smug smile on Ren's face is reinforced by a fresh burst of wanton lust.

As he walks past her, she reaches out and runs a finger lightly down his bare damp arm. He leans over, grinning as usual, kisses her lightly on the lips, then disappears into Emma's bedroom.

'You didn't?' I ask her open-mouthed, totally missing the fact that the toaster, which is temperamental at the best of times, is happily turning my bread to charcoal.

'Well, he had to sleep somewhere.' She grins. 'I couldn't possibly have sent him home in that state, now could I? And you know my motto – waste not, want not.'

Guy, who appears to be immune to hangovers, is dispatched to get his morning suit. Emma is awakened very gently with a frothing glass of Alka Seltzer.

I take two pain killers and contemplate getting ready. I spend an hour contemplating on the sofa, watching cartoons, until Ems, who's made a remarkably speedy recovery considering she was dead just over an hour ago, kicks me into my bedroom for the big transformation scene.

'I wanted to look all fresh and beautiful this morning,' I moan, peering at my hangover-ravaged face in my dusty mirror. 'Still, I want to look fresh and beautiful every morning and don't, with or without getting rat-arsed the night before . . .'

'Don't run yourself down, kiddo.' Emma's standing behind me, messing with my hair, pulling it back and twisting it into an impromptu chignon, then curling it round my ears like a Princess Lea lookalike. 'Don't worry, we have the technology to rebuild you . . . well, Serena does anyway. She brought her entire make-up collection.'

'Oh, right. I wondered why she'd brought a suitcase for an overnight stay.'

Serena digs out her ten-tonne sack of MAC, and

carefully appraises the damage done by three bottles of champagne, a bucket of Frascati, and poor genes.

'What's the verdict, Scotty?' Emma asks.

'It's not good. I dunna think she'll make it, Captain,' Serena jokes back. 'Don't scowl, Alex, it'll give you more wrinkles.'

After an hour of painstaking painting, she stands back, hands on hips, and surveys her handiwork.

She wolf whistles.

'You look gorgeous,' says Emma.

'Do I?' The last time I looked in a mirror, I had bigger bags than a kleptomaniac in Harvey Nicks, and was paler than Marley's ghost.

'Amazing,' Ren sighs. 'If Max has any sense he'll dump her at the church door and whisk you down the aisle instead.'

'In that case, I'm not going!' I protest.

'Look!' Serena chides me. 'I've just spent an age making you look like Cindy C, Emma found you a man so good-looking it would make Narcissus weep to look at himself, and you spent a bloody fortune on an outfit, so *you're going to the wedding, okay*? Now get your kit off!'

That's the first time anybody's said that to me in months. I pull on my silk undies and abandon my robe as Emma reverently removes a polythene-covered outfit, and a Jimmy Choo bag from the wardrobe.

I've also bought myself a big hat. The sort of hat you could only get away with wearing to the society wedding of the year, or Ladies' Day at Ascot. The sort of hat that obliterates faces in all the photographs, that ruins the view of an entire pew in church, that costs a month's salary to buy, and invariably gets sat on at the reception by one of the bridesmaids.

But I don't care because when I put it on I feel like Audrey Hepburn. I may not look like Audrey Hepburn – that would take a large miracle or very expensive surgery – but even to feel like Audrey Hepburn in my current state of battered self-esteem is pretty good going.

I follow the Hepburn theme with my outfit: little black shift dress, cream gloves that button at the wrists, classic black courts, and a small patent clutch bag. Emma lends me the diamond earrings she inherited from her grandmother, hushing my protests with the assurance that they're insured and worth more to her lost than stuck in the fake tin of baked beans in the kitchen cupboard.

Guy returns just after midday to whisk me off to the 'balls up', looking delicious in a dark grey morning suit, and receives even more compliments than I did on how good he looks.

I've avoided the subject up until this point, but he's so bloody Adonis-like I've got to know.

'What was he like?' I whisper to Serena as we head out of the front door.

'Beautiful to look at. But then sex isn't about looking, is it?' she hisses back.

'Hang on a minute.' Emma rushes to the fridge. Coming back with a small plastic florist's box, she carefully pins a lush cream lily to my breast. She grins up at me.

'I thought it was fitting, this marriage being the nail in the coffin of your previous relationship and all that.'

★ ★ ★

We decided I'd forego the dubious pleasure of the actual wedding ceremony, and just stick to turning up at the reception.

'Why put yourself through it?' was Emma's reasoning. 'Max'll be shitting a brick in church. He wouldn't notice if the entire England Rugby crew turned up dressed as Sugar Plum Fairies. Just go to the reception, do your Princess Gracious stuff and then come home again. And don't drink too much, okay?'

The reception's one of these over-the-top affairs and is held in a huge five-hundred-star hotel near Marble Arch.

I arrive to find the Montcrief family out in full force, the majority of whom, along with the bride's nearest and dearest, are all lined up just inside the foyer. The official greetings thing. I hadn't thought about that. Why the hell did I come? It's bad enough facing Max's friends and family without having to walk down that line and kiss every single one of them.

Max's parents, Max himself, Madeleine – you bonked on my sheets, you bitch! – Hurst (sorry, that's Madeleine Montcrief now, isn't it?), her parents, Max's best friend Hugo – a dipsomaniac, self-obsessed, manic-depressive moron whom I've always loathed with a passion – and about eight assorted puffy pink bridesmaids.

They don't look too thrilled at the prospect of duty snogging me either.

I feel like a striker waiting to hit a penalty shot, the opposing team all lined up before me, hands over bits in case I boot the ball somewhere painful.

I used to get on pretty well with Max's mum and dad.

While my family's only wonder is that it took me so long to get out of the relationship, his family wonder why I fell out of love with Max.

They often used to say to me that they didn't know how I put up with him. Now that I've left him, however, he has become a paragon of unappreciated virtue, and I am a whore-bitch-avenger-from-hell, the slapper who should be shot down, the tart with no heart.

I don't know what Max has told them, but I am obviously a fallen angel. My halo has slipped, and from what's been said, it's round my ankles along with my knickers.

I must be the only slapper who's only ever slept with one person. (Okay, make that two now.) The only tart who remains physically faithful to one man for nearly six years. Okay, I'm not oozing virginity from every pore. I've had my mental moments, and I've even had a couple of stolen – and usually drunken – grope-type kisses, but only towards the end, when I knew deep in my heart that it was all over but was finding it hard to let go of familiarity, however shitty, and plunge head first into the cold but cleansing waters of the unknown.

This is good, I'm getting angry again. It's the adrenaline boost I need to sashay down that line up, shake them all by the hand, and look them in the eye without flinching.

The parents of the bride are relatively easy, seeing as they haven't a clue who I am.

Then I get to Max and the new Mrs Montcrief.

At first he looks totally shocked actually to see me here, but then his face changes. He doesn't look like the cat who got the cream. He looks more like the cat that caught the mouse, totally bloody pleased with himself but with a sadistic edge to that broad smile.

Max invited me so that he could gloat, and now he thinks he's got his opportunity. I'll just have to prove him wrong, won't I?

'Alex, so glad you could come,' he purrs like a lion moving in for the kill. 'All alone, are we? How sad.'

I smile sweetly and hold out my gloved hand, like the Queen waiting for it to be kissed by a courtier.

'Actually, I'm not. Guy's just behind me.'

I indicate over my shoulder with what I hope is a gracious sweep of my head, to where the gorgeous Guy, looking totally divine in his morning suit, can be seen handing over the keys of my dream car to a parking attendant.

I couldn't have timed it better if I'd tried.

Max drops my hand . . . closely followed by his jaw.

Ding ding. Round one to Alex Gray.

'So, congratulations. A married man, eh?' I shake my head as though in disbelief. 'Who'd have thought it?'

Max is still gawping at Guy and the Ferrari. The gloating smile he lost a few moments ago swaps allegiance and slides on to my face. Nothing I could say would further enhance the pleasure of this moment, so I move on to Madeleine while I still have the nerve. Unfortunately, she looks gorgeous. There's not even a hint of Pavlova. She's wearing a stunningly simple silk dress that fits like clingfilm on a stick of celery, silhouetting her perfect figure, skimming her contours like fresh cream poured over strawberries. I suppress an urge to spit, take a deep breath, then seize her hand and shake it sincerely.

'Congratulations. I'm *so* pleased for you both.'

I've been practising the line and the hand shake on Emma for a week now, trying to get the pressure, the emphasis, and the tone just right. It comes out a bit insincere politician, but it wasn't a bad attempt.

To her credit, Madeleine manages to smile at me. Guilt's forcing that smile into place, but at least it's better than my reception at the next port of call.

'Hello.' I move on to Max's mother Margaret, who, resplendent in a hat that looks like a pale blue frilly shower cap, looks at me with lip-curling distaste and refuses to take my outstretched hand.

I stand in front of her like a lemon as she looks pointedly beyond me.

For a moment I feel a bubble of hurt embarrassment welling up in my throat, but this fortunately is quickly replaced by outrage. How dare the old bag snub me, after what her son did? She's treating me like *I'm* the one in the wrong and it's not on.

'So lovely to see you again, Marjory,' I say loudly and, leaning in, kiss her hard and wet on each cheek, leaving big red lip marks that stain her skin like a violent blush.

'How are those nasty varicose veins? Still giving you trouble?'

Guy catches me up at this point.

Max's mother's open-mouthed outrage instantly turns to open-mouthed adoration, her frosty eyes melting like ice cubes in sunlight at the sight of the gorgeous vision before her.

'Helloooo,' she purrs, as throatily as Chris Evans spotting Kylie across a crowded room.

I grab Guy's arm before he has a chance to say anything in reply and tow him onwards down the line, shaking hands, kissing cheeks, smiling as though my life depends on it.

Guy's certainly doing the trick. I have suddenly become invisible. All the bridesmaids are eyeing him up like he's hot chocolate fudge cake and melting ice cream, and they've been at Champney's on the strictest of carrot-stick regimes for the entire week. They can't wait for us to reach them, I can see them surreptitiously licking their lips in anticipation. Even Hugo, whose sexuality has always been a bit of an 'access all areas' thing, starts to look all hot and excited.

'Watch out for the tongues!' I hiss jokingly at Guy as we near the bridesmaids' end of the line up.

'Eh?' he replies, looking confused.

'Hang on, where did we meet?' I whisper, my brain a sudden blank.

'Er, at a party in Berkshire, I think?'

'No, not where did we *really* meet . . . where did we *decide* that we met?'

He just looks confused again.

Under the influence of rather a lot of alcohol, Emma had made up some wildly romantic story that would have won a best screenplay award at the next Oscars. I think we'll just stick to the truth. I don't want to go around telling everybody that I met Guy when he rescued me James Bond-style from the jaws of death, if he's adamant that we met at a party.

So much for James Bond. I've decided that Guy is

actually Roger Moore's right eyebrow reincarnated. He said about three words to me on the way over here, just played the Stone Roses very loudly on his in-car CD and grinned broadly at me every time I tried to speak to him.

He's bloody lovely to look at, but he's about as interesting as Steve Davies giving a lecture on the art of watching paint dry.

I'm out with a male bimbo.

He's got beautiful green eyes, well-turned pecs, and his bum is as perfectly formed as the ripest, sweetest peach in a fruit bowl, but where's the brain?

Fortunately it's not his brain that's on display at the moment. The envious looks continue beyond the bridesmaids and into the actual reception room.

This must be a bit what it's like to walk into a room with someone famous. Max likes to think he's a bit of a well-known face. I think his level of fame equates to that of the props that make up Emily Bishop's sitting room. You think you may have seen it before, but taken out of context you can't for the life of you think where.

The reception room is huge, table upon table of polished silver and white linen. Vast arrangements of pink roses, pink and white carnations – natch – gypsophila and buddleia fill the room. I'm highly relieved to see that there are at least three wine glasses and a champagne flute per person, then I remember Emma's and Serena's strict instructions not to get too tight and make a fool of myself.

A board by the door shows the seating plan. I find our names and fight my way through the babbling, honking, couture-togged throng, towing Guy behind me. The table numbers are hidden amidst the central flower arrangements, and I have to peer at several semi-occupied tables like a short-sighted granny before I finally find ours. I thought that bumping into old friends and acquaintances of Max's would be really awful, but as it is, Guy is my salvation, because instead of gawping at me, they're gawping at him. I hear several people whisper that he must be a famous actor friend of Max's, and one girl's adamant that he's Ryan Giggs, but she's wearing glasses thick enough to win a double glazing gold seal of approval.

I've been put on the 'embarrassing relative' table. You know, those people that you never keep in touch with but feel obliged to invite because they always send you a Christmas card, and a gift voucher on your birthday. To my right is Max's Great-uncle Avery, who gets wheeled out of an exclusive nursing home for family occasions, then wheeled straight back in again until the next gathering of the clans. He's nearly ninety, and as bright as a button, but feels that being this old gives him *carte blanche* to behave like a deliberately backward toddler.

He's sitting next to me now, surreptitiously farting away. His face is as deadpan as a poker player with a full flush, but the slight lifting of his right arse cheek every few minutes is a dead giveaway as to who's making the stink.

He also smells of the obligatory old person's stench of boiled cabbage and stale urine. Not much of an appetiser, I can tell you.

Ferreting in my bag, I pull out an atomiser and give him a thorough, yet surreptitious, misting with my Coco, which makes him cough so hard his false teeth almost shoot out into his port-soaked melon balls.

To Guy's left is Max's cousin Marina whom they've tried to keep under wraps since she was spotted as the star attraction in a hard-core Dutch porn movie last year. She's brightened perceptibly since we joined the table, having previously been the only inhabitant under thirty, and is currently trying to swallow Guy with her cleavage, like an advancing black hole threatening to envelop Captain Kirk and the entire crew of the Starship Enterprise.

Every so often Max looks over at me. That smug self-satisfied grin has made a major come back. He waits until he catches my eye, then makes a display of squeezing Madeleine's porcelain white hand or getting jokey with the new mother-in-law. When it comes to the speeches he really excels himself, spouting a load of flannel about how Madeleine has made him the happiest man in the world, how he never thought he could find a love like this – you know, really laying it on with a trowel. What on earth did I think I'd prove by coming? That I'm a sad old idiot who just keeps taking the punishment Max dishes out?

I mean, look at me. I'm so pathetic I don't even have a real love life of my own, I have to persuade some beautiful but brainless idiot to pretend he's mad for me. I study my reflection in the bowl of my spoon, the concave sterling making me look drawn and dour.

I'm about to head off on a real downer when I suddenly realise that Max is getting exactly what he wanted: he's making me feel bad about myself. He wanted me to come to this wedding and feel like crap, and if I'm not careful then his wish will be well and truly granted.

Bolster yourself, girl, I tell myself. You're here now and you either show yourself up or you show off.

I take a fortifying swig of champagne, even though the toast hasn't actually been proposed yet.

It's showtime! I've got the most gorgeous guy in the room sitting next to me, and who cares if he's only here as a favour? I'm going to make the most of it! I discover that a way to make Guy look animated is to get him talking about his gun dogs, so all I have to do is steer him on to the subject of Betsy, his two-year-old Springer, then lean on the table, gaze fondly into his eyes, look rapt and amused, and tinkle with laughter every so often.

'She's such a game little animal.'

'Oh, really?' I put my hand on his arm and slide a sideways look at Max. He's looking less smug now; in fact he's looking somewhat peeved. Bingo!

'A real trier, and bloody loyal.'

'Just how you like your women, eh?' I joke.

'Sorry?' Guy looks confused. 'What? Oh, yes, how I like my women! Good one! Ha ha.'

I sigh heavily.

Speeches and cake cutting over, the band has swung into action, and people are abandoning their tables to hit the dance floor.

Max, who along with his new wife is leading the first dance, is looking over at us again.

'Let's dance,' I say gaily, grabbing Guy's hands and pulling him to his feet. Unfortunately, unlike last night, when he fox-trotted, tangoed and cha-cha-cha'd Serena off her size fours, now he's as

302

stiff-backed as a dead cat with its legs in the air.

He's holding me at arm's length like a kid practising the rudiments of dancing with a kitchen chair as his first partner. Dare I risk getting him drunk to loosen him up a bit? What the hell? It's worth a go. I tip a couple more glasses of champagne down his throat, then drag him back out to boogie. A little bit of life has been breathed back into the dead cat, but although the bubbly has certainly loosened his limbs it's still not quite right . . .

'Guy, look, I really hate to ask you this,' I hiss, 'but could you possibly be . . . well, a bit more . . . you know, affectionate?'

'Sorry?'

'Well, act like you find me attractive or something.'

I could be very offended by the surprised expression this conjures up on his face.

'What do you want me to do?' he asks innocently.

'Well, what do you normally do when you like a girl?' I reply.

'You want me to take you home to meet mother?'

I crease up with laughter. At last! The bloke's actually got a sense of humour. I straighten up and see that he isn't laughing, he isn't even smiling slightly, in fact he's being perfectly serious.

Bloody hell! This is hard work.

I can see that even though we're waltzing, and I'm an old-fashioned girl at heart, I'm going to have to take the lead.

I grab him by the collar of his jacket, pull him to me and stick my tongue down his throat. Like a fearful swimmer on the high diving board for the first time, I just close my eyes and plunge straight in.

The water is warmer and far more pleasant than I expected. I allow myself the luxury of a leisurely paddle with my tongue. Not bad. He could bore for Britain but his tongue could join the official fencing team in the next Olympics.

I suppose he must have had a lot of practice.

My tongue moves on to the butterfly as his hands aim for something a bit less ambitious but far more obvious, and rove their way down my back to my backside. This is more like it. I'm giving Guy my best lip shot and he's responding like a true professional.

I slide a sideways look at the groom through my partially closed eyes. The groom's looking, and the groom looks pissed off.

He catches me looking and, pulling Madeleine closer, plants a big one on her peachy lips. It lasts at least sixty seconds, and is carried out to an accompaniment of 'oohs' and 'aahs' and hankies dabbed in the corners of wet eyes by the assorted watching relatives.

This is another bloody competition, only this time it's not to see which of my friends and I can bonk the most guys, it's to see who between Max and me has made the best life for themselves without the other.

When I stop kissing Guy, nobody but Max notices.

When Max stops kissing Madeleine, there's spontaneous bloody applause.

Round two goes to Max-a-bloody-million, and doesn't he know it? He's got that smug expression back again. Bastard! I want to go and wipe it off with my fist.

Guy and I return to the table. Fortunately Great-uncle Avery's currently got his wheelchair stuck in a drainage channel in a disabled toilet near the foyer, and the air is fresh enough to breathe.

Guy decides to follow his example and relieve his bladder, although hopefully with more success. The minute he's left the table, Max is over to gloat. He slides into the empty seat next to me.

'Strange how things work out, isn't it, Lex? To think this could have been you.'

I can see him watching closely for my reaction to this one. What does he expect me to do, burst into tears and confess that I wish it were?

'Oh, I don't think we'd ever have made it this far,' I reply with a cool smile.

'No?' He looks surprised. 'Don't you wonder what would have happened if we'd stayed together?'

I gaze in what I hope is an affectionate manner over at Guy who's been press-ganged into dancing on his way back from the loos, and is now being pressed rather too firmly to the over-developed bosom of Max's sumo wrestler of a sister Mitzi, as she carts him around the dance floor.

'Not really . . . I think things have worked out for the best, don't you?' I reply, getting to my feet. 'I hope you'll be very happy, Max. Now, if you'll excuse me, I think I'd better rescue Guy from your sister before she squeezes all the life out of him.'

Oh, boy, do I feel proud of myself as I saunter out on to the dance floor. I played that one just right. Cool, but not so cool that he'd think it was an act. I suppose even I wondered, without admitting it to myself for a second, whether I'd wish it were me getting married today when I saw the happy couple. I'm happy to say that I feel nothing but relief that I'm not the one in the white dress.

They do say pride comes before a fall, but I never thought Rod Stewart would be my downfall.

I've just prised thankful Guy away from moronic Mitzi when 'If you want my body and you think I'm sexy' suddenly begins to blare from the speakers. I've never seen music affect a man so deeply, and so instantaneously. From the first drum beat, Guy suddenly takes on a frightening alter ego.

I thought I'd been embarrassed before, but I was wrong.

You see, he knows all the words, every single one of them, and he's singing along with lungs that give him a voice as strong as Pavarotti's, but vocal chords that are far, far less tuneful.

He's also strutting around the dance floor like a chicken on uppers, elbows flapping, head jerking backwards and forwards like a cat about to projectile vomit a fur ball from its throat, threatening the hips of ancient relatives in his own epileptic fit of choreography.

Why on earth didn't I leave him in Mitzi's killer grip!

'Dah, Dah, Dah, Doo, Doo, Dadadadadadada, Dadadadadadada,' he wails at the top of his completely unmusical tonsils.

I know I should say to hell with them all, kick off my new Jimmy Choos and join in with gusto, save face by pretending that he's a really hilariously funny, madcap kind of man and this is his idea of a joke. But I don't, I'm not drunk enough. Instead I go the same disgusting blush pink shade as the bridesmaids' dresses and start to John Travolta side slide the hell away from the sad display that is Guy strutting his not-so-funky stuff.

I'm literally inches away from escape when I feel his hand grip my shoulder and whisk me around in a fast spin that Jane Torvill would have been proud to perform, and I hear three little words that fill me with utter dread and abject fear.

'Alex, let's dance!'

Thank heavens for mad friends.

I'm just standing there like a prat on the dance floor, totally mortified, totally embarrassed, wondering what the hell to do next while Guy jerks around in front of me like a puppet whose strings have been tied to the back of a bumper car, when in whisks Lucian looking like a refugee from the Tour de France in dayglo lime cycling shorts, a zip-up tight-fitting Lycra top, and a black strappy bike helmet.

'Urgent telegram!' he shouts at the top of his voice, shimmying his way through the throng on the dance floor. 'Excuse me, mind your backs, coming through . . . Urgent telegram for Lord Berkleigh . . . LORD Berkleigh . . . anybody seen his LORDSHIP . . . ooh, there you are, your LORDship.

He skids to a halt in front of a totally bemused Guy, holding his chest and panting. 'Soooo sorry to interrupt, but you know what it's like being the head of a multi-million pound business and related to the royal family – you simply never get a moment's peace,' he explains apologetically to the watching crowd.

'The power of contingency planning,' he whispers to me, as Guy, once more looking thoroughly confused, attempts to read the note he's just been handed, which is actually a blank piece of memo pad nicked from reception. 'My boyfriend Justin's the maître d' here. Emma put us all on standby in case of emergency. I've been watching from the wings all afternoon like a little guardian angel, and this certainly looked like an emergency to me! Don't you worry, treasure, Justin and I'll get Rod Stewart out of here, then you can escape down the fire exit.'

His voice reverts to the foghorn tone as he turns back to Guy. 'So of course, you see, you must leave straight away, your lordship. Terribly sorry to poop the party and all that but you know how PC hates to be kept waiting . . .' He clutches Guy by the arm, winks at me and drags my escort out of the room, shouting, 'No photographs, please,' as they go.

'Full of little idiosyncrasies, those royal types,' I hear an aunt of Max's, who nearly lost her false teeth to Guy's elbow-flapping, state indulgently.

I go in search of my hat and my bag. I'll reclaim my belongings, then get Lucian's boyfriend to call me a cab, and get the hell out of here.

Leaving quietly, however, is not quite so simple as I thought. My bag's under my chair, the hat's disappeared without trace, but as I attempt to make my way unobtrusively out of the room, I suddenly find that all of the people who were so ostentatiously avoiding me earlier are now practically queuing up to speak to me. I'm mobbed by a posse of Max's social-climbing relatives.

'Alexandra, angel, haven't seen you for simply ages. Where's that gorgeous man of yours got to? Don't tell me he's gone already? I shall be *so* disappointed!'

'Cooee, Alex. You can't be rushing off just yet, we haven't had a chance to catch up on all your news.'

'Alex, darling! I hear your fiancé's actually related to Prince Charles?'

Oooh, I'm engaged now, how exciting.

'You simply must tell me, how did you two meet?'

I've gone from being social outcast to centre of attention. I could enjoy this.

'Oh, on a yacht in the Med, so romantic.' I smile. Come on, sounds better than at a party in Berkshire, doesn't it?

'You must come for tea next time we're in town, my dear, and do bring that charming man with you.'

'So when do you actually become *Lady* Berkleigh, then?'

'Oh, we were thinking of a summer wedding.' I reply without thinking, 'I've always wanted to be a June bride.'

'But where's your engagement ring? I simply must see your engagement ring.'

I glance down at my naked left hand.

'Um . . . er . . . yes, well. It's in a *vault* . . . yes, that's where it is, all locked up, safe and sound. Insurance, you see. I only get to wear it for State occasions.'

Lord strike me down for such outrageous duplicity!

Max, who always was a complete star fucker, makes his way over to me again.

'So I hear your guy's a peer, eh? My, we are going up in the world, Alex, aren't we? How on earth did you two hitch up together?'

I realise I have an audience of several panting pastel pink bridesmaids, Guy's mother, her two snobs of sisters, and an actress whom I always suspected of having more than a working relationship with Max while we were together, and who usually pretends that I don't exist.

Sod it, may as well be hung for a sheep as a lamb. I make the most of the moment.

'Well,' I begin, smiling in what I hope resembles oh-so-happy reminiscence, 'I was skiing in Klosters last month and just happened to fall down this huge crevasse . . .'

'You, skiing?' Max asks in disbelief. 'In summer?'

'Summer . . . yes . . . Well, that's why I fell down the crevasse, 'cause the ice that was filling it sort of . . . er . . . melted.' I stumble to a halt, a stupid false grin on my face.

'I thought you said you met him on a yacht in the Med?' butts in a red-faced woman in an awful cloche hat.

'Well, that was . . . er . . . where I . . . er . . . oh, yes, I remember now. 'I tap my head. 'Got knocked on the bonce in the fall, still get a bit confused sometimes.'

The matrons in the group nod and tut sympathetically.

'Yes, now, let me see . . . yes, yacht. Now that was where he took me straight afterwards to recover from my skiing accident, and that's where I really got to know him, so when you asked me how I knew Guy, that was automatically what sprang to mind, you see.' I suddenly have a flash of inspiration. 'That and the fact that I was in a coma for a week and didn't really know that it was him who'd rescued me until I woke up . . . on his yacht.'

'Coma? Oooh, how romantic,' chorus the wide-eyed bridesmaids who are drinking it all in faster than the champagne in the crystal flutes they're clutching.

310

'But you can't ski,' Max says dryly, raising a sardonic eyebrow.

'Why do you think I fell down the bloody crevasse?' I growl at him. 'You know, I really need another drink. It's awfully warm in here, isn't it?' I fan myself with my handbag and begin to slide away from the crowd. 'Don't you think it's awfully warm . . . oooh!' I clutch my thigh as though in pain, and begin to limp off. 'It's the old Klosters injury.' I bite my lip bravely. 'Keeps coming back to haunt me . . . better get myself straight off to Harley Street. 'Bye . . . thanks for having me . . . lovely wedding.'

Once out of sight, I cut the limp and head at high speed through the hotel foyer, giggling like a maniac.

I've told so many lies I feel like I should change my name to Matilda. They'll be circulating the room now on the old gossip hotline – at least I'll confuse the bastards. Either that or make a complete prat of myself.

I'm shaking, on a bit of an adrenaline high. All this living on one's wits is hell on the old nerves. The hotel bar is calling me like a siren trying to lure a sailor. I decide to ignore Emma's alcohol ban and order a large one. After all, this has been one hell of a stressful day!

I wish I smoked. This would be the ideal opportunity to perch on a bar stool, signal for the bar tender, and pretend to be Catherine Deneuve. Hell, pretend to be anybody who isn't me.

Parking my bum on aforementioned stool, I manage to get eye contact with the barman.

'A large medium . . .' I begin wearily.

'White wine, madam,' he finishes for me, already

placing my drink on a little paper mat in front of me.

'But I . . .'

'From the gentleman at the end of the bar, madam.'

Well, I suppose this is kind of movieish.

I'm Bette Davis now. I turn coolly to nod my thanks with a stylish tilt of my head. But the stylish tilt and gracious smile go out of the window to be replaced by an extremely surprised gawp.

'What the hell are you doing here?' slips out of my mouth before I have a chance to think up something more suitable.

Jake slowly shakes his head,

'Of all the bars in all the towns . . . Nice to see you too, Alex.' He picks up his own glass and moves down the bar. 'I'm staying here while I'm in town.'

'The newspaper's paying to put you up here? Crikey. Why can't the budget stretch to a few more places like this for me to review?'

'Perhaps you should do a quick write-up while you're here.' He smiles, and sits down on the stool next to me. 'I haven't got a base in London at the moment. I'm still not sure that I'll be staying here long enough to merit getting somewhere. So in the meantime . . .' He gestures around us. 'Here I am.

'I take it you're with the wedding?' he indicates the lily pinned to my boob.

I rub at my aching temples with my fingertips, and nod.

'You see that guy over there, the prat in the cravat?'

'I take it you mean the groom?'

'Yeah . . . well that is Max. Up until three months ago, Max and I, well . . . we were together for five years.'

'Three months!'

'Uh-huh.' I nod wearily, and take a slug of my drink. 'And yes, before you ask, there was a bit of an overlap. Don't ask me how much of one because I've never had the guts to find out.'

'And you came to his wedding?'

'I was invited.'

'Yeah . . . but still.'

'I like wedding cake.' I look at him sideways and smile slightly. 'Besides, *Nil bastardo condemderandum*, as my grandfather used to say. At least, it was something like that.'

'Well, if it's any consolation, the man's a fool. You look gorgeous.'

'You should've seen the hat,' I reply wryly.

'Where is it?'

'Probably being used as a frisbee by some beribboned little brat.' I shrug, taking another fortifying slug of my wine and sighing heavily.

He looks at his watch then back at me appraisingly.

'I'm supposed to be meeting some people for dinner in half an hour,' he says slowly. 'You're obviously not having much fun here, why don't you join us?'

Hang on a minute, is Jake asking me out?

'I don't want to gatecrash,' I mumble uncertainly.

'That's not a problem, it's a work thing. To be perfectly honest you'd be doing me a favour. I'm not really looking forward to it. Some of the bosses at your place aren't exactly . . . how shall I put it? . . . fun to be with.'

'My place? It's your place too, and your bosses, so you'd better not let them know they're not your first choice of dinner date. They'd be mortally offended.' I think of Larry's reaction to my refusal to join him for dinner, instant gossip-mongering in the canteen queue.

'Oh, I think I'm safe. You see, I don't actually work for them. I'm only at *Sunday Best* on secondment from the parent company, on a sort of consultancy basis until I've got you running properly again. And then I shall be off to pastures new.'

'You're leaving us?' I suddenly feel rather disappointed. I've spent so long getting wound up about Jake being here, it never occurred to me how I'd feel if he wasn't.

'Eventually,' he replies. 'When I've got you sorted out.'

'So who's going to take over as Editor when you've gone then?'

'Well,' he scratches his cheek thoughtfully, 'they might get someone from outside, or maybe Damien'll be made up. I don't know yet.'

'Damien? Oh, god!' I shriek without thinking.

Jake looks at me thoughtfully, but thankfully doesn't pick up on my horrified reaction.

'How's that piece I gave you going?' he asks instead.

I take a long swig of my drink, the alcohol sliding blissfully easily down my dry throat.

'Okay,' I reply cautiously.

'Not having any problems with the subject matter?'

'Should I be?'

'Well, it's always easier to write about something you're familiar with . . .' He smiles at me, and just for a second I catch this look in his eye. A look of, well . . . almost . . . *affection*? The same look he gave me when we first fell together in that long delicious kiss by the pool.

I feel a strange mixture of relief and sort of hope. Maybe he doesn't hate me for what I did. Maybe he's forgiven me for my disappearing act. Maybe I can finally broach the one subject we've both so studiously avoided for so long . . .

'You haven't wiped that night completely from your mind then?' I finally venture when my face has stopped burning enough for me to prise open my seared-together lips.

'You think I instantly forget everyone I sleep with?'

Everyone? I think in panic. Have there been lots?

'Isn't that what men do?' I fiddle with the bowl of peanuts on the bar, not able to bring myself to look him in the face. 'You know that sex releases hormones in the body, endorphins and things? Well, I think that in men something hormonal's released that makes them forget who it was they just slept with. It's probably interlinked with the hormone that makes them go to sleep immediately afterwards.'

I drag my gaze upwards. He narrows his eyes, trying to work out if I'm joking or not. 'You know, women get really angry if men generalise about them. "You're all the same". Doesn't that phrase drive you mad?'

'Uh-huh.' I nod slowly, already catching on to the fact that I am about to be made to eat my words.

'Don't you think that men are all different too? You can't lump us all into the same category. Sure there are certain common characteristics, but everybody is an individual, regardless of their sex.'

I decide it's wisest just to nod my agreement.

'Why didn't you say anything?' I finally venture.

'Why didn't you?' he replies, with a half smile.

'*Touché.*'

He looks at me for a moment.

'I didn't say anything because you were obviously extremely uncomfortable about the whole thing. The first time we met at the office your face was as red as that folder you were hiding behind.'

'You mean, you knew who I was straight away?'

'Come on, Alex, do you think I'm stupid? The number of times I thought I should just say something to clear the air . . . but I didn't bring it up because it was obviously something you were highly embarrassed about.'

'Well, I'm not in the habit of having one-night stands,' I mumble.

'Oh, is that what it was, a one-night stand?'

'Well, it was one night,' I half laugh. 'But we didn't do much standing. So far as I remember we were horizontal most of the time.'

Again, a slight quirk of the lips, but then he looks at me sternly.

'You've been playing games with me, Alex.'

'What about you!' I suddenly decide the best form of defence is attack. 'If you think I've been playing games, take a good long look at yourself. What do you think giving me that assignment was if it wasn't playing games?'

'It wasn't a game. It was a way of keeping an eye on you. Making sure you didn't self-destruct.'

'What do you mean?'

He sighs, and takes a slug of his drink.

'Look, Alex. I like you. I like you a lot. What you're doing just isn't you.'

'What do you mean "what I'm doing"?'

'I've been hearing things, Alex.'

'Well, you shouldn't listen to rumours.'

'It's hard not to in a place like ours.'

'Well, you shouldn't believe everything you hear then, should you?' I reply crossly.

'Shouldn't I?' he asks gently. 'What about you and Laurence Chambers? And I know something's gone on between you and Damien. The atmosphere between you is terrible. I tried talking to him about it the other day, but he was about as willing to open up as you are.'

He's not being accusing, but my back's up.

'Not according to the rumours though, eh? According to them I'm as open as a twenty-four-hour café.'

He doesn't respond.

I shake my head.

'You know, you're the last person I'd expect to believe the load of crap that circulates our office.'

'I didn't say I believed the rumours, Alex.'

'No, but you didn't say you didn't either,' I snap angrily. 'Yeah, well, it's all true. I'm just working my way round the office. I might try Nigel next, then perhaps a kinky threesome with Lionel and Sandra, then I thought I might move on to Lucian – I mean, if anybody can convert him it has to be me, doesn't it? After all, I've gone round the entire building more times than the bloody tea trolley!'

I suddenly become aware that I'm shouting so loud that the entire bar can hear me. I once again turn the same unflattering shade as a baboon's bottom, grab my bag, and run.

Work on Monday. The prospect is about as inviting as a quick dip in a freezing cold, shark-infested sewage pit. However, no matter how petrified I am of going in, I'm even more scared of not going in. You see, there's a part of me that just wants to run away, hide, never face Jake again after Saturday's fiasco, and there's another part of me that really wants a chance to set the record straight, to let him know that he was a one off, and that my so-called 'sexual circus' is the equivalent of a clapped out clown in a one-man tent. I'm not swinging from chandeliers with the skill and frequency of a trapeze artist, juggling twenty men single-handed, or cracking a whip at my own pride of lions.

I'm just me. Alex. Steadfastly monogamous, with only one chalk mark to my name and only one name to that chalk mark: Jake Daniels.

He's in a meeting all morning. I sit at my desk trying to work on an interesting fact list Damien asked me to knock up on past monarchs.

He still finds it difficult to face me. He's taken to passing on instruction in memo form, which is highly unnecessary and has the added complication of making Glenda think he must fancy her because he's always popping in and out of the secretaries' office with bits of scribbled-on paper.

Henry VIII had six wives. Well, that's sheer greed for you, that is.

How can I concentrate on work when all I want to do is put the case for the defence to Jake? He must think I'm terrible. I go to bed with him, then leave before he even wakes up. Rumours are flying about me and Larry. People are suspicious that Damien and I are so ostentatiously avoiding each other. Alex Pinter will no doubt have added his own insight into the sordid love life of Alex Gray.

Perhaps I should make myself a banner stating, 'I am not a slapper!' in bold black letters, and parade up and down outside his office.

The blinds that normally shroud Jake's office in secrecy are open today. Through the smoked glass, I can see that he's got Annabelle Stead from accounts in with him. They're going through a computer print out thicker than two box files put together. She's leaning forward in her chair, blouse unbuttoned to an indecently low level, laughing and flicking her hand through her strawberry blonde hair every five seconds. Crossing and uncrossing her long legs with greater frequency than Cupid Stunt. Now if you want a tart, that's one. Talk about giving out signals! She's giving him more come on than a traffic cop with a twitch.

Now she's getting up from her chair and heading around to his side of the desk, pointing something out with her pen, leaning over him, giving him the full benefit of her finely freckled cleavage.

I flick from my fascinating facts file to my piece for Jake, and type up a new heading: 'The predatory female in the work environment – sexual harassment'.

Jake is saved by the jealous Sandra, who bustles in with two cups of coffee and practically bounces Annabelle back to her chair.

I finally get my chance to speak to him in the corridor, both of us having slipped out of the office to use the loo at the same moment.

Unfortunately, when I open my mouth to explain, my brain chooses that moment to pass control of my bodily functions to my libido.

You see, as he stops and looks at me with those strange, intelligent, greeny-blue eyes, a fist of pure lust punches me straight in the face as though swung by Mike Tyson at his fittest.

I'm totally knocked out by the sensation that comes over me.

I want him. I mean *really, really* want him.

Jake waits politely for me to speak.

I try and fail to reconnect my brain to my mouth.

Fortunately, as I'm standing there open-mouthed and panting like a bitch in heat, stupidly silent, and with absolutely no hope of extricating myself from a very awkward situation, Sandra bustles up full of importance and drags him away to a conference call.

For the rest of the day I find myself staring across the office at Jake like a dog contemplating a full supper dish, but being told to sit, stay and beg before it can dive in. He's taken off his jacket and I can see the contours of his lovely muscular back beneath the white cotton of his shirt. I remember running my hands over that flesh, travelling downwards to grip his tight-muscled arse as he . . . I don't need to water my new plant anymore. The drool has soaked it to the roots.

I really must snap out of this. I'm supposed to be uberbabe, the new New Woman, who takes what she wants from men and doesn't get emotionally involved. I am not falling for Jake. I am simply lusting after a bloody good shag. And, boy, was he a bloody good . . .

'Alex . . . earth calling Alex.'

I look up to see Mary grinning down at me. 'I was saying, do you want a coffee? I'm just going to grind some beans.'

'You're joking, aren't you? What happened to the instant crap-in-a-cup we normally have to put up with?'

'Jake bought a percolator.' She beams. 'That man is just so thoughtful.'

Mr Too-Good-to-be-True. I decide I don't like him after all. There's no room for me to like him. Every-bloody-body else in the entire office is already madly in love with him.

I find my gaze drawn to his office again.

Damien's taken over the hot seat in there. It looks like they're having a pretty animated discussion.

Oh, no, what if they're talking about me? How can I concentrate on a piece on the sexual morals of modern-day women when Jake and Damien could at this very moment be discussing my own personal lack of them?

I decide to sod work and call up my much-neglected novel, but I'm even getting cynical so far as fictional romance is concerned nowadays.

The plot has changed from heroine being rescued and carried off into the sunset by handsome hero, to heroine thinking she's found the man of her dreams only to come home from lovingly washing his dirty underpants at the mediaeval launderette to find him in bed with the woman from the castle next door.

Why do most women rely on a man to make their dreams come true?

I feel like buying a vibrator, making a suit of armour out of old baked bean tins and becoming self-sufficient. Then again, I'd have to be solitary if I'd eaten enough baked beans to make myself a suit of armour. Come to think of it, I'd be making my own personal gas chamber. Oh, well, it's a novel way to commit suicide when the loneliness really starts to get to me.

'Hello, people!'

I look up as there's a collective groan from the female contingent of the office. A pencil with large boobs and long peroxide blonde hair has just tottered through the door on a pair of outrageous Vivienne Westwood platforms.

This, 'people', is Ashley Wallace, a minor starlet who has achieved fame simply by being an upper-class slapper who bonks lots of footballers and pop stars, and on the strength of her sexual athletics gets to write us a gossip page once a month.

Emma and I call her the Pop Tart. Perhaps I should interview her for my piece. She's not a bimbo, she has a brain, but unfortunately it has been finely tuned from birth to think of nothing but sex and men and money . . . no, hang on, I think I'll just stick at the nothing.

Ashley has to dictate her 'gossip spot' to Sandra each month. We think this is because she doesn't actually know how to spell, but she says it's because she has weak wrists.

Her left wrist is weak from RSI through flicking her blonde hair out of her face so frequently, and her right wrist is weak from signing up to one hundred credit card chits per day.

'Where's my darling Damien?' she demands, flopping into the nearest vacant chair, and inspecting her nail varnish.

Ashley and Damien are doubles partners in flirting for Britain at the next Olympics.

'He's in with the boss. I think he's in a spot of trouble,' replies Mary.

'The delicious Jake, eh? I wouldn't mind getting a lashing from his tongue.' Ashley giggles lustfully. 'You know, I could seriously set my sights on a man like him. He's wealthy, intelligent, funny, good-looking, seriously sexy . . . I wonder what he's like in bed?'

Absolutely bloody amazing! screams a voice in my head. I know. I've been there and you bloody haven't, so there.

Okay. Reality check here.

Eyes narrowed. Lips curling disdainfully. Nostrils flared. Growl imminent. Prognosis? Well, I've either got severe wind or I'm jealous.

Jealousy? No! It can't be.

I test the sensation by imagining Jake in bed with Ashley. Result? I want to rip her entrails out with my fingernails, wrap them round her throat and slowly throttle her with them.

Okay, I'm jealous.

What's wrong with me?

Ashley's still prattling on.

'Apparently he was seeing someone in Hong Kong, but I gather he's young, free and single at the moment. Perhaps I should offer to reacquaint him with the London scene.' She purses her pouting pink lips thoughtfully.

'I don't think Jake's really your type, Ashley.' I smile to hide the venom.

'Why ever not?'

'Well, he's never married Patsy Kensit, and he doesn't swap shirts after sex.'

The sarcasm goes straight over Ashley's pretty head. She crosses her huge Bambi-like baby blues at me in confusion, and wrinkles her pretty little nose in the way she always does when she tries to kick start her brain.

'Sorry?' she lisps.

You know, I've just had a major brainstorm. I should introduce her to Guy. If ever a couple was born to be together it's them.

'He's gay, Ashley.'

Wash my mouth out with soap and water! Yet another lie to add to the collection. What *is* wrong with me at the moment? It just sort of popped out of my mouth before I could stop myself.

Why am I getting jealous because Ashley fancies Jake? Ashley fancies anything that has hairy legs underneath their trousers and a full wallet – apart from Sandra – and it doesn't usually piss me off this much. It's not because I fancy Jake myself. I mean, I do, I'll be the first to admit that I lust after him rather a lot, but it's not like I want to have a full on relationship with the guy, so why am I worried that Ashley might? Besides, what chance would I stand?

Well, you know that he fancies you 'cause he's already been to bed with you.

No, come on now, Alex. He's a man, remember.

That doesn't necessarily follow, does it? Besides, he now thinks you've got the sexual morals of an alley cat in the mating season, so he wouldn't be interested even if you were. Which you're not, are you?

Sure, I find him very attractive. He has a lot of good qualities, not least that he seems to be the only man I've ever met who knows how to switch on my libido and keep it running for the required period of time – well, pretty much constantly really.

A lot of men don't realise that to turn a woman on you don't just have to stimulate her body. The most important part is to get her mentally gagging to rip off all your clothes.

Jake gets me as mentally excited as a thoroughbred waiting for the off at Ascot. I just have to think about his broad chest, and I'm practically sticking to my underwear. Any amplification of this thought, i.e. me lying naked across said broad chest, and I have to walk with my legs tight together for fear of leaving trails wherever I go. How does this man do this to me? Can somebody tell me why I want him with a passion I've never known before in my life?

Some people say it's all about pheromones and hormones. You know, chemistry. So far as I go, mix Jake's pheromones with mine and you construct the sexual equivalent of an H bomb.

So, yes, I admit, I fancy him rotten. But a relationship? That's another matter entirely. I mean, who mentioned anything about relationships?

Oh, yes, Ashley did.

Hang on . . . Eyes narrowed. Lips curling disdainfully. Nostrils flared. Growl imminent. Yes, it's happening again.

I try to resume a normal expression and end up looking like an entrant in a gurning competition. What on earth is wrong with me? I like Jake, fancy and like, that's all. That's it. Nothing more. I like him. He's funny. We can talk to each other. You know, have a conversation. Living with Max, I didn't think that sort of thing existed, being able to have an intelligent conversation with a man you've slept with.

'How are you getting on with that article, Alex?'

A voice interrupts my manic reverie.

I realise that Ashley's hitched her micro skirt up a few more inches and set her lips to seductive pout mode, and even Mary's fluttering her eyelashes. I look up to see the object of all this untamed lust, and pure and simple *liking* – nothing more, honest – standing in front of me.

As usual the generator that runs my brain shuts down again.

'Sometimes things aren't what they seem . . .' is all I manage to utter, eyes rolling like a rabbit with myxamatosis.

'Right, fine.' Jake looks at me in bewilderment. 'Deadline next week, okay?'

I decide to try and cheer myself up with some pampering.

Why it makes me feel better to go and have some burly, muscular woman spreading hot wax on my legs and then ripping all my hairs out, I don't know, but it does. Perhaps it's the very thin threshold between pain and pleasure.

I also decide to go and get a new hairdo. It is a strange female myth that it doesn't matter how low you feel or how shit your life is, a new hairdo is guaranteed to cure all problems – not.

Getting an appointment with my hairdresser, Harry, is harder than getting a table at the Ivy. You have to book at least three months in advance. Fortunately he's an old friend and when I phone up pleading confusion and misery, I'm immediately allocated a coveted and very rare cancellation spot.

Two days later I'm being shampooed by a junior stylist with severe PMT, who alternately boils off my hair follicles with scalding water, then freezes my scalp with icy blasts from the rubber shower attachment fixed to the taps in the basin.

I then get wheeled, dripping madly, over to one of Harry's mirrors, where I'm given a cup of disgusting coffee and a copy of *Hello* with Fergie in it to wile away the three-quarters of an hour I have to wait for him to finish with his previous client.

He finally strolls over, puts his hands on my soggy shoulders, and beams at my reflection.

'What do you fancy today then, darling?' Harry has a smile like a Red Setter with a large stick in its mouth.

I put down my well-thumbed magazine.

'Brad Pitt and Tom Cruise in a sex sandwich?'

'I'm a hairdresser, not a miracle worker. Besides, I meant with regard to your hair . . . er . . . style? Though I'm using the word "style" very loosely.' He runs a long-fingered hand disparagingly through my limp locks.

'Oh, I don't know . . . just make me look gorgeous.'

'Darling, I told you, I'm a hairdresser, not a miracle worker.'

I pull a face at his reflection.

'You're supposed to be a top stylist, Harry, so do your job and style okay?'

'Well, you need to give me some sort of clue as to the sort of look you're after?'

'I kind of fancy it sort of Liz Hurley meets Rachel from *Friends* . . . a bit of glamour but practical with it. Something I don't have to blow dry for eight hours with eight gallons of hair mousse and a brush that looks like a combat weapon.'

Harry runs both hands through my hair so that it flops limply down on either side of my face, back into my usual boring basic shaggy mess.

'Just a trim then?' he asks.

'Yeah,' I sigh. 'Just a trim.'

'So what have you got to tell me then?' He starts to wield his scissors with the rapidity and deftness of a sword-swirling Ninja. 'What's new?'

'Oh, nothing much . . .'

Harry sighs. He loves a good gossip.

'Only that I left Max and embarked on a rampant rampage of one-night stands.'

'Oooooh!' The light flickers back on in his eyes. 'Tell me *everything*?'

'Well, I'm ashamed to admit that there's not really an awful lot to tell. My rampant rampage has been a bit of a slow shuffle really. I think there's something wrong with my technique.'

'Well, you've come to the right place then. Technique is my forte.'

'It is?'

'I'm not just an artist with the scissors, you know. That's one of the advantages of being a hairdresser: you get to hear everybody's secrets. I'm a veritable Dr

Ruth, I am. I've heard more sex stories than the editor of *Penthouse*.' He picks up a mister and squirts my drying locks.

'Go on, ask me anything?' he says confidently.

'Okay. Will a man have sex with a woman he doesn't fancy?'

'Well, what are the circumstances?'

'A one-night stand.'

'I think it helps if you fancy them, but I suppose if you're desperate . . .'

That makes me feel a bit better. I can't see Jake ever getting to the point where he was desperate. He's too gorgeous for that.

'And do all men go in for one-night stands?'

Harry shrugs.

'I think what you tend to find with men, darling, is that if it's offered on a plate then they'll take it, unless the man in question is in a relationship that he's really happy with. You don't go out snacking if you've just had a four-course cordon bleu meal, if you get my meaning?'

'I think so.'

'However,' Harry continues, before I quite have enough time to wrap my brain around this one, 'it doesn't mean that he wants to eat a four-course cordon bleu meal every night. Sometimes he'd quite like a greasy hamburger and chips.'

Sometimes I wish Harry would cut the analogies and talk plain English. I think I catch his drift though. Variety is the spice of life. I should know, not having had any for over five years. It's either that or he's telling me that the way to a man's heart really is through his stomach.

'So basically, if you want to keep a man happy and faithful, you have to know all of the positions in the *Kama Sutra*, plus a few more, and have some sort of sixth sense that tells you if he fancies straightforward missionary as opposed to being tied to the bed with silk stockings, blindfolded with your knickers, and having his bits covered in warm treacle pudding and custard?'

'Something like that.' Harry grins, chopping away at my split ends.

'God, men get it all ways, don't they? What about what women want? Or is it that we're too busy bending over backwards to accommodate men's wants and needs that we never stop to think about ourselves?'

Harry pauses and looks at his own reflection in the mirror.

'Don't be so hard on us, Alex. I think what a lot of women don't realise is that ultimately they're in control. Sure, if a man is offered a one-night stand, no strings, he's probably going to take it. But that one-night stand has to be offered, doesn't it?'

'What do you mean?'

'What I mean is that in a case of all faculties being alcohol-immune, it's usually the woman who decides whether or not sex happens. Sure, historically men have been the ones to bonk around and act all studly, but they have to find a consenting woman to act all studly with, don't they? Unless of course you're a Roman and then you just sod the consent form, and rape and pillage to your heart's content.

'You girlies have it easier than you think. When God created woman he gave her the gift of subtlety, and you've been using it to your advantage ever since to get what you want from us poor unsuspecting males without us even realising. Men may be the ones who get to run around beating their chests and attempting to spread their genes as thickly as good butter on toast, but that's all they can do unless they find a woman who's happy to divest them of their loin cloth. You set your own parameters, Alex. It's up to you who you let within them, and who you let cross them, and that's pretty much the same for both sexes.

'There. *Fabuloso!*' He wafts a mirror around behind my hair.

I've waited nearly an hour for a trim that takes ten minutes, costs me sixty pounds, and leaves me looking exactly the same as I did when I first walked in here.

Oh, well, my wallet may be lighter, but then so are my spirits, and at least Harry's cheaper than an analyst.

He's made me realise that of all the situations I've been in, I'm the one who decided the eventual outcome. With Mason, Damien and Alex, I was the one who walked out when it didn't feel right. I may have felt like I was out of control, but looking back I did what I chose, not what they wanted . . . apart from with Larry. That one was a narrow escape. Thank goodness the guy had enough integrity not to take total advantage. It's just a shame he didn't have enough integrity to keep his gob shut!

Then again, I think I've finally realised that equality isn't about being able to bonk your way through half of greater London without getting a reputation. It's about taking control of your own life, choosing what you want to do, and then having the freedom to follow it through.

And do you know what? For the first time in a long time I finally know what I want.

I think.

# Chapter Ten

My desk phone rings with the tone that signals it's an outside call, jerking me awake from the mesmeric state watching Jake's bottom all morning has lulled me into. The hard yet gentle curve of firm taut muscle moving sinuously under material . . . slaver, slaver.

'Morning.' Jem's voice booms down the line, with far too much energy and enthusiasm for eleven-thirty on a Wednesday morning. 'What are you doing Saturday?' he demands without preamble.

'Hi, Jem, how are you?' I reply sarcastically, dragging my eyes back to the far less interesting contours of my computer screen.

'Fine,' he replies, either ignoring or not noticing. 'What are you doing Saturday?'

'Oh, you know, the usual. Going out, getting drunk while I watch my friends have a good time, then sloping off home to contemplate my own inadequacy.'

It's our day of reckoning on Saturday so really I should be out in search of that elusive orgy that would take my score from pathetic last place to fornicating first, but there's about as much chance of me doing that as there is of me accosting Damien in the photocopy room and demanding that he put his dayglo condom back on and make good use of it.

'Why do you want to know?'

'I'm throwing a farewell party for Erica, but for god's sake don't tell Mother or she'll expect to be invited and it's not that sort of party.'

After eleven long days of purdah with Mother and assorted WI members, Erica managed to escape back to London on Sunday night. She's still shaky from going over the wall, but I think the nightmares about crocheted tea cosies, bring and buy sales, and curfew at ten are just about starting to recede.

'As if I would,' I reply to Jem. 'What sort of party is it then?'

'Fancy dress . . . sort of.'

'What do you mean, sort of? You're not arranging anything illicit, are you?'

'No, nothing sinister. Bring the girls.'

'Sure.'

'But make sure they're boys.'

Jem finally gains my full attention.

'I beg your pardon?'

'It's a Gender Bender party. You know, men come as women and women come as well . . . men.'

'Oh, I see.' I chew thoughtfully on the end of my pen, returning my gaze to Jake's rear and wondering if I'd fit into his suit, preferably with him still in it. 'Well, Mother should definitely come then. She's always worn the trousers in our household.'

Emma rolls in late Saturday afternoon after another Friday night on the pull. (Without me, might I add, since I yet again opted for a night in with the television and a bar of chocolate – or was it three?)

She never brings her conquests back to the flat. Probably doesn't want to rub my nose in it. Either that or she doesn't want any of them to know where she lives so that they can never attempt to find her again. They all seem to be the same type. Odd. (And I'm being polite here.) I thought the first one was weird, Skidmark of the egg box-blue suit and patriotic hair, but the rest have been well dodgy. A long line of Theo clones with wild hair and grungy clothes.

Serena, who's already arrived to get ready for Jem's party, confirmed that Emma once again disappeared around midnight last night with a weird-haired wonder. Cinderella abandoning the ball at the stroke of twelve to bog off and eat hot pumping pumpkin with the prince – after he's turned back into a frog.

She's carrying several carrier bags, having apparently hit Oxfam on her way home, and once showered and dressed, looks like a Jim Morrison reject, all swirly shirt, fitted flares, long lapels, and eyebrow pencil sideburns. A bit like Theo really. It's very odd, they could almost be twins. The resemblance is kind of scary.

'I bet there'll be a lot of girlfriends missing frilly knickers and suspender belts tonight,' grunts Serena, pulling on a pair of dirty black DMs.

Why is it that when women dress up as men they usually stick to their own gender's underwear, but when men dress up as women they go the whole hog? In fact, the naughtier the undies the better. Forget your staid old granny, up to your armpits knickers. They want the works. Why have comfort fit cotton when you can have satin with lace, frills, and preferably no crotch?

I had a problem deciding what to wear in so far as I no longer have a boyfriend to steal clothes from. I could borrow from my dad, but he's four sizes wider than me and goes for a strange line in Rupert Bear-style trousers of assorted plaids. Please don't ask me why, he just does. He looks like Bob Hoskins borrowing from Rod Stewart's wardrobe. I'd look like a Billy & Johnny clone, so no, thank you.

In the end I borrow a suit off Jem. It's a bit on the large side, but hey, if David Bowie can wear them this baggy and get away with it . . .

Serena's pinned down a protesting Fat Cat and stolen enough fur to make a moustache and side-burns, then squeezed herself into a pair of faded denims and some Doc Martins, a muscle T-shirt, a peaked leather cap complete with studs on the front, and some leather fingerless gloves.

'I'm going gay,' she announces. 'That way I still get to chat up all the men.'

'But the men'll be women, so you have to chat up the women who'll be men,' I explain to her as I pull on a pair of Cats which don't exactly go with the suit, but are the most masculine footwear I possess.

'Oh, shit, I hadn't thought of it like that.' She pulls off her gloves and the hat, then proceeds to slop a bit of cold coffee down the front of her white T-shirt, whilst we watch in appalled fascination. 'Right,' she grins, rummaging in one of the kitchen drawers and emerging with a huge Phillips screwdriver. 'Now I'm a builder, which is actually better because they're lecherous sods at the best of times.'

'You need a builder's bum, though,' points out Emma.

'In these jeans? You're joking, aren't you? They're far too tight. What do you think?' She admires her false facial growth in the shiny metallic side of the kettle. 'Do we make convincing men or what?'

'We look like we're going to a lesbian convention,' sighs Emma.

'Despite the hair?' Serena points to her moustache.

'Makes it worse,' I reply. 'You just look like you've refused to depilate for about six months, out of principle.

We head off in a taxi for my brother's place, Serena seeking revenge for all womankind by wolf whistling at every man we pass, the taxi driver shooting us half fascinated/half terrified looks in his rear-view mirror, which Emma and Serena instantly camp up to by pretending to snog each other, with much waving of tongues and overacted lustful breathing.

The scenes outside Jem's place are like the official opening of a transvestite convention.

The taxi driver sits and watches open-mouthed, and I think slightly disappointed to be left behind, as we get out of the cab and follow a group of female rugby players, a nun with full beard and facial tattoo, and the entire cast of *Priscilla, Queen of the Desert*, complete with plumed headdresses and one hundred-weight of sequins, into the building.

The door to the flat is standing open, and a stream of strangely clad people are staggering in and out, being loudly greeted by Jem, who's dressed as a frightening cross between Lily Savage and Bet

Lynch, in a low-cut leopardskin top with a pair of
Florida Pink grapefruits shoved down the front as
boobs, and a black PVC mini skirt straining over his
arse. He wobbles over to us, his size eleven feet
crammed into the hugest, naffest pair of stilettos
I've ever seen in my life – black patent, very pointy,
with a little bow stuck on the heel. You know, sort
of early-eighties reject. He's also wearing pink fish-
net stockings through which his leg hair sprouts
fetchingly, like hay through juice-stained strawberry
netting.

'Yo, Lex! You made it. Wow, you look great.' This is
directed at Serena whose muscle T-shirt has a ten-
dency to slip at the sides, revealing rather a lot of 36C
boob.

'Help yourself to drinks, they're in the kitchen,'
he says to Ems and me, then turns back to Serena with a
grin, arranging his stocky frame in the doorway of his
room in what I think is supposed to be an alluring
pose. 'And you can help yourself to me. I'll be in the
bedroom.'

'In your dreams.' Serena heads past him.

'Maybe, but they'll be wet ones.'

'Jem! You can be really gross sometimes.' Emma
and I push past as well and follow Serena into the
living room, which is wall-to-wall with cross dressers.
There's one girl strutting around in full motorbike
leathers with eyeliner stubble and a pair of mirrored
police sunglasses, and as well as the rugby team, we
have a mini football squad, five-a-side, I think, complete with studded boots that'll play merry hell on
Jem's stripped wooden floor. Most of the girls, however, seemed to have followed the same theme as me,

and nicked a suit from a male relative.

Come to think of it, fashion is one area where women do seem to get a much better deal than men. I mean, I know there are some pretty good designers around for blokes, but the choice of styles women have to choose from is phenomenal compared with the choice men are limited to.

Unfortunately, despite that endless female resource named couture, most of the men here seem to think that getting dressed up as a woman means struggling into fishnets, Lycra minis, stilettos and huge false boobs hanging out of low-cut tops. They're nearly all clattering round in high heels and blonde wigs, the simultaneous cracking of turned ankles like castanets accompanying the background music.

There is one guy who's dressed as the Queen, in full frock, blue sash, and *papier mâché* crown, and I also spot one Mrs Merton lookalike before realising that it's Jem's cleaning lady who came to do the food and is now making a rapid exit, her lips pursed so hard in disapproval that she's in danger of swallowing her false teeth.

The entire crowd begins to vogue as she heads for the door at high speed.

'Strike a pose!' commands the chorus, so they all start frantically framing their faces with their hands.

Her head withdraws into her yellow plastic pac-a-mac rain hat, like a wizened turtle backing into its shell.

Jem's best friend Martin, who makes a frighteningly realistic Marlene Dietrich, in top hat, tailcoat, fishnets and brandishing a silver-topped cane, nicks Jem's pink feather boa, sticks two plastic cups to his bustier with sticky tape, and starts to high step round the room.

'Vogue and vogue . . .' he lisps over and over, as his makeshift cone bra bounces up and down rather too vigorously until the tape gives way and one of the cups is hanging sorrowfully next to its perkier sister. Jem, wandering past dishing out drinks, pours in some white wine, and chucks in a straw. Martin, sweating like a three-day-old sock in a DM boot, gives up mimicking Mads, slumps down on the sofa next to the Queen who has passed out in very unmajestic fashion, legs akimbo, head lolled sideways, and thin silver trail of saliva beginning to drool out of one corner of the not-quite-royal mouth, and begins to suck wine from his left boob.

'Don't look now,' hisses Serena to Emma, 'but isn't that your ex?'

I look over to where she is indicating, to see a pale blue-rinsed granny talking to a gorgeous emaciated blonde in stack heals and a little silver halterneck dress.

It takes me a moment to realise that the blonde is actually a bloke, one of Theo's long-haired, skinny musician friends. It takes me even more moments to work out that the granny with him is Emma's ex-boyfriend.

'That's Theo?' I rasp in disbelief.

I don't know how Serena recognised him. He looks frighteningly like Maggie Thatcher, dressed in one of his mother's discarded eighties powder blue power suits with shoulder pads so wide you could land a helicopter on them. His usually long flowing locks have been subjected to a home set and tint, and would now sit happily on the most tasteless of grannies. He obviously applied his own make-up. I need say no more than 'blue eyeshadow'. I think you'll get the picture.

'What's he doing here?'

'Must have been invited,' replies Emma casually.

'It doesn't bother you?'

'Why should it?'

'Well, you'd been together for nearly two years when you finished and he didn't even bother to put up a fight for you.' Serena pouts. 'And he hasn't made any effort to stay in touch or anything.'

'He's history.' Emma shrugs in what I think is a far-too-nonchalant fashion. 'Is this a party or what? We've been here for ten minutes without so much as a sniff of alcohol. Let's get a beer.'

My brother's normally immaculate kitchen looks like a bomb site. In fact it looks like the bull's been yanked none too politely out of the china shop and shoved, mooing and mad for it, into a Thresher's.

There are bottles everywhere, the empty mingling with the full, enough to spend the entire morning happily depositing at the bottle bank, savouring the satisfying sound of splintering glass, while a long and agitated queue forms behind you.

The smell of stale beer mingles with stale cigarettes, where the usual charmers have used their glasses for ashtrays.

'Do you want a drink?' Rupert, another of Jem's mad mates, has appointed himself head barman and is currently concocting strange blue beverages on top of the washing machine, which is the only clear surface.

'Not if that's what you're offering,' I reply, sniffing distastefully at what looks and smells like a glass of Blue Loo scooped straight from the bowl.

'There's some wine over there somewhere.' He waves vaguely towards the cluttered worktop. 'And beer in the fridge.'

After searching through dead bottle after dead bottle, I finally give in to the cleaning instincts my mother and Max instilled in me, and pulling a black plastic sack out of one of the kitchen drawers, begin to throw empties into it.

'Bloody hell!' moans Ems. 'We've only just got here, and we're already helping clear up!'

Serena is shoving two empty bottles of Jacob's Creek into my bag. 'Ooh, look!' she cries, turning back. 'I've found a full one.'

I dump the bulging black bag in a corner and accept a glass of the wine Serena's just poured into three plastic cups. It's warm, it's naff, but at least it's alcohol. And, boy, do I need something to help me relax. I'm not really in party mode. I've done nothing for the past few days but think of Jake and my ever-growing – now what would you call it? Lust? I suppose that's a good enough description – Jake and my ever-growing lust for him. That doesn't quite cover it, though. There's more to it than pure and simple sexuality. Can sexuality be pure and simple? Carnal and complicated is probably more appropriate. Hell! I suppose what I'm trying to say is that . . . oh, scrub that, I don't know what I'm trying to say. All I know is that I can't carry on like this, but what am I supposed to do about it? As far as Jake's concerned I'm probably no better than the Damiens or the Larry

Chamberses of this world. I mean, he's had first-hand experience of my hit and run technique, hasn't he?

Jem dances into the kitchen, waving his pink feather boa like a fan at a footie match and shaking his fake boobies with all the vigour of a go-go girl.

'Wow, Lex, you make a good-looking bloke. If you weren't my sister I'd snog you.'

He is, as you can probably guess, already rather drunk.

He straightens his curly blonde Lily Savage wig, and removing huge pink plastic globe earrings swinging like disco glitterballs at his neck, rubs at very swollen red earlobes.

'I don't know how you do it, I really don't,' he sighs, reaching into the fridge for a beer while his other hand ferrets up his black shiny PVC mini skirt to retrieve the string of his tiny G from up his arse. 'I don't know about PMT, it should be PMTT – Panties Much Too Tiny! I'd get bloody grouchy more than once a month if I had to wear this f-ing underwear all the time. Talk about uncomfortable! And as for bras . . . Jeez! I feel like a horse in a badly fitting bridle.'

He straightens up, knocks the top off his Bud bottle on the edge of the worktop, and hauls an errant bra strap back on to his shoulder.

'To think I used to get turned on at the thought of wearing a woman's knickers.' He grins broadly. 'But then again, that was preferably after the woman had just taken them off to get into bed with me. How about it, Ren? Fancy lending me your knicks for the night?'

'Do I have to get into bed with you as well?' Serena teases him.

'That could be arranged. And look.' He pulls down his top to show off his grapefruit cleavage. 'Instant breakfast! Go on, give us yer knickers!'

Ren wrinkles up her nose playfully.

'Well, I'm not promising anything . . .'

'Oh, go on,' he cajoles her. 'Emma lent hers to Theo.'

'Emma did what?' splutters Serena, snorting the Bud Jem's just handed her out of her nose.

'Theo's wearing Emma's underwear,' ploughs on Mr Tact and Diplomacy, heedless of the several surprised, and one rather red, faces staring at him.

'He was joking about her knickers having name tags. I think if Emma can be so generous with her frillies, then you could at least join in the spirit of things, Ren. How about it?'

But Serena has forgotten my brother, and is staring incredulously at our mutual friend who's pretending to be very busy pouring more wine.

'If you dumped Theo three months ago, then what's he doing with his dangly bits happily ensconced in your La Perla? That is . . . if you did dump Theo?'

Emma looks sheepish.

'Well, not exactly,' she finally replies, handing me a full plastic cup and avoiding Serena's gaze.

'You mean, you didn't stop seeing Theo?' I ask her.

'No.' She hesitates. 'Not exactly.'

'Hang on, let me get this straight.' I frown. 'For the past three months, you've still been seeing him?'

'Basically . . . yes.'

'What did he think to all those other men?' Serena asks in wide-eyed astonishment.

344

'Other men?' Emma ask innocently, scuffing her heel against the cupboard door behind her.

'Come off it, Ems. You've been staggering home with legs as bowed as John Wayne after a two-week trail hike, and that stupid après-sex grin you always wear. Don't tell me all these tales of amazing bonking were just bedtime stories?'

'Well, no, they weren't. The amazing sex actually happened . . .'

'But?' I prompt her.

'But the different men didn't,' she finally admits.

'So all of those hot dates you had   they were all with the same guy? All the time you told us you were out on the pull, you were actually slipping out to meet Theo?'

Ems hangs her head, supposedly in shame but she's still smiling.

'What about that guy in the club, what was his name? Mark . . . Skidmark . . . that's it, the one who came home with you?'

'Friend of Theo's,' Emma replies, having the grace to look slightly sheepish. 'Was a total gentleman. Just crashed out next to me on the bed, and left the next morning without even having taken his clothes off.'

'So you were lying to us!'

'Well, we were trying to be like men, and isn't that what they do – lie about how many women they've had when in reality they're practically virgins?'

'Pathetic excuse!' Serena chastises.

'Besides,' I cut in, 'I thought you were all for it, the hit list? You know, being able to pull what we wanted without the guilt trips or the come backs.'

'Well, I was. I mean, I did take Skid home with the

intention of . . . well, you know. But he spent the whole night telling me how cut up Theo was about me dumping him, and how I was the best thing that had ever happened to him and I should really give him another chance. Well, anyway, after that Theo and I had a long talk, and he apologised for not spending a lot of time with me – well, grovelled really – which was a new and rather gratifying experience, and it just sort of went from there.'

'What about all of the other weird-haired wonders you used to go home with?'

'Mates of Theo's,' Emma explains with a grin. 'They'd pick me up in a club, then drop me off at Theo's place.'

'I didn't think he had that many friends,' I say, mentally counting the number of times I saw Ems leave with yet another Theo/Skidmark lookalike.

'Oh, we worked out a pretty good system after a while.' Emma's having a really hard job keeping the smirk off her face. I think she'd let rip and let the laughter burst forth but for the fact she thinks we'd probably lynch her.

'I thought they all looked rather similar.' Despite the fact that we've been well and truly duped, Emma's amusement is pretty infectious. I can feel a giggle tickling my throat like an irritating cough. I take a swig of the Bud Ren's abandoned, but it doesn't help. 'Don't tell me – you had about three on a rota system, and when you got back round to number one again, you just got him to dye his hair and take another trip to the Op Shop?'

Serena has coughed up most of the beer from her lungs and pretty much recovered her composure, and is now staring open-mouthed and incredulous at Emma, her face a mixture of disbelief, disapproval, and yet . . . yes, I spot a glimmer of admiration there as well.

'Ren?' I turn to her.

'What?'

'How about you?' I ask her.

'What about me?'

'Well, you're not going to suddenly admit that you've just been sloping off home to a mug of hot chocolate and your teddy bear?'

'Absolutely not.' Her eyebrows shoot up her forehead with horror at the thought. 'I earned every single one of those chalk marks, had a great time getting them, and I'm proud of it. What about you then? You haven't got anything you want to tell us, have you, Lex?'

'Such as?' I query.

'Well, after what Emma's just admitted, all we need is for you to turn round and say that you've actually bonked three men every night for the past three months, taken part in several wild orgies, shagged your way through your entire male acquaintance, including Emma's brother, my dad and the milkman, and have so many notches on your bedhead any further mattress movement will send it toppling to the ground in a pile of sawdust.'

'Well, if you believe the rumours circulating about me at work, then yeah.' I sigh. 'But no, actually, I haven't. I got stuck at number one, as you well know. I know the hit list was initially supposed to be for my benefit but I'm just not cut out for this game. I've had my offers, but something always seems to go wrong.

Either that or I just chicken out. I don't think I'm made for promiscuity.'

I've decided that somewhere there's a little Off button attached to my libido, and most men seem to press it. Most men apart from Jake, that is. What is it that he's got that meant I could . . . you know . . . go *through* with it . . . relax . . . enjoy myself . . . I mean, *really* enjoy myself. It's kind of sad, really. I could have gone the rest of my life thinking that I didn't particularly like sex. The only problem with my own personal recent sexual revolution – or should that be revelation? – is now I know what I'm missing! Still, I suppose I've doubled my previous score. That's one way of making it sound better, so long as I don't refer back to the fact that my previous score was a sorrowful one.

'Hey, if we're going by percentages then I should win really, shouldn't I? I've improved on my previous balance by one hundred per cent.'

'Nice theory, Lex.' Serena puts an arm around my shoulders, and grins lasciviously. 'But I'm afraid I still win on that score too.'

'You don't?'

She nods slowly, a smug grin settling on her pretty face.

'And, boy, have I had fun adding up that score! Don't look so sad, Lex, at least you get to pass the tab for the restaurant on to Ems. Her score was a big fat faithful-to-Theo zero.'

Emma shrugs philosophically.

'What the hell? It did us good. Theo realised he shouldn't take me for granted, and all the sneaking around didn't half put a spark back into things. If putting my relationship back on track only costs me a few platefuls of pasta, then I'm laughing!'

'So that's it, it's no longer game on but game over?' I ask, actually feeling an acute sense of relief wash over me.

'Sure is.' Emma squeezes my arm affectionately. 'But Serena's been awarded a gold medal in man-hunting, you've kick-started your libido, and I've rejuvenated a junked relationship. So I don't think we've done too badly, do you?'

She looks hopefully at Ren, seeking absolution.

Ren looks back at her for a moment, face initially dead pan then breaking into a huge grin.

'Group hug!' she shrieks, throwing her arms around us both.

'What was that?' Jem, who had previously disappeared discretely with his right size eleven stuffed firmly in his gob, sticks his blonde mop-head back round the kitchen door.

'Did someone say group sex?'

In the corner by the stereo, a couple of guys in pleated tennis skirts, pink Olivia Newton-John sweat bands, and pale pink Fred Perrys are trying to persuade two of the football players to swap shirts.

Somebody's dimmed the lights and put something smoochy on the CD player. The bearded nun is now dancing cheek to cheek with the leather-clad biker. The rugby players are hanging together, scrum-style, arms around each other's necks, drunk and swaying like a large striped blancmange. The Queen's woken up and is dirty slow dancing with a small fat jockey in bright red and yellow silks, one cream satin-covered not-quite-royal knee insinuated firmly between a pair of very overstretched breeches.

Emma and Theo make a strange pair, swaying together to the music, Maggie Thatcher cheek to cheek and groin to groin with Jim Morrison. Ooohhh, now they're snogging. I'm sorry but it's not a pretty sight to watch a former PM getting off with a dead rock god. Serena, despite her fake moustache and side burns made from the pelt of poor old Bic-attacked Fat Cat, looks just like a girl in men's clothes.

She's dancing with a statuesque blond in thigh boots, her head resting happily in his plastic cleavage. It looks like she might get another score on her bedroom door tonight. The statuesque blond has just run red-taloned false fingernails over Serena's bum in a very friendly fashion.

Five minutes later, however, she's back with me – usual position, sofa, alone, glass in hand – and solo once again.

'I was in there,' she states morosely, slumping down next to me on Jem's cream upholstery. 'I'd managed to manoeuvre him into a dark corner for a pretty steamy clinch.'

'What went wrong?'

'Well, everything was going great. We'd just moved on to the tongues bit – and then he suddenly started sneezing. Nearly bit my tongue right off! Turns out he's grossly allergic to cats.'

'Well, why don't you just take off your moustache?'

'Sure, that's not a problem, I can get rid of the moustache easily. But what if I wanted to take him home? I can't just turf Fat Cat out on to the street, now can I? I'm afraid it's a case of love me, love my pussy.'

'I love your pussy.' Jem, who's been tailing Ren practically all night, wobbles over, grinning, champagne bottle from which he is swigging in one hand, head of Martin – best friend – hooked underneath the other arm. 'Take me home and I'll stroke it for you till it purrs!'

Why is my brother such a lewd pervert sometimes? We both give him the sort of drop dead look that comment called for. He drops Martin and falls to the floor, clutching his chest as though shot.

'Oooh, if looks could kill I'd be six feet under, sharing earth with the worms!' he slurs.

'Glad you know your place,' I reply dryly.

'Hey, Jem,' yells Martin, whose plastic cup boobs are now both pointing to the floor. 'Get off the floor, the gusset of honour's here.'

Erica has finally arrived, obviously fully recovered from her ordeal by matriarch and looking totally stunning.

Her dark hair is slicked back with wax, she's wearing a beautifully cut black pin-stripe suit, a white shirt with starched collar and frilled cuffs, and the sort of little black boots you see male flamenco dancers clicking their heels together in. What I recognise as a refashioned lock of her own hair sits rakishly on her top lip. She looks like the smoothly suave, yet wickedly dastardly, moustachio-twirling villain from a twenties silent movie.

Unfortunately she's accompanied by a real nineties villain.

Larry is with her.

He's come as a French tart, with spiked black stilettos threatening his ankles, a black beret sitting jauntily angled on his head, a sleek black bobbed wig, a short tight black skirt with a split up one muscular thigh, and a see through blouse which reveals a bra that must have been made for a breast feeding elephant, stuffed with two pink balloons.

I've tried to get over my animosity, for Erica's sake, but I still have my doubts about him and they're exacerbated by his appearance tonight . . . you see, he's actually *enjoying* being dressed as a woman. I don't mean like everybody else, who's just doing the 'I'm having a laugh' type of enjoying themselves. He is actually enjoying wearing the get up. Everything's silk: his stockings, his short split black skirt, his white blouse. I bet even his undies are. The only thing that isn't is his beret, which is felt, and come on – *felt* is ripe for innuendo, now isn't it?

He has the sort of smile on his face that's normally used by women when they know that they look good.

He thinks he looks good as a woman.

I was worried for my sister before; this is just the final drop of water that popped the camel's hump.

'Rics! Hi! Wow, you look sensational. Come and get a drink.' I shoot off the sofa and, grabbing her hand, rapid tow my sister, blinking with surprise, back to my favourite spot of the evening, the kitchen, determined to have one last-ditch attempt at talking some sense into her.

Unfortunately Larry trots after us, hugging her heels.

Larry the pet lamb – slowly spit roasted and served with mint sauce.

'What on earth's up?' Erica asks.

Larry reattaches himself to her side, and smiles in what I think he thinks is a benign and benevolent fashion at me.

'Nothing,' I reply tetchily, trying hard not to glare too much. 'I just wanted a word.'

'Fine.' Erica now smiles in a benign and benevolent fashion at me too. 'Go ahead.'

'Er . . . in private. You know, it's kind of personal.'

Erica smiles, but her teeth are sort of gritted together. I think she's guessed that she's in for another lecture on the far from finer points of Larry's personality.

'There's nothing you can say to me that you can't say to Larry, surely?'

Well, yes, there are lots of things actually. Like, Larry's a jerk, Larry's a complete and utter fuckwit, Larry is a scurvy flaking infected patch of skin on the Achilles heel of humanity. I mean, I suppose I could say this to him, but I think he might hit me or something.

'You know what I think?' Erica smiles evilly at me, as I stand there dumbly trying to condense a whole heap of insults into one repeatable sentence. 'I think I just need to have a word with Jem. Why don't you and Larry have a nice chat while I'm gone? You know, get to know each other *properly*.'

In other words implying that I'm totally wrong about Larry and he's not the complete slimeball I take him for.

Giving me a 'talk to him' glare, she heads out of the room.

Completely ignoring Erica's eyeballed instructions, I

grab a previously unnoticed bottle of vodka and pour myself a hefty one.

Despite the obvious urge to keep stroking his own thighs, Larry seems to be on his best behaviour tonight. As soon as Erica's out of the room he attempts to toady to me.

'Your sister's great, isn't she?' he enthuses.

'I think so,' I reply coldly, staring past him, swigging neat vodka as though my life depends on it.

He rubs at the side of his neck, face screwing up into a frown as he thinks what to say next.

'Look, Alex, I think you and I got off on the wrong foot.'

'That's just it, Larry,' I round on him, 'we didn't "get off" with each other at all. Despite the rumours you spread to the contrary.'

'Oh, that? Ha ha,' he laughs uncomfortably. 'You're not still worried about that, are you? Just a little spot of office humour, you know. Boys will be boys and all that . . . ha ha.'

'Yep, and arseholes will be arseholes, eh, Larry? Ha ha,' I mock him, turning to walk off.

He grabs my arm.

'Look, Alex . . . I suppose I should, I mean, that is . . . I'm sorry, okay?'

I glare at him as he jerks me back into the kitchen doorway.

'No, it's not okay, Larry. You acted like a complete shit.'

'Well, you certainly got your own back, didn't you? I can't walk past your office without the girls shooting sympathetic glances at my crotch.'

I bite back a giggle.

'Well, you bloody well deserved it after the pack of lies you spread about me.'

'I know.' Believe it or not, he actually looks kind of apologetic. 'If I admit I was a jerk, can we just call it quits and start again?'

'Just let go of me, okay, and I'll think about it.'

'Not until you agree to stop trying to louse things up between me and Erica. I really like her, Alex. Give me a chance, I'm not as bad as you think I am.'

'Well, you can prove that by letting go of my arm . . .'

Larry loosens his grip as though stung, but not because I asked him to. He's looking beyond me.

It's not me stabbing him with mental daggers that has made him drop me like a hot sausage. Larry is being stared at very disapprovingly by a stocky brunette in a little black dress and low-heeled black patent pumps, whose solid calves and steady gaze look vaguely familiar.

Larry just about stops short of dusting me down, and beams broadly at me.

'Well, glad we've finally got all of that nonsense sorted out,' he says far too heartily. 'How about another drink?' He Michael Jackson back slides into the kitchen.

I look closer at the brunette in the rather tasty Nicole Fahri dress, who's had the same effect on Larry as Mace on a would-be mugger.

It's not only the calves that look familiar. Underneath the lustrous golden-brown wig is a face that's haunted a few dreams recently, I can tell you.

Jake! shouts a little voice in my head.

Don't be silly. Jake here? And in a wig and a dress? I don't think so.

I look again.

JAKE!!! the little voice bellows a bit louder, just to make sure I've heard and paid full attention. My body is galvanised into action and attempts to copy Larry's backwards slide into the kitchen without success – probably because I'm not such a slippery little bugger as him. Instead I miss the doorway, impale my left bum cheek on the corner of the sofa table, and come to a rather painful halt.

What the hell is Jake doing here? First the Cotswolds, then work, then the wedding, and now here. He's haunting me. Following me. This is fatal attraction. Oh, my gawd, that means I'm Glenn Close . . . or worse, Michael Douglas! I suck in my stomach and check out my chin for doubles. Fortunately the only double evident is the vodka in my glass. I knock this back in one go and attempt to calm myself. I do not look in the slightest like Michael Douglas, and why on earth would Jake be following me? The obsession's all on my side, not his.

'Lex, are you all right?'

I jump six feet in the air as Erica reappears at my side.

'Are you okay?' she repeats, concerned. 'You've gone as white as a sheet. What's happened? You and Larry didn't fight again, did you . . .'

I clutch her arm in panic.

'He's here,' I hiss.

'He?'

'Him.'

'Who!'

'Him!'

'Lex!' Erica's almost screaming with frustration. 'Who is Him?'

'Jake Daniels, that's who,' I hiss through clenched teeth.

'Where! Show me, show me!' She grabs my arm impatiently so that we're clutching on to each other like two over-anxious toddlers.

'Him over there, the brunette in Nicole Fahri, talking to Nick Preeto and Andrew Wallis.'

Erica's eyes rake over him, growing wider by the moment.

'That's Jake?'

'That's what I said, isn't it? What the hell's he doing here?'

'Perhaps he was invited,' she says dryly.

'Yeah, sure, but by whom?'

'Well, Jem knows him, doesn't he?'

Jem, of course!

'I'm going to kill our brother, very slowly and very painfully,' I mouth. 'How could he do this to me? What the hell am I supposed to do now?'

'Just act naturally, okay?' Erica puts her hands on my shoulders, and begins to knead at my knots like a coach bolstering a boxer before the fight. 'You've managed to work with the guy for the past couple of months without too much hassle, so I reckon you can cope with one evening.'

'But he remembers, Erica!' I wail.

'Remembers what?' she asks me in confusion.

'Who I am,' I hiss through clenched teeth.

She looks at me like I should be wearing a strait-jacket.

'Of course he does, Lexy. Your outfit's not exactly a disguise, is it?'

'No, that's not what I mean. I mean, he remembers

that it was me, you know, that night in the Cotswolds . . .'

She sighs heavily and rolls her eyes in disbelief.

'You can be so naive sometimes, Alex. Did you honestly think he'd forget who you were? From what Jem says he's just not the sort of guy who'd broadcast it to the world, that's all. For heaven's sake go and talk to him. Get this stupid charade sorted out once and for all.'

'I can't,' I bleat pitifully.

'Well, you can't keep avoiding the issue.'

'I can if I try hard,' I mutter, stealing Erica's drink and downing it quickly before she notices.

'Well, if you're determined to avoid him, you're in the right place. It's a fancy dress party, Alex. Nick someone's wig and mingle with the crowd,' she drawls sarcastically. 'He may not even spot you.'

'Mingle . . . right.'

'Alex, I was joking!' she calls after me, as I start to move in the opposite direction from where Jake's standing.

'Alex . . .'

The female rugby players are singing so loudly they're almost drowning out Pete Tong on the stereo.

'Ciiiiirumcision,' they bawl, 'it is our decision, that a willy's kind of crap, when it's got that excess flap!'

I head into the thick of them, seeking asylum.

'And though I'd never dream of having silicone-filled tits, And I wouldn't let a surgeon get his scissors near my bits . . .'

I head out the back of the scrum, deciding that asylum really shouldn't be this rude and rowdy, especially when I'm trying to think of a cunning escape plan.

'. . . When I pick a perfect partner for my horny night time rides, I'd always pick a plonker with a nice short back and sides!' they continue to shriek tunelessly.

I'm just standing wedged between a hot radiator and the fattest rugby player's bottom, which is wiggling rather disconcertingly in time to the music, contemplating my next move, when I spot my port in any storm – my friends.

'Hey, Lexy!' Emma waves her plastic cup at me as I squeeze out of my cramped hiding place and head over. 'Where have you been? Serena's just spotted her conquest for the night.'

'You need another one?' I ask distractedly.

'Well, I know I've already won the competition but I may as well go out on a high. I think I'm going to go and chat him up. What line should I use?'

'Well, I was getting a few pointers from my younger brother the other day,' laughs Emma. 'Apparently his current favourite is, "Excuse me, do you fancy a shag? No? Well, do you mind lying down while I have one?" Isn't he awful!'

'Has it ever worked?' Serena asks with great interest.

'Well, I think he's relying on the humour element. He said to me the way to get a woman into bed is to make her laugh. I told him to just take off his clothes and they'd have hysterics.'

'I think this guy looks a bit too sophisticated to fall for a line like that. I just love his little black dress. Do you think if I could get him out of it he'd let me borrow it?'

'His little black dress?' I ask in trepidation.

'Mmmm. Nicole Fahri.'

'Nicole Fahri?'

'Yeah, last year's but it's still gorgeous.'

'Show me.'

She points over to where Jake is standing out like a high class pro amidst a group of back-streeters, oddly elegant in that gorgeous little black dress.

'He's got good legs, hasn't he?' Serena looks back over at him.

'You ought to see the rest of him . . .' I sigh without thinking.

Emma and Serena look at each other, and then at me with a synchronised raising of eyebrows.

'It's Jake,' I mutter flatly.

'What? THE Jake?' Emma gasps in surprise, craning her neck for a better view.

'The one and only,' I reply morosely eyeing my empty glass.

'That's really him?' Emma can't help gawping.

'Yep, that's the one.'

'You mean, he's the one you . . .' Serena's mouth drops open a little, but she manages not to drool. Just.

'Yep, he sure is.' I pick up her little white plastic cup, and knock back a mouthful of warm vinegary wine.

'Lucky girl,' she breathes.

'You think so?'

'Oh, yes. There's definitely something about him.'

'Bloody horny,' Emma agrees.

'How can you tell in that get up?'

'Nice face, lovely bod. Besides, I told you,' Emma

grins at me, 'there's just something about a man that gives it away. You can just tell. Well, I can anyway. And you already said he was pretty skilful in that department.'

'Pretty skilful must be the understatement of the decade,' I murmur. 'But then again, after Max anyone would seem bloody amazing.'

'Ooh, that's a little bit below the belt, isn't it?'

I bite back the corny innuendo that immediately springs to mind.

'I suppose so.' I shrug ungraciously. 'Just because he and I didn't have any chemistry in that department whatsoever, doesn't mean he can't colour somebody else's litmus paper.'

'He's got great taste in clothes,' murmurs Emma, running an expert eye up and down Jake's body. 'I love the dress.'

'I love what's inside it.' Serena grins. 'I wonder if he's allergic to cats?'

'Oi!' I reprove her.

'Was he really great, Lex? I think you ought to go for a rerun, just to make sure that it wasn't a fluke,' Serena suggests.

'Isn't that against the rules?'

'Well, technically speaking you're only supposed to go in for one-night stands.'

Emma nods. 'Not that you've managed any more since. But the game's over now anyway, so you can go for as many reruns as you want.'

The idea of an action replay of that night runs temptingly through my mind like a big-boobed streaker sprinting across a sports field abandoning clothes as she goes.

'Well, I haven't slept with him yet,' Serena pouts thoughtfully. 'I could add him to my list.'

'No, you bloody can't,' I wail.

Emma and Serena look at each other, then back at me.

'Oh, dear.' Emma smiles ruefully at Serena. 'That sounded like a very heavy blast of good old-fashioned jealousy to me.'

'Which can only mean one thing.' Serena purses her lips and nods slowly.

'You really like him, don't you?' Emma looks me long and hard in the eyes, seeking the truth.

'Don't,' I sulk, looking at the floor like a petulant child.

'Oh, dear,' Emma repeats. 'Is she lying to us, or is she lying to herself? Now why don't we examine the facts? Out of all of the men Alex *could* have bonked, he was the only one she actually did, so that means she absolutely loathes and hates him right?'

'Oh, can't stand the sight of him,' Serena agrees, crossing her blue eyes mockingly.

'All right, I like him, so what?' I admit grouchily, 'I like a lot of people.'

'Yep, but you don't want to sleep with all of them, do you? Well, I hope you don't . . . considering you're supposed to like me rather a lot,' she jokes. 'But you do want to sleep with him, don't you?'

'I constantly want to rip off all his clothes, throw him on the floor and ravish him,' I finally admit. 'Taste every single inch of his body with my tongue, spend three hours just with his . . .'

'I think that means she likes him,' Serena cuts in.

'Well then, what are you going to do about it?'

Emma pushes a stray lock of hair out of my face, and smiles gently at me.

'I can't do anything, can I?' I drag my eyes away from Jake, and refocus on Serena's cup which is sadly, like my life, nearing empty.

'Why on earth not?'

'Well, I've made a complete prat of myself with him, haven't I? He probably thinks I'm some female Don Juan, determined to wheedle my way into the pants of every man I meet for a fleeting fun-filled moment, then shooting off faster than you can say "orgasm" in search of my next conquest.'

'No, that's my job,' Ren jokes, taking pity on me and surreptitiously passing me Emma's nearly full plastic cup. 'Look, Alex, we know that's not true. Don't you think it's about time you let Jake know it as well?'

'I know, I know . . .' I take a deep swig, feel the warmth of the alcohol trail quickly down my throat to swirl acidly around my stomach, killing a few butterflies as it goes, 'But it's not as easy as just going up to him and saying, "Excuse me, but did you know I was a vestal virgin until my early-twenties? Unusual that nowadays, isn't it? Oh, and by the way, I haven't been making up for lost time recently, despite rumours to the contrary." '

'Well, I think you could phrase it a bit better than that,' Emma agrees, smiling encouragingly at me.

Ren's more forceful.

'The only way you're going to get this sorted out is by talking to him.'

'I could write,' I reply hopefully. 'Yeah! That's a great idea. I could send him a letter. I'm supposed to be a writer after all. I'd probably be far more eloquent on paper than I would in person.'

'Just get over there.'

She shoves me in the back and I stumble a few faltering steps forward.

'But I've tried talking to him, my mouth just dries up.'

'How could your mouth dry up when every time you look at him you start to drool!'

'Well, my mouth dries up and other parts take over on the salivation front, okay?'

'Just get over there!' Serena repeats impatiently. 'Before I decide you're not really that interested and move in for the kill myself.'

'You wouldn't?' I breathe, horrified.

'Just watch me,' she growls, giving Jake one of her lustful-look specials.

Cruel but effective.

Before I know it, I'm at his elbow.

It's weird how little black dresses don't really go with hairy muscular arms.

I try to think of an opening line.

'Dry clean only. Isn't that a bastard?' I say, reading the label sticking out of his neckline.

Jake turns to face me as I mentally hit myself round the head with a baseball bat for being such a prat. Something else to add to my ever-growing list of 'stupid things that Alex said'. I bet Jake's raising my moron level from 89% to 99%.

'Er . . . didn't anyone ever tell you that when you wear sleeveless dresses it's always best to use a roll-on deodorant . . . that way you don't get the white marks . . . then again, I don't suppose you wear dresses all that often . . . not to say that if you did there'd be anything wrong with that, I mean each to his own, live and let live and all that . . .'

Oh, god, Alex, what are you saying? I've gone from being struck dumb in his presence, to being totally dumb in his presence.

'I think I need to go and find a rock and crawl under it.' I smile pathetically and apologetically at him, and start to edge away.

'Not so fast.' He reaches out and takes a firm yet gentle hold of my upper arm, 'You're not running out on me again this time, Alex. We need to talk.'

'Where are we going?'

His grip still firm on my arm, Jake leads me through the dancing, laughing throng and out of Jem's apartment, while Serena, thinking quite wrongly that I've just surpassed the world speed record for pulling and Jake is hustling me out of the room so that he can hustle me straight into bed, shoots me thumbs up signals from the other side of the room.

'Upstairs.'

'Well, I'd pretty much worked that one out for myself,' I reply, as instead of heading down and out, we head up two flights to the top floor of the building.

Jake hauls me upright as I stumble on the last step, and parks me, swaying slightly from aerobic effort and alcohol, against a heavy duty pot plant while he rummages in the black patent clutch bag he's carrying as though it's contagious.

'What are we doing here?'

'You know, I could ask myself that,' he replies

quizzically, pulling out a key and opening the door. 'What am I doing here, and why on earth am I wearing these clothes? The things you make me do, Alex Gray . . .'

The things *I* make him do?

He swings open the door, and gestures me inside.

'Welcome to my humble home.'

I walk warily past him, through into an almost identical version of Jem's place without the wall-to-wall perversion. It's slightly 'posher' than Jem's apartment, being the penthouse. The sitting room's bigger, and where Jem has a wall and windows overlooking the street to the front, this place has one wall made entirely of glass and a balcony overlooking the river to the back.

'You live here?' Now I'm thoroughly confused.

'I needed an apartment. This one was for rent.' He kicks the door shut behind us with his heel. 'Your brother put me on to it.'

'But I thought you were leaving soon?'

'I've decided to stick around for a while.' Jake throws his bag on to a plump lemon sofa still covered in its bubble wrap packing, and kicks off his court shoes. I see his calf muscles instantly relax as his feet hit the deep pile of the cream carpet.

His eyes half close with relief.

'God, that's better.'

For the first time I notice that despite the girlie get up, he's wearing no tights and absolutely no make-up.

'I know, I look totally ridiculous, don't I?' he says, aware that I'm watching him.

'Well . . .' I hedge, unsure how to reply.

You get some guys who are eternal boys, with

eternally boyish looks, who never seem to make the transition from youth to man. But not Jake. He is most definitely a man, no doubt about it, and yes, he's standing there in a wig and a dress, so yes, he does look rather odd, but the oddest thing about it is I still think he looks gorgeous. I'd quite like to get him out of the dress and the wig, but my reasons are more to do with wanton lust than a desire to get him back into a pair of trousers.

'How long have you been here for exactly?' I engineer a rapid subject change, hoping that if I concentrate on the full tea chests stacked haphazardly about the room, I might stop thinking about how many bubbles in the bubble wrap would survive a vigorous bout of sexual athletics.

He looks at his wristwatch.

'Oh, about . . . three hours and fifteen minutes.'

'You only moved in today? I would have thought you'd be unpacking, not partying.'

'Yeah, well, ordinarily I would, but I wanted to see you so . . .' he indicates the dress with his hands '. . . here I am. Your brother's a sadist. No skirt, no entry. Those were the rules.'

'You wanted to see me?' I repeat dumbly.

'Do you think I get dressed up like this for fun?' He holds up his hands like a cop stopping traffic. 'No, don't answer that. Look, why don't we have a beer or something?'

Despite being eternally doomed to be only as interesting as their contents, tea chests don't have the same calming effect on my libido as cold showers, or the thought of Damien in nothing but his Mickey Mouse socks.

I think I'd better keep my mouth shut in case of further brain-to-mouth breakdown. Nodding my acceptance with regard to the beer, I do a Larry and trot after Jake into the kitchen.

I can't resist a peek up his skirt as he bends to get a couple of bottles of Becks from the fridge. I'm relieved to see the edge of a pair of very masculine Calvin Kleins peeking out at me.

I walk up behind him, and fingering the hem of his dress, gingerly test the mind-to-mouth connection.

'Can I borrow this sometime?'

Well, that wasn't totally stupid. Sort of humorous really. Ice-breaking. Not that it's particularly icy in here; in fact quite the opposite, I'm heating up uncomfortably even as we speak.

'Do you think it would be small enough?' he replies.

'Well, you seem to be busting out of it somewhat.' I push one of his escaping sock boobs back into the front of his outfit, the back of my hand brushing against his chest as I do so.

'Excuse me,' he jokes, clasping a hand to his breast as though mortally offended, 'just because I'm dressed provocatively doesn't give you the right to maul me whenever you want. What kind of a girl do you think I am?'

I laugh dryly.

'Do you know, that's exactly what I was going to ask you?'

Jake looks at me sideways, but doesn't answer. Instead, he rummages in one of the tea chests, pulls out a tin opener, and popping the metal top, hands me a bottle of beer.

'I had a long chat with your brother a couple of days ago.' He leans back against the clean white work surface, and sucks the froth from the neck of his bottle. 'He filled me in on a few things.'

'Oh, yeah, what atrocities did he tell you about then?'

'Actually he's one of your greatest advocates.'

'He is?' I'm genuinely shocked. Jem's been pretty disapproving since the revelations in the restaurant.

'Yep. Managed to convince me that the Alex I saw wasn't the Alex he knew and loved.'

'And what exactly was the Alex you saw?'

He laughs softly, and without humour.

'Look, why don't we go and sit down?'

We head back into the sitting room, and aim for the long lemon sofa which is the only bit of furniture on view.

'No, don't!' I cry involuntarily as he starts to pull off the bubble wrap. 'It's brand new. I might spill something on it,' I reply lamely, when his inquiring eyes demand an explanation.

Giving me an odd look, Jake sits down and, finally remembering to take off his wig, fluffs his fingers through his flattened hair.

I sit as far away from him as possible, suddenly feeling incredibly awkward, my left hand at my side, popping bubbles as though my life depends on it, as though each tiny atom of air released is giving me the oxygen I need to keep breathing.

'Once you pop, you can't stop,' I quote apologetically at Jake.

He raises his eyebrows at me.

'Jem told me all about the hit list, Alex.'

'Oh,' I say eloquently, suddenly losing all urge to puncture plastic.

'Is that all you've got to say about it?'

'We were just trying . . . I don't know . . . I was just trying . . .'

'You were trying to be a man?'

'No, I wanted the same rights as a man.'

'The right to act like an arsehole?'

'Oh, that just comes naturally.' I shrug self-deprecatingly.

Jake shakes his head and moves a little further down the sofa towards me.

'It certainly explained a few things to me, Alex. Helped me to understand . . . Look, women have the right to equality, but equality isn't about being like a man, it's about having the same freedom, the same opportunities. The right to be yourself and just do what *comes naturally*,' he mimics me.

'Unfortunately, I don't think you've given yourself the chance to act naturally, you've just picked up on the worst aspect of the male psyche that you could possibly emulate. Man's ability to think with his dick. You know, when a bloke acts like a prat it's usually when that one ahem . . . small . . . appendage takes over from his brain. You know I'm right, Alex.'

Of course I know he's right. Look how stupid I get when I'm with him. All of my usual faculties – power of speech, common sense, even movement some-times – go straight out of the window, and all I can do is stand there and drool over him.

'Not all men are complete morons, Lex,' he contin-ues. 'I know Max let you down, but it doesn't mean you have to take revenge on all of us by setting the world record for one-night stands.'

'It wasn't about revenge . . . not really. I just wanted to take control of my life, that's all.'

'And did it work?'

'No,' I sigh. 'Not really. Well, not yet anyway. It was good in a way, though, because it helped me realise a few important things.'

'Yes?'

I look up at him.

'How do you feel about one-night stands?'

'Never do it,' he replies straight away. I look him in the face. I look him straight in the eye. There isn't a flicker of guilt, an iota of insincerity. 'But that's my choice, I'm not condemning anyone who chooses otherwise.'

I stare into my beer bottle and pretend to be absorbed in the amount of sediment that's settling in the bottom.

'So what number was I?' Jake finally breaks the silence.

'On the list or altogether?' I reply, looking up.

He raises his eyebrows.

'We'll start with the list, shall we?' he says with just a trace of irony.

'Number one,' I mumble looking at the floor.

'Oh, well, at least that's something.' He pauses and sucks on his bottom lip. 'And how about altogether?'

'Two,' I whisper.

'What? Two hundred? Two thousand?'

'Just two.' I look up at him, a faint smile gracing my lips.

Unfortunately he's not smiling, just frowning, so I look back at the floor.

'And what number are you up to now? How many computer sheets have you covered in names with crosses by them?'

'Two again.'

'Two?'

'I wasn't very good at it.'

'Is that two including me, or two plus me?'

'Including.'

'Oh . . . I don't have to ask you how far through the *Kama Sutra* you've worked, then.'

I drag my eyes away from the very interesting pile of the carpet, and force myself to look at him again. The frown has gone. This time he's smiling. In fact he's laughing. I'd be relieved if it weren't for the fact that he's laughing at me.

'Oi.' I chastise him. 'It's not my fault, I'm just not cut out for a life of abandoned promiscuity. I've tried, but it's not me. I'm basically a monogamous, give me the romance, hearts and flowers, one man kind of woman. I don't want a succession of conquests, a plethora of notches on my bed head, and trophy Y-fronts in my cabinet. I want to wake up each morning next to the same person, to feel the same skin, to love somebody with the simplicity and complexity that is true love . . .' I tail off, embarrassment washing my face a soft pale pink.

He looks at me for a few agonising moments, silently, appraisingly.

'I'm glad to hear it,' he finally says, and leaning in, eyes never leaving mine, kisses me very gently on the lips.

Oh, the feel of his mouth on mine again. It's like breaking a diet to eat the tenderest, most succulent roast beef with gravy and Yorkshire pudding. I could go on kissing him for ever but he pulls away, leaving me with eyes and mouth wide open like a goldfish gasping for more air.

'I'm fed up of playing games, Alex.'

'Damn! I was just going to get out my copy of *Thirty Fun Ways To Spice Up Your Sex Life*.'

His mouth quirks at the corners.

'Can't you ever be serious?'

I shake my head, unable to tear my eyes away from his face.

'It's a self-defence mechanism. Some people learn karate, I use tongue-fu. Sorry.' I smile apologetically.

'I can think of better things to do with your tongue.' He kisses me again, tongue lightly flicking across mine.

'Now who's not being serious?'

'I'm being *perfectly* serious.' His lips move away from my mouth and begin to trace an erotic line along my throat. 'You know, I think I fell in love with you the first time I saw you.'

'I beg your pardon?'

'You heard me.'

Oh, dear, I'm losing control of my vocal chords again.

'In that case, would you do me a favour?' I just about manage to gasp.

'What?' His lips trail softly and sensuously back to my mouth, silencing me for a few moments.

'Take your clothes off,' I manage to murmur, the warmth of our breath intermingling like our tongues.

His eyes which, like mine, were beginning to close,

blink wide open like a doll whose head's been jerked back too quickly.

'I thought you said you weren't very forward?' he laughs.

'Nooo,' I howl. 'That's not what I meant. It's just, the dress is pretty disconcerting. It feels like I'm snogging a girl.'

'Well, I'll take off mine if you take off yours.'

'Are you trying a line on me?'

'Yep.' One hand smoothly releases the top three buttons of my shirt.

'What about the days of sexual equality?' I reply, sliding my arms around him and slowly unzipping him. 'I'm supposed to try and pick you up, remember?'

'Why don't we just come to a compromise . . . I'll proposition you, and then you can proposition me.'

'Okay,' I croak, as Jake's tongue softly begins to circle the hollow at the base of my throat. 'You go first.'

'You know, you look really familiar.' He addresses my boobs. 'Haven't we met somewhere before?'

'Bit corny that one . . . bit old hat.'

'Can you come up with anything better?'

I place two fingers underneath his chin and tilt his face towards me, my gaze falling on those beautiful, honest, open, funny-coloured eyes.

'How about "Cut the crap and take me to bed"?'

'Yep.' He smiles slowly back at me. 'I have to admit, that's a good one.'